No Gentle Rain

A Novel

ORV CULLEN

Sunshine Publishing Company

Published by
Sunshine Publishing Company
eMail: sunshinepublishing016@gmail.com

ISBN: 979-8-9866150-0-4 (paperback)
ISBN: 979-8-9866150-1-1 (ebook)

Library of Congress Control Number: 2022942725

This novel's story and characters are fictitious. Certain long-standing
institutions, agencies, and public offices and figures are mentioned, but
the characters involved are wholly imaginary.

Distributed by:
Ingram Book Group
(www.ingramcontent.com)

I dedicate this novel to my wonderful wife, Lidia, who not only inspired me to write NO GENTLE RAIN but also read and critiqued every word. Dziękuję

Acknowledgments

I want to acknowledge the following who, in their own special way, made this novel come to light. Thank you all.

Fred H. Keller, Sussex-Lisbon, Wisconsin, historian extraordinaire.

Nancy Lins, Administrator, and Barbara Eigenberger, Research Director at the Oconomowoc, Wisconsin, Historical Society Museum.

The Carolina Forest Authors Club.

Author Ann Jeffries for her assessment of my novel and referral.

First editor, Lynda Bishop, and final editor, cover designer, and publishing consultant, Jessica Tilles.

Finally, to all who influenced my writing.

"Even though the natural inclination of a person is to take advantage of another, those victims who choose to persist will more than survive."

–Author Unknown

Chapter One

"Jakob won't be here this month, Ania," said John. "Maybe next month when it gets closer to the harvest to check on the crop. Go back to the kitchen, or do you want to go back to Milwaukee?"

Ania did not want to go back to Milwaukee. That's why her Polish parents made their youngest girl learn English at an early age. In 1865, Union boys were coming back after the Civil War, known as the Great Rebellion in Wisconsin, plus lumberjacks, dock workers, and coopers making wooden beer casks needed their beer and young girls. They all wanted the girls from the south side for an hour or two, but not for a lifetime. The priest said it would be safer for Ania to live in the village of Sussex, twenty miles from the rum holes dug into the banks of the Milwaukee River. Farms and rolling hills surrounded the little village, and not much more. The black earth could grow hops, and this wealthy farmer, John Williamson, by given name, and his wife, Elizabeth, needed a domestic. John needed his wife's eyes to help watch their workers. He needed Ania to watch their children and help with the meals, and Jakob had already noticed this young woman with golden hair.

Harvest time was a fun time for Ania. Soon, the pickers would gather to work and play at the evening dances. Maybe Jakob would stay a night or two. Maybe longer. No one could believe how he looked—softer and gentler, but he sure could strut. Even Elizabeth would talk to him for hours about the city.

John knew the profit would be better than last year since a little white insect was hitting the New York growers hard, destroying the hops cones and even the vines.

"When will this parasite come here?"

"Not yet, Elizabeth. But it will come. These coming years will be important for us."

Elizabeth knew it, too.

Walking up to his new Beer Garden with his son, Jakob, Heinriche Schmidt stopped to look at the words at the top of the shiny new wrought-iron gate: FUN FOR THE FAMILY! "If you want to make money, Jakob, you have to spend money. This time we added a roller coaster, a fun house, circus performers, and even a real railroad on the grounds. All to draw the crowds to spend the whole day. Some sauerkraut on their wurst and our lager at only five cents for a schooner. Why wouldn't they come?" Heinriche patted Jakob on the back. "Wait until you see this woman, Hilda. She is going to stand on a high platform, and dive into the river at the end of the day. Her breasts are larger than—" He caught himself just in time.

Heinriche thought back to Germany, where he met his wife, Elise. One son later, he was a success in Milwaukee, and he knew it. There were some grabs along the way, but he did not get caught. So, he could and would strut with his captain's cane. Hilda knew that strut, too.

"Is all of this to impress your competitors, sir?" Jakob asked.

"More than that, Jakob. When we went deer hunting, I taught you that you have to make the kill. Otherwise, it's just a walk in the park. You have to learn to take what is given to you. Take what you want. Your relationship with Lieder's daughter, Charlotte. When it leads to marriage, two beer families will merge. You can't imagine what that will do for us... for you. Now, let's see Hilda."

Walking along the gas globe-lit path, father and son made their way to Hilda's new quarters. Entering her spacious building, they saw a dressing room and living quarters for more than one person.

Jacob looked around and then at his father. "Why is there more than one bedroom?"

Heinriche laughed. "Men in the crowds want to look at more than one woman. It's all a show. Hilda on Saturday and a new girl on Sunday. Let's see Hilda."

A knock on her door produced a short young girl with the biggest breasts Jakob had ever seen right at his eye level.

"Come in Ricke," said Hilda. Up and in they went.

Few called his father Ricke. A name his father detested from the old school back in Germany. Who is this, Ricke, in Hilda's eyes?

"This is my son, Jakob, and he wants to see more of you." Heinriche looked at his son. "She's yours." It was all he said to both, but it was enough. Heinriche turned quickly and went back out the bedroom door.

There they stood, and Hilda closed the door. "I have to dress. Next Saturday, this park opens and I want to get my dive just right." Moving behind a dressing screen, Hilda undressed.

Jakob followed and gripped her firm shoulders and kissed her hard on her full lips. "I'm taking you now!"

Ricke was doing the teaching and Jakob loved the lessons. He would see a lot of Hilda. Looking out the window, Hilda saw one more lit globe go out but his entry was just right.

Chapter Two

Going for his cigar after dinner, John confirmed for his wife. "Harvest is about a month away. Fall is close and we might have an early frost. We have to get word out to the pickers. Jakob will be here early next week to walk all the fields. The condition of our crop should guarantee a good price."

After finishing chores for the evening, Ania liked to walk down to the marsh. There she could hear the wren and killdeer. She looked for the male red-winged blackbird sitting on a cattail and singing his song. It would fluff his black feathers and red epaulets and then sing loudly. His strut was so obvious. The female red-winged song was responsive, but her song should have been louder and stronger, thought Ania. It was not. *Why is it like that in love?* she thought. Ania wanted so much more. Of all that she had learned, she had the "one chance" that always stayed with her. Every girl has the "one chance." *Can I get it, right? Mom's dead and my sister didn't get much more than what the right look and the wrong guy can give.* She was stuck now, and no one was going to make it any different for her—not her father and certainly not the priest. "*Have children,*" the priest said. She did, and it didn't make it different for her. "Is it the same for you, my feathered lady? Do they chase you, fill the nest with your eggs, and then just move on?"

John also liked his walk in the cool of this early August evening. Off in the distance was his brother's drying kiln. More importantly, before him was what he had come out to see and touch. In the sunset were hundreds of tamarack poles, twelve feet tall, positioned to form a teepee, each with a green vine winding around each pole. The female vines were so dense this year, they covered the teepee. Taking a cone in hand, John felt it was still very hard and very green. There was no yellowish powder coming off the cone as he squeezed it. It still felt harder than his wife's inner thigh. He reached higher and picked another cone. It, too, was far from ripe. The cones were larger this year. A great harvest. It would please Jakob Schmidt when he came. Soon these fields would be full of pickers and the kiln full of cones.

Late Tuesday, Jakob arrived on horseback. His riding boots were high, and he looked overly confident. Bargaining did not come easily for John. His crop would be good, but Schmidt's reputation belied his words. Each year, Jakob seemed more taken with himself and cared less for others, more like his hard, selfish father. Ania came bounding down the stairs to greet their guest as well. Her steps were light and her smile bigger. There would be more to do the next few days with a guest in the house, but she would find time to catch his glance. A woman could do that. There he stood, greeting Elizabeth and all the children. *We can relax tonight*, thought John. *A walk in the fields will come fast enough tomorrow.*

Easing his guest into the best of spirits, John used only flatteries and pleasantries over dinner. Ania was racing to get her chores done so she could sit with their guest on the veranda that swept around the corner of the house from the north side to the east, overlooking the intersection of Maple and Main. In the evening's shade, the breezes through the enormous maple trees cooled that side of the two-story house best. Soon, Ania sat as close as she dared to Jakob.

Relaxed with her employers, she was not afraid to be direct with Jakob. "Could you tell me more about your home?" She would never see it, they all thought, so what harm would come if Jakob told them of his privilege?

Elizabeth liked to compare as well.

"My house is a long day's ride away. Milwaukee is bustling with people, and new immigrants are arriving almost every day. Factories are springing up everywhere. My home is built on a hill, made of cream-colored brick and is three stories high. The three-story turret looks out over the city and our brewery. I like sitting in my father's office on the third floor of the turret because I can see through the towering elm trees all the way to the Milwaukee River and Lake Michigan. We don't have wrought iron decorating the top of our bay windows like you do, John." There was no mention by Jakob of the new expansion at the brewery. After all, both sides were negotiating.

John listened with one ear and thought about tomorrow. Elizabeth thought about what she was missing twenty miles from the city, and Ania yearned for more. Soon John wanted to go to bed and Elizabeth, being out-fashioned once too often, also made her way upstairs. Staying behind, Ania didn't want to give too much away, but her face betrayed her words. Stuffed with petty grandeur, the words easily fell from Jakob's lips. On he went, describing another beer garden. Travels beyond Milwaukee. It seemed Jakob's shoulders grew broader with each tale. Time slipped away, and so did Ania's defenses. This was all too easy for him.

The next morning's air was cooler and off to the fields they went. Two men. Two positions. One bargain. What buying price would be offered? Did Jakob have full authority to close the deal? Would it be a good walk for John back to the house this afternoon? Would Elizabeth be pleased? Jakob wanted to go deeper into the field where the sunlight did not get to the bottom of the poles, so he could see how healthy the vines and cones were. The cone from the female plant carried what was needed to give taste to their cool lager beers. It was the womb that was so precious to the brewer. It gave birth to the taste he sought. The female cones had to be just right. Light, not heavy with water content and free of pest. Full and just right to the touch. Jakob picked another. It was still too green, but it was coming right along. It was ripening before their eyes, just as Ania had been these past few years. Both men walked back to the house. Satisfied with their business meeting, John convinced the price would be good, and Jakob convinced the crop would be good, but the deal would have to be sweetened.

At dinner, Jakob informed them he would return in three weeks and stay during the harvest. "Would other arrangements be necessary, or could I stay with you?"

Elizabeth nodded. "Of course you can stay with us."

Standing at the corner of the table, a brief smile crossed Ania's round face.

Reaching home after a full day's ride, Heinriche had alerted the butler that before Jakob sat down to eat, he was to report to his father's office.

"Was your trip to Sussex profitable for us, Jakob?" It was more a demand than a question from his father.

"The crops are in good shape. There will be a larger harvest than last year, but too many farmers know of the pest that is decimating the hops crops in New York. Williamson and others will demand more. We must be generous in our offer."

Heinriche settled back in his chair with furrowed brows. "Generous in our offer? Since when do you decide how generous I should be?"

No need to mention Ania and how generous she may be, thought Jakob.

Two weeks later, wagons were sent out in a wide circle around Lisbon/ Sussex to pick up the pickers, mostly whole families. Some would walk instead from as far as the Falls, Merton, or even Waukesha. Their numbers would swell as harvests further north ended, and the pickers rotated south to do this piecework. The word was out, and it was like troops reporting for duty. During the entire harvest, all would camp on the east side of the large barn or near the banks of the millpond, close to the sawmill.

"Here they come," said Elizabeth.

Rolling by were carts and wagons full of men, women, and their children of all ages, piled high with tents, baggage, and anything necessary to live six weeks away from home. A child was suckling her mother's breast as their wagon trundled past the Williamson house. Up Maple Street they went. It truly was a family affair. The word had gotten out, but would there be enough pickers plus hands to work in the kilns? It was harvest time, and a dollar paid in 1870 for three boxes of picked cones was a good wage. The locals would show up each day. *It's time to get this all sorted out and get to work*, thought John. Near the barn, they stood on the horizon and listened as John gave his annual instructions. He would give this same speech a number of times as additional workers arrived at the farm. The men stood up front with women and children off to the sides. Most were tall and slim. Their hands hardened by field work.

"We will begin work each day when the dew is gone. If it's going to rain, we will strip vines from the poles and pick the cones off the vines in the barns. A meal will be served for those working in the field or at the kiln around midday. There will be time for fun and family in the early evenings. Those who cause trouble or waste my time will lose their wages. While working, water only, and no drinking alcohol. Those of you who have your family with you can set your tents near the barns. Those who are by themselves will bunk close to the millpond. Make sure we have all of your names so we can credit you for your work. Pickers here with your kin will work together and will be paid as one. Fill three boxes of cones and you will be paid one dollar. Kiln workers will be paid a like wage. Be ready for some long days. Rest tonight. Get set up tomorrow. We begin work on Wednesday."

At John's side were his wife and Ania. Their responsibilities grew greatly during harvest time. Elizabeth became a foreman and Ania had to take care of all the family duties. It was extra work. Nights were shorter, but it was a fun time most evenings, and especially Saturday nights. John gave his workers Sundays off.

Most field owners did not do this. John looked at his own family standing next to him and he knew rest was important. More than one man noticed Ania standing next to Elizabeth. They would look for her again among all the other working girls trying to look their best at night, no matter how hard they worked in the fields.

Chapter Three

On Elm Street toward the Milwaukee River, grand elms weaved their limbs, hovering over the street. The stately homes peeked through the branches. It was a wonderful evening to visit the Lieder family. It wouldn't surprise Charlotte to see Jakob, but her father was so old German that every visit required proper chaperoning.

Herr Lieder knew why Jakob kept calling on his young daughter. Yet this father wanted to know if this relationship would last, not that it was just proper. Why was Jakob's father pushing this along, if not for the obvious reason? The two beer families led in production. But Lieder, not him, had the bluff cellars lined with cream-colored bricks for barrel storage, preserving the lager at a cool temperature for summer use. Plus, Lieder's horse wagon delivery system was the best in Milwaukee and beyond. Love or business or both. Who knew these days? Why did he not have a son or at least more than one child?

His wife thought the match would be wonderful for both families. She enjoyed saying this to her friends. "Things are moving too fast, so I need to slow this down, for Charlotte's sake."

Jakob's pace quickened, and he ran up the many steps to Lieder's front door. One of Lieder's servants opened the outside door for Jakob and then led him past the inner door to the large foyer. Bigger than his father's foyer, it made an impression on any visitor. A new wrinkle was the five wide steps that led up to the first floor living quarters, wooden staircase, and drawing room. Jakob would have to greet Herr Lieder first in the drawing room. Every visit was the same.

First, greet one parent alone, and then word would be passed to the butler to announce to Charlotte that Jakob had arrived. Jakob would never call Mr. Lieder anything but Herr Lieder. They spoke nothing of importance between them, but the message was clear—tread carefully near my daughter. For now, Jakob would pay heed.

The Lieders were a powerful family, both publicly and privately. Wearing a white dress, Charlotte was from good German stock. She was almost a head taller than her father because her mother was from Denmark. At twenty-one, her blond hair fell across her slim shoulders and her dark blue eyes matched the bow in her hair. Properly schooled, she greeted her father first and then walked deliberately to Jakob's side. Together, they ventured past the pocket doors into the large adjacent room for parlor games. It was a proper slow dance, with muffled laughs and hopeful glances. Marriage was inevitable. They knew it. Charlotte was even secretly building her trousseau. For now, though, it was all look, but do not touch. At least not yet. No chance of an evening stroll tonight. It was getting close to seven in the evening, so this visit would be short. Being close to him was enough now for Charlotte, but wearing thin for this young bull. Jakob was already too experienced. This two-year song and dance, called a courtship, needed a climax soon.

Leaving politely, of course, Jakob reached the front flagstone sidewalk and turned north rather than walking home. The Beer Garden was not that far away. Jakob could slip onto the grounds. If recognized, no one would question him.

Hilda would almost be finishing with her routine and then it would be time for a routine of their own. With the door unlocked, Jakob walked in with purpose on his mind. Noise was coming from the other dressing room next to Hilda's.

Jakob moved forward. The hunt had begun. Sarah was standing facing the mirror. Was she dressing or undressing? It did not matter to Jakob. There was that first look between them. She was not afraid. A heavy sigh left her chest. The time had arrived. There was no doubt who he was. Ricke's instructions were clear and firm. To him, take what you want. To her, yield to him whenever he wanted her. There was no delusion. Just a business arrangement that was to be fulfilled. She would be filled and she would not complain. He would like it a lot, and he would be back for more. He did not even know her name, and he did not bother to learn it.

The next morning, Jakob stood before his father, tongue thick and posture unsteady. "Good morning, Father."

Jakob's father, Heinriche, was much louder. "You have a day's ride to Sussex, so you choose to have a short night. I know you didn't spend the night with Charlotte, so where were you?"

"I was at the Beer Garden with the dark-haired one. She knows much more than Hilda. Father, did you teach her, too?"

"My arrangement with the girls is none of your business."

"Sure, but why do they call you Ricke?"

"None of your business, Jakob. When are you going to ask Charlotte to marry you? Get this done, son."

More work for Jakob.

The old Lisbon Plank Road made for an easy ride to Sussex. It was first an old Indian trail, then a plank road. Now it was nothing more than a gravel dirt road, but it was the most direct route to the Williamson farms. The last toll booth when it was the plank road now stood empty. *Another business venture gone bad*, Jakob thought, as he rode past.

At the home of the Williamson family, preparations were made for Jakob's arrival. Ania was just as eager to receive their mannered guest. Later than usual, he handed his horse over to the groomsman. His lean, long stride made Ania gush with hope, convinced he saw her in a different light than just a domestic. This woman would move slowly, but it was her time; her chance. Even though this was her busiest time with meals for the family and the pickers, she could hardly breathe in anticipation.

John stood next to his wife. "Ten cents more per pound would make up for this year's poor barley crop." *Jakob Schmidt must agree to fifty-three cents per pound*, this burdened farmer thought. *Just ten cents more per pound than last year.* Even though John was also a broker for other farmers' crops, his deal was personal. These were his fields.

Dinner had the same empty flourishes as before. The two men knew it was not the time to discuss business before the family. Some traditions still held. Both parties knew they would discuss the price after dinner on the veranda.

The sun was already setting to the left of them as they sat in the oversized chairs as if they were old friends. John hated this, but he had to open with the first bidding price. "Fifty-eight cents per pound."

"Not possible." Jakob's orders from his father were not a penny more than fifty-four cents per pound.

"All right. You know me, Jakob. I have done business with your father for years now. You know I don't like to quibble. I will not go below fifty-three cents per pound. Nothing less."

Just as fast as he finished, Jakob blurted, "Done!"

They shook hands on it and it was enough. Both needed the other, and both needed to be happy and they knew it.

John walked into the house to share the news with his wife. The price would mean Elizabeth could polish her plans for the house and the children. They would sleep well.

Almost immediately, Ania magically appeared on the veranda. "Will you be needing anything else tonight, Herr Schmidt?"

"Not tonight, Ania."

"Will you be staying during the harvest?"

"Yes, Ania." Wanting her to know he would be available, Jakob added, "I'll be walking the fields and spending time at the drying kiln." He stood up close to her.

Ania stepped back. "Perhaps we'll see each other at the barn dances."

It was becoming obvious to Jakob, just as his father once said, "*The time spent should not be just a walk in the park.*"

The pickers on-site were up early and the locals were streaming up Maple Avenue for the day's work. Jakob did not need to wake up early. Coming to the table for some bread and cheese, he noticed the kitchen was full of women making the day's meal for the pickers. Even the Williamson children were busy running for water or more sauerkraut from the root cellar. Soon, they would load their work onto two wagons. One wagon would go to the field and another to the kiln. Jakob asked if he could ride along. He jumped onto the wagon, holding Ania as it went around the still-standing Civil War Victory Pole in the center of Maple and Main. As soon as the pickers saw the wagon coming up the lane, they stopped working and made their way to the edge of the field, where there was a large clump of trees for shade. The pickers filed past the wagon and received a half loaf of bread, some cheese, plus a bowl of bigos. Ania learned the recipe from her Polish mother. It was a hearty hunter's stew, and it did not spoil, so they served it every day. No one complained. A large barrel of water stood waiting under the trees.

Mothers' hardened faces took their meals, happy they did not have to make it.

Children knew better than to complain. Men did not say much. Since there were no seconds, they all ate slowly, licking their fingers for each morsel. Once finished, they handed in their bowls and spoons, and most found a place in the shade of wagons piled high with marked boxes of cones to rest. Some even nodded off to sleep. This piecework was hard. Jakob marveled they could do this same work, day after day, under the hot sun, even if it was only for five or six weeks in the early fall. He would not do it for a day, and he knew it. *It just worked out that way for me*, he thought. Why? He did not know, and he did not want to care. He smiled at Ania, and she smiled back. He was getting closer. The tallyman for the field pounded on the wagon, announcing that everyone should get back to work. Quickly, the same group surrounded a standing tamarack pole teepee. The vines wrapped around each pole were pregnant with dry cones.

One of the two men in the group cut the vines about three feet above the ground, and the other grabbed the pole puller. Quickly, they lifted the poles out of the ground, laying the entire teepee into a stack. The pickers, sometimes called hoppers, descended on the pile, stripping the cones from the vines. As they worked, they pulled the poles from the pile of vines and stacked them to the side for reuse the following year. One by one, the teepees were falling like bushy trees in a forest. The women talked among themselves and stirred their present children to work faster, while the men would sometimes whistle a song.

Everyone knew what the results meant for themselves or their families. Sufficient coal for the winter, some new furniture, and maybe a bit of savings for another day. Slowly, a family's numbered box filled to be replaced with another and then another. The filled boxes were taken to the tallyman on the wagon. He checked and then accepted another full box, marking who would get credit.

Satisfied, he handed another empty box to the waiting worker. Ants could not work faster or better.

As the wagon heading home rumbled through the smoke from the kiln, Jakob took Ania's hand and helped her down from the wagon. "Tomorrow, I'll check the finished product. Can I help you carry anything?"

"Bring those pots into the kitchen. Thanks, Jakob." Ania could not talk any more. It was time to start the evening meal.

It was the same routine the following morning, but this day, Jacob was on the wagon going to feed the workers at the kiln. The maple trees on the dirt road were showing more red and yellow at the top of the branches. The horses could smell water at the pond, but Elizabeth kept them in check. They could wait, but all the workers streaming out of the kiln could not. The wagon stopped in the shade of the kiln. Already a line was beginning to form. Those staying on-site usually ate only once a day. They didn't have the money to go into town for an evening meal washed down with a beer. This was a time to make money for the family, not waste it.

Jakob jumped down from the wagon and headed for the kiln. John's brother owned this kiln. It made sense for the brothers to keep the hops business in the family. They shared the work, and they shared the profits, even though John owned more land. Divided into two equal-sized rooms on each level, James's kiln stood two stories tall. On the lower level, the room on the left was a large wood-burning furnace. Bins of dry wood were in two corners of this room, with the furnace situated in the middle. The smoke from the furnace vented outside the kiln, and the heat rose through the ceiling to the room right above, where the cones from the field were overspread in a foot-deep layer on a horsehair cloth laid over latticed planks. The cones would be turned twice while they dried for twelve hours. They would then be pushed into the adjoining room to cool. A large trap door in the floor was removed so cones could be swallowed by this hole to fall down a wood chute into large burlap bags. A worker held the bag to the lip of the shoot while standing at the end of the wagon. When one bag became full, another took its place, and the full bag was stacked in the back of the wagon. It was labor-intensive work, but the streamlined process kept the cones moving toward their destination.

Jakob headed straight for the room where the heated cones were cooling. He could tell their dryness by checking the weight before they dropped out of sight into the burlap bags. It was the business reason he was staying longer than he really wanted. The scenery was pleasant, but Jakob's father was the one who had to be pleased. The secret to their lager was in the quality of the hops.

Everything depended on this rewarding process. The best hops made great beer and greater profits for the Schmidt family. Everything else was of little importance, including those evenings the workers would gather to play their fiddles, dance, and socialize. Pleased with what he saw, Jakob made his way outside to the east side of the kiln. Here the fed workers were laying in the shade next to the incline that led to the drying room. Things were just right, it seemed to Jakob. He could relax in a big way.

Jakob took the path close to the sawmill next to the pond. The green rushes were tipped with yellow and the cattail heads were full and dark brown. A red-winged blackbird settled on a cattail, ruffled his epaulets, and sang. It was a glorious afternoon. His thoughts for a moment turned to Charlotte, but they quickly raced ahead to the dark-haired girl at the beer garden. Her fingers were enlightening. Where did she learn such skills? He knew his father benefited.

That's why she called him Ricke, just like Hilda. The path met the road, and just then the wagon Ania was on rumbled by. She waved. Jakob smiled and the same bird called again.

Reaching the house, Jakob sat on the veranda out of the sunlight. It was quiet here. At the back of the house, the kitchen help was combining any leftovers and cleaning all the kettles. Ania was busy with the children. Soon it would be time for the evening meal. He could sit here for a while and close his eyes. Pressure was building at home with his father, with Charlotte, and with growing expectations. Could he settle down? His father seemed to do everything and find relaxation whenever he wanted it. *There is no reason why I can't as well.* Time to empty his head. Try to relax.

Ania came round the west side of the house, and she saw Jakob sitting on the veranda. The children moved on, and Ania walked up the steps to the veranda. The sunlight glistened through her blond hair. It looked as if her head was on fire. *Beautiful,* thought Jakob.

"Do you need something to drink, Herr Schmidt?"

"Not now. Sit here with me for a while. Can you?" Ania could, and she certainly wanted to, sit by him. "How many years have you been here serving the Williamsons?"

"Three years."

"How old are you?"

"Almost nineteen."

"Do you want to stay here doing this all your life?"

For a moment, Ania wondered if she should really answer that last question. She knew she wanted so much more. She saw what little her sister had and how much more Elizabeth had. Somewhere in the middle would not be enough for Ania. *It's time for me,* she thought, but she couldn't really say that to Jakob. "I would like my own house like Elizabeth's and I want children." That probably said too much, but it was true. At times like these, she had one chance, and she wanted it to be the right choice. Had she lowered her guard too much? Would Jakob notice?

"Mr. Williamson has arranged for two fiddlers from the local hotel to play tomorrow night at the barn dance. Will you be there, Jakob?"

"Yes, Ania."

Elizabeth's footsteps echoed in the foyer. "Ania? Ania, where are you?"

Ania tilted her head toward Elizabeth's voice. "Coming, Mrs. Williamson."

The work always seemed easier on Saturday. Probably because there was always a barn dance Saturday night. Everyone then would have Sunday off. The drying kiln hands would work until they caught up, and then they, too, were done for the day. Some chose church on Sunday morning. Some locals invited a person or two to spend the day with their family. The Williamsons wanted it that way.

They went to the Episcopal church, and they had strong family roots. They gave their workers Sunday off, for which they earned the worker's respect and gratitude. Everyone else in the business thought they were crazy, but they were not as successful as the Williamsons. Maybe they knew what they were doing after all. Pickers, kiln workers, and field hands loved working for the Williamsons. They were fair, unlike other employers who would always find an excuse to cut a person's wage or fire a worker. The Williamsons hired the best workers, and they received, in return, the best job for the wages they paid.

<h1 style="text-align:center">Chapter Four</h1>

By eight o'clock that evening, everything was ready for the barn dance. Workers had rolled the wagons outside so there would be space inside, but most people were gathering outside the great doors, where the cooler air gently moved. Those that had food brought something to eat or drink. The highlight of the evening was the fiddlers from the local hotel. Those who brought their own fiddle or mouth organ joined in. The dancing, some called it hopping, easily raised a sweat. It was always the same. The girls of courting age tried to pay no mind to the glances that were thrown their way. Families mostly moved as a group looking for friends. The beat of life here was strong and for a while, everyone clung to the moment. They smiled and laughed, hoping tomorrow would be better.

Ania stayed pretty close to the Williamsons. Light on her feet, work was the farthest thing from her mind. She took a turn on the dance floor. The oldest fiddler could play the best. It was a cacophony of noises that could outdo a marsh full of songbirds. Jakob, leaning against a wagon, saw her there, standing firm in the firelight. She certainly was ready to finalize her dreams. A local landowner's son should have taken advantage of what was right next door. Did the word "domestic" throw them off the trail? Could they not see what was standing right in front of their eyes?

Jakob approached slowly, making sure she could see him walking toward her. It was almost like moving forward to claim the awarded prize. He talked, and they laughed. Elizabeth noticed them as she talked to her brother-in-law, the owner of the kiln. It didn't seem out of place, but she noticed how at ease Ania was in Jakob's presence. Jakob wouldn't dance with her in public, but a dance with her was a part of the plan. He had to have that dance.

Rising late the next day, church was not on Jakob's mind. The two streets of Sussex were very quiet on Sunday afternoon. Jakob walked to the hotel on Main Street to taste the local beer. The brewery was on Maple Avenue. Townspeople had to pass it each day to get to the kiln and hops fields. It was said the brewer stored the beer in a brick-lined cave tunneled into the earth just west of the millpond. The color was pale. The beer was warm and old. Last fall's brew. The brewer had some skill, but there was no need to secure the recipe. There were some local postings tacked to the back wall. The one that caught Jakob's eye was the posting banning a certain person from drinking within. Quiet was deafening on a Sunday, so Jakob thought of his father's beer garden and his girls.

By the time Ania finished with her tasks, going to church and the large Sunday meal for the family, there was little time for herself. She missed Jakob at the family meal but was told he was giving the family time off from his presence. Elizabeth asked her if she enjoyed herself at the barn dance. She pressed Ania. "Didn't Jakob look handsome last night?" Ania would only go so far as to say he was tall and took long strides.

So, this is what excites Ania the most, thought Elizabeth. What compels Ania to think it was acceptable to be attracted to Jakob? Elizabeth surmised the length of his strides was more important to Ania now than the possibilities Ania thought could be hers later. Elizabeth also read everything she already had experienced into the word "possibilities." For some women, possibilities will always motivate them, whether she was building her own nest or feathering her husband's. She did not have to ask Jakob. His actions revealed his attraction. One did not pay that much attention to a domestic. So maybe it could be mutual. Should she pass her thoughts on to her husband? No. He had too much on his mind now to deal with this dalliance. It wouldn't get serious, anyway. She turned her attention to thinking about their friends, who lived in Oconomowoc, west of Sussex, who planned a visit for when the hop harvest was in and everything was shipped out by train from Pewaukee or by wagon down Lisbon Plank Road.

The Williamson's crop would go directly to the Schmidt brewery so it would get the greatest attention. Business details for himself and broker details for area farmers would always be more important to her husband than a domestic dalliance.

At daybreak, John could smell rain on the way, and he gave the order to cut the vines as usual, but instead of dropping them into a heap as before, he ordered poles and hop vines piled onto waiting wagons to be driven to the nearby empty barn. It was not far from the field and close to the kiln. The pickers already knew where to gather and would arrive at the barn mid-morning. The work would be the same as yesterday, just in a different place. The wagons set out at the same time for the early afternoon meal. Jakob rode on one to the kiln and Ania went to the picking barn. A light rain fell as the workers ate, but as they were about to leave, the sun peeked through the heavy clouds. Ania asked if she could walk back to the house. Elizabeth looked out at the sky toward her house and saw no reason Ania could not walk. The wagon left, and Ania set out to her place of employment. The rain cleaned the air, and it smelled fresh, even sweet. She stopped at the marsh and listened to the birds. They competed with each other now that the rain had stopped. Each chirp was prettier than the last. A red-winged blackbird caught her eye just as Jakob came round the clump of trees by the hop field. He stopped to greet her, as the rain began falling again.

Jakob saw a teepee of hops close by. It was the best shelter for this passing shower. He took her by the hand, and together they ran to the teepee. They slid quickly through an opening between the poles. She was laughing, but Jakob said nothing. Inside, the vines were so thick they could hardly see out to determine if the soft rain was going to stop.

As Ania was about to mention how sweet the birds of the marsh sounded, Jakob turned her around with his strong hands. With no clue about what was going to happen, Ania turned her face. She thought to kiss his lips when he drove her down to her knees. Trying to rise from behind, he ripped her blouse down and cupped her firm breast. She knew now. Then he pushed her forward, face down, placing his knee in the small of her back. Her mouth buried in the vines, Ania couldn't move. She cried out, "*No!*" She barely could hear herself. "*No, Jakob!*"

Taught and experienced, Jakob dropped his pants. His shaft was already raised from its home. Keeping her face down, he swept his arm around her very slim waist and pulled her buttocks up. Then he raised the back of her skirt to her head and moved his knee to the inside of her thigh.

Holding her head down, he pushed two fingers inside her. The window had been opened. Ania tried to kick him with her free leg, but Jakob moved his other knee inside the back of that leg and her struggle was over. Holding her head down, he thrust his organ inside her, pulling it out to thrust again. Doing the same again and again. Now Ania didn't move. The fight was gone from her. So Jakob became more methodical. He slowed his pulses, driving deeper within her. Yet he made no sound. All she heard was the movement within her. He raised her tighter into him, then pushed her forward, and, raising her again, did the same. The thrusts were coming swifter now. Jakob couldn't stop this fulfillment. He expelled all of himself inside her, holding steady while he wilted, making sure she would not forget what it all felt like and who took her first. On his knees, while between her thighs, he pulled up his pants and pushed her to his side, remaining silent. Nothing from his mouth. Not a kiss. Not a gentle word. Nothing. Ania rolled to her right to face him, to scream with rage, but Jakob was exiting through the same opening they had entered. It was no gentle rain after all.

Jakob ran from the cone teepee to the path and hurried toward the Williamson's house. Far enough away from her, he stopped to catch his breath and set within the recesses of his mind what had just happened. He wanted to remember for a lifetime the past fifteen minutes as vividly as possible. His shot was true, and the game had fallen before his feet. Just then, he could see John Williamson coming up the path toward him. He couldn't run. He couldn't hide. Why was he coming this way now? Quickly, Jakob made sure all his clothes were in order. Next, he stooped to pick an aster and pretended to be preoccupied as John approached.

"Ah, Jakob, are you on your way back to the house?"

"I am. Please tell Elizabeth that I will be back home before dark."

John moved quickly on toward the barn where the pickers were finishing up their work for the day and would work again tomorrow. As he reached the wagon road to the barn, he looked back and saw a woman walking slowly out of the hops field to the path. Jakob was not moving slowly. He hurried to the stable, saddled his horse, and rode off toward Lisbon Plank Road.

Ania walked aimlessly. She saw nothing. She heard nothing. She hurt everywhere. She stumbled into the house and leaned on a chair when Elizabeth saw her.

"My God, what happened to you, child?"

Quickly, it all spilled out.

Elizabeth did not want to believe a word of it. She led Ania upstairs to her room and helped her undress. Elizabeth saw the large red circular mark on the small of her back, and red marks on the inside of her thighs. Elizabeth took Ania in her arms but could not calm her down. Still sobbing, Ania dropped into bed.

Hurrying downstairs, Elizabeth sent for a stable hand with instructions to find John quickly and ask him to come home. She went back upstairs to make sure there was no doubt about what she heard Ania claim.

Elizabeth touched Ania's hip. "You are sure it was Jakob? Ania, are you sure?"

Turning from the wall, her once bright eyes now empty, Ania whispered, "Yes."

There was nothing more Elizabeth could do, so she went downstairs to wait for John.

Elizabeth rarely interfered with John's day, so this had to be important. Was something wrong with one of the children? John wondered. Barely through the door, Elizabeth asked John to sit down at the table, so she could relay all the details to her husband.

John shook his head in denial. "Can't be. Couldn't be. But wait. How long ago did this happen?"

"An hour ago. Two hours at most."

"Where did this happen?"

"Teepee in the hops field."

"Damn, I saw Jakob walking down the path from the field no more than two hours ago and that must have been Ania walking in the field. I stopped to look back when I reached the road to the barn and I saw this woman walking toward the path from the field. It must have been Ania. How is she?"

"Not good. Crying. Sobbing. A mess." Elizabeth frowned. "Could it have been Jakob?"

"Really?" *What if it is*, John thought. "Where is he?"

John got up from the table to search. First the house. Then outside. Then the stable. The groomsman was watering the horse.

"Have you seen Herr Schmidt?"

The groomsman shook his head. "No, but his horse is gone."

"Gone?"

"Gone."

But not that far. Jakob rode as fast and as long as he dared. Then, walking his horse, he knew that there was a hotel halfway to Milwaukee. Arriving, he took his horse around back for the night. *It will be safe here*, he thought as he entered the inn. He sat at a table in the corner. There was only one other man in the inn. He had finished his meal and was drinking. Jakob gulped his meal and asked for another beer. The stranger joined Jakob for some conversation. Soon that conversation turned to bawdy stories. The stranger offered to buy Jakob another beer and another. Jakob was laughing loudly, spinning one yarn after another. There was one about the dark-haired girl in the city, madam houses on Water Street, and a young blond girl in the country. That story seemed the most real and most recent. Jakob's role was always the same in each story. Take what you want and leave the spoils behind. The stranger was a harness salesman who was not heading to Milwaukee. He was riding in the opposite direction to a large horse barn breeding complex east of Sussex.

John mounted his horse after breakfast and rode toward Lisbon Plank Road, looking for Jakob. The clouds looked menacing. There is work to be done, and here he was chasing a man whose father was his business partner. Ania lived in his house. She was beautiful, and she was only eighteen. He and other men had the moral strength not to rape her. How could he sit with his family in church on Sunday if he at least did not chase down the truth? This was more threatening to John and his family than the clouds above.

Looking ahead, John saw a buggy sitting at a crossroad, and the driver was waving to him. As John drew up close, the driver smiled. "Is this the road to the horse barn at Tower Hill?"

"No, it's not. I'm turning back. Follow me and I will show you the road you need to use."

"My name is August Hoepner, and I sell harnesses for horse teams. These harnesses on my Cleveland Bays are my work."

"Beautiful. My name is John Williamson, and we are nearby in Sussex, where I live. I like your work. Stop by and ask for me. By the way, did you see a tall, blond-haired man riding your way?"

"No, I didn't."

Just then, they were on top of the crossroad, heading north, and the conversation dropped. Parting ways, August headed to the horse barn of a Milwaukee brewer and John headed home without a confrontation.

John gave his horse to the groomsman and marched into the house, meeting Elizabeth next to the stairs. "No sign of him. How is she?"

"I let her stay in bed."

John decided he needed to hear the details. What happened offended him, and he would not let it go. "Let's talk to her, Elizabeth."

Entering her room, Ania looked listless and empty. Innocence no longer existed. Ania questioned herself. *How can I just be forced? Can I not have a part to play? Can I not tiptoe at least a few steps toward the moment I am a woman?*

Elizabeth spoke first. "How are you, child?"

I am no longer a child and it could be worse, Ania thought.

"John is here, and he wants to know what happened to you."

Ania leaned on one arm, hoping she would not be facing an accuser. John looked down at her. It was no different from looking down on a wounded animal, whimpering, laying completely still. It broke his heart, so John softly said, "Ania, tell me."

There was much to tell, but Ania needed only a few words to tell it all. "It was brutal. It was unwelcomed by me. Jakob raped me. He did it without speaking a word."

Stunned, John turned his back, facing the bedroom door. "Has she eaten anything, Elizabeth? Try to make her eat something. I'm going downstairs."

⟿⟐⟞

Convinced he could easily put this behind him, if necessary, lies more than distance could cover Jakob's tracks, but for now, silence would have to do. *Running meant that Ania was a scab that possibly could be picked off someday*, Jakob thought.

Arriving home mid-afternoon, he prepared for his father's arrival. Close to the regular time, Jakob heard his father's familiar rap on the front door with his captain's cane to announce his arrival. He handed his cane to the butler and strode into the drawing room. He wanted to be left alone at the end of each working day to recount what was done that day and what needed to be done the next before meeting his family's needs or problems. It was his disciplined approach to things. Waiting a few minutes, Jakob entered the room. He knew his appearance alone would mean defending his early return from Sussex, but his plans to marry Charlotte should carry the day for him. Jakob believed his father would be surprised with the first, but pleased with the second.

"Greetings, Father."

"What are you doing home so early from Sussex?" Herr Schmidt always went to the heart of the matter.

"I decided I could leave early since the crop looked good, and I believe Williamson is going to deliver a quality product."

"With more than two weeks of harvest left, you can stand there and tell me the end result will be as good as when you were on-site? You are too trusting, Jakob, and therefore you can be easily cheated. We don't get cheated. That's why you were to stay there until the harvest and kiln drying were over. Much can happen in two weeks, even if this crop belongs to the brothers."

Jakob allowed his father to have the last word on this. Quickly, Jakob moved on to something that would be more pleasing to his father. "You need to know that tonight I will ask Charlotte to marry me and then ask her father for her hand."

About time crossed Herr Schmidt's mind, but he did not let it cross his lips. As far as the heart was concerned, that was never of any concern to Heinriche. His son would have enough trouble dealing with Charlotte's father. Both realized this. Jakob could not risk being rejected by Charlotte's father when he asked him for permission to marry his daughter. Charlotte was Lieder's treasure. More important to him than his business. She was his legacy, and he would try to protect her as long as possible. Charlotte, plus her mother, would have to convince Lieder that marriage would be good for his only child. *The match for sure will be good for the Schmidts*, Heinriche thought.

Even though Jakob's steps fell quickly on the flagstone walk to Charlotte's house, he had no idea what commitment was, much less love for one woman. His male juices flowed freely and flooded all of his senses. Once again, there was not much difference between what happened the day before with one young woman and what was about to happen tonight. It was just business. Knocking at the Lieder's door, and after being announced, he was shown to a larger drawing room than their own. Charlotte's mother, Maria, greeted Jakob. After Charlotte joined them, Jakob wasted no time making it a family affair.

Matter-of-fact, before her mother, Jakob stood ramrod straight. "Charlotte, I want you to marry me."

All Charlotte heard was "*marry me.*" It was all she wanted to hear. Months of building her trousseau and months of her mother's lunch whispers to friends about a match were all coming to fruition. The smell of orange blossoms already filled the room even though it was September. The only possible answer from either of them had to be yes. "Of course, I will marry you."

There was no need to plan. Excited, Charlotte would lead the assault on her father, while Lieder's wife would support love's charge from the left. If needed, Jakob would remain in reserve for the final push. Walking into the room, Charlotte rushed to her father. "Jakob wants me to marry him."

"What?"

"Father, you must have known this day was coming and that I would say yes."

Maria approached her husband and put her hand on his shoulder. "Let it be, Karl."

It will be winter soon enough outside, Karl thought, *without a winter's freeze within the walls of their home as well*. Overwhelmed by his women and with his suspicions dormant for now, Lieder parted them to shake Jakob's hand in acceptance.

Jakob saw the offer as capitulation. "Herr Lieder, I want to marry your daughter."

"Yes, Jakob."

The match was struck. Jakob could now leave the two joyful women to make plans. More importantly, he could be quickly away before Herr Lieder could revisit what had just happened. Jakob would only let his family and close friends know of the pending nuptials. He would leave it up to the Lieders to make the formal announcement of their engagement. At that, Jakob was off to where he could really celebrate with softer company.

Chapter Five

After taking orders for his harnesses at Tower Hill, August Hoepner headed for Sussex two miles west of the Tower Hill horse barn. He first drove his two-horse team through Templeton, which was nothing more than a blacksmith forge, store, and railroad track heading north and south. Due west was the quaint village of Sussex, named after the mother city of Sussex, England. Settled some twenty-five years earlier, it had come a long way in a short time, mostly because the good soil produced barley and hop crops easily shipped to Milwaukee. The village had English countryside charm with a large stone Episcopal church, but most of all, an industrious populace that wanted to make things better for their growing American families. August stopped at the Main Street Tavern and asked where he would find John Williamson.

"Look for him at the drying kiln on north Maple Avenue," offered the owner.

Maple Avenue and Main Street were at the center of the village. At one corner stood a beautiful two-story house shadowed by maple trees. West of the crossroads on the other side of the street was an even grander home. One of them had to belong to Williamson. *This stop could be profitable after all*, August thought.

August approached a man who looked in charge of the kiln. "Where might I find John Williamson?"

The foreman gave a slight head nod. "He is in the hops field up the road."

August turned the team back to the main road, and soon the field came into view. At its edge, a man was talking to field hands near the wagons. August waved to get his attention, driving his team to a clump of trees to tie them under a birch.

"Mr. Williamson, remember me? I followed up on your invitation. Are you in the market for some new harnesses?"

John jumped on board. "Take me back to the house on Main Street and we'll talk business on my porch."

Sitting on the porch with a cool drink, they discussed prices and John ordered six pairs plus a fancy ornamental harness for his own team of grays. Taking the deposit, August wanted to leave so he would get as far as the same hotel he had stayed in a few nights before.

"Mr. Williamson, thank you for the harness order. By the way, I was thinking about the tall blond man you asked me about. I didn't see him on horseback, but there was this man in the hotel bar where I stayed. We got to drinking a few beers, and he spun some yarns about his women conquests, including a young girl he called Ania. He thought himself pretty cocky. Called himself Jakob."

Seeing August off, John immediately sought Elizabeth in the drawing room, making sure no one else could hear his whisper. "No doubt about it. The bastard raped her."

After the harvest was in and the nights were colder, Ania was getting sick regularly in the morning and her breasts were more sensitive to the touch. It was not yet obvious, but Ania was showing all the signs that she was pregnant.

Elizabeth was trying to come to terms with the fact that Ania was going to have Jakob Schmidt's child. John felt betrayed and furious that a guest in his house would take license with someone entrusted to his care. Still, they had to be careful and socially not reckless. A timely response would have to wait, determined by events not yet unfolded. What to do and how to do it, for Ania, mattered most now. *She still is our responsibility*, John thought. That was one problem. Another was the planned visit of the Ashworths from Oconomowoc. It was no surprise to John that his longtime friend was doing well in the rapidly growing town of Oconomowoc, since he already owned a gristmill plus two hotels on Lac La Belle. Travelers from Milwaukee often stayed in his hotels on their way to the state capital in Madison, and families from afar enjoyed fishing and boating during summer vacations on the many lakes near Oconomowoc.

Moreover, Elizabeth had no truer friend than Susan Ashworth.

—◦◦◦◦—

At last, the end of October was here. Ania was not showing, and though her mornings were better, it would soon be a growing problem they could no longer disguise. The visit by the Ashworth family was next week, since responsibilities at their gristmill and visitors at their hotels had slowed. Elizabeth finally cornered her husband to review her plans when James and Susan, plus their three young children, would be their guests. Elizabeth had already made most of the preparations, but she wanted to be sure John agreed with her decisions.

Sitting at the large table, Elizabeth approached John. "Our staff knows the date of James and Susan's arrival. They are almost ready for them and Ania is again able to fulfill all of her duties. No one questioned to my face her absence from time to time, but what are we going to say when we no longer can hide her pregnancy?"

"What do you suggest we do? We can't keep her here. People will wonder who is the father. I could be accused. Church members will talk and once that grass fire gets started, nothing will stop it. Our family's reputation, not to mention our businesses, would be ruined. She has to move on. Maybe back to Milwaukee?"

"We can't cut her loose by sending her back to Milwaukee."

As of yet, there was no obvious answer. John looked to leave when Elizabeth spoke up. "What about the Ashworths? What about asking Susan and James to take her to Oconomowoc?"

"Can you bring it up to Susan somehow? I can't do it."

"Let me think about this." As the words fell from Elizabeth's lips, she already was deep in thought.

Ania was feeling better so she could carry out her morning duties without delay or excuse. Elizabeth seemed closer to her now and was willing to give her needed moments for herself. Ania knew she needed someone to talk to but did not know how to start the conversation with the one person who might listen.

Everyone was being so careful and so quiet, but for how long? Where was this heading? That was the big question. Elizabeth's children also sensed something was wrong. Something was different. Ania didn't laugh as much, nor was she interested in playing games with them as before. Alice, the oldest, finally brought this up to her mother. "Why is Ania so quiet? Why does she go right to her room after supper and not read to us anymore?"

"I don't know, Alice. Go play with your brothers."

Elizabeth knew this had to be resolved soon. First, she would have to discuss the subject delicately with her good friend from Oconomowoc.

Arriving by their own carriage, the Ashworths were at the Williamson's by late afternoon. James stepped down from the carriage and handed the reins to the groomsman. Then he walked to the other side of the carriage and helped his slim wife down to the open arms of Elizabeth. John grasped James' hand firmly in a warm handshake, renewing their sincere friendship. Ania was also there to take the Ashworth children to greet Alice and her brothers. They would spend three days together, and it would be Ania's job to make sure this went off smoothly. She took her job seriously and had the temperament to do it well.

The four adults made their way to the drawing room, with Elizabeth leading the way. She pointed out the new ceiling-to-floor draperies that not only provided a rich wine color to the room but also would keep warmth within during the upcoming winter. Sitting close to the large, blazing fireplace, genteel conversation flowed between the four of them. It was a relief to talk about accomplishments instead of goals. The new draperies bore witness to this. Elizabeth had asked one of the servants to give them plenty of time for the adults to freshen up before supper. Ania would take care of all the children.

The two families took their places at the large dining table, and supper was served. Elizabeth was in her element and guided the conversation at the table. John did not mind at all because it gave him time to relax after a very busy six weeks. Now he could step back from all of his duties for at least two months before plans would have to be in place for a new planting year. Elizabeth was fully aware of a farmer's year and she wisely knew the right times to expect more from her husband. Thankfully, this was a night for the after-dinner port wine to warm all of their hearts and also disarm their guests because tomorrow, Elizabeth would speak to Susan about their dilemma.

By design, Saturday started slowly, with breakfast served later than usual in a farmer's house. Since John's brother's family would join them for the afternoon and dinner, Elizabeth sought Susan for a late morning walk. The fallen red, brown, and yellow maple leaves allowed more sunlight to warm their path. Elizabeth knew her words would have to be as perfect as this fall scene. She waited until they approached the turning point on their walk when she voiced her opening gambit.

"Young children sure have a lot of energy. Alice, my oldest, has finally reached the age where she can help me with her two younger brothers. She is also asking me more and more questions about things mothers and daughters talk about." Elizabeth knew the Ashworth's recent financial success could provide the means to take in a young woman to help with their children. Unbeknownst to Elizabeth, Susan and her husband discussed that very need on their way to Sussex. The seed planted by Elizabeth was ready to bear fruit.

"I do need help with the children in my home, but we just don't know anyone. In Oconomowoc, all the reputable women have already been employed by other families."

"Susan, we need your help."

"You need our help? How?"

"Do I have your complete confidence? The only person you can speak to about this is your husband."

"You have my word, Elizabeth."

"Ania, the young woman who cares for our children, is pregnant. She was raped."

"Do you know who?"

"We do."

"Will he marry the girl?"

"He ran off and he comes from a very powerful and ruthless family in Milwaukee who has the means to ruin us, like her. Ania has served us well, and she has been wonderful with our children for three years. We trust her completely. Because of all of this, we feel responsible to shield Ania and us from probable repercussions. The girl deserves some Christian charity. So, John and I think it best for Ania to leave this area before any suspicions are raised or questions asked and rumors fly. Would you and James be willing to take her into your home, where she could care for your young children? She has nowhere else to go."

"We want to help, Elizabeth, but…take her into our home? James and I will need to discuss this."

At dinner, with John's brother and his family, the vivacious Susan was quieter than usual. She kept mulling over Elizabeth's request, thinking it was no small matter for the Williamsons, and it was growing every day. However, how would a pregnant domestic in their own house, even though she would be a governess for their young children, impact their own lives? Furthermore, even though John would pay for any medical care plus her required time off from duties, would Ania still be valuable to them? Susan's husband noticed something distracted his wife during dinner. It was not like her, and he would certainly have to ask why this was the case as soon as they were alone. Probably not until tonight.

On their return to Oconomowoc, Susan and her husband discussed the request again. Financially, yes. For the children and Susan, absolutely! What of the man in Milwaukee and the new woman in the house? *She's pregnant. She's pregnant,* Susan thought. James thought nothing of anything. By the time they arrived home, they had reached a decision and soon thereafter, they sent a letter back to Sussex, clearing the way for Elizabeth to begin Ania's journey to becoming a mother and raising a child in a new home. Would Ania love the solution as much as the Williamsons? Elizabeth would move slowly and first let a different relationship grow between them. This new issue could not be seen by Ania as being just self-serving. Hopefully, at the right time, she would then be open to the suggestion of moving to a new home for her new life. *A tender girl had just been crushed. She must not be hurt again, so this would have to be done just right,* Elizabeth thought.

Ania didn't feel like taking walks to the marsh anymore. It was too close to the hops field where Jakob behaved like an animal. *Like Jakob, the red-winged blackbirds had left the marsh for the winter*, Ania thought. *The birds have gone south and Jakob has gone back to Milwaukee, but I have nowhere else to go. Will my employer keep me on? Do they care and why should they care? Elizabeth can be a stern woman and we really don't talk much. Where is this heading? Where am I heading?*

Chapter Six

Bothered that his brewery was not first in production, Herr Schmidt knew exactly where he wanted his company to be. It was just business at the best possible level. This merger called marriage between two German beer families, had to be good for his business. This had nothing to do with preparing Jakob to run the largest brewery in Milwaukee. Herr Schmidt had no intention of stepping aside.

Walking toward the door on Saturday morning to get his cane and coat from the butler for the final workday of the week, Jakob called after his father. "The Lieders would like to meet with you and mother to discuss wedding plans."

The Lieders would make all the decisions, but it was more than customary at this social level for the groom's parents to know what those plans were. The first decision would be the date of the wedding. The place, of course, would be the beautiful, spacious Lieder home. Charlotte's father was not looking forward to tonight's dinner party. Competitor, now future father-in-law to his daughter, would sit at his table, discussing her future with his son.

His wife was already caught up in the excitement, as if the wedding day was tomorrow. She could not sit still in the large drawing room, waiting for the Schmidt's arrival.

Charlotte cautiously addressed her father ."Did your day go well, Father?"

"So far."

Charlotte knew her father was concerned about his only child, but since he was a man of his word given days ago, he was helpless now. This was the first time Charlotte saw her father in this position. He always was in charge, and now she and her mother had to lead him calmly through this night.

The butler stepped into the room. "Madam, the Schmidts have arrived."

The Lieder family walked toward their door, allowing the Schmidts to enter their lives. They exchanged careful greetings, with only the mothers engaged in conversation. The two short German fathers feigning friendliness, standing as tall as they could like boxers before a match, talked about business. Jakob and Charlotte spoke polite words, but no signs of affection. This was starting like a business meeting between providers so that the finished product would be acceptable. Thankfully, almost immediately, they were sitting down for dinner.

The flower setting at the end of the table was stunning, reaching four feet in the air. Mrs. Lieder had arranged for the six of them to sit at the other end of the long table more intimately. Her husband sat at the head, of course, with his wife to his left and his daughter to his right, protecting him from the Schmidt advances. Servants stood a few paces behind each person, and the butler observed everything while standing farther behind Herr Schmidt, but in the sight line of Herr Lieder.

Dinner went smoothly, but the conversation did not. The men said next to nothing, while all three women tried first to agree on a wedding date in June of the following year. They decided on Saturday, June third since there would be a full moon that weekend to help light the Lieder estate for the expected lavish wedding reception. Staff served the required after-dinner drink at the table to speed things along at this obligatory meal.

With business finished, Charlotte and her mother wisely wanted to separate the two fathers as soon as possible. With the date arranged and their drinks finished, Herr Lieder could stand it no more and rose from his seat. The signal was obvious to all and meant to draw a close to the night's festivities.

Goodbyes were quick at the door when Heinriche Schmidt looked at Karl Lieder. "We soon will have the best possible future for our two breweries." It was meant to be prophetic and complimentary. It was not.

"That will depend on how well your son takes care of my daughter. Goodnight!"

As soon as the door closed, Charlotte pouted. "Father, I'm marrying Jakob, not his father."

"I know you're marrying Jakob, but his father will do everything he can to draw you into his family at our expense. And make no mistake about it, it is his family." He looked at his wife. "You both want this wedding. What I want, Charlotte, is for you to be happy. The price is too great if you are not. I, we, will care for you as long as we live. I am not sure Jakob will do the same." With that, her father ended the conversation, but the discussion about her happiness was just beginning.

Ania's hands were freezing as she carried water from the outdoor pump toward the kitchen. In winter, the pump always needed more priming. The longer it took, the colder Ania's wet hands got, working the cold cast iron pump. She hated this kitchen duty the most.

Watching her through the kitchen window haul two buckets of fresh water up the steps, Elizabeth opened the outside and inner doors for her. Although Elizabeth was not heartless, it was still an unusual act of kindness shown toward a member of her staff. The glance between them betrayed their shared responsibility—pregnancy. Ania could tap into Elizabeth's experiences, since no one had schooled her on the changes that were taking place within her.

Mid-afternoon, Elizabeth asked for Ania. Coming at once into the smaller parlor, Elizabeth wanted to disarm the girl swiftly. Ania took a seat.

"We really have not spoken since you told John and I what happened to you in the hops field. We are both concerned, of course. How are you feeling, Ania?"

Ania dropped her guard. "I'm no longer feeling ill in the mornings. I can carry out all of my duties, ma'am."

"I know you can, Ania. You need not be concerned about that. Of course, we want you to carry on with your work as before. I simply want you to know, Ania, that we are going to take care of you even as things change for you. For now, let's keep this all to ourselves. You can ask of me anything about what is happening to you at any time. I will ask from time to time how you are doing." With that, Elizabeth dismissed Ania, thinking she was one step closer to resolution.

The late November nights were now cold and long. Less was expected of the staff between meals, as if the entire household was beginning its winter slumber. Thanksgiving was near, and with Christmas coming, Elizabeth announced to the staff that the annual December festive parties at their home would be earlier this year, since they would spend Christmas week with their friends in Oconomowoc. The staff now knew of their employers' plans for the end of the year, and soon Ania would know it would be her destination as well.

Thanksgiving was just a family affair and this year they would celebrate at John's brother's home just up Main Street. Staff from both households preparing the sumptuous meal together always provided some jealousy and tense moments as to how to prepare the many courses. Kitchen cooks were an ornery lot. The two female lead cooks in the same kitchen provided some laughs for others doing their best to keep pace and the peace. Since two more families would join the Williamsons, there would be at least twenty people served two meals on Thanksgiving Day.

Things had settled down the afternoon before Thanksgiving and Elizabeth decided she would seize the afternoon to speak to Ania, and if the conversation went well, she would let her know of their decision. Ania would be very busy the next day, so Elizabeth hoped she would have little time to think about this major change in her life, allowing the conclusion to their conversation to evolve into the result needed by John and her. It was quite a move on Elizabeth's part. Hopefully, Ania would think they needed her more in Oconomowoc than with her current employer.

Since the rest of the staff were at her brother-in-law's house or busy in their own kitchen, Elizabeth asked Ania to join her in the small parlor.

"Please be seated, Ania. I have set some tea out for us. Could you pour me a cup with two sugars, please?"

After finishing the task, Ania sat across the small table.

"You have done wonders for our children, Ania. They all respect you as much as they respect me, and in some ways, you are more tender with them than I am. Alice is growing into a young woman and she is asking to do more for me so it is hard for me to keep her busy and she loves to mother her younger brothers. I have a lot to thank you for, Ania."

Ania received the compliment with grace and briefly smiled, because Elizabeth's words were true. The tea tasted sweeter hearing it from the person who employed her.

"Our friends in Oconomowoc have said to us they wish they could find a woman like you who could do the same for their children. Their three children are now of the same age when you came here to serve us, and their father wants Mrs. Ashworth to spend more time with him working in their growing hotel business. So, Mr. Williamson and I have thought this would be the perfect time for you to move away from Sussex to Oconomowoc and work for the Ashworths. You know them and they like you and their children like you. You will be safe there and no one but us here will know of your situation. Oconomowoc is growing faster than Sussex, and it will have more to offer both of you. You may even find future employment in their hotel business when their children no longer need your services. You will then be able to take care of yourself later. We will miss you here, of course, but we and our children will continue to see you when we visit the Ashworths. As I said before, we will see to it that you and your future child will receive all the necessary care from the best midwife or doctor in Oconomowoc. We have arranged for you to join the Ashworths in Oconomowoc when we visit them Christmas week. You must agree, Ania, that this is best for you."

There it was, out in the open. It was all arranged. Moving on was the solution. Already realizing she had no better place to be than with her employer, what difference would it make if that employer was in Sussex or Oconomowoc? It would be new there. It would be different. *It might even be better*, Ania thought.

There was no objection from her, so Elizabeth knew she had not only won the argument, but more than that, she had won the future for them all. They rose from the table together and Elizabeth took Ania's hand and pulled her into her arms. It was a relief and resignation hug they needed.

Now that Thanksgiving Day was over, the staff would be busy decorating the house for Christmas. Garland stretched over every fireplace and every door inside with big red bows at the top. Every year, John insisted on finding the widest and tallest tree for the drawing room. Elizabeth always said that she thought he began his search for the next perfect tree as soon as Christmas was over. Even the three men who struggled to cut the tree down, get it into the house, and stand it up when finished, loved to admire nature's handiwork.

Later, John stood with his hands on his hips before the tree. "This year's tree is the best yet!"

This Christmas, Ania didn't give much thought to such things. The end here was nearing. Elizabeth asked her three children to join her in the small parlor before they would join their father in front of the tree for his Christmas speech to the staff. When Ania came into the room, the children stopped their fussing. With Ania at her side, Elizabeth told the children that their nanny would go with them to Oconomowoc, where she would stay to care for the Ashworth children. Twelve-year-old Alice smiled briefly, but her two younger brothers looked puzzled. This would pass quickly for them, and Elizabeth knew it. A soft wave of emotion rolled through Ania's heart, but Elizabeth quickly moved her to her next encounter before the staff.

The entire household staff, farm employees, and carriage workers had gathered in the drawing room. At the side of the room, large tables held a Christmas feast to be enjoyed by all. John's Christian family roots inspired him to show kindness to those who worked for him. He truly felt this way, especially at this time of the year, and anyone who worked for him knew he felt this way. It was an unusual relationship for the times between him, the employer, and his workers compared to other employers.

With his family, John walked into the brightly lit room with Ania following behind. She quickly joined her place with the rest of the household staff. As John moved to the side of the great tree, a fellow kitchen worker looked to Ania. "Where were you?"

She didn't have time to respond when John raised his hands to get their attention. "Merry Christmas to each one of you. We are here together to celebrate and celebrate we shall. All of you are our guests and I plan to speak with each one of you and give each of you your Christmas present. Before we start our meal, I have an announcement to make. Ania, our long-time nanny, will be leaving with us when we leave for Oconomowoc tomorrow morning to become the nanny for the Ashworth family. She has done a wonderful job with our children and we are sure she will do the same in Oconomowoc." With a prayer before their meal, John closed Ania's employment in Sussex.

The sleigh ride from Sussex to the train depot in Pewaukee took almost an hour. Two sleighs carried family members, presents for the Ashworth family, and Ania and her few things. It was a cold December morning, so heated footstones and bison robes were ready. A rider on horseback would also join them for the trip in case there was some difficulty on the way, so he could go for help. Breakfast was brisk as John kept pushing everyone to leave. After the household staff cleaned up after the previous day's party, they took some moments to say their goodbyes and best wishes to Ania. John and Elizabeth had set the pace for her departure from Sussex, and as far as they were concerned, it could not have been quick enough. As Ania settled in her place on the second sleigh, she felt the baby move.

Shortly after they arrived at the small station, the black behemoth from Milwaukee heading west pulled next to the small wooden depot almost on time. Cases were stored onboard while family members carried the Christmas presents onto the new Pullman's car. As the train pulled away, Elizabeth felt a little uneasy about their decision about whether Ania should have stayed behind or whether she would be better off with the Ashworths. Looking at her husband, she reassured herself their decision was best and so the issue was behind her as fast as the depot disappeared.

Three cutters were waiting for them at the Oconomowoc depot. Two cutters for the travelers from Sussex and one for their luggage and presents. Snow piled higher here confirmed winter's grip had tightened. They passed the largest of the two Ashworth-owned hotels during the short trip to their cream-colored brick home. John noticed immediately that their house had grown in size with a three-story extension on the building's east side, including a larger porte cochère that could serve all three cutters at the same time. Horses were quickly tethered so the riders could disembark.

Standing at the open door were James and Susan Ashworth. James smiled. "Greetings to all of you. Come in and get warm."

Ania was carrying her own two suitcases into the handsome home when James quickly grabbed them from her hands and let her proceed ahead of him into the large vestibule where the staff accepted coats. After James set them down with the rest of the cases in the large foyer, he joined Susan, who was wearing a bright green dress, and together they led them down a short hallway through the pocket doors into the drawing room. Her three children scampered at her heels and finally, she picked up the youngest and placed him on her lap while the older two sat on the thick rug in front of her feet.

The housemaid was told ahead of time to show Ania to her new quarters upstairs and across the hallway from the three individual bedrooms for the children. The nursery for the youngest boy was closest to Ania's room. When she walked in, her room was larger than expected. The wardrobe was to the left of the open door and was more than adequate to hold the few dresses she owned. A dresser, for the rest of her things, was next to the wardrobe. A black library table with a chair was on the opposite wall from the door. From the table, she could look out a window over the backyard, now covered with snow, down a hill to Lac Le Belle. Wallpaper stretched to the top of the eight-foot walls and a small four-poster bed piled high with blankets sat back to the right of the door as you came into the room. Ania could be comfortable here, but would she be happy? The maid told her to unpack her things and then come downstairs for dinner. In this household, the main meal was at night and tonight, Ania would join the two families for dinner. Then the maid turned and left Ania alone in her new world.

Dinner was announced for and served promptly at six. Both families marched past the Christmas tree, out of the drawing room, and into the dining room. Still too small to sit in a regular chair, Richard, the youngest son of the Ashworths, sat in a high chair just to the right of the head of the table between Susan and James. Across from them were the Williamson adults and then the rest of the children, with Ania sitting next to Rosemary, Ashworth's daughter. Ania was to tend to the children from this minute on, and Susan watched carefully for any interaction between her children and Ania. It would be Susan's responsibility to get Ania trained from the start on how she preferred things to be done in this household. This addition to the household would mean less time spent doing what she liked least, compared to being at her husband's side, helping him with their businesses. She liked her children, but favoring adult company, she loved the outside world more. Winter was a good time to train Ania, since there were fewer customers at their two hotels, and the gristmill ran fewer hours so that by spring, when all three of their businesses would need more of her time, she could leave Ania behind at the house and be free of household busywork.

After dinner, the women, children, and Ania withdrew from the dining room while the two men remained seated at the table.

The butler stood at Ashworth's side. "Would that be all, sir?"

"Bring large glasses of our finest port wine and serve them here."

As they drank and enjoyed their cigars, John spoke first. "The addition adds grandeur to your house."

"We needed the additional room for the servants on the top floor and now I have an office in the house. Are you ready for the new planting year, John?"

"As much as I can be at this time of the year. James, I need to say this as soon as possible. Thank you for taking Ania off my hands. Her situation, our situation, was of such a delicate nature that it was best that she be moved out of Sussex. You know, James, she was raped and we could not pursue the matter."

"I don't need to know why, John. That is truly your own business. Such a pretty young girl. We will keep her safe here and make her happy."

The following day, James left early to stop by both hotels. He would join the two families early in the afternoon while they visited the

Christmas shops and stores near the center of town. His wife planned to spend the morning giving Ania a tour of the house and an outline of her duties. Moving from the breakfast table, she went to Ania's quarters and, after a sharp knock, walked into the room.

Learning of Susan's plans the night before, Ania sat at the library table, waiting, looking out the window at the glistening snow. The night before was restful, and Ania had already eaten with some of the staff an hour earlier. Ania stood and gave her new mistress a short curtsy.

"Please sit down, Ania. I trust you find your room adequate and you slept well."

"Yes, ma'am."

"I am not Elizabeth Williamson and I don't do things the same way as Elizabeth. That needs to be understood by you straight away."

"Yes, ma'am."

"I want to show you the house and we will meet some of the staff as we walk the house. Ask your questions as we do if you have any." Finished, Susan spun around and walked out the door, expecting Ania to follow her.

The first stop was the nursery, where Richard was fast growing out of his white zinc crib.

"Ania, one of your extra duties will be to help our youngest, Richard, move from his crib to a regular bed. We will be removing the crib from the room and turning the nursery into his bedroom. It is time for him to move on from being a baby. It will not be easy, for he is of strong will, like me."

Moving into the next room, it was obvious this was their daughter's room. It was not clear yet if she was the favorite of the three children, but her room looked like she was. A small table, flanked by two chairs holding dolls, was set with a miniature tea. The fabric strewed over the four-poster bed matched the pillows on the floor. It was a beautiful room for a five-year-old girl.

Whereas the oldest boy's room was stark, a toy wooden rifle and crude wooden revolver were in the corner of the room. Some books were piled on a small desk next to the bed. A doll was also laying on the bed. Susan saw that Ania noticed the doll and quickly stated that her oldest son probably had the gentlest heart, like his father. "I wish Thomas, my seven-year-old, would let go of his favorite doll."

Susan then moved on to their two bedrooms, joined by a large pocket door. Matching, heavy, dark four-poster beds filled one end of each room. At the other end, there was a dressing table for Susan and a small working desk for James. The two matching chairs in Susan's room matched the two chairs in her husband's room. It was all so over-organized. The only thing Susan said about these two rooms was that Ania was forbidden from entering either of them. When they reached the stairs to go down, off to the right, was a small stairway that led up to the newly built quarters on the third floor for the household staff. Already, Susan was halfway down the stairs to the foyer.

"You have seen the hallway to the porte cochère. The foyer where we greet our guests is often set up together with the drawing room for entertainment."

As they walked out of the immense foyer, they could see into the drawing room. Seated inside were Elizabeth, her children, and the Ashworth children looked after by the young girl who helped in the kitchen. Seeing Elizabeth, Susan stepped in. "I'll join you as soon as I am finished with this business." Moving on, they stopped at the dining room. "Ania, here we have my husband's office and meeting room for people connected with his business. A larger parlor room comes next, where James and I might have a conversation with two or more of our friends. James's man has this next room to himself."

Finally, they stood in the kitchen near the far end of the hallway. To one side of the kitchen was a large table the staff used for meetings and to eat. Sitting at the table were the cook, butler, and head maid, waiting for a formal introduction to the household's first nanny. It was a perfunctory greeting and meeting. All three seemed friendly enough, but Susan hurried along out of the kitchen to the end of the hallway and the tour. It was the double doorway to the back of the house or the path to the street.

"When you go out of the house or to town by yourself, you will use this door. When you do the same with the children, you will use the front door or the door where you first arrived. Is that understood?" Looking out the window, Susan pointed out the carriage house and its adjoining apartments for the workers. "You will be spending a lot of time in the backyard with all the children, but that tour can wait until spring." On the way back to the drawing room, they stopped before the head maid who was sitting at the table. "Judy will introduce you to the other workers. She has been with us since James and I were married. She knows everything about this house."

Judy nodded. "That I do." She smiled at Ania. "We will talk later."

Susan was always two steps ahead and already on her way back to the drawing room. She stopped at the entrance. "The children will be going with us into town, Ania, so you will be caring for them. Plan on leaving soon."

It was time for Ania to go to work. Ania went up the stairs to get her coat and scarf and hurried back down so she could coat the children and wrap them in their scarves. Susan was already in her different world, sitting in the first cutter with the Williamsons. The second cutter held the Williamson children. Ania was in the last cutter, with Richard on her lap, Rosemary on one side of her, and Thomas, the oldest, on the other—her new family, and her old family in the cutters ahead of them. Thankfully, there were enough things in the stores and store windows to keep her new charges happy for the afternoon.

Christmas Eve and Christmas Day helped the week fly by, with no major contests between Ania and the children. Even though the Ashworths asked the Williamsons to stay through New Year's Day, John and Elizabeth excused themselves, saying they needed to get back home to look after their own things. What they really wanted to do was to celebrate the coming of the new year in a quieter setting back home.

With train arrangements for the next day, shortly before leaving, Elizabeth sought Ania, who was with Richard in his room. Ania knew she was leaving, and they clasped hands, drawing each other into a hug.

"Dear child, I will ask about you often and when the time is near for you to deliver your child, I will come back to Oconomowoc and stay to help you. Susan has accepted my offer. Write to me and let me know how you are doing here. We will keep our promise to take care of you."

With Richard on her hip, Ania followed Elizabeth downstairs so that in the foyer she could say goodbye to Mr. Williamson and their children. Even John hugged her briefly before the Ashworths. The parting between Ania and the entire Williamson family was indeed tender. Ania turned to take Richard back to his room, but all Elizabeth saw was Ania carrying her own child up the stairs.

Chapter Seven

Mrs. Lieder's thoughts were way past New Year's Day to June third and her daughter's wedding. The entire weekend needed to be the social event of the year. Winter was nonexistent in her mind, and she needed to move her husband's thinking in the same direction. It would not be easy. Even though household responsibilities were hers, Herr Lieder knew how much was spent and what it was spent on. However, this was his daughter's wedding, and no matter how much money they spent, it could not buy happiness for his dear Lotta. Herr Lieder felt deep down to either indulge his daughter or break her heart, so his wife had to tread carefully when discussing wedding plans with him. Karl grudgingly realized he could not stop the wedding because this would forever damage his strong relationship with his daughter, so the best alternative was to support her wedding plans no matter the cost, so he could be there when their marriage fell apart. It sounded, even to him, like a business prediction, but that was exactly how his competitor, Schmidt, was looking at this union between the two children, and Karl knew it. Despite his inner turmoil, he set these worries aside until the wedding day was over and their married lives began.

Jakob and Charlotte saw each other more often now, and a chaperone was no longer needed since the Milwaukee newspapers had published their wedding bands. More than once in private, Jakob's hands were all over his betrothed. Charlotte fought him off by being sure they were in public places. She did not want to be showing on her wedding day, which was still six months away. Frustration rose for Jakob in her presence, but there was little he could do about it with Charlotte. Since winter curtailed entertainment employment at the beer garden, the two girls Jakob enjoyed the most had taken their entertainment to a different level in a different place on Water Street. There, his frustration level, instead of being increased, would be halved in the company of Hilda or Sarah or both. Hilda, Sarah, and others worked within two unassuming adjoining buildings. Jakob went in the front door of the building on the right and normally chose the girl he wanted to spend the evening with and went with her to the building on the left with an exit to a side street and a second exit to the rear alley. One entrance, but two additional exits were available if necessary.

Jakob and his father never crossed paths here, but Jakob heard an older girl and the bartender talking a few nights back. "Yeah, that's Ricke's kid." It was this girl he wanted to spend an evening with, but since he didn't know her name, he could only look for her each time he walked through that front door. She was not here tonight either, so Sarah would have to do.

Dirty snow was still visible throughout the city even though it was late March, but the gilded wedding announcements were on their way to the post office.

Most people who mattered already knew the date of the Lieder wedding, but formality held fast in the Lieder's home. The wedding would be at three o'clock in the afternoon at the Lieder's home, followed by a very formal dinner and dancing on the veranda. The moon shining full would help light the veranda and steps down to the sprawling grounds, hopefully in full bloom. Relatives would come from Bavaria, and their two long trips would have to be worthwhile. The bride's mother would see to it for everyone. After all, Charlotte was her daughter, too.

Jakob stayed out of Charlotte and her mother's way, letting them make all the plans, but he did not stay out of his favorite evening place. This night he arrived early and there she was, standing close to the bar. Jakob measured her quickly and noted that she was older and heavier than Sarah, but tonight, she would do much more for him. Jakob would be manipulative, touching a nerve and her feminine charms. Control while lovemaking came easy to him, so Jakob knew that by the end of the night, he would know why a few people called his father Ricke.

He approached her slowly. The ladies know the regulars and the regulars have their connections with certain girls. She knew he chose

Sarah, and if Sarah was busy for the night, then he would choose his second best, Hilda.

Tonight, Sarah was busy, but Jakob walked past Hilda. "What is your name?"

"It's Matty. May I be of service for you?"

Jakob took her by the hand and led her to the bar. After purchasing two bottles of his favorite champagne and taking two glasses, they walked arm in arm through the passage to the next building. He asked the bouncer at the end of the hallway if their best room was still available. Rarely needed in this establishment, a bouncer was more of a shepherd for the new girls, making sure clients and girls were both happy with the evening's results. The reputation of the house kept adding prospective clients to their waiting list, which kept the money flowing so that the madam was happy and her financial backers were more so.

Cinched at the side of her waist, Matty's dark blue dress exposed enough of her ample buxom to catch the eye of a potential client.

Jakob opened the door for her. "Please, sit at the table."

Taught to obey but stay in control, Matty took her time to be seated. Jakob stood, opened the champagne bottle with ease, and poured her a glass first. His intense stare marked some danger, Matty thought. As far as she knew, he had never compromised his reputation as a gentleman here. Obviously, he wanted something more, and she hoped she could deliver.

"Tell me about yourself."

Matty sipped from the glass. "You know what I am."

Sitting down, Jakob drank slowly and tried to disarm her. "The night will be worth it for you."

Matty now was on guard. This was very unusual to show any real interest in a girl. There was so much pretending in these rooms. The men wanted to believe, for the moment, that the woman in his company was really interested in him as a man. That ship sailed every night, never reaching its destination, no matter how often the same client was with the same woman. The skill of the woman made the charade more believable, but this voyage was starting differently. Truth made Matty uneasy.

"Pour me another glass, sir."

"No need to call me sir. You know who I am."

"I do, Jakob."

"Tell me about yourself, Matty."

"My parents died in a house fire shortly after we arrived here from Ireland before the war. I tried to find work or a good man. Finding neither, I had just arrived at an awful brothel when a man invited me to leave. It did not take much to get me to leave that place. He took good care of me and I became his. He was married but gentle, so I did his bidding. It was an easy choice because he put me into my own apartment far from the docks, and with his money, I could buy nice clothes so I could be somebody. He took real pleasure in saving me."

"Why do you call him Ricke?"

"He told me as a boy in Germany he defended a village girl tormented by the boys because she stammered badly." *Jakob might as well know it all*, she thought. "The girl called him Ricke because she could not say his given name, Heinriche, and now these same boys terrorized him with his new nickname. Now you know and now I am here."

"Why here?"

"Because I got older and because we could be replaced, we were moved on to work here in this house. There were others just like me. We had no other choice because our reputations were firmly fixed. Hilda and Sarah are the latest additions to this house."

"Does my father come here?"

"He doesn't have to. His other partners in this house do, but he has his own little snuggery somewhere and his own new girl."

She stopped, so Jakob rose and poured him and her another glass. Her green eyes looked empty now. Jakob didn't think it would be this easy to find everything laid out before him. Pleased, he turned to better business. He walked behind her and, with his fingertips, raised her chin and kissed her softly on her lips. She didn't need pity, that was long past. Tonight, she would know a gentleman even gentler than his father. Quickly, he put his hands on her shoulders and helped raise her to her feet. She stood, and he took her into his arms and placed her head on his chest, stroking her hair.

He would be deliberate with each step so that both could enjoy each detail and there would be many details. He kissed her again, gently. He turned her and slowly unhooked the clasp holding her dress, not touching her skin. The dress fell, and she stood before him, stripped of every pretense. He stepped back and admired her, turning her slowly before him. She was blessed with beautiful alabaster skin without a blemish on it, but for a few freckles on her nose. He pulled the covers back from the bed and sat on it to undress. He would not hurry on purpose. Putting his shoes and shirt to the side and then his pants, he took her by the hand, pulled her to the bed, and covered her.

Jakob walked to the other side of the bed and joined her. Sitting up, he placed her head on his lap and stroked her hair, so she relaxed beside him, and then he loved her.

Jakob stayed much longer than ever before, and it was after sunrise when he made his way home. His father was getting ready to leave the house when Jakob walked through the front door. They didn't say a word. The father knew where his son was, but he didn't know that his son knew more than he should about him.

Jakob stared at his father from the foyer, then turned from him and walked up the stairs. This didn't change a thing between them. It just made his father's words *"take what you want"* more understandable.

As the wedding drew closer, Charlotte was inserting herself into every plan and it was wearing thin with her mother. Charlotte wanted to be more than the centerpiece of a well-set table. Now she wanted to set the table, which had Maria caught up in her own extravagance amplified by her daughter's additional wants. Finally, she told Charlotte it had to stop. Charlotte caved for only a day or two, and then she was right back at it, demanding another flower arrangement here or a larger orchestra for the evening dance.

Bickering always seemed reasonable at a time like this, but Karl was determined to put an end to it. "Charlotte, you have to stop with these changes and additions to set plans. I will pay for a European tour for you and your husband after the wedding, but that is the end of it."

They would sail on the same ship that would take their German relatives back home, and from Hamburg, they would go to Berlin, Paris, and, finally, Rome on their two-month trip.

Charlotte knew better than to ask for more.

Chapter Eight

By the end of March, Lac Le Belle was free of ice, and daffodils were blooming along the west wall of the Ashworth house. Each morning, the children couldn't wait to get outside. Keeping them close together in the backyard took all the skill Ania could muster, and sometimes another pair of hands. In place of their mother, the kitchen helper could be called on to help run after these three dynamos. Richard, the youngest, would listen the least.

Warned by his mother that he was of strong will, he did not take it well when Ania moved him from his crib to a small bed of his own. The older children followed Ania's directions, but Richard was a handful.

Ania's second letter to Elizabeth in Sussex spelled this all out and more. The more the children took to Ania's care, the less they saw of their mother. Now, Ania wasn't moving as fast as she used to, so it was hard to keep up with all of her duties. Ania added, *Thankfully, the head maid, Judy, is very sympathetic and would dispatch* the *kitchen girl to help me whenever she saw I was slowing down.* However, the next sentence bothered Elizabeth the most. *Susan has never sat down with me to talk about my pregnancy or what I can expect in childbirth.* Without discussing it with her husband, Elizabeth immediately made plans to visit Susan in Oconomowoc.

By the time Elizabeth wrote to Susan and received a reply, there was enough time to visit Susan before Holy Week and check on Ania as promised. Taking the train from Pewaukee on Thursday, Elizabeth was in Oconomowoc by late afternoon. Met by a carriage at the station, Elizabeth was talking to Susan before dinner while Ania and the three children were still in the backyard.

Arrangements were made, that while she was here, Ania would have the next day off until dinner. Susan acquiesced and acknowledged that

Judy and the kitchen helper could care for the children this one day.

Ania broke free from her duties at ten in the morning, and seeing Elizabeth in the foyer, a broad smile crossed her face. Ania appeared haggard, with two months to go before she would deliver.

After boarding the carriage, Elizabeth immediately peppered Ania with questions. "How are you? What do you feel? Is the baby kicking a lot?"

For the first time, someone was talking to her about what was happening and what would happen to her in just two short months.

"Susan gave me the name of a physician near the center of town and we will see him first of all."

In the twenty minutes it took to get to the doctor's home, Ania felt the most relaxed since she arrived in Oconomowoc. She was always on duty. If Richard cried during the night, it was Ania's responsibility to get up and care for the child.

On the porch, Elizabeth knocked, and soon a middle-aged portly man answered the door and ushered them into his office. The country doctor put both women at ease, asking questions of Ania and taking notes.

Elizabeth clarified she would pay for all costs before, during, and after the delivery. The doctor added that he and the two midwives in the area worked together. The midwife would be called when birth pains began, and then she would send for him when delivery was near. Elizabeth added that she would take care of those costs as well, and that the delivery would be at the Ashworth home. Surprised, the doctor was nonplussed, showing no emotion to this information. There was no physical examination, just a discussion about using chloroform. Finally, the doctor gave Elizabeth the address of the midwife nearest to the Ashworths. It would be their next stop after lunch. The carriage was waiting for them, and soon they were on their way to Mon Bijou on Fowler Lake.

Two women. Two different places in life. Two very different fashion statements as they walked into the dining room. Ania was unaware of the stares, and Elizabeth did not care. They sat at a window overlooking the small lake, and Elizabeth ordered for them.

She put her hand on Ania's hand, beginning the conversation. "My children miss you, Ania. You were wonderful with each one of them. I know you'll be a wonderful mother of your own child."

Out it came for the very first time from her lips. "My child will have a good mother, but no father...no father. Jakob just left me laying there. He didn't even say a word to me. He just left me behind in the dirt. Why did he do that?"

"Men, but not all men, think they can treat women as they please, much like a buck treats a herd of does. They take us when they want and leave us behind if they want. Someday that may change, but not today. I have a good man who loves me and did not just run off. For that and other reasons, I love him. Your man did run off. Let him go and may he never come back into your life. You will be a better mother without him."

With that said, the conversation turned to what Ania would feel before she gave birth and when she gave birth. "Chloroform could be used, but that decision will be made by the doctor with you when the moment arrives."

Ania did not know what to ask, and so she just let Elizabeth talk about her own experiences, nursing the newborn, and the weeks that followed.

"Susan promised she would send for me as soon as delivery was near. I'll help you, Ania."

Nothing more needed to be said, as they ate lunch and left for the midwife's house.

She was home and their polite conversation included timing, payment arrangements, notice that Doctor Jameson should be called, and finally that Elizabeth would either be there or on her way. Elizabeth then told the driver to take them for a long ride through town and into the country so Ania could have some time to herself and rest before working again. The afternoon sun warmed them, and Elizabeth hoped it warmed Ania's spirits as well.

Her charges were waiting for her in the foyer, angry that they could not play outside on this beautiful day. Dinner time was close for them, so playing outside would have to wait until the next day. Rest time for Ania was over.

After dinner, Elizabeth thanked Susan again for letting them have the day. "I plan to take the morning train back to Pewaukee and home. John is expecting me."

The trip back to Pewaukee gave Elizabeth plenty of time to think about Ania, men, marriage, and children.

Chapter Nine

German relatives would arrive soon to stay at the Lieders for Charlotte's wedding and to tour the beer town. Mrs. Lieder was beyond approachable. One day everything was all wrong and the next, everything could not have been better. It was so out of character for Maria. Whose wedding was it anyway, and why do mothers of the bride get that way? Gifts were piling up in the drawing room like Christmas presents under the tree. June third could not come quickly enough for Karl, and now the house had started filling up with relatives, too. Guests he didn't know sat at his table, and some of them brought their children. It was too much for a sane man, and so he spent long hours at work.

His counterpart, Heinriche Schmidt, did not have to do anything other than rub his hands together as the day drew closer. He saw it as nothing more than a business union made in heaven, sanctified by the priest. All Heinriche could think of was his business doubling in size when the priest said they were man and wife. It would be a great day for Herr Schmidt, and on top of it all, Karl Lieder was paying for it.

Two weeks before the wedding, Jakob and Charlotte appeared in public more often. Everyone knew Jakob was getting married, but it made no difference to the girls on Water Street. Almost all of their clients were married anyway, so Jakob was just joining the public ranks of respectability. How well he managed his personal, private appetites was up to him. The girls would always be there for him and others. Did Charlotte know of Jakob's preferences?

Beyond her own hearth, Charlotte did not know much of anything. The outside world of business, commerce, and even the city was confusing to her. She wanted what her mother had, but more children. An older brother for herself would have been nice to inform her of what would be expected of her in marriage. Her mother did not speak of such things and her father was only protective of her, so she hoped Jakob would be patient and gentle.

As they walked in a small park along the Menomonee River, Charlotte tried to broach the subject. "How shall we spend our first days and nights together before we leave for Europe?"

There was only a curt retort from Jakob. "Charlotte, that will be up to me. I will continue to celebrate my wedding with my friends while we wait to disembark for New York and sail for Europe. We will, of course, stay at my father's house. You know our home, just two blocks away from his house, has just started construction, and I have been assured that it will be finished by the time we get back from Europe so we can move in. These things I will take care of. You will furnish the house, of course, and my mother will help. Then we will fill the bedrooms with sons."

It was all the gentleness Charlotte was going to get from her husband. Ania knew the same from him.

Even though Susan had assured Elizabeth that she understood the situation now that delivery was close, she detested the fact that she had to give more of her time to her own children. The busy season for their hotels was beginning and rooms had to be readied, staff prepared, and books managed. Spring fishermen with their families were already arriving and time was getting short before the vacation rush. Though delivery was not imminent, a letter was quickly dashed off to Elizabeth to come and take care of Ania, since Susan had no time for that additional responsibility. Elizabeth arrived and Susan was more relieved than excited that her friend was in town. It was becoming apparent to Elizabeth where Susan's heart was, and it was not with children, not even her own. Even though June arrived full of sunshine, Ania knew instinctively that something was happening within her, and she was so relieved that Elizabeth had arrived the day before.

Saturday arrived at the Lieder's home full of life. It was a glorious day for a wedding. Spring had been rainy, but now the home inside and out smelled of lilacs everywhere. The peony bushes protected from the rain were not beaten down, and most of the tulip heads were still standing tall. *It will be perfect,* Charlotte thought. Her mother's face was radiant as they sat down with Charlotte, Jakob, and his family for the late wedding breakfast. Even Karl, father of the bride, on this day, stood a bit taller. *Perhaps it will be grand. Perhaps it will work,* Karl thought. *Perhaps.*

The wedding would take place at the top of the five wide steps that led to the Lieder's living quarters. Guests could sit in the large lower foyer and to the right in the large drawing room or to the left under the archway that led to the side entrance. The priest arrived early so that time could be well spent with his wealthy flock. This was one of Milwaukee society's highlights for the year, and he wanted to make the most of it. Most of the beer families were represented. Heinriche, Elise Schmidt, and son entered at the appropriate time to gather the most impact. They sat to the immediate right where the bride's parents would sit. Exactly at three o'clock, Charlotte appeared at the top of the staircase, with her parents flanked on each side. At her appearance, Jakob stood and moved to the foot of the stairs. Slowly, all three walked down the stairs, where Jakob joined them at the last step, and the foursome moved toward a small kneeling bench in front of the priest. Maria kissed her daughter first, and then Karl. His role was done here, but Karl firmly believed it was not over. They sat, and the service began. Heinriche could not help but think that his role was just beginning and Jakob's role would not change at all compared to Charlotte's.

Her dress was tight at the bodice, and full beneath her waist. Small ruffles above the elbow joined long white sleeves to white gloves. A single red ruby teardrop joined a silver necklace held tight against her neck, and her sheer veil covered her face and trailed along her head, falling behind her back almost to the floor. Karl thought his daughter stood before the priest, happy and beautiful, and truly an underserved gift to Jakob and his family. The priest spoke in Latin and read two passages from the Bible in German. After kneeling for the prayers, the two voyagers stood and the priest, speaking in Latin and German, joined them as husband and wife, pronouncing the same to all in attendance: Mrs. Jakob Schmidt. The couple turned and faced their witnesses. It could not be undone. The parents of the bride rushed forward to congratulate their daughter and Elise joined them. Herr Schmidt, standing still with the captain's cane in hand, surveyed the scene and smiled.

Once the wedding was over, the servants scurried from their hidden vantage points to begin a long day. Thankfully, the weather had cooperated, so that men and women began spilling out onto the large terrace and estate grounds. Even Lake Michigan participated, shimmering with sunlight in the background.

Guests were further pulled toward the uncovered tables of sweet cakes and pastries. Barrels of Lieder beer, encased in blocks of ice, stood on tables under chestnut and linden trees. Small tables with blue umbrellas were scattered on the lawn. Slowly the rooms emptied, so that inside the drawing room and foyer tables could be set up and fitted with flowers and plates. The orchestra had arrived and was already in place for dinner, music, and dancing later under the full moon. Those in attendance would not forget this bountiful wedding banquet. Maria had seen to it.

The wedding and reception were everything that Charlotte hoped they would be. She found a moment to thank her mother and father, clasping him tightly. Jakob was standing with friends at the white carriage bedecked in flowers. The driver held the reins of the two white steeds, waiting to carry them off. Even though it was a short distance to the Schmidt residence, there was no need to hurry, and so Jakob instructed the driver to take Lake Drive to the point and then to his borrowed father's residence. The moon was behind them and shone on the water that Charlotte hoped deep in her heart that the start of their marriage would be as bright.

By design, there was no one to greet them at the door so that their beginning would have no witnesses. Determined, Jakob took Charlotte's hand and led her to his room full of moonlight. They were not with a chaperone or in public view, so there was no stopping him. Without a moment for her to undress privately, he turned Charlotte's back to him and undid the two buttons at the nape of her neck. Then he pulled at the ties that held the bodice tight. With her back still to him, he pulled the dress from her shoulders and it fell to the floor. The point was surely made to Charlotte.

"Stand here and take everything off now."

She didn't hesitate. Charlotte knew Jakob always took the lead in beginning their conversations, but demanding was new.

Standing now completely naked, she waited for further instruction.

"Turn around."

She turned this new chapter in her life the best she could and faced him. He sat on the bed, but said nothing. There was no awe, no word of kindness, nothing.

"Come here."

He took his two fingers and touched her lips, and then parted them, forcing them inside her mouth. Pulling them out of her mouth, he traced her body, trailing his fingers over the top of each breast and then to each nipple. They were not erect yet, but Charlotte's whole body shuddered. Jakob was not being tender at all, but rather teaching her that her body, all of her body, was his to do with as he pleased when he pleased.

"I'm cold. Could we get into bed?"

"Not yet. Stand right there."

Now his fingers found the inside of her knee and he forced her to move her leg out so he could put his feet and knees between her legs. With his knees, he forced her to open her legs.

"Jakob, let me get into bed."

"You will not move. Stand still."

He took his fingers and tweaked her nipples slowly between his thumb and forefinger, increasing the pressure so that Charlotte cried out.

"Be still."

Her nipples had to obey, and they now stood erect, as did both breasts. He moved his fingers to the inside of her thigh and they moved to what she knew he wanted, but he pulled them back and then walked them up closer to her again and again. Without touching her, Charlotte felt him. Each time his fingers drew closer to her and now split apart on each side of her, they rubbed against her, and then, without warning, he drove both fingers as far as he could inside her.

Charlotte gasped. He had broken the seal. Slowly, he pulled them out, only to drive them in again and again.

"Now you can get into bed. Lay on your back."

"But I'm bleeding."

"I don't care, and neither should you. Lay on your back."

First Jakob took off his shoes and then, standing, facing her, on purpose, slowly removed his waistcoat, shirt, and pants. "Take me in your hand."

"Take what?"

He pointed to his erection. "Take this in your hand and pulled me to you." He made her believe this first time that she was forcing Jakob to come to her. It could not have been more obscene for Charlotte. She tried, and Jakob grabbed her hand and placed her fingers on his penis.

"Touch me here and here. Move your hand up and down the shaft."

Now Jakob climbed into bed to her side and grabbed her by her hair.

"Open your mouth and take it inside your mouth."

As soon as she opened her mouth, he jammed himself into her. "You will do this when I want. Do you understand?"

He pushed her away. It was a whirlwind for her, moving quickly from this lesson to another lesson, and then to another. For far experienced Jakob, he was taking his time teaching and taking what he wanted.

"Lay back." With his hand, he stroked her until her wetness was obvious to both of them. "Pull your knees up."

He slid inside of her. Jakob pulled out again and again so that he could thrust into her as if each thrust was the first ever within her. Turning her over and as her head hung over the side of the bed, first with his fingers and then with his reddened penis, he drove into her again and again until he could hold it back no longer, and Jakob filled her with everything he could muster.

Quickly standing to capture the moment, Jakob walked around to her side of the bed. "When I come to you to take you, you will do exactly as I say and you will want me to do anything and everything I want to do to you. You are not in England and you surely are not Queen Victoria. You are my wife. That is what you married, Charlotte."

Then he walked back to his side and fell into bed. Turning away from her, he quickly fell asleep, leaving Charlotte alone in the dark, hurting everywhere, especially in her heart. It hardly seemed that she had slept at all when he was on top of her again, pushing his knee between her legs for the same. Charlotte died at night and Mrs. Jakob Schmidt was born.

There would be no going to church at St. Paul's Lutheran Church this first Sunday in June. Ania was in so much pain that both Elizabeth and Susan agreed it was now time to send for the midwife. After she arrived, they sent word by the same driver to the doctor, alerting him that Ania, at the Ashworth residence, was giving birth. The midwife assured everyone that everything looked good, but it probably would be a long night. Things were made ready in the room for Ania and the new baby. Nobody could do anything now but witness Ania's pain. Elizabeth sat at her bedside, wiping her forehead or holding her hand. The baby was in charge now. The rest of the household staff wanted to know how she was doing, and at regular intervals, one of the six would look in the room to check. At six o'clock, the butler called Elizabeth and Susan for dinner, but only Susan left to have dinner with her family. Elizabeth stayed with the midwife, attending to Ania as best she could. Sunlight was disappearing from the room when Doctor Jameson arrived. He and the midwife walked out to the hallway, and softly, she told him the birth of this baby would be soon, adding birth pains were coming closer together and the mother-to-be seemed to be weathering the storm quite nicely.

"She is young and strong. She'll be all right."

The doctor nodded. "You're in charge."

She was in charge, and so the doctor went downstairs to Mr. Ashworth's office to discuss with them what they could expect in the next few months.

Back in the room, the midwife went to Ania's side. "Control your breaths and push down hard when you feel the next pain." The full moon's brilliance filled the room while the midwife attended to her charge. "Push down hard, girl. Again. Push hard, Ania."

The child's first cry was long and loud. Even the doctor, who was slumped half-asleep in an office chair, heard it. All the noise, plus the comings and goings, kept everyone up in the house. For the Ashworths, things could finally settle down.

The doctor checked the exhausted woman before him first, and then, taking the child from the midwife, laid him at her breast. "Your son is strong, Ania."

"My son," was all Ania could say.

Everyone needed sleep. Elizabeth went to her own bed and the midwife snuffed the last candle in Ania's room while the baby introduced himself to Ania's breast.

Chapter Ten

Soon, the baby in her arms would be baptized privately by the pastor at St. Paul's Lutheran Church. So, with little difficulty, Ania chose a name dear to her heart. Henryk, after her father. Ania loved her father's gentleness and his desire for his whole family to have a better life in America than life in Western Poland. Poland under Prussian rule was no more, and since they were close enough to Germany, there was a corridor to get out. He did not have the chance to enjoy that better life in America before his death on the docks. He had brought his daughters halfway, so Ania vowed, as she held his namesake in her arms, that she and her son would have that better life. She would no longer be a victim and slowly, if need be, fulfill her father's dream. It would not be any easier for her than any other girl alone with a baby in this part of the New World. The next step was to give her son a Christian middle name.

Ania whispered, "I will carry the dream forward for you, Henryk Piotr Sobieski."

The pastor at St. Paul's Lutheran Church trusted the sponsorship of the Ashworths, so the private baptism was carried out with no difficulty and no fanfare. It suited Ania perfectly. Afterward, Elizabeth spoke with Susan, who assured her that for the next two months, Ania would have light duty, and with that in hand, she promised Ania to return soon to check on them both.

Henryk made the time go fast for Ania by nursing well, and he was sleeping longer periods at night so that Ania could get some real rest. Henryk expected the most, and Susan was waiting in the wings to expect more, since she wanted to be back in public view, at the hotel's desk or making her way among the guests. Susan's husband was getting impatient as well because they were in peak season. Susan's children wanted Ania back on full duty, too.

Finally, transition day came, and everything was Ania's responsibility again with help from the kitchen girl. Henryk would just have to fit in.

The Ashworth children helped Ania with baby Henryk, giving him plenty of attention. Henryk could not move much, but the three children wanted to see what he would do next like a new toy. Breastfeeding him before them bedazzled them all, and Henryk was more than willing to steal the show. Bedtime was chaos at first, but he took it all in stride and it tired him out for a good night's rest. Time just ran away for the five of them.

Because of the heat, the children, with their new cocker spaniel puppy, did not like going outside, even though the days should have been cooler by the middle of September. July and August had been so hot and dry that crops withered and farmers were already killing off their dairy stock. The gristmill the Ashworths owned was mostly silent because of the drought. However, business had been brisk at their two hotels, so Susan could keep going about her business, moving among their guests and hotel staff. Guests wanted to get on the water or in the water during the summer and early fall to escape the heat.

Late September and October stayed the course. The fall rains did not come, and the wind from the southwest kept bringing the heat. Farmers could not remember a year like this, and even the cynics were getting itchy, wondering when the rains would finally come. Then, news of the huge fire in Chicago and later, reports about a greater woodland fire in northeast Wisconsin, with hundreds perishing in each fire, filled the papers. Letters received by the Ashworths from their Chicago clients were full of horrible stories of loss and suffering.

Heinriche Schmidt read every paper he could get his hands on about the tragedies. The stories about the great city to the south of him interested him the most. Most of the Chicago breweries had been destroyed in the fire. Those that were left would never keep up with the population's thirsty demand.

He sent for his son, who recently returned with his pregnant wife from their European trip. Charlotte, now carrying her first child, had become quite reserved. She was dutiful and respectful toward her husband, but was more concerned about the coming birth of her child than about paying him much attention.

According to Jakob, she was busy taking care of herself or furnishing the house as he had preordained. It was pretty clear for now that Jakob had won his rightful position, according to his father, and would be better off for it. Jakob didn't even bother to tell her he was leaving to see his father or when he would return home. After a quick two-block walk from his own newly built house, he found his father in his office, bubbling with business possibilities.

"Have you been reading the papers, Jakob? Do you know what this means for our business?"

His father made all the business decisions anyway, so why should he pay attention to such matters was all he could think of as he answered, "What story are you talking about, Father?"

"What story? The Chicago fire!" H father placed his hand on his son's shoulder. "We have much to do."

"*We!*"

"I want you to make contact with the steamer companies and railroad shippers. We want to corner this business. Go to their offices. Learn what is available and how much it will cost for the transportation of our beer barrels on ship and train. Reserve what you can using my name. I will be traveling to Chicago soon to find a distribution center close to both the docks and rail yard. Is that understood? A cab has been arranged for you here so you can leave immediately."

Jakob understood, and he was quickly off to get the information needed and make deals if necessary. The quicker done, the sooner he could relax at the establishments of his choice. Already, Jakob's moral compass did not point toward home and his wife, but back to Water Street and the girl of his choice.

Finished with her on Water Street, Jakob made his way home just before sunrise. Charlotte was long awake as Jakob finally came down the stairs for breakfast. His place was still set for him, as usual, although the times he ate breakfast alone were becoming more frequent.

Charlotte walked into the room to silence but sat at the table anyway, choosing not to be diplomatic. "You got in late last night, Jakob?"

This opening line had to be met with resistance. "I was sent on an errand by my father yesterday concerning our business and the Chicago fire."

This intrigued Charlotte because Jakob hardly ever spoke of his father's business. Business would burden his time, but his success, she felt, would be good for their growing family.

She hoped to please him with questions about his work and draw him closer to her. "What did your father want you to do?"

She thought it to be an innocent question, but she was not ready for the barrage that followed.

"Woman, you know nothing of these things. You have said before that these business items are confusing to you, so why should I bother you with them now? You wouldn't understand. I don't care if you don't understand. I don't want you to pay attention to my work or to my time. Take care of yourself and the baby. Be sure the nursery is ready. That is what you should spend your time on. When I come to you, it will be on my time and then you can take interest in me."

Renewing her memories of his demands in the bedroom was all Charlotte had to hear to leave the room crying. It had not become easier for her, and there was no reason to believe it would change any time soon. Anger must have aroused him as he made his point to her again in her bed. She warned him to be careful, but Jakob didn't even hear her. Laying there, Charlotte thought that perhaps a child—a son—would soften his heart.

Jakob left early the next morning and headed for the brewery. Workers took notice since they didn't see Herr Schmidt's son often. Jakob climbed the stairs to the third floor and through a wall of windows, the brewing vats stood in a row as far as he could see. For a moment, he marveled at all the activity he could see out those windows on his way to his father's office with the information requested two days earlier.

Moving past all the clerks, he made his way into a large paneled room. Stopping just past the door, he recalled he had not been in this room for years, and from what he remembered, it had not changed. His father's office at home had all the trophies of travel, but here there was only an oversized desk, chair, and a side table. Few were allowed to see his home office, and here his coworkers were allowed only to see stark power.

His father walking in behind Jakob, marched to his desk and spoke while he sat. "I thought I would hear from you yesterday with the information I requested. Each day we delay puts us a day behind on this opportunity. When I ask you or anyone else to do something for me, I want it done immediately. I will not remind you of this business tenet again. What did you find out?"

Bypassing his father's criticism, Jakob delivered the information. "We have a steamer on standby for our sole use and five boxcars have been booked on each southern run of the Chicago and Milwaukee railway beginning the first week in November."

"Well done! That gives us a week to secure a distribution center along with storage for the beer, plus horses, and wagons close to the rail yard and docks. I am sending Otto, my foreman, who runs our distribution here to Chicago to choose such a place for us, and I want you to go with him."

"I thought you were going to Chicago?"

"I changed my mind. I am needed here to increase production. You need to go in my stead. Expect to be gone for two weeks or more. Plan to leave later today. You can meet Otto here, this afternoon, and then take the streetcar on Water Street to the railroad station."

Finished, Heinriche Schmidt stood up and moved to the door with new production orders for the plant foreman. Jakob also knew it was his time to move his business career forward and leave family matters behind.

Packing his suitcase would be done by a household staff member while Jakob told Charlotte where he would be for the next two weeks or more.

Charlotte feigned loss, speaking with him while looking forward to quiet for two weeks or more. *Perhaps a visit with my parents*, she thought.

"Be careful in that burned-out city."

"I will be careful. My father is sending a bodyguard with us."

A peck on her cheek and he was gone. It was a short ride for them on the horse-drawn streetcar to the train station. The discussion of what was needed in Chicago took up all their time during the three-hour ride to Chicago. Arriving before seven in the evening would allow them enough time to make arrangements at a good hotel. The next day would be busy gathering information, looking at maps, plotting the burn area, and choosing the main storage center and at least three outlying potential distribution centers, like spokes on a wheel close to the remaining thirsty population centers. Contacts would have to be made with horse and wagon owners to secure a regular stream of their product. This would not be easy since every builder in town would want their use. Otto had already told Heinriche that some of his own stock would have to be brought in from Milwaukee. It was no surprise that Herr Schmidt had chosen Otto to be the foreman at his Milwaukee distribution center. *He certainly is the man for the job here*, Jakob thought.

After settling in for the night, they asked for the nearest saloon so they could ask the owner about his current situation. After pouring their second schooner, the bartender offered what he knew about the local situation.

"The breweries are all gone, and so are most of the saloons. My saloon was one of the lucky ones, but I cannot keep up with demand."

They promised they would return, and on the way to the hotel, Jakob turned to Otto. "My father is right. We can make a name for ourselves here."

The next morning, after securing a cab and driver who knew the area, Otto asked the driver to take them to the ship docks and then the rail yard that served the Chicago-Milwaukee line. Between these two delivery points, Otto decided they would seek an existing storage facility. They would immediately rent it and fit it for their purposes. From there, they could set up a network of delivery points, including saloons, that would be owned by the company. Things would move fast with building contracts for purchase or signed rent agreements. Liveries and horse teams would have to be reserved. Men were hired and immediately put to work. A sizable web would have to be fashioned, and Herr Schmidt would be at the center of it.

Jakob quickly sent off a letter to his father, saying they would be in Chicago until at least Christmas. He also asked his father to send three capable men to help make all the necessary arrangements and encouraged his father to initiate local banking ties. These ties would help with the supply of credit, plus money for purchases and wages. Jakob listed in order all of his business needs for Chicago, and his father smiled as he read each paragraph, convinced that his son was finally taking an interest in his own future fortune, especially since the letter included no words of concern to pass on to his pregnant wife. Jakob was finally getting it.

One whole month and not a single word from Jakob in Chicago, Charlotte thought. *What is that saying, "Distance makes the heart grow fonder?" I have not yet been married for a whole year, and this distance between us gives me more pleasure than if Jakob was in the same room. Should I talk to my parents about this? What would Father say if he knew how miserable I am? What am I going to do? I have to see them, but I think I am not going to tell them anything; not until the baby is born.*

Heinriche sent three men to help Otto, who was really in charge, but Jakob had the impression he had his father's ear. They carried two letters: one for Otto that contained more business directives for the operation, and a personal letter for Jakob. The letter had two revealing sentences, which Jakob read with great interest. The first, his father wrote: *I have sent notice to your wife that you are still busy in Chicago and would not be coming home soon,* and the other was shorter but to the point, *You are coming along in our business, son.* The first was just information for Jakob, but the other was good news, confirming that he was entering his father's world. This was something that needed to be celebrated. *A good relaxing night had been earned,* he thought.

It was not too hard to get the information he needed at the saloon they had visited the first night they were in town. Even though all the known brothels had been sacrificed in the fire, there still were places of interest available if the right money was forthcoming. Jakob had the money, and so the connection was made. Jakob told Otto that this coming weekend he would be gone over Saturday night. Nothing else needed to be said. Hell, everyone needed a weekend off, but they were not the owner's son.

Otto turned to their bodyguard. "I hope we're home by Christmas."

Reconstruction work in the city slowed as the winter weather set in. The cold, damp winds off the lake were horrible, so it was time to leave their work in the hands of the three men recently sent by his father, who would primarily spend their time refitting the large storage distribution center. This all could be done out of the weather and so progress would continue until winter passed and then work in other places could start or finish.

Otto, Jakob, and their bodyguard left for home on the late morning train to Milwaukee. After saying goodbye to their bodyguard at the station, Jakob and Otto headed for Herr Schmidt's office at the brewery to report on their progress. Heinriche announced to both they would be going back to Chicago at the end of January and again in February to review progress. With that phrase said, Heinriche thanked Otto and handed him an envelope. Jakob surmised it contained a well-earned bonus.

Then he turned to Jakob. "Well done."

It was the best Christmas gift Jakob could have received from his father. The trip to Chicago in January was called off because of the weather and this meant that their scheduled trip in February was moved up by two weeks, not because of Charlotte's due date but because it was time to roll out a full delivery schedule by mid-March. Deliveries were at a trickle so far, and competitors late to the challenge were exploring how they, too, could capture some business for themselves. They would go begging because Herr Schmidt had a six-month jump on all of them.

Jakob and Otto left for Chicago in the late morning while Charlotte, close to delivery, did not even bother to see him off. She hoped in her heart that he would return before she gave birth, but she had also reached the conclusion that nothing any longer was certain with her new husband.

Looking out the train window, Jakob was certain about everything. He thought himself successful at manipulating women. He could buy what he wanted. He was going to be a father. He knew his wife, and she knew her place. His father appreciated his work in Chicago. He had even said so. Looking at the world go by, he thought, *I am quite certain of my situation. I know where I am headed.*

Both Otto and the bodyguard had a good nap on the ride south. They were more interested in getting this inspection over with. Starting in March, the first full boatload would arrive dockside. The first full load of boxcars that same week would hold beer wagons and horses. A quick tour of all the facilities proved that their delivery system was ready. Icehouses to keep the barrels cool and additional saloons owned by the brewery would be added to train stops up and down the Chicago Milwaukee line. The product was ready in Milwaukee. It was time to tap the barrel and let the beer flow to the people of Chicago.

Everyone wanted to see it happen, and most of all, Herr Schmidt. He could not be more pleased with himself, his plans, his son, and their fortune, and Jakob heard it again and again in his brewery office. The brewery and his office were feeling more and more like home. With his father's blessing, it was time to celebrate. He took the streetcar down Water Street to his favorite place, and Sarah was still available for the night.

Baby Schmidt seemed to be quiet, now getting ready to appear, and Charlotte was more than ready to get this done. The doctor said that the delivery was still two weeks away, and it was not unusual for the baby to be quiet at this time. Charlotte would be well attended to by her doctor from the Lutheran hospital, a nurse, her mother, and servants in the house. Everything was ready, but the baby was not.

During these dreary days of March, all three families were hoping the arrival of this baby would brighten their lives. What a blessed event it was going to be for two brewery families. Saturday morning, March fifteenth, the clouds broke, and finally, the sun appeared. It was going to be a wonderful day when Charlotte cried out from her room to send for the doctor.

Successive birth pains were greater now in the afternoon and everyone was in place. Even Jakob was downstairs, waiting with his father, and so was Charlotte's father, a safe distance away on the other side of the room. *At least the baby chose a decent time to arrive in the afternoon*, thought Jakob.

The men could hear Charlotte's cries. Then everything went quiet. Then a scream. It seemed to take forever before the doctor came down the stairs, stepping slowly.

He took Jakob aside. "The boy baby is dead, and it appears he was dead for some days. I have to go back to attend to your wife. I will tell you more later."

Jakob approached his father. "Not this time. The baby is dead."

Heinriche grasped his son's shoulder and then turned for the door, leaving the comforting to others.

Charlotte's father saw the scene and knew instinctively what it meant. He turned to the wall and waited for his wife to come down the stairs with the news.

The birthing room was deathly quiet. Charlotte was trying to deal with the absolute opposite of a crying baby. Everyone spoke in hushed tones. The doctor had no answers while the baby was spirited away. Charlotte could not cry yet, but her mother would not stop crying. A staff member sent for the priest. Finally, the doctor took charge and told everyone to leave the room.

Sitting on her bed, he asked what he didn't want to ask. "When did you notice, Charlotte, that the baby was not moving or kicking as much?"

"A little more than two weeks ago. You said that was normal. Are you saying that I was carrying a dead baby for the past two weeks? How could that be?"

"I don't know."

"Will I be able to have another child?"

"We'll see." The doctor stood. "I'm going to speak to your husband and try to answer any questions he might have. I'll be back to see you tomorrow." He moved out the door and out of the situation.

Charlotte's mother came back into the room, sat on the bed, and took her daughter's hand into her own. She held it tight and didn't plan to let it go for a long while.

Jakob didn't really have anything to ask the doctor, and what the doctor had to say was already said. "I'm sorry Mr. Schmidt."

"Can I speak to my wife?"

"Let her rest and then talk to her."

Waiting until it was almost dark, Jakob finally climbed the stairs and walked slowly into her room. Standing above them, he told Charlotte's mother to leave.

When she was gone, he turned to his wife. "What did you do wrong? What did the doctor say? What did you do?"

With what little strength she had, Charlotte glared at him. "*Get out! Get out of my room!*"

More than surprised she would talk to him like this, he stormed out of the room, past her mother, down the stairs, and out the door. Charlotte's mother took back her place and her daughter's hand, but said nothing. Charlotte closed her eyes, but she had definitely opened a new chapter in her young life.

Chapter Eleven

Now that Pepper, the cocker spaniel, was five years old and Richard, the youngest of the Ashworth children, was seven, he wanted a dog of his own. He already had a name for it: Salt. His parents, James Ashworth and, especially his wife, Susan, were hesitant to get another dog, but Ania did not really care. Her son, five-year-old Henryk, probably would like a puppy to play with, too. Thomas, the oldest, was turning twelve next week and late May would be just right for an outdoor birthday party. His godparents, an aunt and uncle, plus the Williamsons, would be at the party. The day could not have been better for the Saturday party at the back of the house near the lakeshore. Pepper was having a great time among all the children when Uncle Charles had the dog sit at his feet. The dog seemed to be hypnotized as he waved his hand repeatedly before its eyes.

Because Pepper kept barking and barking, James told a staff member to tie him to the doghouse behind the kitchen. The dog just wouldn't stop barking, so Richard went to the dog on his hands and knees to quiet him when the dog lunged at him, biting him in the face just below his nose. Running right to Ania, she took him to his father, where she repeated what Richard told her. Blood was pouring off his face, so his father suggested taking him to Doctor Jameson as quickly as possible.

Susan said to her husband, "I can't go. I have to take care of my guests," when Richard asked his father, "Could Ania go?"

On his way to the buggy, James turned to a staff member. "Make sure you shoot the dog."

Driver and buggy were waiting at the side entrance and all three jumped in.

As the horse began trotting to the center of town, Richard laid his head on Ania's lap and she stroked the young boy's head to quiet him.

"You sure have a way with my children. You treat them as if they were your own, and all of them love the attention you give them. If only Susan—"

James stopped himself mid-sentence. He had said too much, and he knew it.

"I like taking care of the children. Susan likes working with all the people at your two hotels. I'm sure she is a big help to you."

After a quick exam of Richard laying flat on a table, the doctor turned to James "Your son will need some stitches."

Approaching Richard with needle and thread, the doctor did not expect the left cross that came from this seven-year-old. It glanced him across his cheek and knocked him down, more by surprise than by strength.

The doctor smiled and looked up at the boy's father. "That's quite a punch your son has there. Ania, take his hands and hold them tight. Mr. Ashworth, stand behind him and hold his shoulders down so I can get this done. Lay still, Richard."

Just to be sure, the doctor's wife held his feet.

After all the excitement, the doctor, his wife, James, and Ania shared another laugh about Richard's behavior. "There will be no extra charge for my fall to the floor."

There was more laughing on the way home by everyone as they shared the story with the driver, and Richard's father acted proud, more than embarrassed, at his son's behavior.

"Doctor Jameson and his wife are nice people. After all their years together, they can still laugh at themselves. How wonderful."

Thinking of the doctor's marriage and his own, James mused how Ania was more beautiful and wonderful than even she realized. Of course, the same story was repeated over and over again at the party. Richard now thought of himself as some kind of hero decking the doctor. The dog, however, was nowhere to be found.

On the way into the house after the party, Ania was holding Henryk's hand with Richard and Rosemary in tow when James addressed her. "You should bring the younger two children to each hotel when I am there so that I can show them what I do at work."

"I'll do that, sir."

It was a warm day in mid-June when Ania could follow up on Mr. Ashworth's request. Thomas had been to the two hotels enough, so he wanted to stay home on his own, while Ania, her son, and her two younger charges went first to the downtown Oconomowoc hotel. Since things had settled down at the hotel late morning, James would take them on a tour of the three-story brick hotel and then have lunch with his visitors. They met in the small paneled lobby where James was waiting for them.

"We're going to the basement first, where most of the work is done like repairs, storage, and food preparation."

Each worker was very busy with their task, but James greeted each one by name and with respect.

"Few see this area, and now you have. From here, we are going to walk up to the second floor so you can see one of the rooms. And from there we will stop at the dining room for lunch." After lunch and finishing their ice cream, James turned to Ania. "This has been great fun. I've decided that I'm going to go with you to Mon Bijou, so I can show it to you myself."

James, Ania, and the children boarded the carriage. "It's such a nice day, driver. Take the long way around the lake to the hotel. I want to drink in this day." James leaned back in the carriage, lifting his arms above his head and sliding his right arm behind Ania's neck, glancing her head as he did so.

She looked at him.

"I'm sorry, I didn't mean to."

"That's all right, Mr. Ashworth."

"Call me James."

"Yes, sir—James."

They passed a few ragged cattails at the water's edge, and sitting on the cattails, red-winged blackbirds were singing, each one searching for a mate.

Ania smiled. "I love their song."

"Stop, driver. Let's listen to the birds."

Pointing out the birds to his children, Ania thought about her favorite marsh in Sussex and reflected that no matter what happened there, she still loved their song.

James looked at Ania. "Are you thinking about someone?

"No, I just love the sound of the birds."

"Move on, driver."

They reached the driveway for the Mon Bijou with stately elms protecting them from the afternoon sun. The doorman immediately recognized his employer and so he stood taller than usual, and, with great aplomb, opened the buggy door for his companions. James stepped out first and eagerly took Ania's hand as she stepped down from the cab. She turned to the children and made sure each one was safely on the walk.

Peony bushes alternated with lilacs dotting the edge of the walk. The lilacs were in full bloom, with purple and white blossoms everywhere. Their perfume filled the air, wafting into the lobby of this grand hotel on Fowler Lake. James took his time pointing out the fancy columns to his children, and the new patterned tin ceiling in the large lobby. Only Ania paid attention.

"The tin ceiling was shipped from West Virginia, installed, and painted white just last week. I'm very proud of it."

Ania admired the craftsmanship. "It's beautiful."

"Susan thought it too expensive, but I went ahead with it anyway."

The children were losing interest fast, but James seemed to linger at each stop, explaining to Ania how this or that worked, going to great pains to answer any question she might have.

James realized that sending things up and down the dumbwaiter did not hold the children's attention for very long. "Let's take the children down to the water and to the gazebo at the end of the walking pier."

Looking out over the water, James seemed to be in another world, totally relaxed in Ania's presence. Getting later than planned, James knew it was time for them to leave, so they walked toward the carriage house. "Thank you for bringing my children. I hope we can do this again."

"It was wonderful, James."

Susan looked for Ania when she got back to the house to inquire about her day of visiting the two hotels. "Was it difficult keeping the children occupied during their long day?"

"Oh, no. James loved explaining the workings of each hotel to them. We all had a wonderful outing."

As usual, Susan hastened on, turning into the small parlor, and then stopped to consider Ania's comment. *Since when does he want to spend that much time with his children? Oh well.* Sitting at his desk to look over impending food orders for the two hotels, it hit her. *James! Since when does Ania call her employer by his first name?*

Business was very good in 1876. Grant was president, and the centennial celebration of the birth of America lasted a whole month in Oconomowoc. Shopkeepers joined city fathers decking out the village in red, white, and blue bunting everywhere. Visitors saw the people of Oconomowoc in the relatively new state of Wisconsin, proud to be American. Since the Transcontinental Railroad Express had made it across the nation to San Francisco the month before, advancement and growth were in the hearts and minds of everyone in town.

It was turning out to be a very good year for the Ashworths, too. Business at the hotels could not have been better, and the gristmill was expanding to keep up with demand. Susan indulged herself in some new things for the house. Her work had earned it, and now the debate in the house between her and James was when they could get away for a vacation, but the answer from him was always the same—no time and too much to do.

This time, winter was extreme. Freezing temperatures started early, and this demanded everyone's attention to their three businesses and even their home. Staff at each place buckled down and shuttered anything and everything that could be closed. Since the horses had to be brought into the barns earlier than usual because of the weather, feed would be at a premium.

Still, the approach of Christmas warmed the hearts of everyone despite the bone-chilling cold, and James seemed to be caught up in the spirit of the time, being more generous than usual to all the staff but especially to the household staff. Ania received from ostensibly both James and Susan not only her money envelope but also a necklace.

As winter tightened its grip, the primary need for every household was firewood. Individual wood supplies split and stacked had run out, so foraging for anything that could burn had begun. Seeing the potential problem for all hunkered down in the town, James started up a cooperative effort to cut down known old and dead trees in the surrounding area. Horse teams dragged the trees on the ice of both lakes to town so that families could cut them up for their own use.

The following spring, many people stopped James on the street and thanked him for his efforts. It would be a very long time before this act of leadership would be forgotten. It was a new dimension of kindness in James that Susan had to come to terms with in her own heart. She was uncomfortable showing kindness to strangers and especially to people in their employ. She wanted to lead using strength, coldness, and her sharp tongue if necessary. Weakness, emotional or otherwise, was not something she was comfortable with, so she had to be tough and cold. It worked for her in the past and it was the first method she always turned to. She wasn't a harsh woman. It was just not in her nature to be kind to anyone. The more kindness James showed, the more her personality hardened.

If James would not accompany her on a well-earned holiday, she would go alone. New discussions with him in early spring about a future trip went nowhere, so Susan announced first to Ania that this coming May and June she would be on her own caring for the children as she planned to visit relatives in New York and then Boston.

Susan's demeanor was curt. "If you have a concern during the time I am gone, ask your employer."

After making travel arrangements for Susan, her departure date of May third came with chilly rain. It was just as well, since Susan's parting at the train station was cool as well. A last-minute change for the trip was that their oldest son would join her. Relatives back east had not seen the boy since his birth, and because he would go off in the fall to a Lutheran prep school in Watertown, his exposure to the east would be good for him.

Chapter Twelve

The entire house seemed to relax at her parting. Things had to run normally, but everyone could walk a bit slower, smile at each other, and enjoy the day while they worked. More than one person can be on vacation when the manager leaves on a long trip. It was expected that James's time away from the house would have doubled since Susan was not able to tend to their business affairs, but he found twice as much time to be in the house or available for his children. He would seek them out and join in on their play or plans for the day.

The day's directions for both hotel staff would be completed by early morning so that James could find time to accompany Ania and the children to town. It all looked so happenstance that there was no reason for concern, but the serendipitous coincidences took place just about every day.

Late Thursday afternoon, James walked into the new ice cream parlor on Wisconsin Avenue after Ania and her three charges arrived. James joined them, of course, and the laughter began. It was great fun for all.

"It appears tomorrow is going to be a sunny day. Bring the children to the Mon Bijou, and we will take a boat ride on Lac La Belle to the Islandale island for a picnic. We will all meet at the walking pier at ten a.m. Does that give you enough time, Ania, to get the children ready for the day?"

"Of course, James. We will be there at ten a.m. How long will we be there?"

"All day."

The largest launch in the hotel's fleet was waiting for them with picnic baskets, blankets, and even a large umbrella onboard. James was already in the boat and each child jumped in. Then he politely took Ania's hand and helped her to her seat next to him.

"I'll teach you to row, Ania." He smiled and off they went.

After some small half-circles and much laughter, their strokes were in sync. The island came into view as soon as they passed Deer Point. Each child had to carry something from the boat and soon they had arranged everything overlooking the water.

Ania watched the children make their way onto the sand of the narrow beach.

"It's almost perfect."

"You're right, the weather couldn't be better. Could you watch the children, James, while I get the lunch ready?"

"Of course."

As James walked down the small sand bluff to the water's edge, Ania's mind raced first to the idea that this was what it could be like. *Will I ever have another day like this?* She called to them and lunch could not have been better. *Especially when everything is almost perfect.*

Richard looked from his father to Ania. "I want to explore the island."

Henryk, of course, had to keep up with his older friend.

Rosemary stood and looked at Ania. "Can we go?"

James nodded. "Let's all do it. We can pretend to be pirates looking for buried treasure."

The island had been used for picnics and lovers before, so a path at the water's edge circled the small island. The children walked ahead, challenged by their minds, to find any treasure along the way. Unbridled innocence followed their soft footsteps, seeking only joy. Walking close behind them was the pair already touched by most of life. Each turn on the path reminded James that he was further along, and turning back was impossible, while each turn for Ania was full of new possibilities. Years separated their dreams. His life was already carved in wood while her life was waiting for the right timber.

James broached the subject. "Do you have plans to be more than a nanny for the rest of your life?"

"I hadn't thought of life beyond working here with your children."

"But my children will not always be young children, you know. Thomas is going to prep school and Rosemary will soon be twelve. Life has to change for all of us."

"It does."

The boat ride back was just as much fun. Carefully, all three children took a turn trying to row with James at their side. Henryk, nor Ania, would never forget this day.

As they approached the pier, Henryk tugged at his mother's dress. "What are we going to do for my birthday?"

James spoke up immediately. "Let's have a birthday party for the boy."

"A birthday party? Can we, Mother?"

James didn't give Ania a chance to reply. "Of course, we can. Leave it up to me."

James alerted the kitchen staff of the date and his plans to celebrate Henryk's birthday. His two children would be there, plus the entire household staff. Twelve people sat at the dining room table for the evening meal and birthday cake. After the meal, a member of the staff placed a large tray of presents before Henryk. His eyes shined with wonder, taking his time to admire each small present from the staff. From James and his two children, Henryk received three children's books. The boy thanked everyone, hugging his host. It was innocent. It was perfect. It was memorable.

Planned for late June, Susan's arrival was delayed by two weeks. She surreptitiously arranged it this way so that she could make the point, *how well he does without me*, to her husband. Instead of being upset by the delay and Susan's absence from her regular duties, James seemed only bemused. He took the additional time to connect with veteran staff members. Guests affected by the Chicago fire still wanted to talk to anyone who would listen, and James always had a story to exchange. The Fourth of July passed without incident, except for the boating accident on adjoining Fowler Lake. A local family lost a child, putting a damper on lake activities that soon passed as new guests arrived.

James was dutifully standing at the depot platform when Susan and their son stepped off the train. The greeting was warm, and both travelers returned from the east full of news from their travels. James, however, could not find space to add his own news. The only question from Susan was, "Is business good?" The heat and flies bothered the waiting horses as the bags were loaded onto one buggy and the family boarded the other. As soon as they sat down, Thomas began again, telling his father of all the marvelous things he had seen. He liked Boston better than New York because there was more history to discover in Boston. The short ride to the house did not give him time to add much detail, but James knew his son wanted to tell him more.

Everyone at the house was on the lookout for the buggies to arrive. They rushed outside to stand under the porte cochère, almost at attention for their return. Ania was first in line with Richard and Rosemary on each side of her, while Henryk stood behind her, almost out of sight. Susan put on her best fake smile as she strode by, stopping briefly to greet her two smaller children, leaving James to follow in her wake, softly saying that everyone looked nice and adding, "Thank you."

Rosemary was the most deflated. She wanted her mother to notice her while Richard didn't care, at least not yet.

Susan hastened down the hallway, and as she approached the stairs to her bedroom, she turned to her husband. "Before dinner, I would like to talk to you about our business accounts, our profits, and if our staff is carrying out their instructed duties as expected."

"Will you have enough time before dinner at six p.m.?"

"The things I want to talk about will not take much time. At dinner, I can tell you about my parents in New York, my sister in Boston, and then Thomas can add his stories about Bunker Hill and Boston Commons. Could you ask Judy to report to my room?"

Her steps in the house were all business, and soon James would have to make his report as well. Judy had been with the Ashworths since their marriage. Though her primary responsibility was to care for the lady of the house, she was also her eyes and ears while Susan was gone. Necessary reports had to be made about the staff, of course, but she was careful how she spoke about Mr. Ashworth. Judy liked James's demeanor very much and did not want to hurt him in any way. Softer men could be taken advantage of even if they ruled their own house. Some men would rather not fight, even if they held the upper hand in society's design.

"You called for me, Mrs. Ashworth?"

"Yes, Judy. In the next few days, we will talk about things concerning the staff while I was gone. I am only interested in things that happened within the house. I can talk to someone else at each one of the hotels. We will meet privately in Mr. Ashworth's office while he is away."

It seemed innocent enough, but this was the first time in their marriage that Susan was gone for more than a few days.

James was waiting in his office for Susan and mistakenly thought their conversation would be quite short, since business at the hotels was as good as last year and business at the gristmill would be better. With Susan, more often than not, he always thought wrong.

She rushed into the room, asking the first question before she sat down. "Will we surpass our goals for this year?"

"Hotel reservations are up at both hotels and since the crops of barley and wheat both look good, I expect that business at the mill will be better than last year. Do you want to hear about the children?"

"Not now. That can wait. Any problems with the staff here in the house or at the hotels?"

"Everything went well here in the house. Ania works wonders with the children. The only problem we're working on is the need to add more horses to each livery for our guests to use, which will mean building additions to each barn. Plans are being drawn up now to get the additions done before winter. I should have seen this coming, but this summer we can borrow horses and carriages from our local friends. They will not mind the additional income. Next spring we'll be able to take care of the demand ourselves."

"You should have seen this coming, James. Either business grows or it dies. We are growing and you should have been ready. That is our income we are giving away to our friends."

So it went, again. *A problem I solved has now become a source of irritation,* thought James. *She is not home more than three hours and we are feuding once more.* Before six o'clock, Ania brought the children downstairs to meet their parents in the dining room. Both children wanted to share their adventures to the island, rowing a boat, and trips to the ice cream parlor. Richard waited patiently for his parents while Rosemary could not keep still in anticipation.

Instead of smiling parents eager to meet their children, both were solemn, with Susan walking ahead of James as usual.

The oldest of the three children took most of the time at the table telling stories of his adventures, while Rosemary only wedged what she had done with Ania and their father.

Dinner went quickly since only the children were doing any talking when Susan announced she wanted to retire early. "We will talk again about this profit loss."

James stood and watched his wife depart through the open pocket doors. Sources at the two hotels dutifully reported to Susan when called upon.

Everything seemed in order. There was not much to glean from their reports other than the odd comment concerning Ania's tour of the Mon Bijou with the three children, and readying the best boat at the hotel for James, Ania, and the three children for their all-day picnic. Susan let some time pass before sitting down with Judy in James's office, where she carefully put her maid at ease. There were questions about the kitchen or problems with the staff, and if she needed anything immediately. Judy carefully responded that everything ran quite well in her absence.

"Tell me about James and the children."

Judy's face brightened. "James could not have been more relaxed with the children, playing with them on the grounds or on trips into town."

"How delightful. Tell me more."

"All of them went into town to the ice cream parlor more times than I can count. Ania, of course, kept everyone in order. The entire staff had great fun at the birthday party for Henryk, too. James wanted the day to be special for the little boy. He made sure there was a big cake and presents for him. I never saw him take charge of a household matter like that before with such a smile on his face."

It was that last sentence that bothered Susan the most. Leaving him behind was supposed to draw them closer together, not open the door of his heart.

What should I do about it? she thought. Her answer would not arrive until fall, when she could not shake off a bad cold.

"It's the change of the seasons and this rainy, cold weather. That's why you are feeling so poorly."

"I have had this cough and cold for three weeks now, James. It could be pneumonia. People die from pneumonia. I want Doctor Jameson to come to the house."

"He will tell you that it is nothing to be worried about.

"You don't care what happens to me."

"I care. Call the doctor, Susan, if you want. I'm on my way to the mill."

I am running myself down, thought Susan. *Maybe, I should spend less time at the hotels. I could be here running the affairs of the house. Thomas is off to school in Watertown. Rosemary is getting older and could tend to Richard.*

Maybe my sister in Boston is right. I have earned my place here, so why not enjoy it? Ania could move on and I could move back to being in charge in my own house. Then I will not have to share James with anyone. Doctor Jameson had listened before when I told him I didn't want more than three children. He advised me to take an active role in our businesses. I wonder what he would advise now.

It was late morning, and the sun was peeking through the dark clouds when Doctor Jameson arrived for his appointment.

Judy led him to Susan's bedroom and after a few minutes, his diagnosis was no pneumonia yet, as he packed his bag. "Susan, you must sleep sitting up. Drink lots of water mixed with honey."

"Could you stay for a few minutes?"

"I can, Mrs. Ashworth. What is it?"

Susan dismissed Judy and turned back to Doctor Jameson. "I need your advice, Doctor Jameson. Please pull up a chair and sit down. This may take some time."

Pulling the chair from the dressing table, Dr. Jameson sat near Susan's bed.

First came silence from Susan and then a few tears. "After Richard was born, I told you I did not want any more children. I followed your advice to get out of the house and I took a very active role in our businesses. I liked helping James with the everyday work at the two hotels and my help was appreciated by him as he turned more and more of their operation over to me, but I have become a stranger in my own house because I cannot do both well enough for me."

"What do you mean, well enough for me?"

"After I returned from my trip to the east, the house and hotel staff confirmed for me that I need to take on a different role for the benefit of my marriage. James needs to see the softer side of me as the head of his household affairs, hostess, and especially the mother of his children. Rosemary is old enough now. She can help me in the house with Richard so that Ania can move on."

"Is Ania a threat to your marriage?"

"I have no reason to believe she and James. I don't think so, but I don't want her to stay here any longer so she can become one. Ania is a very talented woman. She is younger than I by some dozen years, so I fear I have to do something."

Doctor Jameson gave pause and for a long while said nothing. It was obvious he was thinking something through. "I think I have a solution. Ania can come work for me. She and her son can live with us. We have the room and I need the help. My wife is getting older like me and she should not have to help me any longer with my work. I can afford to pay her and give her a place to stay with us. Let me discuss this at home and I will let you know at my next appointment with you when I check on your progress."

"Thank you, Doctor Jameson. Thank you."

After Doctor Jameson left, Susan closed her eyes and began to heal.

Chapter Thirteen

Heinriche paced his office. "Sit down, Jakob. You have been married for seven years and I still have no grandchildren. Do you know why Charlotte can't give me an heir?"

"Three more miscarriages and all the doctors say is that she's a healthy woman. They are of no help. They don't know why. I should have married someone else, anybody else!"

"No one else would do. That is still true today, Jacob. She is only twenty-eight years old. I may still get that grandchild from her."

"I don't want to go anywhere near her. Some days, she cries all day. Some days, she is cold and distant. We don't talk much anymore. She doesn't want to go anywhere. The house is so deathly quiet I seek my comfort elsewhere. I should divorce her."

"The Church will not allow it just because she can't have a child and our friends and business partners would not accept it either. Go home, take care of your wife, and give me a grandchild."

Caught between a demanding father and a sullen wife, Jakob could not fulfill his father's demand by issuing another decree at home. No fruit from her womb bedeviled him on all sides. Family and friends silently wondered why he was still childless. Charlotte was beside herself with trying and grew more and more distant, while Jakob tried to grant his father's wish.

This failure to become a legitimate father before Milwaukee's society shadowed Jakob everywhere. Especially within his own mind. It dogged his steps no matter where he went. His world shrunk so much that the only two places where he could escape were in his new office at the brewery and the friendly confines of the house on Water Street. Jakob did not hide these two places from Charlotte. In fact, he was enjoying rubbing them under her nose whenever he could. He delighted in seeing her anger, which so easily could be turned by him on its head, by simply referring to the empty bedrooms in his own house as the reason her bed was empty as well. Slowly, justification for any irritation, he chose to belittle his wife and, at times, himself replaced what little remorse he had. It was self-flagellation and the same kind of punishment for his wife. This would drive him into the arms of others, where the very climax he experienced again and again only drove him deeper into more self-deprecation and disappointment. Why bother talking to Charlotte about it when she was the very source of his irritation and nothing she could say would smooth this over? He trained her. Her mechanics were flawless, but the results were always the same—disappointing.

Charlotte would speak to one doctor and then to another as far away as Chicago, and then to her mother. Her father could not comfort her, not about this. All of them felt the shadow of disappointment creeping into their lives.

They had no answer for allowed questions and no satisfying retort for whispers and side glances. They all knew what others were saying or thinking, but all they could do was suffer in stifling silence. Charlotte's womb was unsuccessful, so three houses were empty of joy.

Once again, winter appeared early in Oconomowoc. Despite how dreary it was outside, Susan felt there would be more joy in her marriage and her house if Ania was no longer in their lives. If Doctor Jameson would employ Ania, it would be easy to explain this to Elizabeth in Sussex. After all, her children were getting older, which was the reason Elizabeth used as one reason Ania should move on. It was, of course, not the main reason, but it bolstered her proposal. Doctor Jameson was coming at the end of the week to see how Susan was progressing. Carrying in his bag of wonders, she hoped for a solution to her own irritation.

Judy showed Doctor Jameson to Susan's room, now filled with sunlight and good cheer. Susan was all smiles, expecting good news from her friend.

She never felt comfortable talking to the young minister, so Doctor Jameson was her man. Now about her father's age at his death, the doctor was the only person she could talk to about her feelings. He seemed like he wanted to listen, so why not use him for her purposes?

Doctor Jameson was all business with a brief examination first, followed by questions about her health. She looked good and sounded better. So, Doctor Jameson pronounced her healthy enough to resume all of her duties. Susan just knew that would be his verdict, and then there was that pause that would lead to the most important conversation between them. Would he—would his wife—take on her problem? She could easily handle the proclamation to others that Ania was moving on, and as far as how James felt about her decision was of little importance to her. After all, he was too busy to join her on her travels. Ania would not be out of Oconomowoc, but she would be out of their house. Would Doctor Jameson agree? This time, the doctor needed no inducement to pull up a chair and sit before her.

Doctor Jameson was right to the point, as usual. "We agree to have Ania and her son join us, but one condition must be met."

"What is that condition?"

"That my wife and I get to ask Ania to join us in our home. Nothing must be said to her by you about this change in her life before we speak to her. Is that agreed?"

Why wouldn't I agree? Susan thought.

"I agree to your terms and I will meet your condition. When will you speak to Ania?"

"It will be soon and it will be at our house. You could arrange to have her bring Henryk for an examination. Can she handle a buggy?"

"She is good with the reins."

"Let's plan for next Tuesday morning at about eleven. She probably will not return until after dinner, if that is all right with you."

"It is, Doctor Jameson, and thank you."

The ruse worked. Tuesday morning, Ania boarded the carriage with Henryk and took the reins of the single mare to see the doctor. Ania took her time, holding the mare to a walk. It was not very often that she was in charge of anything more than telling a child what to do. The pace was different this morning for Ania and she looked forward to seeing the doctor, hoping that everything would be all right with her son.

At the top of their front porch steps, Mrs. Jameson met Ania and Henryk as if they were guests at her home. Jane was a little plump for her height, but her smile, and especially her laughter, was infectious. She stepped forward on the porch and stooped low, hugging the boy tight, and did the same with Ania. Her greeting could not have been warmer.

"Welcome to our home. We want you both to feel at ease here."

Doctor Jameson stood at the open front door, smiling at the three of them.

"Come here, Willy. Don't just stand there at the door. Come greet our guests."

So that is Doctor Jameson's first name, Willy.

"I call William, Willy, whenever I want to get his attention."

Doctor Jameson listened when he heard his wife call, "Willy," and he stepped forward almost immediately. He shook Ania's hand and then quickly stooped to shake Henryk's hand more vigorously.

Ania couldn't have been more overwhelmed by this display of unexpected kindness. Even though it was so spontaneous and so warm, it was to be the first of many kindnesses shown to her in this home.

"Willy, take Henryk into your office for his examination while I talk to Ania. Come with me, my dear. The two boys can take care of themselves."

Doctor Jameson motioned to Henryk to follow him, and the doctor led him to a room immediately off the hallway while Ania and Jane Jameson went the opposite direction into the simple parlor of their two-story home. There were no servants in this household. Jane and William liked it that way, sharing chores each day together and happy to treat each other with respect while admiring what each of them brought to their union. They shared this love and wanted to offer Ania and her son the same opportunity Jane received from William's mother years ago. Not only did William's father and mother get an eager assistant, but William also married her, and Jane had said that one day she would like to do the same to some other young woman that needed a little help on her own way in life. Knowing Ania for over seven years, Jane and William had decided that Ania was that person.

"Please sit here, Ania, while I get us something to drink."

While stepping out of the room, Jane motioned. "Don't be afraid to look around."

Two chairs on each side of a table sat in front of the fireplace. The small mantel above the fireplace held a vase and a small daguerreotype picture of a young, handsome boy. On the rug in the corner was a small rolltop desk. The tambour was up and same-sized slips of paper stuffed the cubicles.

Jane came back into the room as quickly as she left, placed a tray on the table, and poured the coffee. "What are you going to do now that the Ashworth children have grown older and they no longer need your help?"

"Mr. Ashworth said the same thing to me four months ago." Ania took a sip of coffee. "I have thought about that a lot ever since James said it, but I don't know what I'll do or where I'll go. I don't know of anyone that will hire me because Henryk must come with me."

"Perhaps there is an answer right here. Oh, look, here comes your boy now. How is he doing, Willy?"

"Mother, Doctor Jameson says I'm a healthy boy. He let me listen to his heart, too."

"He sure is healthy, Ania. What have you two been talking about?"

"We will tell you while we eat lunch, Willy."

"I don't think we can stay for lunch, Mrs. Jameson."

"Please call me Jane. Of course, you can stay for lunch. We have much to talk about."

Jane led the three of them to the kitchen at the back of the house. Doctor Jameson pulled out the chair for Ania and let Henryk pull out his own chair. Bread, butter, cheese, and two kinds of sliced apples graced the table. Then Jane was gone again, getting the coffee tray from the parlor.

Doctor Jameson motioned to her. "You first Ania."

Ania took care of Henryk's plate and then her own and then passed everything on to Doctor Jameson.

Jane reappeared with the coffee tray and poured fresh milk for Henryk. "Yes, we have a cow."

When Jane sat down, the doctor spoke. "Now let's get down to business. Ania, there is no other way to say it. Jane and I want you and Henryk to stay with us and we want you to help me in my office. You will learn how to work in a doctor's office. You can live here and I will pay you a little income."

"But—"

"Let me finish, Ania. We see in you a young woman who is very capable. You'll help me in my office and help Jane here in the house. Then you'll be able to spend more time with Henryk. We all can teach your son to read and write. We both want you and Henryk to become part of our home."

Nodding, Jane dabbed the corners of her mouth with a linen napkin. "I believe it's time for Ania to take care of Ania. Willy will talk to the Ashworths. All we need to hear from you is your decision."

"I…I don't know what to say."

"Say nothing now. Finish eating with us. Why don't you take Henryk for a walk in town this afternoon and think about it? You have all afternoon and you both can join us for dinner. It has been all arranged."

Jane Jameson changed the subject. "Tell us about your family."

"My older sister and I, with our parents, came to Milwaukee from Poland. My mother died shortly after we came here and my father was killed in a work accident on the Milwaukee docks two years after my mother's death. My sister lives in Milwaukee and has three children, the last I heard from her. I came to Sussex nine years ago and then Oconomowoc, doing the same thing in both homes. I met your husband seven years ago when Henryk was born. That is my history."

"It's a lot like my story." The warmth in Jane's smile echoed in her voice.

"Jane, I think it's time for Ania to be alone with her thoughts. All I would add, Ania, is for you to make plans for the rest of your life and Henryk's life. Take a long walk and come back to us with your answer."

Doctor Jameson got up and walked out of the kitchen toward his office. With her hands, Jane covered each of Henryk's and Ania's hands and squeezed them. Standing, she went to get their coats for that walk in town.

After they went down the six steps to the front yard, Ania stopped and turned around to look at the house. Looking past the modest structure, there certainly was no comparison to the Ashworth house, so her first thought was more of a question. *What will it be like to be almost an equal in a household among people who love me, not love what I can do, or how well I can do it? They are asking me to stay. They are asking me to decide for myself and not telling me what to do. In fact, they want me to take care of me and Henryk.* She turned again and took one more step closer to being herself.

They started their walk toward the train station, then across the tracks past a church. Turning east, Ania finally spoke. "What do you think about the Jamesons, Henryk?"

"I like the doctor. He's funny. He made me laugh when he tickled me and the lady likes to smile and laugh, too. Can we go back now?"

"We'll head back to their house soon."

They crossed the tracks again and headed back toward the main street of Oconomowoc.

"Let's walk past the lake."

Across the street was the marsh and then the clear waters of Fowler Lake. Main Street overflowed often when the water was high in the spring. Walking past the worn cattails, a lone brown feathered bird with white eyebrows sat high and proud. It was a female red-winged blackbird, and she sang so loud the sound bounced off the brick walls of the nearby Lutheran church where Henryk was baptized. She didn't fly away as they approached. She just sat and sang, "It's time for Ania."

As Ania walked to the doctor's house, she saw it very differently than when she arrived this morning. Her borrowed horse and buggy now sat near the barn, reminding her that she belonged here. She took Henryk's hand and picked up her steps, ready to move forward.

Her knock on the door was resolute, and Jane answered the door. "Yes, we will live and work here."

The red-winged blackbird song was right.

Chapter Fourteen

Doctor Jameson and his wife, Jane, watched Ania and Henryk in their buggy disappear down the road. Both stood by their invitations to Ania and her son.

Perhaps they could now pass a little of themselves on to them, since they couldn't do the same for their dead son.

After putting Henryk to bed, Ania lay in hers, looking up at the dark ceiling above. Her thoughts rambled from Milwaukee to Sussex to Oconomowoc, to the birth of Henryk, to the Jameson's invitation to what was next. Another move; another change. *I'm tired*, she thought, *and I'm only twenty-five years old. But it is time for me. Time for Ania* was the last thought she had before deep sleep took over.

Doctor Jameson waited until after Thanksgiving to relay Ania's decision to Susan and to plan for her move to their home. This time, Judy led him to the parlor across from the dining room. Susan was sitting, relaxed and confident that the good doctor was bringing her good news. There was no need for an examination. The red flush of Susan's cheeks told Doctor Jameson everything he needed to know about her health.

She stood and shook his hand strongly. "Welcome to our home again, Doctor Jameson. Please be seated here at the table with me."

Their business meeting had begun.

"Ania has accepted our invitation to live with us and work in my office. I trust you are pleased, Susan."

"I am delighted for her."

"And delighted for yourself, I am sure, Susan. I want her to join us as soon as possible. Is there any reason why there should be any delay?"

"There is no reason here why this can't be done before Christmas. There will be some goodbyes between her and the children. We will wait until Thomas comes home from school so she can say goodbye to him as well. After all, she has spent seven years with us. Once that has happened, she will be on her way."

"Good. That will give us enough time to get everything ready at our house. Let us know the day and I will come to get Ania, Henryk, and their things."

The transaction was over and both parties were very happy. Now Susan's attention turned to breaking the news to James in the right way, giving him no cause to believe she had initiated this change. He needed to never know the truth. Ania would be removed from the house, and this possible temptation would be far away, not completely out of possible sight, but hopefully further out of his mind. *The time will have to be soon before James hears this news from our children*, she thought, *so why not tonight?*

After dinner, James wandered into his office to enjoy a cigar. Walking out of the dining room, Susan looked into James's office and saw him relaxing at his desk and thought the time was right to speak with him.

Entering his office, she mustered a relaxed tone as much as she could. "Enjoying your cigar? The second time Doctor Jameson checked on me, he made a peculiar request."

"What was that, Susan?"

"He asked me if Ania could move to their home and help Jane in the house and him in his office. Thinking about it briefly, I saw no reason why Ania should not be given the chance to learn how to help a doctor in his office. After all, Thomas is off to school and Rosemary is old enough to help with Richard. Before Thanksgiving, Ania and Henryk spent most of the day with the Jamesons and they asked her if she and Henryk would move to their house and help them. She said yes and Doctor Jameson told me of her decision today."

"So, it has all been arranged."

Was there a bit of reluctance or even mistrust in his choice of words? Susan thought. *No need to visit his suspicions, even if they are true. Ania's decision has been made.*

"I guess Ania wanted to move on with her life. I am sure the doctor will take care of her. She will be leaving as soon as she can say goodbye to Thomas when he returns from Watertown. It is time for me to look in on the children."

Susan left James alone with his thoughts and was gone as quickly as she brought up this change in their lives.

Thomas was returning for Christmas vacation the following week, so parting words with Ania would have to wait until then. During that time, Susan kept James busy whenever he was in the house to limit goodbyes between him and Ania. Christmas would keep the children busy, making the break between them and Ania with Henryk easy as well. Susan was sure there was no need to shed any tears at all. She wanted everyone to move on with their lives so that James and she could move on with theirs.

Late morning, on a rather warm day for December seventeenth, Doctor Jameson arrived at the side door. Susan looked down the hallway as Ania walked alone to the door, carrying Henryk's suitcase. A stable hand was waiting at the door for Doctor Jameson's arrival. At his feet were Ania's two suitcases. Opening the door for Ania and her son, he quickly lifted all three cases into his buggy, and just as quickly, Ania and Henryk were gone from the Ashworths.

Henryk sat between her and the doctor. The drive was not long, and as they drew closer to their new home, Ania couldn't help but notice that all of them were sitting together as a real family. For Ania, it had been seventeen years ago, when she stood on the ship with her parents, looking at Milwaukee from the water, that it felt like family.

Seeing Jane at the open front door, Willy stopped in front of the house. "I'm going to take the buggy around back, and I'll bring your two cases in. Just take Henryk's case with you, Ania. After lunch, we'll take them up to your bedrooms."

Ania helped Henryk step down from the buggy, and they walked up the steps to Jane's open arms.

"Good morning. Good morning. How are you both? Are you hungry? Take off your coats. Henryk, Willy added a lower peg on the hall tree for you so that you can hang up your own coat. Then let's go into the kitchen to eat lunch."

After the horse and buggy were cared for in the drive-thru barn, Willy came through the back door and small hallway into the kitchen, lugging the two cases. He took them to the front of the stairs and came back into the kitchen.

"I think we're going to have our first big snowfall. The dark clouds are hanging low in the sky and it's getting colder. There is no wind, and it even smells like snow is in the air."

"I'm serving the soup, Willy. Go back and hang up your coat and hat next to Henryk's and sit down at the table."

After lunch, Jane led Ania and Henryk upstairs. She stopped first at the small room just off the landing. The slanted ceiling mimicked the roofline. There was a small chest next to the window of the outer wall, and a small bed was tucked to the left of the door along the inner wall.

"This is your room, Henryk."

"My room? My own room."

Across the hall was a much larger room for Ania, with a dresser, desk, and comfortable chair next to a window looking out from the opposite side of the house as Henryk's room. A small wardrobe was tucked in the opposite corner. Both beds for Ania and Henryk were piled high with feather blankets and soft pillows. At the other end of the hallway was the bedroom for the Jamesons.

The fourth room served as a storeroom for the house and Doctor Jameson's office.

After they placed all three cases in Ania's room, Jane stood with her hand clasped. "We'll add your own touches to each of your rooms later. Put your things where you want them and then join us downstairs."

Henryk kept walking up the last two steps of the stairs and then into his room, and as he did so he kept mumbling, "My own room."

Ania stood with her hands on her hips. "So Mr. Big Shot, where do you think you're headed?"

"Just to my own bedroom, Mom."

"Put your own things away in the dresser. Clothes in the top two drawers and your gifts from your birthday party in the bottom drawer. Then come into my bedroom to help me."

"Yes, Mother."

Coming down the steps, Jane and Willy were sitting by the fireplace in their small parlor. At their feet were some books for Henryk to look at while Doctor Jameson talked to Ania. As soon as she and Henryk entered the room, Willy stood up and walked over to the rolltop desk in the corner.

"Ania, one of the first things I want you to do is to organize these records for each one of my patients. This desk is stuffed with names, things that have been done for each family member, and payments made or payments still owed. I, we, don't want to spend any time with this, so we just stuff more slips of paper into each cubbyhole, and then we forget about them. Your first job in my office is to organize this mess. You can also help Jane in the kitchen. We need to work together and help each other in this house. Henryk, there will be jobs for you as well."

Christmas was quieter at the Jameson's, but much warmer than it had been since Ania arrived in Oconomowoc. The tree was smaller, and the presents were fewer, but the feelings all around were true, and love for each other was taking root. By the end of January, Ania had sorted through all the records in the rolltop using the new Dewey Decimal System, now popular in libraries. The rolltop became a library shelf, and each cubbyhole started a new surname letter or group of letters. The parlor held a Christmas tree in one corner, and the rest of the room's floor space was now papered over with piles of family bills and records for each letter of the alphabet. Ania put play letter blocks on each pile to keep them straight and then sorted each pile. When Willy couldn't make it to his favorite chair, he put up a fuss, but progress was being made and soon the piles disappeared into each correct cubbyhole of the desk.

When she was almost finished, she explained the system to the doctor. "If you attend to more families, you'll have to get a bigger rolltop desk."

"That won't happen, Ania. I'll never get rid of this old desk. Instead, Henryk and I will build small wooden boxes and stack them on top of each other for you, and you can stuff them with papers instead of chickens and we'll call it Ania's paper roost."

They laughed so loudly that Jane had to come into the room from the kitchen to find out what was so funny, and when Willy repeated the story to her, Ania knew she belonged.

Henryk brought wood into the house for the kitchen stove or fireplaces in the parlor and examination room. By now, he was getting pretty good with a mallet and a wedge. His first free wood stacks did not stand for very long, but he was getting better at it. Ania caught Doctor Jameson watching Henryk through the window, and she was pretty sure she saw a look of appreciation on his face, as one by one, Willy taught Henryk little jobs around the house that lightened his own load. Henryk loved learning from him, and when he knew how to do it, the little guy could work alone for hours.

By spring, the small parlor had become the doctor's waiting room and office, both run by Ania, plus Henryk's classroom, where Willy and Jane spent their spare time teaching the boy. At night, all four would rest by the fire. Jane noticed it first. Henryk's feet, as he sprawled out on the floor, were almost in the hallway. Willy sat on the other side of the small table between them with his face buried in one of his medical journals, so Jane bumped his elbow.

"We need a bigger room for the four of us, Willy. We could switch rooms. This could be your examination room. It's smaller than your room across the hall, but it will do. Then all of us could spread out in the other room. We could add a small table for Henryk so he wouldn't have to lay on the floor to do his book work and we could add a couple of extra chairs in the corner for waiting patients while you're busy in the examination room. What do you think, Willy?"

"I think you're a pretty smart woman. We'll move things tomorrow morning. You'll have to buy some furniture. Ania can handle the buggy and all three of you should stop at the bank, too. It's time for Ania to get her wages and open her own savings account."

It did not take long to exchange the furniture in each room. Willy asked Ania to take one end of the rolltop desk while he took the other to move it out of the corner of the room. They swung it around to get through the first arched doorway and then the smaller arched doorway. As they tipped it backward, just a little, to ease it into its new home, it caught Ania's eye. On the back edge of the desk were three carved letters: P.W.J.

Ania couldn't help but ask, "Why are these three letters here, Willy?"

Willy's face turned pale, and suddenly he was years and miles away, to the back of his old house in Milwaukee. Horror covered his face, and he looked as if he was going to scream. His mind revisited Peter running into the burning barn, and he couldn't stop him.

Willy reached for a chair. "I've got to sit down, child. Those three letters were carved by my son shortly before his death. I was angry with him when he did it, but now it's the only thing we have left from him besides his picture. Those are his initials—Peter William Jameson. He died in a fire while we lived in Milwaukee. Our barn caught fire, and he ran into the barn to save our horse. Neither one of them made it out. We moved here after the fire to get away from that terrible place. Now you know why we'll never get rid of this old desk. Jane and I loved that boy so much. It was like losing a son in the war. I hate fires."

"I'm so sorry, Willy."

"Jane and I try to forget, but each day when we look at this desk, we remember him. We don't talk much about him anymore because it hurts too much."

The next day in early May, when the daffodils were popping through the softened earth, the three of them rode the buggy down Walnut Street, passing the gabled cottage on Pleasant Street, which Jane adored, to Milwaukee Street. As they turned the corner onto Milwaukee Street, they could hear the pings on anvils from Sorenson's blacksmith shop. The sound reminded Jane that their horse needed new shoes soon. Their planned destination was a furniture store on Milwaukee Street. However, Jane said to drive on and then added to turn left on Main Street and come back around and stop at the corner before the bank.

"Why are we stopping here at, ahh, Summit Bank?"

"Before you moved in, Willy and I said that not only could you live with us but that we were going to pay you a small salary for your work in his office. Today is the day you open your own savings account with four months of pay."

"You don't have to do that, Jane. Henryk and I are happy just to live with you."

"We promised it, and as a woman, you need to learn to make sure people keep promises they make to you. The bank promises to protect your money and pay you some interest on your account."

"What is interest?"

"Let the banker explain that to you. Here is your twenty dollars for your first four months of work."

Ania took the money and walked hesitantly into the bank with Henryk and Jane. A half-hour later, all three walked out of the bank and boarded the buggy. As they drove back to the furniture store, Ania held a slip of paper given to her by the banker in one hand, and the reins in the other, plus words she had never heard before, were swimming around in her head. These lessons were just as difficult as Henryk's lessons.

At the furniture store, it did not take Jane long to pick out the items she needed for the larger parlor. After loading and tying the twin chairs, desk, and small chair for Henryk in the back of the buggy, they took a longer way back to their house, stopping under a large maple tree, almost leafed out.

Another new large house was going up on North Lake Road. The new turrets were visible across the water.

"Oconomowoc has grown since I moved here."

Hearing that, Jane sighed. "You should have seen this place when we moved here twenty years ago. There were no wooden sidewalks and I could see the end of town from here. It's better, I think. The wealthy from Milwaukee, St. Louis, and Chicago have found this place for their cottages. They call them lake cottages for summer use even though they are three and four stories tall. It's just not the same at all."

Back at home, they put the twin chairs along the wall just inside the large arched doorway, and Henryk asked if his desk and chair could sit next to the doctor's rolltop desk. It was obvious to the adults Henryk felt at home here, too.

With client lists and bookkeeping chores now arranged and easily maintained by Ania, Doctor Jameson began calling her name more often instead of his wife to help him with patients. The females, especially the younger ones, appreciated Ania's presence in the examination room when delicate questions were asked. Some mistook Ania as the doctor's daughter, but when one farmer thought her to be the doctor's young wife, Jane set him straight right away. At the dinner table that evening, all three had a good laugh about his confusion. Jane had nothing to worry about. Their relationship was rock solid.

Summer evenings were spent outside on the front porch or in the backyard, sitting on the curved wooden benches surrounding the trunk of a large box elder tree. Early mornings after breakfast, Jane would ask Henryk to join her in either the vegetable or flower gardens to teach him some new bit of information about growing things while the doctor would nudge another medical journal into Ania's hands so she could read one more article about anatomy or a successful treatment for an illness. After Ania read the article, she would ask a flurry of questions, taking Willy back to his days teaching young prospective doctors in the classroom. The journals Ania read came from one of his former students working in a new Milwaukee hospital. The doctors would share letters and, from time to time, a missive would contain another request for Doctor Jameson to return to Milwaukee. It would never happen, of course, but the doctor in Oconomowoc liked reading the words.

The month of July was passing slowly in town and there were no patients, so the doctor said to Ania that he was going to help his wife and Henryk pick raspberries for dinner. Five minutes later, two men came tumbling through the front door in terrible haste.

"Is the doctor here?" said one of them.

Before Ania could answer, the other said, "He's got to be here."

"He's here."

"Tell him to come quick to North Lake Road. He'll see the buggy accident there. Two people have been hurt bad."

Ania ran out the back door toward the garden, taking the doctor's bag with her.

The doctor was bent over with Jane and Henryk, looking under the leaves for the hidden fruit, when he heard Ania yell, "Doctor, two people have been badly hurt in a buggy accident on North Lake Road."

"Get the horse, Ania, and hitch it to the buggy. I'll get my coat and wash my hands."

Meeting Ania in the barn, he jumped into the buggy.

Jane looked at Ania. "What are you doing standing there? Get in the buggy, Ania, and help Willy."

Ania was barely onboard when Willy told the Gray to giddy-up. Even the horse sensed the urgency and her gait seemed faster than usual. Turning north on Lake Road, just past the dam, they saw a crowd gathering on the street. With two horses tied to a nearby tree, and a third horse laying on the ground in obvious distress, Willy stopped the buggy just short of the wounded animal.

As they got out of the buggy, one man said to the other, holding the rifle, "You have to shoot that horse. Do it now."

Then they saw the tangled mess of a turned-over buggy and wagon laying on top of it. A bleeding woman was laying next to the buggy, with a man pinned under it. While waiting for a doctor to arrive, nobody did anything for anyone.

Doctor Jameson approached. "Help me get this wagon off of the carriage, men! Do it quickly."

"Now lift the buggy to its side. Careful now. Slowly."

The man was moaning, but the woman was still. Hoofprints were tattooed on the woman's face and neck. Clenching her teeth, Ania kneeled over her and wiped the blood from her face with her dress. "Can you hear me, Ma'am? Can you hear me?"

Rolling her head toward her, Ania heard her whisper, "My children, children."

"She's alive, doctor."

Looking up from the man, Willy pointed to the white house across the street. "Take her to that house, Ania. Put her on a table and wash the blood from her wounds. I'll follow as soon as I can."

Rolling the man over, Willy saw it was the shoemaker. His pants were torn open, with bruises on the back of both legs, just above the inner knee from the imprint of the buggy wall which had pinned him to the ground.

He looked to be the better of the two injured, so the doctor said to some bystanders, "Lay him on his back under that shade tree. Get him some water and I'll be back as soon as I can."

Willy walked across the street to the house the men had taken the woman. The front door was open and just inside the doorway, the doctor stopped in the foyer and listened for the room that was the noisiest. Entering the large dining room, the woman was laying on the dining room table, and Ania was washing the blood from her hands and face.

Willy walked into the room. "All the men, get out. Is the woman of the house here?"

An older, gray-haired woman stood in the corner of the room. "I'm here."

"You stay here. I might need something. Start unbuttoning her dress, Ania, and pull it down off of her arms to past her waist."

More hoofprints became visible, especially on her chest and also on her stomach. Willy looked at Ania and frowned. "A horse must have danced on her chest. Can you hear me, ma'am?"

The woman tried to speak, but whatever she said, they could not understand.

Willy leaned in closer. "Try again, ma'am."

She kept gasping for air, and when Willy gently pushed on her rib cage, the woman moaned, and then he pushed just as gently on her stomach. She moaned louder.

"Ania, I want you to wash off all the blood and dirt from her while I go outside to check on the man again. Don't let her move. She's probably bleeding internally. Keep her still. Talk to her, Ania, and don't let anyone but me into the room."

Willy was already gone when Ania dipped another clean cloth into the bucket of water. Sadly, a pile of dirty, blood-soaked rags was growing at her feet.

The doctor was back sooner than Ania expected with the man from the street. Seeing his wife on the table, he took her hand and cried.

The woman of the house kept to the corner of the room, and the doctor turned to her. "Could we all stay in this room for the night?"

"Of course you can, and I'll take care of your meals, too."

"Ania, take the buggy home and tell Jane that I plan to stay here for the night. Come back after breakfast and by then, I'll know what we'll need to do next."

Ania turned the corner onto Milwaukee Street and walked the mare slowly toward home. She kept thinking that the man had just walked away from the same accident that the woman, probably his wife, could not move without convulsing in pain. *He's going to live*, she thought. The mare had already stopped before their house and bowed her head, as if she also knew what was going to happen to the woman.

Ania told everything to Jane, and Henryk and Jane agreed with Ania that probably there would be nothing Willy could do for the woman.

"Her ribs have probably punctured her lungs, and that's why she has trouble breathing. It's not going to end well, Ania."

It was already dark, and Ania hadn't eaten anything. Jane insisted that she at least have some bread and soup. Eating it quickly, Ania dragged herself up the steps toward her room.

Jane called out after her. "Henryk can take care of himself."

The next morning, Ania ate breakfast as quickly as possible and left the house. Arriving on North Lake Road, there was no one around. The horses, wagon, and buggy were all gone from the street. Even the leaves were still as she knocked on the door. It opened slowly to the woman of the house. "Come in. The doctor is waiting for you."

On the table, a sheet covered the woman's face and body. Sitting in the corner of the dining room, the husband was slumped over with Willy's arm on his shoulder. Ania stood still and said to herself, *Jane was right*.

Walking over to Ania, Willy gave her a weak smile. "The shoemaker is well enough to make all the arrangements for his wife. We can go home."

They were quiet as the buggy slowly rolled toward home. Ania could see defeat in the doctor's eyes. She wondered how he could keep doing this.

Almost home, the doctor finally spoke. "You really did well, Ania. Keep reading those journals and asking your questions. It doesn't always end this way. You know that already."

Chapter Fifteen

Jakob's and his father's offices were full of men carrying rolled-up blueprints of potential changes to their brewery because of recent advances in the industry, especially in refrigerated transportation and the malting processes. The changing landscape for breweries meant either keeping up with these advancements or being buried by those who did. Jakob had earned his chops with success in Chicago, according to his father, and now was in charge of keeping up with brewing advancements both in America and Europe. Though his father still made all the final decisions, Jakob was allowed to sort through people and ideas that he should consider for renovations at their brewery. It looked like a glorified secretarial position, but both knew it was the only way for Jakob to be schooled in the industry that he would one day manage. It was Jakob's future, and even his father knew Jakob liked taking care of his own future wherever he could. If his wife could not take care of matters at home, Jakob could at least take care of business here.

Personnel working in the brewery offices did not drink their product as much as those on the line who normally worked twelve hours a day. Jakob felt it was a hassle to leave his desk these busy days, so the bottom drawer of his rolltop desk was just deep enough for a bottle of whiskey, a water bottle, some bitters, and a full sugar bowl. Blended, his newest best friend these days was a whiskey cocktail, and it was always within reach, comforting him during the day like the girls at night. While there was little comfort at home, work, whiskey cocktails, and the depths of Water Street were enough to keep his personal demons at bay.

Reaching early evening, and after one too many cocktails, Jakob pressed his case for a change at home even though it was the week of Thanksgiving. The short walk to his house invigorated his resolve, but did not clear his mind.

Throwing open the door, he stood in the foyer. "Charlotte, get down here."

The housemaid coming down the hall for Jakob's hat and coat turned on her heels and disappeared. She had heard that voice before from him, and did not like its consequences. Charlotte took her time coming down the staircase, but she did his bidding. She followed him past the mouth of the staircase toward the parlor, when he turned on her.

"What are you going to do about our situation, Charlotte?"

"You're drunk again, Jakob."

Jakob tumbled to the floor. "Vickers has three sons. I have none. Ulrich has two children and they married after us. You are useless to me."

Charlotte leaned over him, repeating her position. "You want me to leave you, Jakob, don't you? You want me to walk out that door and never come back? I will not do that. I will never do that. I am your wife. You are my husband. It's done and only God can change it."

Grabbing her hair to pull himself and her up the stairs, Jakob reached the second step and thought differently. He threw her down. "God is not going to change this. God is not going to change you and God is certainly not going to change me."

Jakob turned and staggered toward the front door.

"Where are you going now, Jakob?"

There was no answer. Steadying himself, he was out the door and down the steps. Jakob headed for the intersection of Water Street and the cabbie stand.

Reaching the post, he waved for the next cab and fell when a huge paw from nowhere grabbed him by the coat collar, speaking in his best Irish brogue. "The trip back up is harder than the fall down. Lean against this post while I get the cabbie's attention. Are you headed downtown?"

Jakob appreciated the hand up. "I am headed to where I can get drunker than I am now and then sleep it off, where I won't have to answer any questions tomorrow whenever I wake up."

"Sounds like a good plan for this evening. I know a very good first stop. It's just an Irish hole. Would you like a partner? They call me Dan for Danny. You might've guessed I'm Irish."

"Now what would make me think that of a redhead. That a freckled man, almost twice as big as me, would be Irish? I'll call you Danny. Let's see this Irish hole."

Jakob slowly climbed into the very black Hansom cab while Danny walked around the other side and squeezed in. The cab slouched, bearing the Irishman's weight. With forearms the size of fence posts, Jakob was well protected for a raucous evening of drinking.

Danny yelled up at the driver. "Cullinn's Pub."

The longer drive past Jakob's shelter on Water Street to Danny's Irish pub served Jakob well, giving his head time to clear and get ready for their drinking marathon. The pub was not much to look at from the outside, but inside, the air was warm and filled with smoke and laughter. At the far corner, a few men were singing some well-worn Irish ballads even though they didn't know what they sounded like and they didn't care. Everyone in the house wanted to be there, and despite the rumors that fights always broke out in an Irish pub, everyone had a smile on their face.

"Jakob, in this place, the drinks are on me." Jakob and Dan occupied two wooden stools at the bar. "Donovan, your finest Irish whiskey for my new friend and beer chasers."

Jakob's cut of clothes looked out of place in this Irish pub and within the hour, he didn't care, and neither did his new friend.

Several drinks later, Jakob propped his hand on Dan's shoulder. "Danny, you could not have been more generous, but it's my time for me to be the host. Get us a cab."

A few waves and words later, they were out the door, promising to be back soon. Just as easily, they stumbled through the door to Jakob's well-worn place of relaxation.

As best he could, Jakob made for the madam of the house. "I need two girls to undress us and keep us warm for the whole night."

This night, it didn't matter who they were.

Two girls were summoned and the taller of the two sidled up to Danny. "You're a big one, aren't you?"

During the night, the two girls had it easy enough. The following morning, whenever morning would come, they wondered if it might not be so easy. Jakob and Danny had forged a new partnership in Irish whiskey and song.

Rolling her to his side, Jakob yelled across the room. "It must be time for lunch, Danny. I'm going to take you to the Newhall House Hotel for lunch. We have things to discuss."

"I'm not awake yet. These girls have skills. Mine would not let me go to sleep until, well, you know."

"Maybe she wanted to be able to say to her sisters she made love to this huge Irishman."

"That she did. That she did."

After a soft tap on her small, rounded derriere, she looked up at Jakob. "Tell Mildred we both want to take baths."

Bathed and dressed, the two made quite the pair walking past the ladies. One was tall and broad and the other was short and slim.

The pair, who shared their beds the night before, waited for them at the side door when Danny's girl grabbed his arm. "Ask for me when you return. My name is Gretchen."

Noting that a cab was already waiting for them, Danny looked at his newfound friend. "People do immediately what you ask. Girls for the night, a bath when you ask for it, this cab waiting for us. Who are you, Jakob?"

"Danny, I'll tell you that and more over lunch. Driver, Main and Michigan. Front entrance of the Newhall House Hotel."

As they entered the hotel, walking under the high, wide rounded arches into the lobby, one gentleman and then another greeted Jakob. A table was immediately readied and two waiters stood next to the table, each waiting for instructions to serve their guests. Sitting, Danny asked again, "Who are you, Jakob?"

"My name is Jakob Schmidt, son of Heinriche Schmidt, owner of the Schmidt brewery."

Unclear yet where this was exactly heading, Danny was certain this partnership would have to be pursued over a full belly. This Irishman was not going to waste the opportunity to have a big meal in a famous hotel.

"Let's talk business, Danny." Jakob sipped his coffee. "You have the experience and I have the money. You have the brawn and connections with the right people. I'll back you financially and together we will have our own respectable, fancy house. I can supply the beer and liquor and you can hire the girls and run the house. I'll pass the word on to the best clients who have the money and will want to be discreet. The business will be in your name, Danny. All profits will be split fifty-fifty. Are you in?"

"I'm in all the way, but you are Herr Schmidt. You have all the money you could possibly want. Why do you want to get into business with an Irish brawler?"

"For me, it's my very own business to run the way I want to with you, of course. I won't have to take orders from anyone. I'll be able to give them. We'll do very well together, but from now on we also have to be discreet. We should meet at Cullinn's Pub in a week. Let's say seven p.m. We need to think about a name and where the place should be located. Remember, we want only the finest of Milwaukee's gentlemen to make use of our place."

Danny and Jakob walked out of the side door of the Newhall House Hotel. "Here's some money for a cab. See you in a week at seven p.m."

"Cullinn's pub," Danny said to the driver. As he boarded the cab, he was already thinking about who he should talk with and Gretchen immediately came to mind. He liked her, and she appreciated him. It wasn't too often a girl would say to him, *"Ask for me when you return."* His mind was spinning faster than the wheels underneath him, saying to himself, *This is my start, and I have got to play this smart.*

Ideas fell from their lips a week later, faster than Jakob could write them down. Jakob liked the idea of using Gretchen as the contact person between Danny and the girls. She had experience so she would know how to handle the stable and where to find new talent. Whenever Jakob saw her, she always had this peaceful look on her face. *Girls will trust her*, he thought, and he believed she could keep them in line. She stood a head taller than most of them, and that alone could intimidate any newcomer. She was also bigger than most, so no wonder Danny liked her.

"I know you like her, Danny. Her face is like a white dove, but I know she can handle you."

Danny didn't know where to locate their house. Jakob thought it best to be near the edge of the business district, probably north of Grand

Avenue and east of the river. "It has to be two, no three stories tall, facing two or three streets. It needs a respectable front, with a foyer opening to a large room for coffee, a dessert table, card playing, and maybe even billiard tables. Connected to this will be a hallway to a larger room with a stocked bar with the finest choices supplied by me. We'll also have a fireplace, a raised music platform with an open floor before it, and tables surrounding it to greet and entertain the ladies. It will have the look and the air of high fashion and respectability."

"What did I call Gretchen before Danny?"

"You called her a white dove."

"We'll call our house the White Dove! We'll etch the outline of a dove in the glass of the front door and the calling cards will be circulated among the few with the same outline of a white dove. The girls will be the best of the Germans, Irish, Poles, and Serbs living among us. We'll pay them well and they'll want to work for us."

Danny could not keep up with Jakob's ideas, but this was one ride he was not getting off. There would be much to do after they located a building, but he was ready to put his shoulder to it. *Jakob wants to spend the cash, so why shouldn't I add my sweat to the project*, Danny thought.

Finally, Jakob slowed down. "Danny, we've been at this for two hours and I need to relax. Let's go to my favorite spot."

"Jakob, don't you have to go home to your family?"

Jakob turned red with rage. "Don't talk to me about my family ever again."

Danny didn't talk to Jakob about anything up Water Street. He saw his new partner seek refuge in the arms of strangers instead of going home. It wasn't clear yet to Danny why he chose a whorehouse, or for that matter, why he wanted to be a business partner in a whorehouse. However, it was something he needed to find out about this man he now found himself tied to, he hoped, for years to come. Heads turned again as this pair walked into the house and immediately, Danny asked for Gretchen.

Gretchen was lounging in the room where the girls rested, waiting to be summoned. Word was passed to her that the Irishman had returned and asked for her. She waltzed quickly through the throng of girls, who gave her those foolish smiles worn by competitors, and she confidently passed through them all with a wicked smile on her face and approached her man.

Danny smiled at her. "Could you join us for the evening, Gretchen?"

Funny to be asked, she thought. *No one asks anymore.* "I'm yours for the night, Red."

As she led the way to Jakob's favorite room, she looked over her shoulder to see if another girl was joining her. Seeing none, she worried, but she was too far into the room to do anything about it.

"What did my trusting heart get myself into again?" she mumbled.

Danny closed the door behind him, and Jakob saw a look of worry on her face. "Don't be afraid, Gretchen. We both want to talk to you. Please sit down at the table and listen to what we have to offer you."

Still worried, Gretchen sat down and Danny sat closest to her while Jakob pulled a soft chair up to both of them.

"Danny and I are going into business together. Your Irishman will run the business with you if you accept our offer. We're going to open our own place for the very best clients to spend time with the very best women Milwaukee has to offer. You will find the girls and manage them while they're employed by us. You will be paid well and so will each girl and they'll room together on the premises of our establishment and all their needs will be attended to, such as meals, clothing, even the services of a doctor. But to be employed by you, each girl must be clean and they must know how to read and write. They must be able to add and subtract and carry on a meaningful conversation with their clients. They will be required to read the latest newspapers and know the difference between a fine wine and a cheap wine, a good brandy and garbage."

Like Danny, it didn't take Gretchen long to say that she wanted to join this venture. She knew the Schmidt name. She wanted to know Danny better, and she also knew what any madam didn't have to do any longer. Since she was relatively new to the business, her remaining contacts were with fresh face, clean ones that would be best for their new house.

"When do I start working for you and how many girls do you want?"

"First, we have to find the right place and set it up properly. We hope to receive our first clients when the weather turns cold this fall. That will give you all the time you'll need to find the faces we're looking for. Start with five girls and remember our requirements. You can't talk to anyone about this. I'm sure you know why. And from now on, the only person you can talk to about our business is Danny. Is that understood?"

"Yes, it is."

"If Sarah is still here, could you get her for me?"

"If we're through, I'll get her for you now."

The meeting was over, and Gretchen stood to leave.

"I'd like you to spend the rest of your night with me, Gretchen."

She nodded at Danny. "I'll be back to you."

As she sought Sarah and the key to another room, she recalled what she had to do first, and even though Danny was the bigger of the two, there was no question that Jakob was the boss. *He has thought this all through and he likes giving orders. I can handle Danny*, she thought, *but I am glad I don't have to deal with this coldhearted man.*

Sarah was more than willing to oblige Jakob's request. With a key for another room and Sarah in tow, Gretchen left her in Jakob's room and took Danny to another. Her new position had already begun. Seeing him already getting into bed, she decided this was not the time to talk to Danny.

Jakob was up early, long before Danny opened his tired eyes. Gretchen was snuggled up against Danny at peace, no longer at work. It was a strange feeling for her and one she would like to visit more often. Danny stirred and instinctively pulled her closer to him. He wanted her close to him. Gretchen closed her eyes again and thought this new responsibility could wait for a few more hours.

After settling the account for his and Danny's evening, Jakob took a cab directly to his office. His work there had slowed for now, since contractors had been chosen, plans adopted, and contracts signed so that the physical changes to the factory could begin and the new brewing processes could be implemented. Instead, Jakob could sit at his desk and concentrate on his new business venture, or leave his desk to find a building under the guise of expanding the brewery. Furthermore, he had the time to find out if a business would be closing so that he could purchase a property on the cheap. Properly placed questions led him to two current possibilities. The better of the two buildings faced three streets, but was too close to the residential areas where he would draw his clients. The other building had all the internal prerequisites required, and was a safe distance from the homes and wives his clients would come from. It was three stories tall, had a cream-colored brick front, but faced only two streets.

Soon Danny would have to make face-to-face contact with the owners, asking for a first refusal contract while he looked for a better property if there was a better property available closer to the intersection of Grand Avenue and Water Street. If the money was right, the owners would not care who they were dealing with, especially if they wanted to sell quickly. Danny also had the size to intimidate the sellers, and yet he could be steered to say the right things in the right way to close the deal.

Jakob reached into the tall bottom drawer of his desk and poured himself three fingers of a new brandy. Leaning back, he thought that Danny probably relished the idea of being a businessman, carrying out business deals. *I must remind him often that I can turn off my cash spigot whenever I want, or remove him, even if his feet do not fit my shoes,* Jakob thought.

After draining the glass, Jakob headed for the front street to catch a cab. The plan was to drive the streets around each potential business site. He wanted to view them as if he was a new client choosing to stop or not. *Will the client feel safe no matter the hour, and will he protect his reputation if he had to make a quick escape? Will their disorderly house be close enough to the right clients, and yet far enough away from the public's eye? This cab driver will have to be employed into the night,* thought Jakob.

"Driver, can I keep you in my service for the rest of the afternoon and tonight?"

"Sir, I'd be happy to do as you ask."

"First, take me downtown to Grand Avenue and Water Street, and then we'll head east."

By nine o'clock, Jakob was home. His long cab ride was over and he had finished dinner downtown two hours earlier, so Jakob headed for the parlor. On the small table next to his chair, the butler placed a silver tray with a brandy cantor and one glass, fulfilling Jakob's regular evening request when he was at home. The first two belts went down quickly and Jakob was enjoying the third while pitting the two properties against each other. Which one of the two would best satisfy his requirements? It would take at least two months to ready the White Dove and another month to stock it, furnish it, and train the cooks, bartenders, girls, and the rest of the twenty-four-hour staff. Jakob planned to add a doorman at the front entrance and a guard at the back. Both would add muscle to the operation. Danny and Gretchen would always be on-site, so they would need their own rooms or maybe one room. Laughing at his last thought, he could hear the front door open and Charlotte dismissing the butler. Jakob gulped the last swallow from the glass and poured another.

"I saw the light in the room, so I thought I would say hello.

"You're out late. Where were you?"

"What do you care, Jakob?"

"Where were you, Charlotte?"

Charlotte slipped into her role as a wife. "If you must know, I was at the Cathedral."

Jakob laughed. "Praying I suppose."

"A priest has gathered some of us women together to find ways we can help girls and women who are pregnant or who have babies but no husbands to care for them. We—"

"That's funny. That's really funny. Get out of my sight."

"I'll leave you with your best friend." Charlotte smirked.

Thrust and parry. Thrust and parry. She is getting better at this, Jakob thought as he threw the glass at her.

"Bring me another glass," he yelled to anyone who was listening.

Chapter Sixteen

Sitting next to Jane at the kitchen table, Doctor Jameson announced to Ania and Henryk that City Hall had recently reported that a new common school was going to be built just one block east on Fowler Street, next to Oconomowoc's finest, Binzel's Brewery.

"Students will be able to attend in the fall of 1879," said Willy.

"That's a funny place to build a school," Jane piped up.

Henryk was not paying attention to the chatter since he was busy finishing his fourth ear of white corn.

"I think Henryk should go to school there," said the doctor.

"He'll get enough schooling from us," said Jane.

"No, he won't. I think—"

"Willy, who can I talk to about schooling for Henryk?"

"Ania, go speak to the principal at the Methodist Church School when it reopens after the harvest. I hear they now have five female teachers. After speaking to the principal, maybe you could speak to the teacher who has children in her classroom Henryk's age."

In late October, after harvest time, children could begin another school year. Ania steered the buggy up North Lake Road late afternoon to the Methodist Church School on Pine Street. Enlarged the year before, Ania walked up the steps and asked one of the older students for the principal. Politely, the girl led Ania to an outer office, where a young woman was sitting at a desk.

"May I speak to the principal?"

"You can. What is your name?"

"My name is Ania Sobieski."

Just as she was about to get up, a short, spectacled man came out of the inner office carrying a stack of papers and set them on the desk. "May I help you?"

"This woman's name is Ania Sobieski, and she would like to speak with you."

"Come into my office. I have a few moments before my meeting with a teacher."

Ania sat down across the desk from the principal and asked the many rehearsed questions she prepared for this moment. The principal took interest in all of her questions but stopped her when she mentioned Henryk's age.

"Before you go on, you should speak with Miss Adams, who teaches our youngest students. She should still be in her classroom. I'll introduce you to her."

Miss Adam's large classroom was on the same level as the principal's office, and when the principal led Ania through her open doorway, she immediately looked up from her front desk set before a large slate wall blackboard.

"Miss Adams. This is Ania Sobieski. She would like to speak with you about schooling for her seven-year-old son."

Leaving the school behind thirty minutes later, Ania's head was full of reasons she should enroll Henryk, but the tuition required was beyond her means. Miss Adams made it quite clear that a child entering the twentieth century needed, at the very least, a common school education. The words of Miss Adams, *"Do this for your son,"* kept ringing in her ears as the buggy made it down Milwaukee Street to home. It was after dark by the time the gray was unhitched and Ania made it into the kitchen.

At the dinner table, it didn't take long for the conversation to turn to Ania's visit to the Methodist Church School. There was resolve in Ania's words as she revisited the teacher's comments and encouragement, but there was also just as much hesitation when she spoke of enrolling Henryk at the school. Since his name was mentioned so often in the discussion, Henryk listened carefully but held his tongue. He decided he could talk to his mother later, when she was alone, to ask her what words like common school, geography, and mathematics had to do with him.

"Why don't you enroll Henryk in the school since you have said so many good things about it?"

"It costs too much, Willy."

"Jane and I could help with the tuition."

"No! I couldn't accept that. You're already helping both of us. We live with you and you have given me a job. No, this is something I have to do."

"We can teach the boy here, Ania, just as I said before when Willy first brought the subject up."

"We will, Jane, but the teacher is also right. We will teach the boy here until they open the public school next fall. Then he can go there. The taxes I pay will help build the school, so Henryk might as well attend it. Until then, he can learn from us."

After stepping down from the Milwaukee taxi, Jakob stood under a short awning and watched the engraver put his finishing touches on a slender dove etched in the glass of the front door. The front room had all the comforts of home, and it looked innocent enough, with card tables, billiard tables, and a coffee service on a side table large enough to hold cups and saucers. The slender hallway past the kitchen led him to the greeting room, but it told a different story. Furniture was stacked to one corner while one set of carpenters was working on a long bar and the other set was working on a raised platform.

Jakob nodded to one of the carpenters. "Where's Danny?"

"He's upstairs. I'll get him."

Jakob had time to fume within before Danny walked into the room. "We don't open in two years, Danny. November first. We open in eight days." Jakob looked straight up into the Irishman's green eyes and yelled louder. "November first, Danny!"

Danny walked toward the open staircase that led to more carpenter noise on the second floor. "I know it looks right now that we'll not be finished, but I've been assured by the lead carpenter on each floor that both floors will be ready two days before we open. That will give us all the time we will need to position furniture in each upstairs room and properly stock the bar. Finishing touches, if needed, can be done off-hours. Rooms on the third floor for the girls and my suite will be finished last. We'll be ready, Jakob."

"All right, Danny. You didn't wilt before my concerns or my yelling. I believe you. Are the iceboxes in place?"

"On each side of the mirror behind the bar opening on the other side of the wall is an icebox large enough to hold a raised barrel of your finest beer. You didn't notice them because all you can see from the bar is the beer tap. Gravity will deliver your best to mugs, each etched with a dove."

"Great idea, Danny, great idea. What about the girls, bartenders, servers, and kitchen staff?"

"They will all be here the day before we open. Do you want to meet them?"

"No, Danny. You and Gretchen are the faces of our business. You handle the girls, too. We'll get together privately, here, the day before we open, so I can let you know how many clients you can expect. A few cards with the name of our house have made their way into the hands of the right people. Word has even made its way back to me that a new house called the White Dove is opening Friday, November first at nine p.m. Where are the girls?"

"They're all staying with Gretchen until we open Jakob, and then they will stay here. Even though their rooms are not finished on the third floor, they will have to make do. Gretchen has assured me they meet our requirements. I meet them tonight."

"Our guests must be pleased, Danny, or they won't come back. Be sure they have the right talent and that they look good, too. Their job is to entertain our customers for an expensive evening, disarm them but satisfy their wishes so they'll return again and again. Keep that in mind when you examine them tonight. I'll see you in a week."

As Jakob headed for the side door, he yelled once more, "November first, Danny."

Jakob can be demanding, Danny thought, *but hell, he wants to succeed and so do I. It's time to put a burr in the pants of each of these workmen. Jakob won't be pleased if we're not ready on November first, and there is only one person who will feel his wrath.*

"Fitz! Fitz, I want to talk to you!"

"How many of your men can work on Sunday for additional pay?" asked Danny.

Fitz held no hesitation. "Just about all of them."

"Plan on it, Fitz. You know armed guards will now be posted at each door around the clock so your workers can stay here as long as they want. I'll see you tomorrow morning."

Danny turned on his heels and walked toward the front door. Standing for a moment next to the guard at the open front door, he looked at the etched dove and smiled. Boarding a cab, Danny told the driver to take Milwaukee Street seven blocks south to an address on East Chicago Street, where Gretchen housed her eager charges. She recruited each experienced girl with Jakob's requirements always on her mind. One was a former elementary teacher from a well-known family in St. Louis, who took to teaching and correcting the social skills of Gretchen's girls. She was driven to this business by a former collapsed relationship torpedoed by her father. Another girl was Sarah, who was Jakob's favorite. Many guests knew her youth and beauty, and Gretchen assumed her reputation would draw business. Only one girl needed more seasoning.

Now that Gretchen had recruited all five girls, Danny planned to check on their progress. First, he wanted to see how each one would handle his personal attention. Tonight, they wouldn't have to be dressed in their new working clothes. That would come later next week. Gretchen brought the teacher first into the room and then took her seat behind the woman. Danny sat at a table in the center of the room and asked the teacher to stand before him. She approached him slowly, a tactic recognized immediately by Danny that Gretchen had confided in him as a secret of the trade to make the client grow with desire.

"Take off your dress."

Again, she moved slowly, unbuttoning the button at each elbow and down her bodice. She turned to one side and then the other to slip the dress off of each arm, slowly lowering it to the floor, teasing him. There was no embarrassment in her eyes, just readiness to please.

"Beautiful," Danny said to no one. "You can get dressed."

There was no need to bring Sarah into the room. Of the remaining three, only a very young German blond girl seemed hesitant during her audition before Danny.

Gretchen saw it, too. "She'll get better. I'll talk to her."

A few minutes later, over dinner, Danny assured Gretchen that he liked what he saw. "They are all different and all beautiful."

"I noticed you were pleased," said Gretchen with a bit of sarcasm.

"Jakob will be pleased, but will they be sophisticated enough?"

"They know what to say and how to say it, but, Danny, do you really think their future clients are looking for sophistication in bed? They are looking for pleasure along with something new in bed they have never experienced before with a beautiful young woman who speaks words of kindness to them. When you draw me closer to you, even while you're sleeping, are you appreciating my ability to read or write, or my thoughts about who is running for president from which party? Or are you appreciating my kind words spoken to you, my warmth, my touch, and especially my willingness to do what you want, when you want me to? That's exactly what our customers will get from all of our girls each night or day."

"I like how you think, Gretchen."

"You like me for more than that, Danny."

"You're right, Gretchen. Show me."

The next week went by too quickly, but thankfully Fitz was true to his word.

With the first and second floors finished, two days would be enough for the three bartenders to arrange the bar and for the chef and servers to ready the kitchen, and Danny to direct the workers on where to arrange all the furniture on both floors. Furthermore, two rooms would be ready on the third floor. Danny walked about on each floor, pleased with himself. It was his first real project on this scale, and he had pulled it off. *Jakob will be pleased as well when he arrives,* Danny thought.

After telling the taxi driver to wait, Jakob knocked on the side door. The guard opened the door slowly and let Jakob pass. Danny had alerted him of a visitor coming at eight o'clock. The guard didn't know who he was, but he looked important enough that the guard didn't need to question him. Jakob passed the new stairway to the third floor and met Danny in the finished greeting room.

"Nice, Danny, nice."

They sat on upholstered chairs next to a side table where Danny had placed two glasses and an unopened bottle of brandy. Jakob quickly opened the bottle and filled two glasses. Taking a long pull from his glass, Jakob filled it again.

"The White Dove is ready for business." Danny saluted his partner with his raised glass. "To our success."

"You know, Danny, this is all window dressing. What happens upstairs will either make or break us. Take me upstairs where the real work will be done."

The very visible, open staircase led to a hallway that overlooked the room below. Jakob stopped and looked down on his investment and pronounced it ready with a wink. They turned the corner to a center hallway with four large rooms on each side of the hallway.

"We only have five girls?" asked Jakob.

"Our business will grow quickly when the customers see what we offer them. There will be no need to disturb business because the extra rooms are ready now. And if we treat the girls right, other women will quickly want to work for us. As you can see, each room is decorated in a slightly different way. I especially want you to see this room at the end of the hallway."

The door was closed, which puzzled Jakob as Danny opened it. With black hair piled on her head and held tight with two needles, Sarah stood in the middle of the room, wearing a tight, dark-green velvet dress with a slit at the side, revealing her slim leg to mid-thigh. Draped over one shoulder was a dark red boa. A silver choker circled her slim neck and held a dark green teardrop resting above her breasts.

Danny could see Jakob was pleased.

"Will each girl be dressed as beautiful as Sarah?"

Danny nodded in the affirmative. "I thought you should have a restful evening before we open tomorrow night. Your favorite brandy is on the table next to the bed. You'll not be disturbed. Good night, Jakob."

"You'll have to tell the taxi driver at the side door to leave."

"He's already gone."

Danny closed the door and walked to the end of the hallway to the new stairway, and climbed the stairs to the third floor to his own two rooms, and for some reason, he whistled an Irish tune. There Gretchen would be waiting for him.

By seven o'clock the next night, everyone was in place, waiting for the first man of means to walk into a new house for a new experience with the same result.

One and then another and more arrived to enjoy the White Dove's opening and the teacher's lessons, which were secret no more.

<h1 style="text-align:center">*Chapter Seventeen*</h1>

Two years had passed since Willy and Jane first discussed Ania and her son staying with them. As Henryk grew stronger, he could do more household chores, and Ania was more proficient in the doctor's office as well. She took to being a nurse easily, and that allowed Jane to be the woman of her house. Willy's practice kept growing as Oconomowoc grew. Each summer, more guests arrived at the expanding hotels, and those who had built their summer cottages brought their families and staff to enjoy the Hamptons of the Midwest.

Owners or their rich family members were arriving earlier and staying longer. Even though there was a second younger doctor in town, there was enough caring to be done by both of them. He had the newer and bigger house, but the Jamesons were just fine with their place in life. Since Ania and Henryk had graced their home, their lives were as full as they could be.

Ever since the October morning fire in the third ward destroyed the Humiston house, each fireplace and the kitchen stove had a full fire bucket at the ready.

One of Henryk's chores on each even day of the calendar was to check and fill every bucket to the top. Jane had arranged this so that Henryk could learn even and odd numbers, plus days and months of the year. Today, writing with his left hand, he placed a small letter X in the corner of Friday, March 28, to show he had made his fire bucket rounds.

Coming down the church steps Sunday morning with Ania and Henryk, Willy saw his wife talking on the sidewalk with two other women. Bidding them a good day, Jane continued with the same topic as the four of them walked home.

"Willy, when is this town going to buy its very own fire wagon? Watertown has two of them. Articles in the *Free Press* since the October fire have repeatedly called for the town to raise the money and buy one. What if that fire had happened at our house? What would we do? People are worried."

"The town officers are talking about it."

"Talk is not enough," said Ania.

Willy and Jane looked at each other, surprised.

"Ania?" asked Willy.

"I believe we'll get a fire wagon if and when a store owned by one of the town's officers burn down."

"She's right, Willy. They'll do nothing. They always do nothing."

The debate ebbed and flowed in town while the stores were waking up after a long, depressing winter. The movement of goods from shopkeepers to customers had slowed to a trickle after Christmas. Now, wagons for more than a week were going back and forth to the train station to load up with goods mostly shipped from Milwaukee or Chicago for delivery to the shops on Milwaukee Street, and North and South Main Streets.

Another quiet Monday evening had begun and optimism was high for another good business year in Oconomowoc. Shopkeepers, wives, and their hired hands were putting in long hours to fill the shelves and store their new wares. Near eight o'clock on the first evening of the workweek, most of the activity in and about the stores had ceased. Just about all the owners and their helpers living on or off premises had left their work for the night. The horses and wagons were long gone. The streets were desolate except for a pair of mangy dogs working their way down North Main Street, sniffing at each doorway until they lay down at the foot of the dry goods store window with a single lantern still glowing in the darkness.

A woman's voice pierced the night air. *"Fire! Fire!"*

A man, screaming even louder, quickly joined her. "Fire!"

It wasn't long before the bell of the Lutheran church downtown began a continuous ringing.

"Grab the fire buckets and let's go," yelled Willy. "You too, Henryk."

Within a moment, all four were standing on the street, waiting to hear which direction they should run. Noticing people running west on Milwaukee Street toward the center of town, they also ran in that direction, and when they turned the corner from Walnut, they could see it. Flames were already shooting out of the upper windows of the dry goods store, and the roof of the next building was on fire as well. Two lines of people were already forming a bucket line from Fowler Lake to the fire. Men were running in and out of stores, piling goods on the street. Soon, wagons arrived to move what they could out of danger.

"Always stay together," yelled Willy as they joined a second bucket line.

Flames had jumped the street and now there were two walls of fire on each side of the street, moving north and south. The fire would soon run out of buildings on North Main Street, but if nothing stopped this surge on South Main Street, it would destroy the center of town or more. People were coming from everywhere to help, knowing their houses or businesses could be next if this raging inferno was not stopped.

Luckily, a week earlier, an old building was torn down to its foundation, creating a fifty-foot breach between buildings on the east side of South Main Street. This might save the east side of Main Street. Still, if the flames devoured the tall mill building on the opposite side of the street, nothing would stop the flames in any direction. Even though the fire was two buildings from the mill, the front bucket line was now at the mill. Water drenched the wood walls facing the fire, and men were carrying buckets of water to the roofline, throwing water on anything in the mill that faced the flames. The two buildings in line with the mill would have to be sacrificed to the fire. The fire had to be stopped at the breach of the buildings on one side of the street, and the mill on the other, or the blaze could devour the whole town.

Two men were running up and down the bucket lines, calling for Doctor Jameson.

Willy stepped out of the line. "Over here."

"We need you to come with us."

"Come along, Ania. Henryk, you stay with Jane. Don't go near the fires."

One of the two men took his place in the line, while the other led them closer to one of the burned-out buildings.

"We found him just inside the door."

The badly burned man was now laying in the street. They had thrown water on him to cool his arms, hands, and more. Pieces of black flesh hung from his arms like burned wax drippings on a candle. Willy yelled to some men to help him move the burn victim to a long horse's trough just emptied of water.

"Put him inside the trough with his hands and arms at his side and fill the trough with well water to his armpits. Give him a lot of whiskey or brandy."

"How much whiskey?" someone asked.

"Get him drunk, man!" said Willy. "Ania, find Jane and Henryk and tell them to go home and fetch my doctor's bag. Tell Henryk to stay home. Then go to a house and get some clean sheets and two scissors."

Fifteen minutes later, Ania was back with the sheets and scissors, and she found two more men sitting on the ground, leaning against the opposite end of the same wooden trough. Willy was looking at the leg of one man while the other just sat there, moaning.

"I've got two burn victims here, Ania, and more may be coming. Watch me tend to this burned man, so you will know what to do if we have another."

Willy cut away the remnants of the burned sleeves from the man's arms. Then he poured garnered whiskey on his own hands and scissors, and cut the burned black flesh from the man's hands and arms.

Taking a nearby stick, he stuck it in the man's mouth. "Bite down on this when I tell you. Bite down hard." He poured whiskey over the burned areas of the man's hands and arms. "Ania, lightly wrap the man's hands up his arms and tie them off at each elbow. Make sure he has a lot to drink, too. You know now what to do with bad burns. I'm going back to the man in the trough. When you're done here bandage the man with the gash on his leg. Use water and then alcohol and then bandage him."

Ania turned back to the man with the burns. He was in so much pain he couldn't cry or even scream. "I'm sorry." She went about her business no matter how much he screamed. "Give him something more to drink," she ordered to an old man standing nearby, "and get more bottles of whiskey."

Moving to the next man, she looked at the gash of weeping blood down his leg. "I'm going to cut away your pant leg."

He didn't answer. He just sat there, saying the same thing. Something about no insurance.

"This is going to hurt."

Water first and then alcohol. He flinched when she poured the alcohol on the wound, but didn't say anything. Dazed, he just let Ania do her work.

Cutting wide strips of cloth, she wrapped the bandage tightly around his calf and tied it off. Moving back to the doctor's side, they quickly looked in on the man in the trough, while two more burn victims lay close by.

Willy pulled on Ania's sleeve so she looked toward him and whispered, "He's going to die, Ania. Jane will stay with him and feed him more alcohol, so his mind stays numbed to decrease the pain. We have to work on those who have a chance of living."

Ania turned to one of the burn victims while Willy went to the other. She poured alcohol on her hands and scissors.

Taking a piece of wood, she placed it in his mouth. "Bite down on this." She was in charge and she knew it.

She gave orders to the two men standing nearby. "You hold his feet down," she said to one, and to the other, "you hold his shoulders." She looked at the burn victim. "Sir, this is going to hurt. Bite hard."

He looked into her eyes. "Do it."

She nodded. "Hold him tight." Ania parsed her lips and poured whiskey on the man's arms and hands.

The man jerked his arms and snorted. Immediately, Ania started cutting away burned flesh from his hands and arms. Blood squirted from one arm, so she fastened a tourniquet above his left elbow and kept cutting.

"Give him the brandy to drink and then put the wood back into his mouth." She finished cutting. "Bite hard."

Again, she poured alcohol all over his arms and hands. The man, spitting out the piece of wood, kept cursing, and finally his head dropped to his chest as he passed out.

As instructed before, she loosely bandaged his arms and hands. Willy had already finished with his patient and was kneeling behind her, out of her sight, watching. He smiled just before Ania turned to her right side to see if somebody else needed her attention. Then she turned back the other way and saw the doctor smiling. Not speaking, she moved off to the side, sat on the wet earth, and closed her eyes.

Willy went back to Jane, who was still softly talking to her patient. His breathing was shallow now. This twenty-year-old helper was going to die soon and die alone except for Jane's calming voice in his ear. Maybe he heard her and maybe not, but at least there was a kind voice. Willy looked at her and she slowly shook her head. They had seen death's grip before. It would not be long for him.

"I hate fires," Willy said to Jane. "I hate 'em."

Down South Main Street, the fire engine that arrived from Watertown two hours ago was still pouring a high stream of water onto the mill. The fire stopped at the mill, and would go no farther. Its flames satisfied, devouring the buildings already lit up. The bucket brigade could breathe easier, and so its pace slowed, realizing that victory was near.

Looking down the street, Willy saw two men escorting another young man who had a bad gash in his hand from breaking a window. Opportunist or not, he never answered their questions about his purpose for breaking the large store window. The doctor and Ania, busy with the wound, did not further their inquiry and the young man volunteered nothing. After Ania tied off his bandage, he gave her thanks, and, since his escorts were gone, quickly disappeared into the crowd.

Jane watched as men gently lifted her young charge from the horse trough and into a wagon. His lifeless burned body rolled to one side of the wagon like cordwood. Standing next to the wagon, Jane bowed her head and was crying when Willy dropped his arm around her shoulder. Ania joined them as the wagon pulled away, but said nothing.

Knowing it would be too painful to discuss this event with them, she stepped between them, and, of each of them, she took a hand in hers. "We've done enough. Let's go home."

Willy and Jane did not answer Ania. They just started walking home with her. Finding Henryk asleep in the parlor, Ania woke him, and the four of them aimlessly climbed the stairs together and drifted into their rooms. Tonight, Ania needed to lay next to Henryk and hold him tight. Calmed by his presence, Ania, totally exhausted emotionally and physically, fell into a fretful sleep.

Chapter Eighteen

At six o'clock in the evening, Charlotte walked alone across the park to the Cathedral for Mass. The grime of Milwaukee's smokestacks had stained the cream-colored bricks of the church right down to the steps before the great door but their work was especially visible on the tall brick bell tower, turning it sooty black. For Charlotte, her world was the same. Outside of this building, everything in her life was dark and sooty, and yet when she walked within, she found a touch of happiness, respect, and purpose. Following Mass, the priest was holding a meeting to discuss the new charges that had come to the church for care. The outside world was sooty for these babies, but here at the Cathedral, they would wash them clean, feed them, and, if possible, find new parents for life.

Father Timothy stood before the nine women huddled in the first pew and remembered when a dying woman two years ago asked him to find someone to raise her toddler. He found a couple willing to add her son to their family. This success story spread and soon thereafter, another baby was left on the church's doorstep. It didn't take him long to recognize the need and seek help from his members. The fledgling group had grown over two years, from two women to nine generous souls sharing their time and money. He started each baby orphan's monthly meeting with a prayer and the second homily of the night.

These homilies were usually short, but this night, the priest was more pointed in his remarks. "We built this church to be a safe place for all who come to us, and that includes the babies no one wants to care for. It is not their fault these innocents have entered a cruel world, but it will be our fault if we do not care for them. We will not be so innocent if we do not find parents and homes for these children."

Each word of the priest's homily echoed in Charlotte's ears. Since she believed the words in the Bible, "*Suffer the little children to come unto me,*" she attended these meetings and when needed, took turns caring for a child at the church until the foundling was in a parish home.

The priest, witnessing her generosity, asked Charlotte to stay after the meeting. The monthly reports at the meeting confirmed the need was growing, so he knew finding parents was critical.

"Charlotte, you like to do this work, don't you?"

"I do. These babies are so beautiful and they need homes, Father."

The priest had seen emptiness in her eyes before, and he knew there was an emptiness in her heart. Charlotte's failure to bring a child to term haunted her, and she had already spoken to Father Timothy about what this had done to her marriage. Charlotte would not walk away from her marriage, nor would the priest advise it. However, as it sometimes happened, the solution was close at hand.

Charlotte had already held the solution in her arms. All she needed was support at home.

"Charlotte, you need to take one of these babies home with you. Talk to your husband. Convince your husband."

"He will not agree."

"You must try, Charlotte. You are not alone. Try."

Charlotte's face brightened at the thought of a baby, but her face darkened just as fast when the priest suggested she convince her husband.

"Father, I will pray about it and you will know what I decide."

"You can do it, Charlotte."

"Good night, Father."

"God bless you, my child."

The words "my child" kept ringing in her heart as she walked home. *Is it a good omen?* Charlotte thought.

Jakob was celebrating tonight. The child he recently gave birth to was one year old. The White Dove was more than a success. It had become the place to go to for the best time with the best girls in town. Danny and Jakob also saw that their need had already taxed their ability to keep providing enough living space for the best working girls. Word of mouth was all the necessary advertising, and it was a good thing Danny had readied twice as many rooms for occupants than originally planned. Doubling to sixteen available rooms suggested by Danny made sense to Jakob and would mean only a minor investment in profits. Increased traffic at the bar would easily pay for the construction of rooms and their furnishings.

Jakob raised his shot glass. "Danny, congratulations on our success."

They were sitting again late afternoon at Cullinn's Irish Pub, where it all began more than a year ago. Both were dining on steaming shepherd's pie and, according to the barkeep, his best bottle of Irish whiskey was sitting on the table between them. Two very large glasses were already wet, and so was Jakob's whistle.

"Danny, I agree with you. Double the number of rooms and do it quickly. I leave it up to you how they should be decorated, but one idea I have is to decorate one like a Roman bath with water to the waist and Greek columns. The room could be double in size and serve four or five men at a time with massages and more. Group activities could be arranged for a special price."

"Great idea, Jakob."

"Can we get enough girls, clean girls, Danny?"

"Gretchen will find the right girls, Jakob. In fact, girls are coming to us, wanting to work for us. Most that come to us have nowhere else to go. Benefits offered here are what keep them coming."

Approving the barkeep's whiskey choice, Jakob motioned to the barkeep. "Drinks for everyone."

These Irish laborers would never see the inside of the White Dove, but that did not mean they should not be able to celebrate his success.

"Barkeep, give Danny the bill. Here are two gold double eagles to finish the night off for my Irish friends. Danny, it's time for me to go to the White Dove and really celebrate. Let's go and I want another bottle of this Irish whiskey."

Stopping at the bar on the way out of the pub, Danny said to the bar owner, "Another bottle of that Irish whiskey," and dropped a ten-dollar gold piece on the bar.

"Here are two bottles. One for each of you."

In the cab, Jakob grabbed the bottles out of Danny's hands. "I need both of them for the night."

The cab pulled up at the side entrance, and Danny went in first. Dismissing the guard inside the door, Jakob made his way surreptitiously to his favorite room at the end of the hall next to the back stairs. He stumbled through the door, and Sarah, already waiting for him, closed the door. Taking the two bottles from his hands, she placed them on a table in the center of the room.

Holding himself upright as best he could, Jakob moved toward the bed. "I want to go to bed with you now."

Sitting on the bed, Jakob struggled with his clothes as Sarah slid past him to the other side of the bed. Jakob, with his shirt still on, rolled on his side to her and tried to enter her, but it was of no use.

She warmly coaxed him to try again, but Jakob rose to one elbow. "Get the bottle from the table. I saw you put it there."

Sarah rose quickly, grabbed the bottle, and sat at his side. Jakob took the green, stout bottle from her and gently caressed it lovingly in both hands. Then he drew it to his lips and kissed it long for himself. Consummated again, he gave the bottle back to her and slowly lowered his head to the pillow. Once more satisfied, he slept in his own stupor. Placing the bottle on the table, Sarah walked to the other side of the bed and cuddled close to Jakob, imagining herself in a different place. Wondering if there would be hell to pay with him in the morning or if it would be just another work night stretching into midday. She closed her tired eyes in her own stupor.

Waking before Jakob, Sarah did not move beside him, prolonging her idle dream. *Women did leave this work and marry*, she thought. *Gretchen has her man. Maybe, just maybe, I could.* She couldn't finish her thought because Jakob was calling her name.

"I'm here for you, Jakob."

"My hands are shaking. I need a drink, Sarah. Get the bottle for me."

Sarah didn't want to argue. Her only leverage, really, was to please Jakob in every way he asked. Could she one time? Dare she speak to Jakob. "Love me instead of the bottle."

"My hands are shaking, Sarah. I need a drink."

"Alcohol is going to kill you."

Jakob drained the bottle. "Not now, Sarah. Come here."

⸻◦◦⸻

Every glance from the parish priest at mass reminded Charlotte of their conversation to discuss the possibility of raising a foundling as her own. Since the family's seasonal parties were all inspired by the birth of a child, the timing seemed right. With daily prayers on Charlotte's lips and the air full of Christmas hope, she told the priest that she intended to ask her husband if this new arrival at the church could become a part of their family. Jakob had been reasonably sober and actively engaged in conversation with her and others during the holidays, so maybe he would say yes.

Each breakfast, Charlotte checked off mentally the details of her plan. Dress, dinner, their best brandy, even arguments she would use, and the best day of the week to do battle. Her plan sounded good to her.

On the afternoon of New Year's Eve, Jakob had come home early from the office, since the snow was falling and more was on its way. Most would be staying close to home for the evening and maybe longer. Jakob seemed pleasant at the dinner table and conversation flowed easily between them. Charlotte's blond hair fell loosely around her shoulders and darkened lashes. She felt confident in her shimmering white taffeta dress, tight at the hips but falling gracefully around her bosom. She let Jakob slip away alone to the red sofa in the large drawing room. A great fire burned close to his feet, and quite full of himself, Jakob was enjoying his evening cigar. Charlotte told the butler to take their finest brandy to the room and pour two glasses. Finishing her order, the butler passed Charlotte in the hallway. At the door, Charlotte armed herself with her best smile and made a cat-like entrance into the room. She picked up Jakob's full glass and handed it to him. Taking the other glass, she sat on the sofa and slowly turned to her husband.

"I want to apologize to you, Jakob."

"What for, Charlotte?"

"I've not been able to bring a son to your arms. We have tried and now the doctors say I'll never bring a child to term. For this physical shortcoming, I'm very sorry."

"You should be."

Dismissing Jakob's lack of empathy, Charlotte continued. "Listen to me, please, Jakob, for this is difficult for me. We want a child. I know you want a son. Your father wants an heir. There is a way we can have that child."

"Are you going to steal one?"

"I don't have to. We've been caring for a young baby boy at the parish. The child was left in the church three weeks ago. I've held the child in my arms. He's a beautiful boy. We could have our son."

"You mean a bastard son, Charlotte, with bastard blood flowing through its veins? You want me to bring someone's rejection, someone's garbage into my house to take my name?"

Standing up, Jakob took his glass, threw it into the fireplace, and slapped Charlotte's face. "I should have never married you. You have failed me. You have failed yourself. You are worthless to me and this house. What you want to do out of this house is of no concern to me. You can suckle the baby boy at your dry breast if you want to. I don't give a damn what you do. I should just kill you."

Already prone on the sofa from the blow across her face, Charlotte cried tears of despair and then hatred. She willingly entered a celebrated marriage and found herself stuck with being a burdened wife. Her reward was never to be a mother, and there was now nothing Charlotte could do to change it.

Paralyzed, the slapped woman lay there sobbing on the red sofa, her homemade sooty black mascara staining her white dress. Void of any feeling, Charlotte waited for another empty new year to arrive.

Grabbing his coat, Jakob stormed out the door, choosing the white snow of the street instead of his wife.

Jakob could not seek Sarah at the White Dove. She might have been engaged for the night. Plus, he did not feel like answering to another woman about anything. He needed a woman and then he wanted to pass out from alcohol or exhaustion or both. The street car passing the stop for the White Dove continued moving down South Water Street and deeper into Jakob's abandonment of anything socially acceptable.

He had heard of Lili's, but had never been there before this night. Passing through the doorway into the meeting parlor, the first thing he noticed was the smell. This place had been well used for years. The girls looked older and had fallen farther, but this would have to do for the night.

Jakob stopped at the bar and purchased the house's best brandy and then turned to the woman that had to be the madam. "Let me see your girls."

Already noticing him, the girls flocked to Jakob, eager to do business with his money.

"I'll take that one for the whole night in your best room." He dropped a double eagle at her feet. "This should cover the cost." He took the hand of the tallest, youngest girl in his view. "Lead the way."

The madam eagerly picked up the twenty-dollar gold piece from the floor.

Entering the room, Jakob asked, "How long have you been working?"

"Long enough to know how to take care of you." She approached the bed. "Shall we get started."

The night would be hard for them.

Chapter Nineteen

Finally, the ground's frost had lifted from the soil foundation and work could begin on Oconomowoc's first common school on Fowler Street. Willy and Henryk often walked to the construction site so the boy could watch the workmen lay the cream-colored bricks on top of the white stone foundation. The two-story, four-room school opening in the fall would be an easy walk for Henryk. Henryk could start with the girls and the town boys on the first day, while the farmer's children would delay their attendance until the harvest was in.

Nine-year-old Henryk was taking his fishing trips along the south Fowler Lake shoreline. He walked west on Milwaukee Street to Main Street, rebuilt from the devastating fire. He vividly remembered that night and quickly learned how fire changes people's lives, including a friend his age who moved back to Milwaukee since his parents lost their business in the fire.

With Henryk busy during summer days, Ania could spend some of her own time outside of the doctor's office. It had been ten years since she had enjoyed this freedom. When she allowed herself, Ania would think back to those days in Sussex, walking along the marshes to watch and listen to the red-winged blackbirds. Even though those days of great expectations were long gone, thankfully, as she walked, the blackbirds' songs were the same along Fowler Lake. Looking toward Milwaukee Street, she recalled her innocence and wondered if she could listen again to any male song. *These thoughts are for the birds*, she thought. She smirked and turned toward home.

Henryk and Willy were part of the crowd, watching as men hoisted the square bell tower, with a slanted roof and zinc ornamental lattice at the very top, to the roof of the new school.

"When that bell rings, Henryk, you should be in your classroom or close to walking through that door." Willy pointed to the large single door tucked in the corner of the joining classroom wings.

Henryk was getting suspicious of this schoolhouse he was told he was going to enjoy. Like the school, it was all going to be new to him as well.

Picking the sweet corn for Friday's dinner was a chore Ania enjoyed doing with Henryk. Henryk would put darkened corn silk threads from a corn cob inside a rolled husk and pretend he was Willy, smoking his cigar or he would put some of the corn threads across his upper lip like a mustache. Ania laughed, although she had seen it many times before when she heard Willy's voice booming through an opened window.

"I need your help in the office, Ania."

Willy was stitching a long, deep gash on a young man's muscular arm.

Ania walked into the office. "Get another bowl of clean water, Ania. When I'm done here, clean the man's arm again and bandage it. Ania, this is Tom."

Finishing up, Ania addressed Tom. "How did this happen?"

"I bumped a scythe hanging on a wall in the barn, and the blade caught me along the arm. I live just west of town on my parents' farm. They're getting older and, well, someone has to take care of them and the farm."

As Ania tied off the bandage, Henryk peeked his way around the door frame. "Dinner is almost ready."

Jumping down from the doctor's table, Tom smiled at the boy. "Who's this?"

"That's my son, Henryk."

"Hi, Henryk." Tom faced Ania. "Please tell the doctor I'll stop by in two weeks to pay my bill. He wants to look at my arm anyway, and that's when I'll settle up with him. Thank you. Good day to both of you."

From the porch, Ania and son watched him untie his horse from the black metal hitching post and turn south on Walnut Street. Jane was hollering from the kitchen for dinner, and she was not to be denied.

⸺◦◉⸺

Scheduled for the evening two weeks later was the school dedication ceremony with the best local dignitaries promoting education for every child in front of the finished building. Newly hired teachers and the principal would also be in attendance. Elementary children who would attend the school came to the ceremony with their parents. Even though opening day was more than a month away, Henryk was getting a bit skittish about this change to his schedule. The idea of sitting at a desk near some girls for six hours a day, five days per week, did not appeal to him.

Mid-afternoon, the day of the school dedication, Tom showed up at the Jameson house as promised, to have the doctor give his arm a final look and to pay his bill. He hoped the doctor would be alone because something else was bothering him and he wanted to discuss it with him. Tom knocked on the door and his face fell when Ania opened it and led him into the doctor's office. She removed the stitches and collected his money, but the doctor was nowhere to be found. Ania thought he was moving too slowly for a man who had a lot to do, or so he said. *He did not talk much,* Ania thought, but it was just as well since she had to get ready for the ceremonies at Henryk's new school.

The four of them were going to have an early dinner and then go on to the ceremony, but Tom did not want to leave.

At last, Ania got him to the front porch when Tom blurted out, "When is the doctor going to be here so I can talk to him?"

"He will be along soon. You can wait on the porch if you want." She closed the door.

Tom walked down the steps to check on his mare when he saw the doctor strolling up the street in no hurry. Quickening his step, Tom met him and turned to walk back with him toward the doctor's house.

"I might as well just say it, Doctor. Is Ania married, or is she seeing someone?"

The doctor laughed out loud. "No, she's not married or seeing someone, but I think you should find that out for yourself by asking her. Talk to her."

The doctor entered his house and invited Tom to follow him and wait in the hall. Hearing voices in the kitchen, the doctor walked down the hallway.

Willy walked through the doorway with a big smile on his face. "Ania, Tom is in the hallway, and he would like to talk to you."

Ania looked up with puzzlement written all over her face. "About what? Did I do something wrong?"

"No, Ania. Go talk to him."

As Ania left the room, Jane looked at Willy and furrowed her eyebrows. "What's this about, Willy?"

"Let's see what Ania has to say when she comes back."

Ania walked right up to Tom. "Is there something wrong?"

"Nothing wrong. I was hoping I could call on you. Maybe tomorrow in the afternoon. We could walk to the ice cream parlor downtown."

"Yes. Yes, we can do that. Would it be all right if I brought Henryk with us?"

"Of course. I'll be here at two p.m. if that's all right with you."

"That would be fine."

"It will be." Tom turned and was out the door.

Now that she had a moment to think about what had just happened, her mind spun back to Jakob in Sussex, and a cold shiver swept down the nape of her neck and gripped her heart. She shuddered and said to herself, *That will have to change.*

Ania walked back into the kitchen. "The man you met two weeks ago with the cut on his arm is taking us to the ice cream parlor tomorrow afternoon."

Jane didn't have to ask Willy any more questions, but noticed that Ania was rather quiet while they ate. She didn't brighten until later at the school's festivities and was especially alert when meeting Henryk's teacher but silent again, during their short walk home.

The next day, before two o'clock, the whole Jameson household was on alert for Tom's arrival. Jane seemed to be the most interested in minding the front bay windows, watching for the farmer. Shortly before the appointed time, she saw Tom hitching his horse to the post out front.

Jane's voice, with a touch of glee, rang up the stairs. "He's here."

"I'll be down."

Tom knocked sharply on the door.

Slowing her step, Jane opened the door and produced the best blank face she could. "Welcome to our home. I am Doctor Jameson's wife. You may call me Jane."

Leading him further into the parlor, past Ania's desk, and three empty chairs, Jane told Tom to be seated, and she sat in her chair. Willy wanted no part of this and kept himself busy out back.

"Tell me about your farm, Tom."

"It's not my farm. My parents own one hundred thirty acres west of town. Most of it is in hay, corn, and pasture. We milk Holsteins morning and night and the new breed to Wisconsin called Jerseys. We have—"

"Hello, Tom."

Tom stood, fumbling with his hat. "Good afternoon, Miss Ania and Henryk."

The thought of getting a bowl of ice cream appealed the most to Henryk. He didn't realize he was being a nine-year-old chaperone for the afternoon. Ania wore a simple pale brown cotton dress, but this afternoon would not be very simple for her. It was not her best dress, but it was right for the occasion. Henryk didn't care what he was wearing. The only thing on his mind was ice cream.

Walking to the ice cream parlor on Milwaukee Street on this breezy afternoon was easy enough for all three of them, although Henryk was steps ahead or lagging behind. *He is no help in this situation*, Ania thought. Tom didn't help either, since he still had said nothing to her or Henryk.

"I heard you talk to Mrs. Jameson about Jersey cows. I've seen the big Holsteins, but I've not heard anything about Jersey milking cows. Can you tell me about them?"

"My father is switching out his herd from Holsteins to all Jerseys for a number of reasons. My parents are both rather short and the full-grown Holsteins are taller than they are and they weigh up to thirteen hundred pounds or more. They can easily push my father around. Jerseys are much smaller by five hundred pounds than a Holstein, and they eat a lot less.

We milk twenty cows every morning and evening. Jersey milk is richer and is very good for making cheese at the creamery. I have named them all and my favorite is Rena, daughter of Maria, our biggest producer. All total we have twenty-nine cows including one bull and four new mothers and three female calves. We only keep the females."

"What are some of the other names you have given to the cows?"

"There is Jane, Shirley, Betty, Lily, Bertha, and Sheila."

"Why do you name them?"

"They seem to know their names when we call them in the pasture or when we milk them. They like us to talk to them."

"Talk to them?"

"I know it sounds funny, but you should come to the farm and watch us milk them. Bring Henryk. The doctor and his wife should come, too."

They walked past Summit Bank and crossed Main Street.

"How big is the farm?"

"We have one hundred thirty acres, mostly in hay and corn, to feed the cattle."

"Is there just the three of you to work the farm?"

"I did have an older brother. He was part of Wisconsin's Iron Brigade and was killed at Gettysburg. He's buried there."

"I'm sorry."

On that dry note, they were at the ice cream parlor.

Henryk stood at the door, looking up at the sign that read Palace of Sweets over the door. "Can we go in, Mother?" Then he made it his business to choose a table for the three of them.

Again, it turned quiet as the three dug into the two scoops served to each of them in frosted glass bowls. Henryk wanted more ice cream, but Ania just shook her head.

They were finishing their treat when Tom asked, "How did you come to work for Doctor Jameson?"

"He asked me to help him organize records and statements in his office, and then he began teaching me how to help him with his patients. I enjoy the work very much, especially helping people."

The walk home went fast enough, and Tom stopped at the first step leading up to the front porch. "Ask the doctor and his wife, Ania, if they would like to come out to the farm for an afternoon. I'll ask my parents and let you know."

"Thank you for the ice cream, Tom."

As Tom marched to his horse, Ania and Henryk climbed the steps to the house. Both waved as Tom wheeled his horse south to ride home.

Jane met Ania and Henryk in the hallway. "Did you have a good time?"

Henryk headed out the back door.

"Tom has invited all of us to his parents' farm for an afternoon."

"That could be fun."

"Could be."

⟡

Tuesday, after picking up the mail from the post office, Henryk laid it on his mother's desk for sorting. Under another medical journal from Willy's doctor friend in Milwaukee was a letter for Ania from Elizabeth Williamson in Sussex. It was a short missive, and tucked between a few news items were two phrases summarizing a sad fact and a mother's feelings: *Our fourteen-year-old daughter, Alice, has died. Diphtheria took her home too soon. Somehow, Elizabeth always finds a way to go on with life no matter what falls between her pages as her life is written down*, Ania thought. Then Elizabeth added: *Hold Henryk tight*. Ania had promised herself she would do that, but could she do it well enough, and where would that leave her?

⟡

Leaves were turning colors when the four of them readied to visit Tom's dairy farm. Willy hitched the buggy in the barn for the drive and pulled it to the front of his house, tying their horse to the post. Henryk came down the porch steps, followed by Ania and then Jane, carrying a freshly baked apple pie covered with a gingham cloth. Even though

Willy did not like to leave his post, he relished the idea of a thirty-five-minute drive in the country with his wife on a beautiful early fall day. As he turned the horse off Milwaukee Street onto South Main Street, Jane saw the sun shining on the beautiful gazebo in the middle of City Beach Park near the water of Lac La Belle. The white gazebo was the place they liked to sit in the early evening and watch the sun go down over the lake. Driving on, they passed over a small hill and off to the right of the road, when they saw Tom walking his herd toward the barn for milking.

"Can I help him, Mother?"

"Of course. Be careful. The cows are bigger than you."

Henryk jumped down from the buggy and was soon alongside Tom, repeating his words, "Hey, bossie. Come, bossie." The cows marched ahead to their tune, eager to relieve their udders.

Willy pulled his buggy into the driveway, stopping between the house and barn. A small collie ran out to meet them from the back porch, making sure he was being heard. Tom's parents followed. Willy stepped down from his buggy, reins in hand, and grabbed the horse's halter so Ania and Jane could step down to greet Tom's parents. Then, he walked the horse and buggy to the east side of the barn, and tied the horse to a post in the shade.

"Welcome, Mrs. Jameson, and this must be Ania."

"Please call me Jane. Here's an apple pie for later."

As the cows guided themselves into the barnyard, Tom quickly closed the gate to the yard and hurried to his parents' side, with Henryk in pursuit.

Met by Doctor Jameson, there were introductions with Tom making a special effort to introduce Ania and Henryk to his parents. "Mother and Father, may I present to you Ania Sobieski and her son, Henryk? This is my father, Rudolph Kaderbach, and my mother, Frieda. You know Doctor Jameson and this is his wife, Jane."

"I didn't know you had a son, Ania," said Frieda.

"Father, the cows are waiting."

Everyone walked toward the barn and down the steps to the lower cooler level of the barn, while Tom climbed over the barnyard fence and waited for his father to open the door to the barn so the cattle could find their places inside. Once they chained the milkers, Frieda got out the buckets and three milking stools while her husband set out the metal milk cans. The cows, busy with their individual small piles of hay, waited patiently for their turn. All three Kaderbachs took their turns milking and then dumping the milk from the buckets into the metal milk cans. The four visitors stood off to the side out of everyone's way, and watched in awe. Tom asked Henryk to stand close to his side and then squirted some milk toward his face. Then he did the same, squirting milk at several cats sitting nearby, hitting one cat with a short stream square in the mouth. A cacophony of sounds filled the barn, from the cats to people's voices calling cows' names and the animals bellowing in return.

Finishing the last cow to be milked, Frieda poured the milk into the milk can and walked up to Mrs. Jameson. "While Tom carries the milk cans to the milk house, we should go into the house and sample that pie."

Frieda led the way onto the back porch that ran the width of the house. She took off her shoes, and while putting on another pair, she laughed. "Shoes in the barn get messy."

"Should we take off our shoes?"

"Oh no, Ania. You didn't get close enough to the cows to get them dirty, girl. Now let's have that pie."

Rudolph and the visitors sat down while Frieda filled water glasses for all of them. Tom sauntered into the kitchen and sat next to Henryk. After cutting the pie, Frieda laid the largest piece before Tom.

A few minutes later, after the pie was devoured, Frieda's question sliced through the polite conversation at the table. She looked right at Ania. "What happened to Henryk's father?"

The question moved everyone at the table to silence.

Ania responded without a second of delay. "The man and his family did not think I was good enough for him."

Jane smiled within, recognizing the impact of Ania's words. "I want to thank you, Frieda, for allowing us to visit your farm. We need to get home before dark. Willy, could you get our buggy?"

The women in the room all knew what had just happened while the four men were more interested in their slice of apple pie, not realizing at all that Ania had just served up a big slice of humble pie. Ania took Henryk's hand and followed Willy out the door. Tom followed Ania while Jane, pie plate in hand, turned away from Frieda's sight, thinking even if Ania didn't realize it, she couldn't have chosen better words. The girl had grown up.

Tom stood next to the buggy while Jane boarded. "I hope you and Henryk enjoyed yourself."

Ania smiled. "Yes, yes, I did."

"May I call on you again?" Tom was not a bit wiser about what had just happened.

"If you wish."

The sun was hanging low, and Willy knew it was time to leave.

Henryk bubbled over with excitement from his afternoon at the farm. Frieda's question and Ania's retort had flown over his head, but someday, soon, he would ask the same question and Ania would need to have a different answer. The boy was not yet ready for the truth, so when and if Henryk asked, a half-truth would have to do.

In their bedroom, Jane and Willy compared their reactions to Frieda's statements and Ania's response to her question.

"I think Frieda knows that even though she can run her farm any way she wants, she would not be able to run Ania. That farm is not the place for Ania."

"I wonder how she will handle Tom?" asked Willy.

"Ania will handle him. I wonder how Tom will handle it. No matter what happens, Frieda will keep on running her farm. What a day."

The first day of school came with a rush of early morning activity. Henryk looked smart with the new suspenders over his white cotton shirt. He objected only briefly when Ania slicked his hair off to one side.

His clean shirt made it through breakfast untouched, and the adults pronounced him ready to make his entrance into the new school. The school bell was already ringing when Ania took his hand on the porch and they bounded down the steps toward his future.

The four classrooms were all the same except for the sizes of the wood and metal desks. Henryk's third- and fourth-grade classroom was on the lower level to the right of the entrance and past the school office.

Miss Crowley stood to the right of her large desk and greeted Ania and Henryk as they separated just inside the doorway with the same words said to each parent, "Your child will do well here," and to each child, "Find a seat and sit down."

Leaving the room, Ania had to look back and give a short wave to her son.

Miss Crowley's dark eyes matched her black hair pulled in a tight bun.

Henryk watched her from his seat and noticed that she was shorter than most of the adults at the door.

After the last child came into the classroom, she waited at the door for a few moments and then closed the door tight.

"Stand at your desks, children, and listen. Third graders will sit up front. Fourth graders will sit to the rear. Girls will sit on this side and boys closest to the windows. You may now move to your correct desks and sit down."

Her charges with their lunch pails shuffled quickly to their places before her approving eye, and then all was quiet. Henryk's school day had begun and finished at exactly three o'clock, with a bow before Miss Crowley from all the boys, and a curtsy from all the girls.

Henryk ran all the way home, up the porch steps into the parlor, and slumped into his chair across from his mother.

"Well, Henryk, you're back. Tell us what happened on your first day."

"I sit in the back behind the third graders, away from the girls. After lunch, we learned what will happen to us if we disobey a rule. The teacher drew a circle on the blackboard and put a dot in the middle of the circle and told a third-grade boy to put his nose on the dot and keep it there for fifteen minutes. He had to stand there and not move at all. The teacher also made a dunce cap and said we would wear it in the corner if we did not know our lesson. She also taught us a new word: ferule, which is a stick she can use to slap our palms or knuckles if we do something really bad."

Willy winked at Jane. "I don't think that will ever happen to you, Henryk."

Ania side-eyed her son. "Don't be so sure, Willy."

By the end of September, everyone in the classroom knew the rules and the two men who were running for President of the United States. Willy favored Republican James Garfield, so Henryk did, too. Miss Crowley held a mock election in the classroom for the boys, since only men could vote in the upcoming election. The boys in the classroom elected James Garfield by eleven votes to one vote for the Democratic party nominee, Winfield Scott.

Stopping at the doctor's office after spending time at the blacksmith, Tom ran up the porch steps and knocked on the door.

Ania opened the door and stepped out onto the porch. "I didn't expect to see you today, Tom. What's on your mind?"

"It's going to be a nice day tomorrow. Would you like to go with me on a buggy ride around Lac La Belle?"

"I'd like that. What time will you be here?"

"I plan on being here before one in the afternoon. Is that time all right?"

"Let me speak to Doctor Jameson."

Leaving the porch, Ania asked Doctor Jameson and came right back to Tom. "Doctor Jameson said it would be all right for me to leave the office tomorrow afternoon."

"Wonderful. See you tomorrow."

At the dinner table, Ania told everyone of her plans for tomorrow afternoon. As Ania spoke, Jane furrowed her brow briefly, and Ania caught her doing it.

After Henryk joined Willy in the barn for chores, Ania asked, "Jane, is something bothering you about my plans with Tom for tomorrow afternoon?"

"Oh, no. I just wonder what Tom's plans are for you."

"There will be no plans for me in that household. It's not what I want and there would be one too many cooks in Frieda's kitchen. That's one kitchen I plan to stay out of."

"That makes me feel much better, Ania. Be choosy. Will you be all right going alone?"

"I'll be all right, Jane. Thank you for asking."

Even though Tom was early again, this time, Ania was waiting for him in the doctor's office. Jane answered the door with a smile and ushered him into the room.

"Are you ready?"

"I will be in a few minutes. I have to put this paperwork away and then we can go."

Tom held the shiny bridle of his well-combed mare while Ania boarded the gleaming black buggy. A blanket was set to the side, so Ania had to sit more in the middle of the bench seat. Believing she would not need it, she moved it to the middle of the seat and took its place. Turning onto North Main Street off Milwaukee Street, a bright sun was shining over the water of Lac La Belle, and with no wind, its warmth felt good on their shoulders. Most of the maple leaves had already fallen while dry brown oak leaves were hanging on for dear life.

The green branches of the pine and the balsam trees leaped brilliantly off their deep blue canvas.

Driving past the large homes straddling the street, Ania started the conversation. "Are all your crops in?"

"We only have to get into the barn the last hay of the year before it rains again. Then Mother wants us to build another corn crib before the snow flies. My work never seems to end."

"Do you always want to be a farmer?"

"I never thought about it much. With my brother not coming back from the war, I reasoned it was my place to look after my parents and the farm."

Reaching the outskirts of town, Tom turned the buggy onto a road that ran lakeside. Pulling up to a marsh, Ania recalled her buggy ride with

James Ashworth. Here, the cattail reeds had already turned brown, and most of the life in the marsh had gone out of it. Two female red-winged blackbirds, which had not yet fled for the winter, were sitting on adjoining ragged spikes. When one female red-winged flew to another spike, the second female followed, and then a third time, it did the same. *Related or not*, thought Ania, *I could never follow another female from place to place in her marsh.* A third female, red-winged flew in and sat on a cattail spike on the other end of the marsh. She skipped to another spike and sang for a moment. *Funny,* Ania thought, *the other two birds did not break into song at all.*

Tom broke into Ania's reverie. "This area would be a great place to grow marsh hay after all the cattails are removed."

"But then the red-winged blackbirds would have no place here to sing."

"They're just birds."

"I could use more help on the farm, Ania. I want you to know of my intentions."

"Does your father or mother know of your intentions?"

"My father does not care, and my mother does not know."

"Your mother is in charge of your household, Tom."

"You're right, Ania. The loss of my older brother at Gettysburg destroyed my father. When the news came to us that my brother had been killed, my mother vanquished my father's role in the family. You see, he gave his blessings to my brother leaving the farm and traveling to Camp Randall in Madison against my mother's wishes, where he joined the 6th Wisconsin Regiment, part of the Black Hats Iron Brigade of the West. She blames him for his death."

"Tom. Your farm is not the right place for me. Your mother lost one son many years ago, and she has no intention of losing another now. Take me home, now, Tom."

The ride home was quick and silent. As soon as Ania stepped down from the buggy, Tom stirred his mare to pull away.

Entering the kitchen, Willy looked surprised that she was home so quickly.

Jane inquired, "How did it go?"
"I sent him home empty-handed."
Jane's approving smile said it all for Willy.

Chapter Twenty

By the early 1880s, Milwaukee had grown to be a vibrant city of over one hundred twenty-five thousand people. Germans, Poles, Irish, Scandinavians, Blacks, Italians, Brits, and Serbs supplied the workers for the industrial factories sprawling across the Menomonee Valley and beyond. Even though the wheat trade market had been lost from the Milwaukee docks, iron manufacturing, multiple breweries, meat packing, tanning, and flour milling, plus tradesmen to build anything everywhere surpassed the loss.   The Milwaukee Iron Company in Bay View alone employed over one thousand workers turning out rails as the train network pushed westward. Ten, twelve-hour days, six days a week were the norm at wages of $1.25 per day for the most unskilled workers. Milwaukee backed the growth of a nation pushing toward the Pacific. As always, those who saw the financial rewards reaped much, while the worker and his family found only the leavings among the chaff. Men and women from both sides in churches and labor halls tried to blur the lines, but with few gains to change.

Months passed since being slapped from possibility to truth before Charlotte could work again with the abandoned babies at her parish because they were the very embodiment of what was wrong with her marriage. Father Timothy's private counsel or homilies to his congregation about marriage and family life only increased her hidden pain. She still could not hold the babies when they cried for her to pick them up.

Gabriele walked into the room. "You can't just let them cry."

"Right now, I can. How long have you been doing this, Gabriele?"

"Ever since the priest allowed the little ones to be dropped off here."

"Will they ever stop coming?"

"No. Women have babies. Husbands die in factories or leave their wives or worse, and the women can't take care of them. My husband works in a meat packing plant in the valley as a foreman. His hours are not as long as the meat cutters and packers. He tells me their working conditions are worse than his, with no heat in the winter and no fresh air in the summer. His boss pushes him constantly to make his men work harder and faster. It seems like every day he has another story of a man getting injured by an animal in the yard or cut bad at the table. Workers in other factories have it just as bad or worse. No wonder men leave their families or drink themselves to death. It's a city stupor, and it's going to boil over."

"I didn't know."

"Nobody knows except the workers and their families. The papers don't write about it and the business owners want to keep everything quiet. There are rumblings here and there, and some brave people are speaking out secretly among the workers. If anyone mentions out loud the word union, he's shown the door and replaced by another worker. My husband has mentioned a group called the Knights of Labor, and I think they have a chapter that meets here at church. He doesn't talk about it with me. I've said enough. You can go home now, Charlotte. I will handle them until the sister arrives later tonight."

As Charlotte walked down the front steps of the church, she mumbled, "I have a house, but it's not a home. I have servants but no children. I have a man but no husband. What a joke—when she says I can go home."

Crossing the park to a cab stand on Oneida Street, Charlotte saw a woman on the ground huddled next to a large tree. She barely looked up.

Because her fine clothes belied her situation, Charlotte stopped. "Can I help you?" Hearing only sobs from her, Charlotte asked again, but louder. "Can I help you?"

"No one can help me."

"I can help you." Leaning over, Charlotte pulled on her upper arm. "Come with me. Where's your coat?"

"I don't have one."

"Are you hungry?"

The stranger's eyes answered Charlotte's question. Reaching the cab stand, she told the driver, "Take me to Barney's on Water Street."

Composing herself, the slender, young woman smoothed her hair in the cab. "Where are we going?"

"You're going to a restaurant to have dinner with me."

Laying her head onto the side of the cab, the woman closed her eyes and fell silent. The short ride did not allow the woman enough time to rest, but it gave her enough time to think. Stepping down from the carriage, Charlotte ushered the woman toward the restaurant door.

"I don't know your name."

"My name is Darla. You should not be seen with me."

"Why is that?"

"I'm not your kind of woman."

"Come inside the restaurant and you can tell me what kind of woman I am," said Charlotte.

Charlotte ordered a hearty Irish stew for them, followed by a few soft words to put the woman at ease. It would not be easy, since Darla feared recrimination from anyone just as much as the harsh treatment she just received from her employer. Ever since she turned into a beautiful woman, her mother condemned that same beauty. Darla was no temptress, but she was judged to be so in her own home by her mother.

There was no escape other than to leave, to find her place, and she found worse. Learning early never to trust anyone, especially another woman, Darla was hesitant to accept anything more from Charlotte than a hot meal.

"Don't judge me."

"Together, we can do some judging later. Tell me, why were you on the ground huddled next to a tree sobbing?"

"I left Sheboygan six years ago and came here for work. After six years of putting smiles on the faces of men, they threw me out because the pig they used for a doctor said I have some disease that I can give to their money men. They told me to get out. They used me up, and now I have no place to go and nobody cares. I'm finished."

"If you're finished, Darla, then I guess I'm finished with my barren life, too. We can help each other. First, you'll need a place to spend the night. You can spend the night at the Cathedral."

"But I'm not Catholic."

"It doesn't matter. You need a place to sleep. After we finish eating, we'll take a cab back to the church."

Recognizing Charlotte at the door, Mother Superior needed only a brief explanation. She led them both to a room near the sisters' quarters, which was used for visitors.

Charlotte assured Darla she would be comfortable for the night. "I'll be back at noon tomorrow so that I can take you to my doctor." Turning quickly away, Charlotte added, "Be sure that you're still here," leaving Darla in the sister's care with no chance to respond.

Walking down a hall of the Cathedral the next morning, Charlotte wondered if her new ward would still be there. Darla did not disappoint her. Striding into her room, Charlotte saw Darla's buried face in her hands. Putting her hand on her head like a blessing, the girl looked up into Charlotte's eyes, hoping her new benefactor could make her future better.

"Here, I brought you a coat. Put this on," said Charlotte.

As soon as Darla fell into the cab's seat, she looked at Charlotte. "Why are we going to your doctor?"

"You need to see a doctor who knows what he's doing. Not some drunk who calls himself a doctor. I'm going to help you, and you're going to let me help you so that I can help myself."

"Could you see the doctor with me?"

"We'll see him together after we have had lunch."

Charlotte trusted this elderly doctor she first met as a child. He had helped her in the most meaningful ways during her lost pregnancies, and even though he was getting older, he always had some new information to pass along. Her female friends had sought younger doctors for fresh answers, but Charlotte saw no reason to leave Doctor Buetner behind. Talking to Charlotte, the doctor did not question her request to examine Darla or her motivation for making that request. He took his work seriously and had learned long ago that most questions about why this or that happened to a person were irrelevant to his patient's care.

With the nurse assisting and Charlotte sitting close by, Doctor Buetner took his time, leaving nothing to chance. Even if some hack doctor had drawn a conclusion, he needed to find out if that conclusion was medically correct.

When finished, the doctor sat before Darla and Charlotte with a glum look on his face. "I didn't see anything wrong with you until I looked into your mouth and under your tongue. Here's a mirror and you can see it for yourself as I lift your tongue up and to one side. Do you see these white areas in your mouth and on your tongue? Those sores could be proof that you have the French disease. It is called syphilis. Do you know what that is, Darla?"

"I've heard other women talk about it, but that's about all I know about it."

"It's a disease inside your body and people can die from it. I'm going to send you to a hospital on the outskirts of the city. The address is 2222 Cedar Street. You will receive care there and I pray for a cure for this disease. I will write a letter of introduction for you and they will take you in, and with your permission, I will write a letter to a doctor who volunteers there so that he can see you when he visits patients at this hospital."

As they walked out of the building, everything was different for Darla, but nothing had really changed. She had a new coat and a new friend. She was eating at restaurants and would spend a second night at the Cathedral, and then there would be another cab ride tomorrow. Everything was moving around her, within her, and for her, while she stood still.

The doctor and deaconesses at the hospital would play along with Darla with help from Charlotte, even though this French disease held all the cards and it would keep raising the ante. It was unknown to Darla, just as Charles Guiteau was unknown to President Garfield. Each slayer would be successful. Hers was the kiss of death, and his, the assassin's bullet. The president's doctors, although well-meaning, were clueless, and so were Darla's.

President Garfield lingered for eighty days until September 19, 1881, while Darla would have to battle her invisible enemy longer. After Darla was received at the hospital, Doctor Thatcher saw her a week later. He was tall and slender, with still a twinkle in his eye. He said little, but he listened with interest and smiled often. Walking into the ladies' ward, two deaconesses followed close behind. They each took turns writing orders after the doctor stopped and checked on each woman's condition.

He stopped at Darla's bedside. "So we have a new patient. Doctor Buetner wrote to me about you. How are you feeling?"

"I feel well."

"Let me see your hands," said the doctor. "And now the bottoms of your feet, please." Seeing a rash on both, he asked, "Do your feet or hands itch?"

"No. They don't itch at all."

"This French disease is a tricky one. I'm going to have the nurse rub this mercury cream on your feet, legs, and hands daily until the rash goes away." Making sure his helpers wrote down his instructions, Doctor Thatcher turned back to Darla. "I'll see you again soon and we'll see if this cream helps your rash."

Morning and afternoon, the nurse, as instructed, put on her gloves and rubbed mercury cream all over her feet, hands, and legs. After almost two weeks of this regimen, Darla's spirits lifted as the rash seemed to be disappearing.

On Monday, the doctor was pleased with Darla's progress. "When Charlotte Schmidt stops to see you, ask her if all of us could meet here a week from this Friday, on June twenty-third, in the early afternoon."

"I will ask her."

One week later, when the three were together, Doctor Thatcher said, "There's no reason why you should not be able to go home. You say you feel well, and this hospital bed could be used for someone else."

"I don't have a home."

"Yes, you do. She'll come home with me, Doctor. We'll leave today."

"Then I'm going to give to you some bottles of this calomel cream the nurses have used. Apply it if the rash comes back anywhere on your body, Darla. If you apply it, Charlotte, use gloves. Should you need more cream, you can get it from Doctor Buetner. I hope I never have to see you again, Darla."

"Thank you, Doctor Thatcher. You've been very kind."

As he left, Charlotte turned to Darla. "Let's go home."

—◦◦◉)

Jakob avoided home as much as possible. His parents excused his actions since they had no grandchild, and Charlotte's parents did not care if they ever saw him again. His office at the brewery, a room at the White Dove, or another place of lesser quality were his desired places for respite. What little work he did was window dressing, especially for his father or those around the office.

Trying to look busy was hard work for Jakob, so the bottle at his fingertips became an easy lift. The son had given up fighting this inclination, but did not want to expose this weakness to his father. Since there was no one close he cared to talk to or reveal himself to, Jakob resorted to talking to himself, as he had all the answers to anyone's questions. "Should I have another drink?" was not really a question at all, but only a way to mark the time until everything went black again.

"Who is pulling my sleeve?"

"What are you doing sleeping at your desk?" asked his father. "Nobody else can sleep at their desk. Do you think that because you're the owner's son that you can sleep at your desk? I can't even sleep at my desk. I can't drink at my desk. I work at my desk. I *work* at my desk. All of this that you see out those windows is there because I work at my desk. I can't sleep at my desk. I don't sleep enough in my own bed. This is supposed to be yours someday and you're supposed to pass this along to your son, but you cannot even produce a grandson. It is supposed to be so grand, and it's not, but at the very least you damn well will produce work for me. When I took you hunting, I told you there are all kinds of game to be killed in the forest. You kill because in life you can't stop hunting."

Standing and brushing past his father for the door, Heinriche grabbed his arm and spun him around. "Get sober."

Pulling away from his father for the door, Jakob slurred, "I'll do as I damn well please," and mumbled under his breath, "if you only knew."

"What was that?"
Jakob was already gone.

—❧—

Danny and Gretchen were working long hours, and the White Dove was working out well. Two more Milwaukee aldermen were regulars, and a few police officials were happy to receive the soft favors offered at the White Dove. Danny worked hard to curry those favors, so the law and the politicians were no threat to the business. It was primarily the socialistic press that wrote condemning articles about prostitution or white slavery to increase revenue, but no one of means did anything about their clarion calls. Once in a while, a group of hard-nosed bitter women of one religious group or another would raise cane in some torch-lit parade, hoping to secure freedom for misguided teenage girls. The watching working girls would make fun of them as they paraded down the street, encouraging the marchers to join their ranks. Blind eyes made their business secure so much so that discussions were being held between Jakob and Danny to open a second Dove south of their current location. Danny also held some other ideas for expansion, but Jakob suddenly turned toned-deaf to any idea preoccupied with greater concern.

Chapter Twenty-One

Two years had passed since the death of President Garfield. Oconomowoc, by unanimous city council vote, renamed the new common school Henryk attended for the assassinated president, at the same time keeping quiet that his assassin had spent time within their city as a guest at Draper Hall. A girl and a boy were chosen to pull the rope, loosening the banner covering the chiseled stonework renaming the school. Tall, left-handed Henryk was the boy of choice since the seventh and eighth grade boys were still in the fields at the opening of a new school year. The Jameson household was excited. Even though two teachers had failed to change Henryk from writing with his curled left hand, Henryk was the teachers' unanimous choice to pull loose the banner with an eighth-grade girl.

Ania was proud of her son, who had come a long way in his twelve years. She had come even further as an accomplished nurse under the private tutelage of Doctor Jameson. Willy had constantly reminded her that a good attitude passed on to her patients would help with the patient's healing process. There was no doubt that she used this wisdom in her medical practice.

Slicking his hair to one side for the early evening event, Henryk stood just two inches shorter than his mother. It was also obvious to the adults in the house that their sixth grader had grasped the importance of the event.

Turning the corner onto Fowler Street, the four of them had to walk through throngs of people who had come for the renaming of the common school. The town band was present and local dignitaries were making the rounds in the crowds, seeking future votes. Somberness for the assassinated president met head on with the joy of naming a grade school in his honor.

Willy leaned over to Jane. "Funny how respects are paid after someone is dead."

Jane shushed him with a wave of her hand.

Ania took Henryk up front so he could stand near his teacher. With a rope hanging down on each side of the bunting covering the chiseled stone, it was obvious what Henryk would have to do when the time came to do it. Near the other rope, a freckle-faced girl stood with her eighth-grade teacher.

After a short speech by the mayor, extolling the Civil War hero, Ohio Republican congressman and the twentieth president, the principal of the school introduced the sixth- and eighth-grade teachers and the two students who would pull down the bunting. Following the directions of the mayor, passed to the students through the teachers, the bunting came down with aplomb and loud applause. Then, as before, students with parents met their new teachers in each classroom while the rest of the crowd moved on.

When everyone was back home in the parlor, Willy reached into his pocket for his jackknife, and after opening it, handed it to Henryk. "Henryk, to commemorate this date, I would like you to carve your three initials H.P.S. in the side of my desk, just below my son's initials."

Ania looked surprised. "Are you sure?"

"Just as sure as Henryk is twelve years old.

Jane smiled with a head nod. "Go ahead, Henryk."

Carefully, Henryk carved his initials just below P.W.J. for Peter William Jameson. "We have the same name, Peter."

Jane cried and Willy pronounced, "This boy is going places."

November was a dreary month except for the addition to the Jameson house on a Thursday afternoon. Willy was carrying a wooden box under his arm as he came through the back door into the kitchen, and on his heels was a tall, slender man in bib overalls carrying a toolbox and a spool of wire.

"It's here," Willy said to Jane. "Where do you think we should install the wall phone?"

"I think it should be installed on the wall close to Ania's desk so she can answer the phone while you're with a patient and we'll be able to hear it upstairs when it rings."

"You're right."

Marching into the parlor, Willy stopped at Ania's desk. "Put it here behind her desk on the wall to the right of her chair."

Ania stood at her desk. "What are you two talking about?"

"This man is going to install a telephone."

"A telephone?"

"That's right, a telephone. Hotels here are installing them. Even some of the homes are installing them because if they need a doctor, they want to get word to us immediately. So, we have to get a telephone installed."

Jane looked on. "You'll learn how to use it, Ania. It made sense to me when Willy brought it up. We'll all need to learn how to use it. Things change all the time. I've seen enough of them in my fifty-six years, but they keep coming. I just read the other day in a Milwaukee newspaper that people back east are replacing kerosene lamps with gas lights in their homes. What will they do next?"

By dinnertime, the man was gone, and a new wall phone, with two large shiny bells on the front, a crank on the right side, and a large hook on the other side, was staring back at them.

"Soon our wire will be hooked up to a station downtown, and then we'll be able to take a call." He pointed at the mouthpiece. "We'll talk into here, and this thing on the hook here we put to our ear to hear someone talking to us from their telephone. I don't know how it works, but it works. When we know it's connected downtown, I'll call you from the station and each of you will be able to talk to me. Then you will call me downtown."

On Saturday, two days later, Willy walked to the central station and made the call. Jane knew it was coming, and made sure Ania and Henryk were in the parlor. The bells rang louder than Jane expected, startling them all.

Jane slowly picked up the earpiece and held it close, but not too close, to her ear. She heard Willy's voice.

"Talk into the mouthpiece, Jane. Say something."

"Willy?" That was all she could say.

"You have to put your mouth close to the mouthpiece so I can hear you."

"Willy."

"That's better. Now give the earpiece to Ania. Can you hear me, Ania?"

Ania heard Willy's voice and looked straight at the earpiece as if it was Willy's face.

"Talk to me, Ania. Put your mouth close to the mouthpiece when you speak so that I can hear you."

Ania yelled into the mouthpiece.

"I can hear you now. Now give the earpiece to Henryk. Get him the stool to stand on."

At first, Henryk did not want to take the earpiece from Ania.

"It won't bite, I don't think."

"Are you still there?" asked Willy.

Henryk dropped the earpiece and took two steps back. "It talks."

"Of course, it talks. It's a telephone."

Just to be sure, Henryk went into the hallway to make sure Willy was not there.

Ania took up the earpiece and told Willy what Henryk had done, and when Henryk took back the earpiece from Ania, he did the same.

Walking out of the parlor, Henryk was shaking his head. "It's a miracle."

After dinner, while the four of them sat in the parlor and looked at the telephone, they all laughed and agreed they could handle this new thing, and then they laughed some more.

The next morning, after breakfast, Jane and Ania were sitting in the kitchen, making plans for their own Thanksgiving Day feast.

"We should take the buggy and do some shopping to get ready. We need sugar and flour and you need a new dress, Ania."

"A new dress. I have two brown dresses. They're still worth wearing."

"Then you will have three dresses and a day dress for church, too, and maybe a hat. I'll do the buying. It's our Christmas present to you. You are a fine lady, Ania, and there is nothing wrong with looking the part."

Ania lowered her head, and Jane took Ania's chin in her fingers and saw the tears trickling down Ania's cheeks.

"You've been so good to us."

"We have, but you both have been very good for Willy and me. We're going tomorrow afternoon. Willy knows, so you'll not have to ask him if you can leave. First, we will have lunch downtown and then we're going shopping, Ania. We're going shopping!"

Fern frost covered the windows the next morning, but by eleven, the sun had warmed the day enough that only a light blanket was needed for the buggy. After lunch at the hotel restaurant, Ania drove the gray onto Milwaukee Street to the women's dress shop on South Main Street.

While tying the horse to the black metal hitching post in front of the shop, Ania protested again. "My two dresses are just fine."

Jane took her hand. "It won't hurt you to look. Isn't that a pretty dress in the window?"

The shop was divided into three areas. Mrs. Jameson was greeted by name and her young companion with a smile at the door in a small front room with a windowed floor case on one side of the room. It doubled for the place where purchases were made. On the other side of this room, shoes and ribboned hats filled shelves. Between this room and the two small changing rooms was a room full of bolts of material, colorful dresses, and, of course, stays and petticoats.

Jane walked in and looked around. "I always like this room. It's like walking into a different world on a gray November day."

Ania held the sleeve of a forest green dress in her hand. "There are so many colors."

"I think a blue day dress and a straw bonnet with matching blue ribbon would be perfect for you to match your blue eyes."

The clerk smiled. "Oh, I so agree. Let me see what I have over here. Yes, I thought so. Here is a light blue dress that will fall gently down around your slender waist with white lace at the neck and at the ends of the sleeves."

"Try it on." Jane pointed to a stay on a mannequin. "We'll need this, too."

The clerk motioned Ania toward the changing room. "I'll help you change."

Jane started looking for another dress that Ania could wear during the week. *Now where was that simple wine-colored shirtwaist and skirt… this could serve well for other things besides work.* Slipping both items off their hooks, Jane turned around and saw Ania standing in the doorway.

"Perfect! That dress was waiting for you." Walking over to the floor-length mirror, Jane studied the dress. "We can hem it a bit and take it in a little bit here at home. What do you think, Ania?"

Ania looked at herself in the mirror. "It is pretty."

"Do you have a ribboned bonnet to match?" Jane asked the clerk.

"I'll get it."

After putting the bonnet on, Jane took a quick look at Ania and said with emphasis, "Yes, we will take both and this, too." She held up the skirt and shirtwaist. "Mrs. Frye, could you package up these items, and after we're done at the general store, we'll stop back and pick them up later this afternoon."

"Of course, Jane."

Ania looked at Mrs. Frye and then back at Jane.

Jane smiled wickedly. "Let's hurry on. We have other things to do. See you later, Judy."

After picking up the five packages from the dress shop, the ride home went quickly. Jane gathered some things up into her arms and stepped down from the buggy.

Ania began leading the gray by the bridle into the barn.

"I will send Henryk out to help bring in our packages, Ania."

Jane had laid everything out on the kitchen table and propped her hands on her hips. "We sure were busy. Take your dresses upstairs and hang them up in the wardrobe. We can hem them tomorrow. Now we have to get supper started."

Since there was only one service on Thanksgiving Day, it usually was very crowded, especially if the farmers had a good year. If the farmers did well, Oconomowoc did even better than just depend on visitors from St. Louis, Chicago, and Milwaukee during the warmer months. Ania was taking longer than usual upstairs, and Willy was becoming impatient, waiting in the parlor with Jane and Henryk.

Jane poked him in the ribs with her elbow. "It'll be worth waiting."

Almost as soon as she finished her sentence, Ania was standing in the archway of the parlor, in her blue day dress and bonnet covering her blond curls.

Henryk stood. "Mother."

Willy stood beaming, and Jane had the biggest smile possible on her face. "I told you, Willy."

Willy didn't move. He just looked. "May I have both of my ladies on each arm?"

Just outside the front door, each lady took an arm, and he proudly walked them down the steps of his house, and did the same up the steps into the church. Heads of men and women turned as Ania passed by, and the four of them took their seats in their regular pew.

Leaning over to Willy's ear, Jane whispered, "Our girl is smart and beautiful. I told you."

Sure enough, Ania received more attention than usual after the service, and Willy was not interested one bit in leaving for home. He was enjoying the scene more than Ania.

Walking home on this day of thanks, Ania's level of self-assurance and confidence had reached their apex. There was no longer any doubt within her. This gentle, demure woman's heart had not turned bitter, hardened by her trial, but rather every experience had strengthened her will, so she felt she could handle herself anywhere with anyone. No gentle rain would stop Ania from singing a song of her own.

Chapter Twenty-Two

Henryk wanted to play with his Christmas gift from Jane outside, but the snow was too deep to play football with his friends. He did not care much for the pajamas his mother had given him, but she kept saying they were so practical. Willy wanted to give Henryk a rifle of his own for Christmas, but Jane would not allow it.

In its place, Willy gave him a bag of clay marbles and a thick European history book so he could either play Ringer or read inside on these cold days.

The last week in December and the first two weeks in January always seemed to be the coldest in Oconomowoc. Wednesday, January 10, fit the bill. Henryk had finished his schoolwork after dinner and everyone was cozy around the fireplace when the telephone rang.

"Could you get it, Henryk?"

"Hello. Is Doctor Jameson there?"

"I'll get him."

"Doctor Jameson?"

"Who is this?"

"Doctor Jameson, this is Doctor Thatcher."

"Sam. Blessed New Year to you."

"Willy. I need your help. Can you come to Milwaukee right away?"

"Why? Are you in trouble?"

"No, it has nothing to do with me. Do you remember the wood frame Newhall House Hotel? It burned down this morning."

"Burned down?"

"Burned to the ground. Many have been killed and there are a lot of burn victims. I need your help."

"I can't leave. The other doctor in town is gone. My nurse could help. She knows how to handle people who have been burned. Do the cuttings and dressings, everything."

"Whatever you say, Willy."

"I'll ask her. Hold one moment." Willy returned to the phone. "She'll come. She'll be on the nine a.m. train out of Oconomowoc tomorrow."

"I'll pick her up at the train depot downtown. What is her name?"

"Ania Sobieski."

"Thanks, Willy. I'll be waiting for her at the train station. Tell her about me. Goodbye."

Willy slowly placed the earpiece on its hook and turned, saying under his breath, "I hate fires."

Sitting in his chair, he gave pause to the news, wondering for a moment if he had made a mistake in recommending Ania. No doubt that she could do the work, but she would be alone in Milwaukee. *I'll have to write a letter to Doctor Thatcher that Ania can take with her.*

Satisfied with his plan, he turned to Ania. "Let me tell you about Doctor Samuel Thatcher. He's tall, slender with brownish, blond hair and he walks with a slight limp from a farming accident, I think. He was in a few classes I taught at medical school in Milwaukee. We became friends because he was so down to earth. When I mentioned that to him, he said, 'Of course, I am down to earth. I was raised in a small town.' He's a good doctor who cares about his patients. His patients are the only thing that interests him. He's the one, Ania, that sends us the medical journals. I told him you would be on the nine a.m. train. He will meet you at the Milwaukee Reed Street Depot. Do you remember where that is, Ania?"

"Yes."

"Look for a tall man with a limp."

"Mother, you're leaving?"

Jane spoke up. "It'll only be for a short time, Henryk. It'll be a short time, right, Willy?"

"I don't know. Ania can call us after she has been there for a few days and let us know."

"I have to get my things ready to leave," said Ania.

"Let's help your mother, Henryk," added Jane.

"I'm going to put together a valise for you, Ania, with medical supplies and things you'll need to use caring for the burn victims. I'm also going to write a letter for you to give to Doctor Thatcher."

Willy went to his desk, and the women headed upstairs with Henryk shuffling behind. It would be a short night for everyone, especially Henryk.

After breakfast, Willy tied the horse and buggy out front and, going in the front door, returned with two same-size valises and placed them on the buggy. The heaviest blanket he had was waiting on the seat to do its job. The ride would be cold, but at least short to the train station. Going back through the front door, Willy saw Ania on her knees, speaking to her son.

"See, you are taller than me, Henryk. Take care of Jane and Willy. Mind your teacher. I'll come back home as soon as I can. You know I will. All that I love is in this house and you more than anyone else."

Henryk stepped back from his mother. "I'll take care of things while you're gone."

Then he stepped forward and hugged his mother. Jane saw it from the kitchen doorway and Willy saw it from the front doorway. They similarly thought, *She is special.* After Ania stood, Henryk took his mother's hand and headed for the front door.

The short ride to Garfield school was quiet and crowded on the only seat. Jumping down from the buggy, Henryk took a few steps toward the school and then turned to wave. Ania knew it was coming.

At the train station, Willy got down first, and while Ania held the reins, he took the two valises out of the buggy and placed them on the plank wood platform. He then helped Jane and Ania down from the buggy.

"You both should get out of this cold. Go home. I can wait for the train inside." Ania hugged Jane. "Thank you for everything."

"Goodness, child, you're coming home to us. We'll take care of Henryk."

Then Ania hugged Willy just as long. "I love you both, you know."

"We know. Say hello to Doctor Thatcher for us. Remember, you know what you're doing, and don't let anyone tell you differently. Godspeed, girl. I can hear the train coming. You better get onto the platform."

The heated coach felt good. She placed her valises in the empty seat next to her, and looking out the window, she saw the buggy heading north. *I hope Willy is right and I know what I am doing*, she thought. The train pulled out of the Oconomowoc Depot early and headed east for the Reed Street Depot in Milwaukee.

Many say that a third-degree burn inflicted the greatest physical pain on this Earth as flesh melted and dripped like candle wax before it turned crisp and black. Ania had seen it before, and she would see more of it today. Doctor Thatcher waited impatiently inside the depot, turning to the wall clock every few minutes and willing it to move faster. He wanted to go back to Cedar Street. He did not want to leave the hospital, but his friend and teacher had entrusted a woman nurse into his care, and he was not about to put her in any danger. He waited.

Her train pulled into the depot behind schedule. Walking toward the train, Doctor Thatcher scanned the passengers, stepping down from the carriages, and was sure he had spotted Willy's nurse. Their eyes met from a distance and both knew.

"I'm Doctor Thatcher. Are you Ania Sobieski?"

"I am."

"Let me take your heaviest bag. We can talk in the cab."

Then, turning on his heels, he looked for the best door back into the depot. A cab was waiting for them on the street, and in a moment they were off.

"I'm sorry I hurried you, but we have much work to do for the injured and dying."

"Can you tell me what happened, Doctor Thatcher?"

"Call me Sam. Early yesterday morning, while everyone was sleeping, the six-story wood frame Newhall House Hotel caught fire. Firemen reports say flames shot up the elevator shaft and the roof was on fire by the time they left the fire station. It went up like a flaming straw stack. People were trapped in their rooms. Because ladders used by the firemen didn't reach the top floors, people jumped to the street from their windows. We have people at the hospital with burns, broken bones, and worse. More are coming. Tell me why Willy spoke so highly of you. Don't be shy. I need to know what you can do."

"For five years, I've been helping Doctor Jameson. First in his office, and then taking Jane's place as his nurse. I have dressed and bandaged all kinds of wounds. Four years ago, we had a fire in Oconomowoc that destroyed most of the downtown."

"I remember Willy telling me about that. He didn't mention you by name. You were the woman who did all those things at the fire."

"It was a long night."

"I'm glad you're here. Willy spoke highly of you. We're here. Are you ready to go to work?"

"Before I forget, Willy wrote you a letter, Doctor. It is in the heavy bag that also contains medical supplies and my instruments."

"Deaconesses will take care of your things, and you will stay with them at the hospital. You will dress like one of them and work with me. When you're ready, you'll find me in the room with the burn victims."

The first floor of the small building had been cleared to receive victims from the fire. Men were on one side of the room and women on the other side divided by hung bed sheets. New arrivals would have to make do in the hallways. Beds were made up on the floor. Ania made her way into the room and looked for Doctor Thatcher. He was standing in the back corner talking to a priest who was placing a stole around his own neck. It was not a good sign.

Ania weaved her way toward him as the doctor moved on to another patient. "Good, you're here. This woman needs her arms and hands redressed. Cut away all dead flesh and rinse with clean water. Here's another pair of scissors so that you can boil one pair in water while you use your own boiled pair with a different patient. Deaconesses will do the boiling for you. When you're done with this patient, find me. I'll have another patient for you. Even though you do your best, some of these people are going to die."

Ania began with the young woman at her feet. Her screams pierced the room as Ania cut and pulled her wrappings away from her hands and then her arms. Her right arm and hand were mostly bone and muscle. There was nothing to save there, so Ania concentrated on her other arm, slowly, carefully, cutting away burned skin and tissue. Perhaps she could use this arm someday. Her eyes rolled back and finally, she passed out, maybe to dream that she was only dreaming. Finished with the improbable, Ania said to herself, *I will look for him when I am finished here.*

"I'm done with her, Doctor Thatcher. One arm is good, I hope, and one is just bone and I believe it will have to be amputated. She's so young."

"See that woman next to the wall. Do what you can with her. Boil your scissors."

Women and men who would survive, cried, wailed, and screamed the most. Those who were dying turned quiet as their breathing became shallow and then death claimed them for their forever. Were they on vacation at the Newhall House or on business, or just a night on the town? Word was trickling into the hospital that many burned to death in their rooms as the whole hotel came tumbling down around them. *What is worse,* Ania thought, *to die immediately or slowly when the result is the same? No wonder Willy hates fires. I've seen enough of them myself.*

This new patient had no burns, but her legs were full of wood splinters. Ana gripped her hand. "I will be right back."

She walked up to Doctor Thatcher. "Do you have any drinking alcohol here?"

"Why? This is a Lutheran hospital. I don't know. Why?"

"The patients could use it to deaden their pain."

"You're right. Lutherans drink. I'll find out."

Ania returned to the woman. "You're going to drink some liquor before I start taking out all of these splinters. How did you get these in your legs?"

"I had to kick through some wood panels to get out of my room. Something was blocking the door. I broke through and ran down the back stairs and somehow got out. They brought me here."

"Here's a bottle of something. Keep drinking it until you think you're going to pass out. What's your name?"

"Judith. I've never had a drink before."

"It's time to start. This is going to hurt. Keep drinking."

Ania started with the small splinters. It did not take much of the hard liquor, and she was out. The largest piece was through her calf muscle and would take some time to free. When Ania finished, she took the rest of the bottle and poured its contents wherever she worked on her legs. Ania wondered if she was alone in her hotel room or if she had lost more than some blood.

The cabs and wagons with the injured finally stopped coming. The wagons did double duty, taking away the latest corpse, and making space in the room so a new arrival could move in. The coroner's duty helped alleviate the hospital's overcrowding. For now, he was the end of the line.

A younger man made his way into the room looking for his parents, who were visiting Milwaukee from Fond du Lac for the first time. Slowly he weaved among those laying on the floor, hoping to recognize either his mother or father. Ania watched him leave worse for his search. Doctors, deaconesses, and Ania paid no attention to the clock. Pastors and priests came and went. It didn't seem like they were very far away. When it was too dark to change a dressing or cut more flesh, Ania moved from one patient to another that she had already worked on, comforting them. If all she could do was say a few words or stroke a forehead during the night, she would do it. It was the right thing to do, even if it was the only thing she could do.

Doctor Thatcher watched her move from one patient to another, speaking a kind word or drawing close to their faces just to smile or stroke their hair.

He knew she had to be exhausted. Walking toward her, Doctor Thatcher waited until she stood. "You have to get some sleep. We'll have to do this all over again tomorrow and the next day. Speak to a deaconess in the hallway and she will show you where you can rest. They will wake you. You know I'm right. Get some sleep."

Ania didn't protest. "Wake me at first light. Good night, Sam."

"Go to sleep, Ania."

The next day's morning paper started adding details about the fire and posting the long but not final list of those who perished in its pit. Confirmed dead by coroners count were forty-four individuals, but he expected that total to rise significantly. The paper also said that some victims were just ashes and would be impossible to identify. Ania learned that two more burn victims under their care died overnight.

Finishing her rushed breakfast, a deaconess came up to her. "Doctor Thatcher is asking for you."

"Good morning, Doctor."

"Did you sleep well, Ania? Can you help me with an amputation? You worked on her."

"Of course." Ania wondered how Doctor Thatcher could go about his work so calmly.

"What are you thinking, Ania?"

"How do you keep going?"

"There's no other choice. Just like you last night. You kept visiting each patient, speaking to them, praying for the best, and you stroked their foreheads. They have nobody else but us right now. We have to make them believe we know what we're doing, and there is hope for them in the things we do for them. Willy taught me a long time ago that believing you're going to get well helps a person get well. You and I give them hope. Follow me."

They went into a smaller room, which the deaconesses had converted into another operating room. Wilma was laying on a table unconscious and about to lose her right arm at the elbow, and maybe her life as well. She had lost a lot of blood, but surgery could not wait.

"I hope she stays unconscious. We have chloroform on hand. Some patients make it, some don't. Let's get on with it, Ania."

The long blade and saw were ready. "I'm going to wash my hands. You do the same, Ania. There is a basin over there. Doctors are doing this more and more now, even though Doctor Semmelweis in Philadelphia was ridiculed for encouraging this twenty years ago."

The surgery went quickly. A deaconess carried the amputated right forearm out of the room quickly to be disposed of with the rest of the trash.

Three hours later, as Ania and Doctor Thatcher made their rounds, a deaconess rushed up to Doctor Thatcher. "Your patient is thrashing about and screaming. I can't keep her quiet."

"Let's go, Ania!"

Her thrashing about had opened the stitches at the end of her elbow where a forearm used to be. Blood was pouring from the wound.

"Hold her shoulders down, Ania!"

A deaconess grabbed her legs.

"We're going to have to move her to a bed and tie her down so that she can't move at all."

Doctor Thatcher took Ania's place to lift her from the floor and Ania moved to the center of her body while the deaconess lifted the women's legs.

As Doctor Thatcher said, "Lift together," the woman gasped and her body went limp. Laying her back on the floor, Samuel just shook his head. "She fought herself and lost."

Five days later and at the start of a new workweek, those who were going to survive their burns had already left the hospital, or relatives had found them and arranged for their trip home. Six more patients had died, so the room and hallways were quieter. Ania knew her purpose for staying was drawing to a close, but she waited for Doctor Thatcher to say so. She did not have to wait long.

"Ania, your work is finished here. You can go home on Wednesday. The other doctors and I want to thank you for all of your work. Would you do me the honor of spending tomorrow with me? I would like to show you the city, and you could call home. Later, we could have dinner together at a restaurant. Have you ever been ice skating?"

"I don't know how to ice skate."

"I'll teach you. Can I call for you at one o'clock tomorrow?"

"I would like that, Samuel."

"So will I."

Tuesday morning, the sun was shining in a deep blue sky. Samuel made his rounds at the hospital, and by one o'clock, the cab for the two of them was waiting at the side door. The two met in the hallway, looking for each other, and laughed loudly, almost bumping into each other. It was a laugh long coming and needed by both.

As they stepped outside, Samuel smiled at her. "Let's put this hospital behind us for a day."

Reaching the heart of the city, Ania's sight turned inward, thinking of her arrival in Milwaukee with hopeful parents. Her planned departure to a small village called Sussex was to protect her, not from growing up, but from crushing her dreams. It was obvious that Milwaukee had grown taller and stronger these fifteen years, but not wiser. That was left for Ania and others who dared to face living here or anywhere. Her parents had brought her and then sent her far away, and now her migration had brought her back.

"What are you thinking?"

"I was remembering the Milwaukee dock where we arrived."

"How did you wind up in Oconomowoc with Willy and Jane?"

"They took us in so that Jane could take care of the house while I did the work in the office. Willy didn't want Jane to have to do both any longer. Tell me more about the city."

"I wish I could show you more, but the snow piles make it difficult for the driver, so I told him before we started out to head to an ice skating pond near the lake. I've been there before. We can rent skates and there's always a fire going on shore if we need to warm up."

"I don't know how to skate. I never had the time to learn."

"It's easy. You just glide on the ice. I'll show you. We'll do it together."

"Easy for you."

The pond was so close to the lake that the frozen lake shore looked more like streets of ice houses and castles glistening in the sunlight over their shoulders.

They walked toward a shed, shielding the man from whom they would rent their skates and the wood for the fire. "It's perfect for skating. The sun and the fire will keep us warm."

Sitting on a large log near the ice, Samuel first fixed the skates to Ania's boots, and then did the same to his own.

"Watch me." He stood and pushed off.

Hands clasped behind his back, he took long strides and glided before her.

"You want me to do that?"

"No, no. We'll hold hands and we'll slowly move on the ice."

He crossed his hands in front of him and told Ania to do the same. Taking her hands into his own, they slowly stepped onto the ice.

"Push like this with your left foot and glide with your right foot and here we go. I won't let you fall."

That did not last long as they went down in a heap.

"Up we go. Let's try again. Relax. Push with your left foot and glide with your right foot. That's it. You're skating Ania."

Ania was sailing on the ice as her wine-colored skirt swirled around her.

"You can do anything, Ania," said Samuel, and then he saw it.

The sun was shining through her blond hair, and there was, for a second, a blush on her face. Round and round they went together until the sun lowered its head and shadows covered the pond.

"It's time to go, Ania."

"It's like gliding in a boat on the water."

"It is. Please call me Sam. As I said before, we can go to my office so that you can call Willy and Jane. Your son should be home from school by now so you can talk to him."

The same cab was waiting for them and made its way to Doctor Thatcher's simple office of two examining rooms and a second, smaller private office for the doctor. His office was full of books and medical journals. The telephone was in the front office where patients could wait, and files were arranged not much different from Willy's office, just a bit larger and in a tall building instead of a house.

"I'll wait in my office while you make your call home."

Pulling from her pocket a small piece of paper, Ania laid it on the desk next to the wall phone. Dialing the number, she waited and waited until Jane finally answered.

Recognizing her voice, Jane asked, "When are you coming home, child?"

"I'll be on the three p.m. train to Oconomowoc tomorrow. I should be in Oconomowoc by five p.m. I can walk home."

"Dinner will be waiting for you, and you can tell us everything. Let me get Henryk."

"Mother, are you okay? Is everything all right? When are you coming home?"

"I'll be on the three p.m. train tomorrow."

"Tomorrow! That's wonderful!"

Jane took the earpiece from Henryk. "Willy will be waiting for you at the train station. It's supposed to snow tomorrow evening. Godspeed, Ania," and Jane was gone.

Smiling, Ania replaced the earpiece on the hook. "I'm finished, Sam."

Sam came into the waiting room. "Let's get something to eat. I'm hungry. I know this place around the corner. Maybe we can get in."

Walking into a small restaurant called Bella, they spied a table for two at the side of a window, ready to draw two people closer.

After Sam pulled the chair out for Ania and sat down, he began the conversation. "I didn't read the letter from Willy you gave to me when you arrived until last night. I presumed Willy would write wonderful things about you, but I wanted to watch you in action for myself and make my own judgment. Willy was right and more, and as I said before, not only do you have the required skills, you also give of your heart to help heal the patient."

"Thank you, Sam."

"I want to say something more, Ania. In the same letter, Willy invited me again to visit him. I never took the time to visit them in Oconomowoc, even though he and Jane have invited me many times. I always said I was too busy. But now I have an even better reason to visit them. May I call on you when I come to Oconomowoc?"

"I would like that Do you know that I have a twelve-year-old son?"

"Willy mentioned him in his letter to me. I'll call on you both. I plan to come in the spring if that is all right with you?"

"Of course. I have a favor to ask of you, Sam. You said you were taking me to the train station. My sister, who I have not seen in years, lives just south of the train station. Could we stop at her boarding house before the train station?"

"We can. If I called for you at one p.m., would that give you enough time to visit your sister?"

"Yes, it would be enough time. Thank you, Sam."

"Our meal is here," said Sam. Looking over his plate of meat and potatoes with a fork in hand, he added, "This should fill us up."

The next morning, Ania thanked the deaconesses for their hospitality under terrible circumstances. Both valises were at the side door, waiting for the cab, and soon Sam was at her side as well. The cab arrived on time with the same driver as the day before. Samuel loaded the valises and offered his hand to help Ania in.

He joined her from the other side. "What is your sister's address?"

"She lives at 300 Pierce Street."

The driver looked at Doctor Thatcher with a frown on his face.

"I'll pay you extra," said Doctor Thatcher.

They passed the train station on Reed Street and headed south for Pierce Street. Next to a two-story boarding house was a small house. There were no numbers on the small house, but the boarding house address read: 310. The driver looked at the doctor "It must be the house."

Samuel helped Ania step down from the cab and watched her walk up to the door. Ania knocked, and the door slowly opened. Samuel could see a slender woman slightly taller than Ania, with sleeves rolled up to the elbow, and it looked like a girl of about four was holding onto her skirt.

"Can I help you?" asked the woman, looking at the cab in the background.

"Aga, it's me, Ania."

"Ania!"

Aga looked stunned and took her younger sister into her arms.

"Come in." Slapping the chair with a rag in her hand and clearing the crumbs from the table before Ania sat down, she added, "As I wrote, this is my daughter, Beata."

By those letters, Ania knew Aga's circumstances, and now she saw the toll on her older sister by four years. Aga's youth drained from her, replaced by the shell of a woman. Thin, her face drawn and with matted hair, Aga tried to compose herself, forcing a smile, but it was obvious life had already passed her by.

"Who is this, Mother?"

"This is your Aunt Ania. She's the woman I write letters to in Oconomowoc."

"How are you doing here, Aga?"

Sitting at the table while Beata moved to her side, Aga gathered her thoughts. "The owner of the boarding house allows me to stay here with another girl. We clean the rooms for the dock and railroad workers living at the boarding house. Most are immigrants and some have families. I have a place to live, meals, and a little money for other things. It's not much, but at least we're not on the street. My two older children are grown and have gone their own ways. I'm a single mother but finally wiser for it. I saw the fancy cab. Why are you in Milwaukee, and who is that man by the cab?"

Ania gave her sister all the details she thought she could handle, including how she got there with the man standing at the side of the cab.

"Aga, I really must go, so I don't miss my train to Oconomowoc."

Tearful hugs and promises to see each other fell away as Ania left, closing the door behind her. It was painful to see and more painful to hear how lives were bent and broken under their own weight. Sam stepped down from the cab and then helped Ania step up into her seat.

After coming around the cab and joining her, he said to the driver, "The train station on Reed Street."

Arriving at the station after a six-block ride, the driver stepped down to hold the horse by its bridle, giving his riders inside the cab some privacy before they parted. Samuel spoke first, offering his thanks again, and then turned to a more important subject.

"I have two letters here. I wrote one for Willy and Jane and the other to your son, Henryk. I left them unsealed so that you could read them both while on the train to Oconomowoc. Spring cannot come fast enough for me."

"I'll look forward to your coming."

"I'll telephone you in early May, after I make arrangements at a hotel in your city."

Stepping down from the cab, Samuel came around and helped Ania step down. Still holding her hand, he placed it on top of his and raised it to his lips, kissing it in parting. It was brief but meaningful to both. Then Sam escorted her to the station and bought her train ticket. Ania waited at his side. As Ania passed the gate into the boarding area, she turned and waved.

"Practice your skating."

Ania laughed and waved again.

The trained pulled out of the station, slowly passing boarding houses and factories with multiple stacks, belching dark smoke. Ania's first-class seat was very comfortable, and it was not long before her mind whirled with the events of the past nine days from the telephone call taken by Willy. Instances could change lives, change places, and change futures. Her mind stopped first at her sister's house, close to the bowels of the city. Her first question was, would Aga's life ever be better, and what about her daughter still clinging to her skirt? When she finally lets go, would it be the same or better for her? At least they were living a life currently unchanged. What about those who died in the fire, or worse, those who were burned and are still living? Ania skipped over in her mind, skating and dinner with Sam. Those thoughts would have to be dwelled on later, separated from everything else, and some time.

West of Milwaukee, Ania pulled the two letters from her coat pocket and laid them on her lap. Unfolding the letter addressed to Willy and Jane, she read: *Dear Jane and Willy. Thank you for sending such a capable nurse and woman. You were right, Willy. Ania can do procedures that even doctors shy from. I look forward to seeing you both in the spring. I trust your invitation still stands so that I can see Ania as well. Samuel.*

Jane, and probably Willy, too, will want to know from me what the end of that last sentence means. I will have to have an answer ready for them, Ania thought. She placed the letter back in its envelope and then pulled the second letter from its home and read: *Dear Henryk. Your mother is a wonderful woman. I watched her and saw her strength and compassion. She could handle anything that needed to be done. I saw grace as she wiped tears, stroked foreheads, and removed fears. I looked within and saw her heart, and I look forward to meeting you this spring when I visit all of you and your mother in Oconomowoc. Samuel Thatcher.*

The train from Milwaukee to Oconomowoc was on time, and Ania could not be happier to be home. Although small snowflakes were already falling, portending a major snowfall, Henryk was standing on the platform as the train approached, waiting for his mother while Willy stayed with the buggy nearby. Ania stepped down from the train with one valise in hand, while an older man politely carried Ania's second valise behind her and stood it next to her on the platform. She thanked him, and he tipped his hat. Turning to pick up the second case, Henryk was already before her and wrapped his arms around her waist.

Ania kissed the top of his head. "I've missed you, son."

"Willy has the buggy across the street. I can handle this valise for you."

"That you can." Ania smiled.

Holding the reins in the buggy, Willy smiled as Ania approached. "It's good to have you home, Ania. Get in. A storm is coming."

Even the harnessed horse was impatient to get out of the wind, and so the ride home went surprisingly quick. When they stopped before the barn, the blown snow bit their faces head on.

"I'll get the horse and buggy into the barn. You two get into the house."

Hearing them tromping their feet in the small entryway, Jane stood by the table and waited for Ania to come through the door.

Before Ania could brush the snow from her shoulders, Jane hugged her. "Welcome home, child."

The kitchen felt warmer to Ania than when she first arrived five years ago.

"You must be hungry, Ania. Wash up. We'll eat in ten minutes."

Ania put the valise from Willy in the office and took her own valise to her room upstairs. The water already poured into the basin from the pitcher on the washstand was cold. After quickly washing her hands, she took the two letters from her suitcase and hurried downstairs into the warm kitchen. Waiting was hot stew sitting on a cast iron trivet. Sitting down, Ania placed the two letters to the side of the trivet. After Willy said the table prayer, questions from Henryk and Willy peppered Ania while Jane focused her attention on the two letters sitting there waiting to be heard.

Ania glossed over the stories of the patients she and the doctor treated for Henryk's sake, with plans to share those medical details with Willy later, since all four knew enough about fires. Then Ania turned to her time with her sister, making sure Henryk heard that he had an aunt and a cousin close to his age.

Then Jane turned the conversation. "How did you get on with Doctor Thatcher?"

"Sam was very kind to me, meeting me at the train station and taking me to the station for the trip home after I saw my sister. We worked together long hours at the hospital, especially the first four days I was there. You have trained him well, Willy. Sam always shares hope with his patients, believing that healing is stimulated when patients have hope."

Jane couldn't hold back her question any longer. "What are those letters laying there?"

Trying to look as innocent as possible, Ania picked up the letters. "Samuel wrote you a letter, Henryk, and a letter for both of you, Willy and Jane. He wanted me to read both of them, and I did. Why don't you read your letter first, Jane?"

Jane took the letter and scanned it before reading it out loud to Willy.

Hearing the letter, Willy smiled. "I'm glad Samuel will finally take some time off and visit us."

Jane was more taken with the last sentence, mouthing the words, "*So that I can see Ania as well,*" and then she smiled broadly.

She knows, Ania thought.

"Why don't you read your letter out loud, too, Henryk?"

Willy and Henryk didn't catch it, even though it was right there before their eyes. It did not get by Jane as she heard the words: *When I visit all of you and your mother in Oconomowoc.* Jane gently nodded, confirming for herself that her intuition was right. Standing and turning away from the table to get the hot apple dumplings for dessert, Jane thought, *Ania and I will have to talk.*

Cleaning up from dinner, Jane waited before she made her way up the stairs and into Ania's room. "Do you need help unpacking, Ania?"

"It's almost done, Jane."

"It's Sam, is it?"

"Doctor Thatcher wanted me to call him Sam."

"And he wants to see you and us in Oconomowoc?"

The gig was up, and Ania knew it. "Yes, he wants to see me."

They clasped their arms and smiled at each other.

"He's a kind man. We even went ice skating together yesterday afternoon."

"Can I mention all this to Willy? I don't think he got it from the letters."

"Sure."

As Jane left the room, she said over her shoulder, "Willy will be pleased."

Chapter Twenty-Three

In late March, left from a brutal winter, were small piles of dirty snow. In Darla's room, Charlotte was translating into English from the German paper delivered to the house the latest news about the Newhall House Hotel fire. The coroner's office was still receiving letters from relatives trying to trace the whereabouts of missing loved ones in Milwaukee. His reply was always the same to each one writing: *We are still looking.* He could not give his petitioners hope or a release from their worst fears. Charlotte could only do the same for Darla, as it was time for her to go back to the same hospital where she started two years earlier with so much promise. The disease didn't care how much Charlotte wanted Darla to get better. Syphilis was only interested in ravaging her body like a scythe, cutting through golden grain.

"At least try to drink your calomel tea. I'll hold the cup for you."

Darla sputtered the liquid over her lips and it ran down over her withered chin. "I can't even drink something without making a fool of myself. I can hardly see the cup."

Charlotte dabbed her chin with a napkin. "I'm taking you back to the hospital. We have to try something else there. The rash on your body has been gone for almost two years, but you're not getting any better. You're weaker than when you first came here. These calomel pills in your tea don't seem to be helping."

"Jakob will be glad to see me go."

"Not really. With you here, I'm not only out of his mind but out of his sight as well. Caring for you gave some life to this house. I don't want you to go back to the hospital, but we have to try something else."

Charlotte squeezed Darla's hand and turned her face away to cry. Three days later, they were at the hospital, waiting for Doctor Thatcher's arrival.

Darla was a wisp of a woman and could barely find the breath to answer the doctor's questions. After the brief examination was over, Doctor Thatcher was more than polite as he spoke to Darla and Charlotte. His words were brief, warm, and full of resignation and frustration. "I love what I do, but I can't fight an enemy I can't see."

"I'm tired of fighting, too."

"Don't say that. We're not going to stop fighting."

Doctor Thatcher spoke over Charlotte's words. "I'll make you as comfortable as I can. Charlotte has told me already that she will stay with you. I'll do everything I can."

"Jakob will want you at home," said Darla.

"He doesn't care. Once, he said to me, 'Do what you want outside of the house.' He's never home, anyway. I'm not leaving you."

For weeks, Charlotte stayed close, holding Darla's hand, mostly wiping her brow, and reminding her she would stay close. It was easy work for Charlotte, but it was of no use to Darla. Doctor Thatcher would speak to Darla, but neither knew if she heard anything that he said. They say hearing is the last sense that disappears. Even if true, it would not matter soon.

Charlotte looked down at her and then at Doctor Thatcher. "She's so young. What a waste. She was used up by men who sought and played with her youth and took it all from her. It's not right, Doctor Thatcher."

"Do something about it."

"Do what?"

"There are groups of people, mostly women, of course, who want to shut these whorehouses down, but they have little support from the politicians or the press and little money. The politicians use the women themselves and then pay off the press to keep the truth from their voters. Politicians' wives keep quiet so they can continue to live their lives of ease and these poor girls recruited from across the state pay the price. It's got to stop. You could help them, Charlotte. Shut these places down. I can put you in contact with a group of women who need your help with this crusade because syphilis is turning up everywhere in this city, even in babies born of good women infected by their husbands. Let me know."

Darla could barely swallow now and her morphine shots were coming more often to quiet her and stop her from thrashing about. Charlotte pulled her chair close to the bed and took Darla's hand and squeezed it.

"I'm still here. I'm not leaving you."

Powerless to help Darla did not mean Charlotte was helpless. Charlotte would not turn empathy for Darla's life into just pity for her situation. It would be fuel for her new anger directed at whorehouses and the men who owned them and those who used them.

"Darla, I don't know if you can hear me or not." Charlotte squeezed her hand. "You'll not be forgotten as long as I live. I'll take you with me every day of my life and draw strength from your fight. The press and politicians will hear your story and I'll use my means to shut these places down, no matter where the fight takes me. Did you hear me, Darla?"

Maybe Darla squeezed her hand, or maybe not. It did not make any difference to Charlotte now.

"I won't allow my sorrow, Darla, to shadow my life so that your dying, and especially your life, is just lost under your tombstone. I don't intend to just nick this problem during my lifetime. Do you hear me, Darla? I'll make a deep kerf, cutting across the grain of anyone who resists me trimming back new branches of an old evil tree."

Darla's dying took two more long nights and days. The priest was long gone.

She didn't whimper anymore or stir. When daybreak approached, her eyes rolled back within her gaunt face and her hand slid free of Charlotte's hand. A deaconess confirmed Charlotte's diagnosis that Darla was gone.

Charlotte looked at the deaconess. "I'll take care of everything for her."

Darla's funeral mass was at the Cathedral, with three people in attendance.

Charlotte would bury Darla on a hillside close to Charlotte's parents' waiting mausoleum in Calvary Cemetery, with enough room between the two for her own final standby tombstone. Even though the burial would have to wait until the ground frost had left, Charlotte's new work began immediately, meeting with a group of women from Milwaukee and Chicago on Water Street in view of the Water Street brothels.

Eight blocks away, Gretchen addressed Danny. "Are we going to expand or not? Have you talked to Jakob? We could open a second house by the end of October if we secure the site now and get started."

"I know. I know, Gretchen. But he always puts me off. If I push him too hard, I don't know what he'll do. When he drinks, he gets angry and he always starts drinking when I sit down with him. Something else seems to be on his mind. I'll try again as soon as I can, Gretchen. You could manage the second house while I handle the White Dove. I'll ask him again."

No one could really talk to Jakob anymore. He had not spoken to his wife in months, nor did he want to. He used a room at the White Dove for his own, rather than going home. Jakob's favorite, Sarah, stopped trying to find the good in him and building a life on it. His drinking had not yet turned him violent with her, but there was no future in it for her to spend time with him. She was ready to turn him loose to the other girls, since he loved the bottle more than her, even if he denied it when he was alert enough to talk about it. Sitting in the room they used, Sarah thought they could have him and she knew they would take him. When Jakob stumbled into his room at the White Dove, Sarah was waiting for him.

"Oh, it's you, Sarah. Could you get me a bottle?"

With her head held high, she spoke as sternly as she could. "Not yet, Jakob. Don't ever ask for me again, and if you do, I won't come to warm your bed. Others will, but I will not. You love the bottle, any bottle, more than me, so take any girl you want, but not me."

"It's not just the bottle, Sarah. I have syphilis. According to the doctor, I have had it for more than a year."

"You bastard! You didn't tell me! You don't care about me! You don't care about anyone except yourself, and I don't think you even care about yourself."

"Not anymore, Sarah."

⸻❦⸻

Before Thursday afternoon ended, a twenty-foot-tall harbinger of spring lay in front of Henryk's school, waiting to be raised for the coming weekend. On Saturday morning, mothers of the sixth-grade girls would add long streamers to the top of the newly cut birch Maypole. Mothers of the seventh- and eighth-grade girls planned to go into nearby fields during school on Friday to gather wildflowers to weave that night into garlands to be worn by their daughters at the Maypole dance.

Saturday afternoon, the sun broke through the threatening clouds. Before the girls took the stage, the boys planted two trees, celebrating a newly arrived custom recently imported from Nebraska called Arbor Day. Near the school's front door, tables laden with pies and cakes were waiting to be devoured.

Henryk could not help but keep his eyes on Jane's cake more than the girls in their white dresses milling nearby. His watch was rewarded with an extra-large piece of his coveted cake.

On the way home, Willy broke the silence. "The weather cooperated. I thought it was going to rain again. For this late in May, the farmers are still having trouble getting their crops in the ground."

Jane shrugged. "As good as last year was for them, there is no guarantee that this year will be as good."

"It's not off to a good start."

As Willy was coming through the front door, the telephone rang.

"Can you get it, Willy? Our hands are full."

Henryk followed Willy into the office as he answered the phone. "We should have named the two elm trees we planted."

Ania followed them. "What would you have called them?"

"President Lincoln and President Grant."

Willy extended the mouthpiece. "The telephone is for you, Ania."

"Jane, Doctor Thatcher asked if he could visit us at the end of May. I said it would be all right with us. He's talking to Ania now and asking her if it would be all right with her, too. I hope she says it's fine."

"Willy, are you trying to be a matchmaker?"

"Not me. But after what you told me, I agree they would make a nice pair."

Ania's smile said it all.

Jane beamed, too. "Well, tell us, Ania."

"Sam is coming on the Saturday afternoon train next week and is staying at a hotel. He's going to church with us on Sunday morning."

Jane clasped her hands. "That sounds good. We can have dinner here after church and then you two can have the rest of the day to yourselves."

After Ania disappeared upstairs, Willy eyed Jane. "Now, who is trying to be the matchmaker?"

The week crawled by for Jane, and especially for Ania. Ania knew Sam's intentions and was fully aware of the situation, but she decided she would not immediately fly to his side when he arrived at the train station. Instead, she would wait for Sam to come to the house Saturday night to greet the Jamesons. The only certain thing was that she intended to wear the wine-colored shirtwaist and skirt she wore when they went skating and to dinner. Jane's intentions could not have been more transparent than Ania's, since Sam had never been to Oconomowoc, but she realized that she and Willy were not the reason he was coming to their city. Willy looked forward to seeing a good doctor and a good man he could call his friend, while Henryk could have cared less at this point that a stranger was arriving Saturday for a four-day stay.

⊷⊙⊶

Walking slowly from the train station to the hotel on Oakwood Avenue, Doctor Thatcher decided he wanted to relish this visit that had been long since coming for many reasons. The Townsend House Hotel was only five blocks away and gave him plenty of time to recall the real reason he was here in Oconomowoc. He would not quicken his purpose just as he could not quicken his step. *Damned leg*, he thought. *I hope Ania won't think less of me because of this limp.*

Slowly was exactly what Ania needed. This relationship, if it was to be a lasting one, needed to be planted slowly and carefully. Ania reminded him of the good earth of his father's farm back in Fond du Lac. When tilled for planting, the ground felt warm to the touch, but it dare not be overworked and abused less it dry out quicker in the hot months of July and August. Maybe a limp is a good thing.

Walking toward the four-story hotel, he asked a passerby on the bridge, "What is this lake called?"

The friendly man tipped his hat. "Fowler Lake."

"It sure is beautiful."

As the man moved on, he called back. "Soon, all the red-winged blackbirds will be back and their songs will make the lake also sound beautiful."

The Townsend House Hotel was grander than Doctor Thatcher had expected. Making his way to the main entrance, the blooms of the Blue Flag Irises along the walk were already in the shadow of the evening. Once his bags were in his reserved room, Sam made his way to the restaurant, and even though he was underdressed, he enjoyed his meal without regret since only one thing was on his mind.

Ten minutes later, as he was walking up the Jameson steps, Samuel said to himself, *I can't wait to see all of them.*

Henryk answered the door.

"You must be Henryk, Ania's son. I am pleased to meet you. I'm Doctor Thatcher." He offered his hand to Henryk.

"You're the doctor from Milwaukee that my mother calls Sam. Can I call you Sam?"

"Of course, you can. May I call you Henryk?"

They shook hands.

"You have a good grip, Henryk."

Closing the door, Henryk led Sam into the parlor. "Mother, here's the man we've been waiting for."

Willy moved forward to hug his former student.

Pushing Willy's shoulders back, Sam looked at him. "Time past does not kill real friendship."

"Ladies, Doctor Thatcher is here."

Jane greeted Sam first, whom she had met once when Willy invited him to their house for dinner.

Sam then turned and took one step toward Ania, who stood to his right.

Seeing her in the wine-colored skirt and shirtwaist, he smiled. "Did you do any more skating when you got back home?"

"You were not here to hold me up." They laughed. Sam turned very serious. "I'm glad to see you, Ania."

"And I, you, Sam."

A fifth chair was waiting in the parlor for their guest. Sitting, the hour went quickly as words tumbled from all of them. The subjects were not important, just the warmth felt by all in the room. There was no need to be careful about what was spoken or even how it was spoken. It was a family making a newcomer one of their own.

Sam stood. "I'm staying at the Townsend House Hotel and I should get back. What time should I be here for church tomorrow morning?"

"Since we are walking, be here by ten a.m.," said Willy.

"Until tomorrow morning, then. Good night, everyone. Good night, Ania."

"I'll walk with you to the door."

"Thank you."

Walking her to the door, Sam raised her hand again and kissed it gently. It was a gossamer kiss felt by Ania.

"Good night, Sam."

Early morning mass bells from the Catholic church across the lake woke Sam from a very deep sleep. Sunlight creeping into the room was held back by the clothes press at the side of the window. Following breakfast, Sam took his second cup of coffee to the open veranda and studied Fowler Lake, barely seeing the Norwegian bridge to his left through the trees leading to Ania. The birds were at the height of their morning calls, and Sam listened as one called loudly and another responded. Sam did not have to sing. All he had to do was walk across the bridge.

In the Jameson house, everyone was ready for church earlier than usual, waiting for their guest. Looking out the window, Henryk alerted everyone that Sam was coming up the walk. He opened the door and offered his hand to Sam.

Sam shook it with a smile.

"You have a good grip, Doctor."

Jane and Willy were first through the arched parlor door, walking past Sam and Henryk to the porch, trailed by Ania. Jane turned Willy around to watch Sam as Ania came through the parlor door. It was obvious to them, as Ania stepped into the light of the open door. She was wearing her light blue day dress and held her bonnet by her side.

Sam smiled broadly and bent closer to Henryk. "Your mother is beautiful."

It wasn't just the dress. Ania wore it well, and they all knew it.

"May I have your arm, Mrs. Jameson?"

"May I have your arm, Ania?"

Henryk closed the door behind them and watched his mother walk down the porch steps, arm in arm with Sam. He had seen his mother arm in arm with Willy before and he liked it, but this was different.

At this worship service, there was an extra man in the pew the Jamesons filled most Sundays. He sang with gusto, drawing a few approving nods. Then, after the service, the beautiful spring day slowed the steps of everyone leaving the church. The pastor enjoined Samuel and Ania in a brief conversation at the door, asking where Samuel was from and inviting him to return, to which Sam heartily agreed.

Not far away, Susan was talking to a friend when she glanced to her left and saw her husband staring at Ania on Samuel's arm. At that moment, it became obvious to Susan that her husband's buried feelings for Ania were very much alive. Her problem, even though on another man's arm, was still too close.

Ania appreciatively held Sam's arm tight as he helped her down the narrow church steps. Feeling secure in each other's presence, they realized there was no need to enrich the recipe with unnecessary words or actions. The unspoken understanding between them was already in the air so they could relax and enjoy the time Samuel would be in Oconomowoc.

On the walk home, Jane was mentally rehearsing her menu for the Sunday after-church dinner, thinking of putting the seasoned pork roast into the oven immediately. She could prepare everything else while the roast was warming.

Following dinner, Jane offered, "Because the porch is cooler, let's take our rhubarb pie out front."

Before sitting down, Sam asked Willy, "How many years have you enjoyed this cooking?"

"We've been married for thirty-two years and Jane's cooking was this good from the very start."

"You're a blessed man."

Jane smiled briefly at Willy. "It's been a good thirty-two years, Sam." Jane looked at Sam. "What do you two plan to do with the rest of the day and tomorrow?"

"Ania is taking me on a long buggy ride tomorrow to show me some of your lakes and your fair city. Today, I could just sit here and enjoy this beautiful day."

"Willy, we'll be gone most of the day tomorrow. Is that all right with you?"

"We have no appointments scheduled for tomorrow, Ania. Enjoy yourselves."

Finishing her pie, Ania took Sam's empty plate with hers to the kitchen to help Jane with the dishes.

"Tell me what's happening in the medical world in Milwaukee?"

"There's much to tell, Willy. Analgesics are being used as painkillers, either swallowed or rubbed on the skin. Chemists in Europe are working on all different compounds to hinder pain with or without surgery. But the scourge in Milwaukee is syphilis. Poor choices by men are bringing the disease home to their wives, and even children are being born with the disease. Some of the cases are pitiful with great pain endured by the patients, not to mention all the disfiguring to the face and other parts of the body. If the disease affects the mind, people are sent to insane asylums, and if the disease attacks the internal organs, death is imminent. Prostitution is the fuel for this plague. Someone has to control this before it destroys the city."

"The La Belle House in town had such a reputation, but it burned down in 1879 and so far, thank God, I haven't had to treat any syphilis cases here."

"You don't want to."

Ania joined them on the front porch.

"Ania, would you like to take a walk with me? Henryk could join us and show me where he goes to school."

"You three go on. I'll still be here on the porch when you get back. I like these spring days when it is still cool."

Ania found Henryk in the backyard. "Sam would like to see where you go to school."

"Right this way, Doctor." Henryk took the lead, but he did not get why his mother and Sam did not keep up.

In front of the school, Henryk pointed out his classroom on the second floor and the plaque over the entrance explaining to the doctor why the school was named Garfield School.

Turning the corner, Sam asked, "Is your son going on to school after he graduates from here?"

"We're considering sending him to a preparatory school in Watertown fifteen miles from here. He could live at the school, and yet be close enough so that he could come home on weekends by train."

"You said, 'we.'"

"Willy and Jane have recognized Henryk's abilities and have offered to help me with the tuition at Northwestern Preparatory School. They want to help because they lost their only child in a fire."

"I know. That's why Willy stopped teaching at the medical school in Milwaukee and left for Oconomowoc. Which has all brought me to you, Ania."

"What time does your train leave on Wednesday?"

"It leaves at one-thirty."

Walking back to the house, Henryk was waiting for them on the front porch. "You two sure do not walk fast."

Seeing them, Jane took Henryk with her to get the coffee and cookies readied for their return. Another two hours on the porch did them all good. Sam had not felt such warmth since he left home for medical school.

"What time should I bring the buggy around to the hotel?"

"I'm going to finish reading a medical journal in the morning so that I can leave it with you and Willy. I think ten a.m. would be just right."

It was not a hint from Ania, but still, a good time for Samuel to leave this day behind. It was his practice to make notes following each patient visit, and he thought, *There is much to mull over from this visit.*

Ania smiled. "I'll see you at ten then."

Without a flourish, Sam stood and took Ania's hands into his. "Until tomorrow morning, then. Good night, everyone."

After breakfast, Henryk had left for the last week of school and Willy was already in his office when Jane said to Ania, while packing lunch for her and Sam, "Samuel sure can sing. Do you know what song he's singing to you?"

Ania picked up the basket without blushing. "So far the tone sounds right to me."

After harnessing the bay to the buggy, Ania drove the buggy out of the barn, stopping for Jane standing next to the driveway. Jane placed two jugs of water next to the picnic basket. "The weather looks good for the day. Where are you going?"

"Through town and then around a part of Lac La Belle, stopping for our picnic either on the way or in the park." The bay wanted to go, and so did Ania.

Sam was waiting for her and eagerly climbed into the buggy. "Just over four months ago, I waited for you at the railroad station. You were on time then and on time today. Where are we going first?"

"We are driving downtown to post a letter for my sister in Milwaukee. That will take us close to Lac La Belle and from there we can ride north past some very fine homes built between both lakes. The white and purple lilac bushes should be in bloom along the way."

As they drove past the large houses, Ania described what she knew about each family. After paying the toll, Ania drove the buggy across the road on top of the dam between Fowler Lake and Lac La Belle. Turning west onto the road that was closest to Lac La Belle and going about a mile, the road dipped close to a marsh near the water.

"Please stop for a while?"

"Sure." Ania smiled.

Their horse didn't mind stopping to rest, either. Getting down from the buggy, Sam held the halter so Ania could join him.

"Listen," he said. "Do you hear all the birds? What a lively chorus of sounds."

Standing there silent, it seemed to Ania that Sam was drinking in the sounds to take with him to Milwaukee.

"These sounds are so different from what I hear in the city. Listen." Enthralled by the sight of the sun dancing on the water and the sounds of all kinds of birds coming and going, Sam smiled. "I haven't heard this in a long time. My mother warned me that the city doesn't have everything. Thank you for bringing me here."

Back in the buggy, Ania controlled the reins. "We're going to stay on this road until it leaves the lake, and then we'll turn around to go back into town."

Reaching the center of town and kitty-corner from the Summit Bank, Ania pulled to the side of North Main Street and stopped before the corner.

"It was here where Willy and I worked to help burn victims from a fire that destroyed both sides of North Main Street to the water and the right side of South Main Street to the mill. If that tall mill had caught on fire, most of the town may have gone up in flames. And right there on the street, Jane comforted a young man while he died from his burns. It was really hard for her and Willy to see that after losing their young son in a fire."

Ania stirred the bay and turned onto Milwaukee Street and headed west for the village park. She stopped the buggy at the water trough.

"Tie the horse, Sam. We can have our lunch here. I'll grab the picnic basket. Could you bring the water jug and blanket?"

Sam spread the blanket on the grass overlooking the water. Two willow trees allowed the sun to dance through their wispy branches across the blanket.

"I'm sure many couples have used this spot for a picnic. It's an open-air cathedral. We should be in a painting."

Breaking out the sandwiches, Ania smiled. "It's a beautiful spot for a park. Willy and Jane come here to watch the sunset over the water."

The same scene hushed their voices as they ate.

"How many years have you been in Oconomowoc?"

"I came here eleven years ago, first working as a governess responsible for three children, and then the Jamesons invited us to live with them six years ago. So much has happened since Henryk and I moved into their home. He challenged me to set up his office, and then he taught me how to be a nurse.

"Henryk became part of a family and because of them, he has been in school for three years. They took us into their home, taught me skills, and made it possible for Henryk to go to school. They don't just love us. They love us as their own even though... Tell me about your family."

"My parents own land west of Fond du Lac, which they farm, and my father has a lumber business on the land as well. I have an older brother and sister with families of their own. Their homes are on my father's land, and both men help on the farm and in the lumber business."

"You didn't want the same for yourself?"

"You know I have a slight limp, Ania."

"Willy told me about it before I came to Milwaukee."

"I was Henryk's age when a doctor set my broken leg. A tree my father was cutting twisted and came down around me. A limb caught my leg and knocked me to the ground. It could have been worse. The doctor saved my leg, and even though I had a long recovery time, I kept going to school and beyond, right on to meeting Willy and becoming a doctor. I will always limp, but it doesn't hurt or hinder me in any way."

On the way home, Sam asked, "What happened to Henryk's father?"

"Let's not spoil a nice day talking about him."

Reaching the barn, Sam helped Ania unharness the buggy. Then she gave a body brush to Sam so he could groom the mare while she went to get some grain from the bin, hay, and new water for the stall. When they finished, they went in the back door, carrying the empty picnic basket and two water jugs.

"I see your faces caught some sun today," said Jane. "It looks good on both of you."

"I'm pretty much of a paleface," said Sam. "I don't get out enough in the city but I do tan easily."

"You work too much," said Jane. "The same sun shines in the city."

"Ania, since tomorrow is my last day full day here, could we go for a walk in the early afternoon? Maybe we could catch some more sun, and I would like to take you to dinner at the hotel."

"I have to ask Willy."

"You two go on with your plans for tomorrow. Willy and I can handle everything here. Let's have our coffee on the front porch. Sam, do you want to eat with us this evening?"

"Thank you, Jane, but I promised myself that I would finish this new book on internal medicine before I left here. I'm going to get a quick meal at the hotel and then read tonight until I finish the book. I left the medical journal behind for Willy this morning, but I'll bring it by tomorrow."

"Willy will be sorry he missed seeing you today," said Jane.

Before Sam said his goodbyes to Ania, he turned to Henryk. "May I talk to you alone for a moment?"

"Sure, Doctor."

Walking down the porch steps, Samuel looked back over his shoulder and smiled at Ania and Jane.

"Your mother tells me you are going to be thirteen years old this summer. That's getting pretty old, so I thought I would ask you if I could see your mother again? I want to be sure it's all right with you."

"I know you like my mother and I like you myself, so sure. You're a lot like Willy."

As Henryk was coming back up the steps, Ania smiled at her son. "That didn't take long."

"Men don't talk as much as women."

Sam turned to Ania. "Thank you for a wonderful day. I'll be here after lunch if that's all right with you."

"I'll be looking for you, Sam."

After Samuel left, Ania turned to Henryk. "What did you two talk about?"

"Man talk, Mother, man talk."

Ania joined Jane in the kitchen. "What do you want me to do?"

Jane stopped what she was doing. "I want you to listen to me for a while, Ania. I know Samuel likes you and you like Samuel. Willy was like Samuel before we married. He loved caring for people. I didn't change that because I didn't want to change him. He was the kind of man that would change himself when he learned that being a doctor meant caring for himself so that he could care for others for a long time. Caring for himself meant me caring for him. Without us even discussing it, he soon loved me as much as his work.

"That is all a woman can hope for. Early on, I worked with him and for him so that our lives were entwined in everything we did. The loss of our only child then brought us even closer together because we were already one. Not just in some spiritual platitude, but in reality. I see the same kind of man in Samuel.

You can't change a real man, but you can become his greatest interest by loving him in every way he wants and needs. We have enjoyed great unity in our marriage because we respect each other and trust each other. Willy knew even before we married that no one could love him more than me. I've said enough. Here comes my man."

After finishing the dishes, Ania slipped out the back door to think and started walking toward Fowler Lake. Soon the water came into view, and as she looked west, the low sunlight parted the sentinels standing secure along the water. Ania felt secure and melted into the Jameson household at the edge of life. But now, close to Samuel, there was more she could have. Reaching down deep, she mumbled, "I love my son but can I, should I, want more with Samuel?" Approaching the water, the cattails were already in the shadows, and there were no perched red-winged blackbirds in sight to soothe her mind with their song or answer her greatest concern. "Should I tell Samuel what happened to me in Sussex or not? Willy and Jane have never asked me what happened before I came to Oconomowoc. Maybe Samuel will never ask me either, but if I tell him everything, will he love me more or will he love me less? I know it's on his mind because he asked the question, 'What happened to Henryk's father?' Should I tell him and let him decide if he wants to keep seeing me? He has a right to know and I have a right to say nothing to him if I choose. The steps I take on our walk tomorrow afternoon will determine what steps Sam will take tomorrow night at dinner. I would ask him if he had a child. I think it best not to leave him in the dark." Satisfied with her conclusion, Ania turned back to the Jameson house, hoping the twilight would last until she was home.

The next day, Samuel was at Jameson's door a few minutes after one o'clock. Willy answered the door. "Hi, Sam. I know you're here for Ania." Jesting, he added, "Do you think you could save some time for me before you leave?"

"Ania has offered to pick me up at the hotel tomorrow morning, and then you and I will have time to talk before I take the afternoon train back to Milwaukee."

Coming down the steps into the hallway, Samuel said to Ania, "Are you ready to catch some more sun?"

As Willy held the door open for them, he smiled, remembering having those same days with Jane. "Have a good time."

Walking toward Fowler Lake, Samuel basked in the day. "It's another beautiful day here. It's so different from hearing horses and cabs and people as I walk to my office every morning. Milwaukee was a great place for me to begin my work. You have to be where the people are to face their diseases and injuries. That's the only way medicine advances enough to stave off dying for a little while. Some people expect miracles, but all we really do is hold on to a person as long as we can so that next time we face the same problem, the new patient might be able to hold on a bit longer. Each dying patient moves us a step closer to saving more time for another. Enough talking about my work."

"You are dedicated, Sam."

The same cattails Ania had seen the night before were now on their left, stretching across a small bay. They were full of marshland birds raising a ruckus, seeking a mate or a nesting space near the ground, sprinting from here to there and back again. The birds were all busy, happy, and singing.

"From a young girl, I have always loved this sound when the marsh is bursting with life. Sam, I need to—"

"It's beautiful, Ania."

"Sam, I need to tell you something important."

"Of course, Ania. There's a fallen tree. Let's sit there."

"Sam, you asked me, 'What happened to Henry's father?' Henryk has no father. Let me explain. My parents sent me to live in the small village of Sussex when I was sixteen, to work in a household, taking care of a family's children so that their parents could pay closer attention to their business of raising hops and selling hops from local farmers to a single brewery in Milwaukee. The son of that brewery owner raped me in a field and then fled back to Milwaukee. I fought, but… Then my employers thought it best that I leave Sussex and move to Oconomowoc. I—"

"Stop, Ania. You have said enough."

"I have said enough."

"Does Henryk know?".

"He only knows that his father left. It was enough at the time."

Samuel fell silent. *Too silent,* Ania thought. *Should I say more? Should I have said anything?*

"I should get you back home. We are going out to dinner tonight at the hotel, my last night, before I leave. I'll pick you up at six. Let's head back to the house."

"I know you're leaving."

Sam was giving Ania too much time to get ready. Why did he need all this time before dinner? *The male red-winged blackbird comes and goes as he wants, so why not Sam? It is like that with all of them,* she thought.

Waiting in the parlor was not easy for Ania. Ready for the evening, she was wearing her blue day dress and her bonnet. She did not like feeling uneasy, and Jane saw it in her eyes. Samuel did not keep her waiting long, knocking on the door before six o'clock.

Samuel, wearing his best, walked into the parlor, and before them all, lifted Ania's hand to his lips and kissed it.

"Our cab is waiting."

"Have a good time," Jane said.

"We will," replied Samuel, heading for the door.

On the porch, Samuel said to Ania, "May I take your arm?"

Then, helping her step up into the cab, Samuel said to the driver, "Back to the hotel."

Both were quiet for the short ride to the hotel. The cab pulled up to the main entrance of the four-story hotel, and Samuel quickly paid the driver and helped Ania step down. *He is acting very formal,* thought Ania.

The doorman pulled one of the four doors open for Ania, and tipped his hat to Samuel as he passed by, and followed Ania into a huge parlor.

"This room is larger than Willy's entire house."

"I was told by one of the staff members that the house cotillion band offers evening music for the guests and some nights dances are held in this room. The grand concert piano being played off to the side of the bandstand can also be used by a guest. The wide staircase in front of us heads to the rooms on the upper floors and the down stairs next to it goes to the dining room where we are headed."

"The red velvet carpeting looks so soft."

Walking past one of the inner doors, she reached out to touch the white Greek lace curtains on one of the doors. Just inside the dining room entrance, the lead waiter met them and led them through the spacious room to a table close to the windows, stretching the length of the dining room and facing the lake. Warm breezes filtered into the room off the lake through the end windows, while shadows from the large trees close by danced across the white tablecloths.

"Look, Sam. The sun is beginning its descent over the water. Beautiful."

As the sun shone through Ania's blond hair, Sam looked past her and out the window, "It is a beautiful sight."

Pulling the chair for her, Ania sat to Samuel's right and automatically smoothed the white starched table cloth in front of her with her gloves.

The waiter assigned to their table immediately appeared, and sat glasses on the table from his wheeled cart. "Would you like me to pour a glass of water for you?"

After placing the menu to their right, he asked again, "May I suggest a glass of white wine?"

Ania nodded to Samuel, who placed the order.

"Are you in a hurry to eat, Ania?"

"No, Sam. I am in no hurry."

"Good. Let's talk over this glass of wine before we order our dinner."

After pouring the wine into each of their glasses placed to the left of their water glasses, the waiter asked, "Do you wish to order now?"

"Please return in fifteen minutes."

Then Sam turned his face from the waiter and looked directly into Ania's blue eyes. There was no doubt he was going to say something very serious to her.

"First, Ania, may I take your hand in mine?" Taking her hand in his, he held it ever so gently. "I don't care one wit what happened to you twelve years ago. Of course, I'm angry that this terrible thing happened to you in the first place, but if it had not happened, you and I would not be sitting together right now. I'm very fond of you and I marvel at all that you have gone through to be the woman you are. In spite of what happened to you, you are the mother and had to be the father of Henryk, and you became an accomplished nurse as well." Ania looked down as he went on. "You have no reason to look down. You have every reason to look up and look ahead." Samuel gently squeezed her hand. "May I be part of that future, Ania? May I see you again?"

Looking up, Ania returned the pressure with a gentle squeeze. Then Samuel raised her hand to his lips, and both knew nothing more needed to be said. Watching from a distance, the waiter caught this important moment and immediately planned a surprise for the couple.

After perusing the menu, Ania said to the waiter, "I'm going to have the beef roast with potatoes and carrots."

Samuel laughed. "How did you know what I was going to eat?"

They ate heartily as the sun danced on the water before them. Other patrons came and sat around them, but Samuel and Ania paid them no mind, their sparkling eyes set only on each other as they made plans for Samuel's next trip to Oconomowoc. The waiter, seasoned by a longer life, saw possibilities leavening before him, and he thought back to an earlier time.

Seeing they were finished, he quietly approached. "May I suggest our dessert for the evening?"

Samuel hesitated.

"We don't have to have dessert, Sam."

"Yes, you must," said the waiter, "compliments of the house. We like serving people who really enjoy each other's company."

In a moment, he was back with a strawberry torte and ice cream in two large, fancy bowls.

"Thank you, sir," said Sam.

"No, thank you both."

As they were leaving the dining room, Ania smiled. "That was the longest dinner I have ever enjoyed. We are the only two people left in the room. Thank you, Sam."

Helping Ania step up into the cab, Samuel joined her. Taking her hand, he held it in the seat between them, thinking that he had no intention of ever letting it go again. Unlike earlier this evening, the ride to the Jameson's house was too short.

At the door, with darkness near, Sam asked, "Would ten a.m. be too early?"

"We all want to see you before you go back to Milwaukee."

Samuel lifted her hand to his lips and kissed it, bidding her a good night. Then Sam opened the door for her and watched her disappear into the dark hallway.

Hearing the door close, Jane came out of the parlor. "How was your evening?"

Lifting the bottom of her skirt, Ania ran up the stairs halfway and looked over her shoulder. "It was a lovely dinner."

Smiling, like the waiter, Jane knew it was all unfolding before them.

The next morning, after checking out from the hotel, Samuel stood on the Jameson's porch. With the valises at his side, he knocked at the door with mixed feelings. In a moment he would see Ania and in three hours she would take him to the train station where he would say goodbye to her. On the other side of the door, Ania opened it to the man she did not want to leave. There were smiles on their faces when their eyes met.

"Good morning, Ania."

"Good morning, Sam."

Said simply as if they had been greeting each other for years.

"Is that you, Samuel?" Willy said from his examining room. "Send the boy in here." Samuel walked into the room, but he couldn't wipe the big smile from his face. "So, you do have some time for me. Let's go onto the porch and talk."

Ania walked into the kitchen and asked Jane if there was something she could do to help. "Samuel is leaving soon, so you should spend your time with him. I can handle everything here."

Time always goes quickly when you want it to stop—talking for two hours on the porch, and lunch seemed to go by in ten minutes, and then it was time to leave. While Samuel finished his goodbyes to Jane and Willy, Ania went out the back door to get the buggy. Coming out the same door, Sam placed his two bags in the back and then sat next to her. Ania flicked the reins, and the gray stepped off down the driveway to the road and shortly turned right onto Milwaukee Street. Looking west down the street, the white clouds were thickening and turning darker.

"All the time you were here, Sam, we enjoyed sunshine after a very wet spring. Now it looks like it is going to rain again."

"I brought the sunshine." Sam laughed.

"That you did, and more." Riding along the water, Ania added, "The marsh has already turned quiet. The birds know it's going to rain this afternoon and have found their cover."

After tying the gray to the horse post at the station and lifting out the two bags from the buggy, Sam refused Ania's request to carry a bag. Crossing the rails, they stood close to each other on the platform, looking down the tracks and hoping the train would be late. Hearing the engine before they could see it, Sam drew Ania into his arms and kissed her on the forehead.

Ania looked up. "I don't want you to go."

"I'll be coming back."

After the train pulled into the station and groaned before them, Sam picked up his two suitcases and headed for the second Pullman's car. Ania took his arm and together they walked toward the car. The conductor could see it in their eyes and gave them an extra moment at the steps.

Once more, and very deliberately, Sam raised Ania's hand to his lips and kissed it. Lowering it, he looked directly into her eyes. "I'll be back soon." Then he turned from her and boarded the train, with the conductor stepping up right behind him, waving at the engineer. Both Ania and Sam were now alone. As he looked for his seat Sam thought, *my limp didn't matter to Ania at all*, while Ania boarded the buggy, thinking, *Sam can't come back to me quick enough.*

Chapter Twenty-Four

Walking up the back steps of the White Dove to his apartment, Danny finally had news Gretchen was waiting for.

"There you are. Jakob will meet me at Cullinn's Irish Pub tomorrow afternoon at three to talk about the business. Maybe he's come around to starting a second house."

"It's time he lets us know if he plans to finance a house that I can manage. We have to think about us, Danny."

"You're right, Gretchen, but he owns everything, and I can't antagonize him or we might be on the street. Our business partner can get angry in an instant. I have to be careful when I talk to him."

"Remember, Danny, he needs us to keep his business running. Think it through tonight."

Since it was too early in the afternoon for the regulars, the darkened pub was almost empty. As Danny drank his second shot of backbone whiskey, Jakob walked through the door and headed straight for Danny's table.

Sitting down, he yelled at the bartender. "Bring me a bottle of whiskey." Then he looked at Danny. "We talk better when we're drinking."

Bringing the bottle, the bartender filled both glasses. "Do you want anything to eat?"

"A bowl of your stew for each of us. Now Danny, let's talk business. You wanted this meeting. What's so important?"

If there was one thing Danny had learned from Jakob, it was not to waste words, so thinking about it the night before, Danny was convinced that the past profit performance generated by the White Dove was the best proof to open a second house.

"Jakob, you've enjoyed strong profits on your investment and we have benefited from working as your managers at the White Dove. We are losing business. If we turn away clients, they go somewhere else, and we could lose them for good. Gretchen and I want to open a second house. It'll be good for business."

"Are you finished, Danny?"

Since his boss did not dismiss the idea out of hand, Danny became hopeful, thinking he was working the numbers in his head.

The bartender carried the tray over his shoulder and placed part of it on the table so he could serve their stew.

Jakob still said nothing and dove into his stew. Still not a word.

Let him enjoy his stew, thought Danny, and he ate as well.

When both were finished, Jakob took his time, wiping his lips with the napkin. He waited for Danny to do the same and then looked directly at him. "No. We're not adding a second business."

Danny kept calm. "Why not? We're making money. Let's make more."

To Danny's surprise, Jakob didn't raise his voice. Instead, he seemed resigned, so why not nudge him again? "Why not expand?"

Pushing the bowl farther in front of him, Jakob folded his hands and laid them on the table in front of him. "I'm going to die, Danny."

"We're all are going to die, Jakob. What are you talking about?"

"I have had syphilis for some years now, and it has turned worse."

"I didn't know."

"I don't want you to tell anyone. If you do, you'll no longer be working at the one house we do have. There's another reason why we're not expanding. There is a growing resentment among the powers that be in the city against young girls working in places like the White Dove and women of means are now leading the charge. My wife is one of the pack leaders attacking our business, and if they can get some crusading newspaper writer or blowhard politician to take up their story, we could lose more than just our business. Now I want you to leave so that I can drink."

Danny rose from the table and offered his hand in sympathy rather than friendship, but Jakob held it tight in friendship.

During his cab ride to the White Dove, Danny realized explaining to Gretchen why she would not have her own business would be easy, wondering for the first time what kind of future they would have.

"He's dying?"

"That's what he said, and I believe him. If he dies, what happens to the White Dove?"

"If he dies, what happens to us? Have you thought about that?"

Charlotte's three meetings on Water Street with women wanting to do the right thing so far had produced no results and no attention from anyone. Most who listened denied there was a problem, and those who agreed there was a problem said there was nothing they could do about it. What they were really saying was there was nothing they wanted to do about it. They had not pulled the right thread.

Charlotte met with the group again in early November. "The politicians won't help us until we get the public involved. A person who writes for the German American newspaper by the name of Vincent came to me for financial help so that he can get started in Milwaukee politics. My price for him was to consider writing a series of articles on prostitution in Milwaukee, focusing on the young age of the girls. Since he was sure he would lose nothing by doing it, he's willing to begin the series next month. Do you think we should do this? It could be traceable back to me and then to all of you."

No one at the meeting objected.

After the first snowfall of November finished falling, the phone rang. Henryk gently said, "Mom, Samuel is on the telephone again."

"Hi, Samuel. How are you?"

"I'm fine, Ania. I've asked a fellow doctor to cover for me so that I can come to Oconomowoc for Christmas."

"That would be wonderful, Sam. How long can you stay?"

"I'll arrive Christmas Eve afternoon, but I have to leave before New Year's Eve so that the doctor working in my place for Christmas can go home for a few days. I'm going to stay at the less expensive hotel on Milwaukee Street. The one I've been to the last two times. I'll be on the afternoon train just five weeks from today."

"I can't wait to see you, Sam. Goodbye."

At a Milwaukee restaurant, Vincent struck a bargain with Charlotte and went to work immediately. He started gathering facts about the houses of prostitution in the city while he began a series on the young women who worked at these houses. Charlotte demanded that these girls, hidden by the night, should be revealed to the public as the same women who could be wives or daughters. Vincent felt the same as Charlotte that these girls "*shall not remain nameless as they are being used up,*" quoting her to his editor. The editor demanded hard evidence of his new writer so that his paper could stand behind anything he printed.

Vincent listed the names and addresses of each house, and then he sought the civil records, looking for the real owners of the buildings and exposing them. He visited as many houses as he could, avoiding their real purpose by only drinking at their bars and gathering any information from a girl who would join him at his table. After each of Vincent's articles, readers wanted more, as he dug into the underbelly of Milwaukee life. The more evidence he revealed, and the more certain parties wanted nothing more to come to light, the more Vincent would dig. The coroner's office freely offered statistics, and doctors gave him stories of suffering and death, hiding names, but not the havoc syphilis was causing in the city. As the public demanded more information, questions were finally being asked of the aldermen if a house of prostitution was in his ward. As each successive week went by, the reaction from those who had a stake in the businesses went from jokes to whispers to "Who is this Vincent?" and "How can we get rid of him?" Politicians could no longer turn a blind eye because even the clergy were making them feel uneasy in the pew with a comparison to women in the Bible. This next election year for Milwaukee government offices, incumbents would not appease voters with empty promises. Changes were being demanded as Christmas closed in on the city.

"Have you been reading these articles, Danny, written in the paper by a man called Vincent?"

"What articles?"

Gretchen pointed to torn pages from newspapers on the table. "These articles!"

Reading each article slowly, Danny lowered his chin into his left hand in thought. "This isn't good for us, Gretchen."

"Damn right this is no good for us. We might have to think about moving on."

"Where? To do what?" Danny bellowed.

"Figure it out, Danny, figure it out."

The afternoon train heading west out of Milwaukee on Christmas Eve was full of passengers. Sitting in the leather seat next to the window, Samuel held two matching boxes on his lap and a big grin on his face. As travelers departed the train, "Merry Christmas" was said sincerely, often, and without hesitation, to people they would never see again. Samuel's turn to pass on well wishes came at the Oconomowoc station, when, for a few seconds, his mind turned away from Ania to others.

Henryk beamed. "He's here."

Samuel's grin broadened as soon as he saw Ania.

Henryk eyed the packages Samuel carried. "What do you have there?"

"This is for you, Henryk, and this one is for your mother. But neither of you can open them until after church tomorrow morning. Merry Christmas, Henryk." He handed the boxes to Henryk to place underneath the tree in the parlor. "Who hung the tinsel on the tree?"

"Mother and I did."

"You didn't have to bring us presents."

"I wanted to. You'll see. Merry Christmas."

"Here's the city boy." Willy laughed. "Merry Christmas, Doctor."

"Where's Jane?" Samuel asked.

"She's still in the kitchen. She wants to make tomorrow's Christmas dinner the best ever for us. Here she is."

"Merry Christmas, Jane."

"Merry Christmas, Samuel."

"What time is the church service tonight?"

"The service is at eight o'clock. Why don't you eat and change here and then you can leave for the hotel after tonight's service?"

"Thank you, Jane. Then I won't have to rush around."

Singing filled both the Christmas Eve and Christmas Day services. The Lutheran pastor finished his two-part sermon on Christmas Day, standing before the twenty-foot-tall Christmas tree. He was answering the question of why Jesus was born in Bethlehem.

Jane bumped Ania's arm during the singing of "Hark the Herald Angels Sing." "Samuel is in good voice this morning,"

The snow crunched under their heels, and their cheeks were quite red as they made their way home.

"For some reason, temperatures always go lower beginning Christmas Day. The older I get, the colder it gets."

It was too cold to answer Willy, and as soon as they were back in the house and brushed off the cold, he went right to the fireplace and stoked the fire.

Willy sent Henryk to the shed to get more dry wood. "It's just too damn cold."

The hot Christmas dinner warmed their insides and Jane announced the cleaning up could wait so that everyone could gather near the tree and open their treasures. The parlor warmed from the fire, had enticed its guests to sit near the tree. Handing out his presents last, Samuel asked Ania and Henryk to open them together. Henryk beat Ania to it and held up a pair of ice skates matching the ones given to Ania.

As Ania held hers, she thought back to almost a year ago and her first attempt to stay upright.

"I hope the three of us can go skating tomorrow afternoon. Is there a place on Fowler Lake?"

Henryk answered quickly. "Lac La Belle and Fowler Lake both have skating areas, but Fowler Lake is closer."

"Can we go tomorrow afternoon, Ania?" Samuel asked.

"Of course, we'll go."

Willy then stood up and reached behind the tree for one more gift for Henryk. "This is for you, Henryk." He handed over his old .22 rifle to the boy.

Jane frowned a little at her husband and then sat back to relish the sight.

Henryk hugged Willy, thanking him, and then he did the same with Samuel.

It was near perfect, thought Jane.

The following day, the early afternoon sun finally broke through the clouds, and thankfully, there was no wind.

Ania looked at Samuel, all bundled up inside the doorway. "You sure came prepared to go skating."

Sam looked down upon the cleared area for skating that was not as large as the ice-skating pond near the lake in Milwaukee. "There's plenty of room for all of us."

Not too far away was another cleared area where children were using their sleds to go down a small hill onto the ice, and in between, there was an open fire blazing away with a shed on one side of it and a fallen tree trunk on the other side where people could sit and watch or put on their skates.

Walking over to the tree trunk, Samuel quickly put his skates on, and while Ania and Henryk were adjusting their new skates to their shoes, Samuel first stood and then kneeled on both knees before them as if he was going to help them with their skates. "Ania and Henryk, stop for a moment."

"What is it, Sam?" asked Ania.

Looking at both of them first and then solely up at Ania, Sam asked softly, "Ania, would you please be my wife? I fell in love with you the first time we went skating. I promised to hold you then, and I promise it to you now, and I will always be there to pick you up if ever you should fall. I don't have much, but it is all yours. Ania, will you be my wife?"

Ania looked surprised for the moment as she glanced at Henryk and then back to Sam. "Oh, yes, Sam. I want to be your wife!"

Reaching for her, Sam lifted her into his arms and offered his hand to Henryk, who now stood tightly next to them. With their skates firmly on and with nothing more than a whimsey that turned water solid, all three were off to begin their glide together. Then her men took each one of Ania's hands and made sure she did not fall. Love for each other and not whimsy would steady them for the rest of their lives.

Three cold people came through the door, laughing and talking loudly but warmed by all the possibilities.

"Who is making all that noise?" Jane came out of the kitchen.

Ania beamed with excitement. "Where is Willy?"

Willy came out of his office. "I'm here."

"We have something to tell you both. Samuel asked me to marry him and I have said yes."

Willy pumped his fist in the air. "Wahoo! No wonder my gift from Samuel was two bottles of wine. Jane, bring five glasses. We are going to celebrate."

Taking Ania in her arms, Jane leaned back and then took her in her arms again while Willy bear-hugged Samuel and then tousled Henryk's hair.

Overjoyed, Jane was beside herself. "Where are you going to have the wedding?"

"Can we have it here this coming May?"

"Where else would you have it? Of course, you'll have your wedding here."

Willy, Samuel, and Henryk broke from Ania and Jane to sit in the parlor while the two women went to get some glasses from the kitchen.

In the kitchen, Jane reached for her best glassware. "Will our house be large enough for your wedding?"

"There will be only us and Samuel's family, including his mother and father and his older brother and sister and their spouses. I don't know if their three children will come. Perhaps my sister will come and her daughter. Do you think the pastor will officiate?"

"Of course, he will."

Willy had already opened the bottled wine, and he did the pouring. "To Ania, Henryk and Samuel. May their happiness fill many years."

Meeting Doctor Thatcher the first Wednesday after New Year's Day, Jakob was unusually quiet during the examination. Both knew the news would not be good, and Samuel was already girding himself for his patient's reaction. There was none, not even a word, when the doctor laid out what would happen to him.

Walking out of the building, Jakob called for a cab and headed directly to his house to confront Charlotte.

Their butler met Jakob at the door. "It is good to see you, sir. It's been too long."

"I'm here to see Charlotte. Is she in?"

"I will call Miss Charlotte for you. Will you sit in the parlor?"

Charlotte was sitting at her small desk in her bedroom, looking over a list of Milwaukee aldermen, when the butler knocked.

"Yes, Charles."

"Your husband is here and wants to talk with you. He is in the parlor."

"Charles, about ten minutes from now, come into the parlor and ask Jakob if he would like a drink."

"Yes, Madam."

Taking her time to enter the parlor, Charlotte stood near the couch where Jakob was sitting. "You do know where your home is."

"I do. It is Miss Charlotte's now."

"Does it matter? Why are you here?"

"I have syphilis, and it's your fault, Charlotte. You couldn't be a mother and God knows you are no wife. I blame you for this, and I wanted you to know while I can still make sense."

"You would blame me. You didn't get syphilis from me. Thank God I would not allow you anywhere near me, husband or not. Mostly not! You are a detestable man who reeks of self-pity. Nothing is your fault. You are a failure in your father's eyes. Even though I could not bring a child to term, at the very least, I tried to be a respectable woman as your wife. I even tried to bring an orphan baby into our home and raise him as our son. You called him 'garbage with bastard's blood' and left me crying on this same couch you're sitting on now. You have no idea what you could have become and what we together could have been. You are a disgrace to everyone. Go on and die. You won't receive any comfort from me. Return to the streets where you belong."

Charles walked in on cue, prepared to say his prearranged line, when Charlotte interrupted him. "Jakob is leaving. Would you please see him to the door?"

Turning her back on her mistake, Charlotte walked out of the parlor and headed for her room.

Realizing he was only two blocks over from his parents' house, Jakob said to himself, *I might as well. It's time they heard it from me before they hear it from someone else.*

Jakob's parents were quite comfortable in the parlor, sitting before a roaring fire, when their butler announced their son was in the foyer.

Heinriche lowered the newspaper. "Show the sot in."

His mother, Elise, furrowed her brow. "Shush, he'll hear you."

"He is a sot."

Sitting closer to his mother than to his father, Jakob lowered his head and just looked at the floor, speechless.

"Well, what is it that brings you here during the shank of the evening?"

Raising his head, Jakob's face held no expression. "I want to move back in here. I have an advanced case of syphilis, according to the doctor, and I'm hoping I can spend whatever time I have left here. The doctor is sure the disease is starting to affect my inner organs. I may linger for some time, even disfigure, so I wish to do it here beyond the city's eye."

"You have your own home!" Heinriche bellowed.

"I'm not wanted there, nor do I want to spend any time there."

"That doesn't surprise me. For some reason, you were and still are better at handling things that are not yours."

Elise held her tongue and waited for what would come next, knowing the decision belonged to her husband.

"Come and go as you like. Your former room will be made ready and I will alert the staff. You are a Schmidt, and I will take care of your name."

Just that easily, another business deal was made without terms and no one was happy.

Chapter Twenty-Five

Danny burst through the open door of their apartment. "Have you heard, Gretchen?"

Gretchen was opening the window and warming the room with April breezes off the lake. "Heard what?"

"Two young girls working at the Steamers House were found murdered in the alley at their back entrance. One of the girls was naked from the waist up. Our women already know about it, and they're afraid."

Moving to sit at the table, Gretchen paused in thought. "Wait until the newspapers pick up this story. The people will be demanding more changes from their aldermen. Priests and pastors with their women's groups buzzing around are going to make it more difficult for us to stay in business."

"What are you getting at, Gretchen?"

"It's time for us to move on. Do you think your idea will work?"

"It will work if Jakob will back the purchase of the large day boat at the dock that I have my eyes on. He owes us a favor. We could give him a share of the profits while we pay him back the price of the boat. What about the girls?"

"They'll go along. What else can they do and where else can they go? They might like traveling from port to port on Lake Michigan. Go to Jakob and ask for his backing and we'll put the White Dove on the waves."

"You're right, Gretchen. The tide has turned here, and it's time for us to move on. Getting word to Jakob for a meeting is the problem. He doesn't show up here anymore."

While Danny and Gretchen were contemplating their next move, Jakob was busy doing nothing. He was deliberately taking his time before sending men to pick up his personal effects from his house and move them to his parents' house, so the separation to Charlotte's liking was painfully slow.

When the movers walked out the front door for the last time, Charlotte felt free for the first time since her wedding. Tired of Jakob's bullying, Charlotte's staff of three stayed with her and shared in her new freedom.

Confirmations came by letter to the Jameson's home from Samuel's family in Fond du Lac and Ania's sister in Milwaukee that they would be in Oconomowoc for the wedding. Jane was getting nowhere, trying to convince Ania that she should have a new dress for the wedding.

Ania's retort was always the same whenever Jane would raise the issue. "Samuel likes my day dress. I like my day dress and I'll be married in my day dress. Buy me something I can use in my own kitchen, like some pots or pans or dishes, not a new dress."

Jane couldn't argue with her logic and finally gave up trying.

Ania and Samuel would not need much. According to Samuel, his three-room apartment in Milwaukee had little room for anything. Samuel wanted a different place for Ania to start their new life together, but they decided it could wait until they could choose their new home together. By telephone, Samuel asked Ania if he could come to Oconomowoc and spend most of his time with Henryk. He suggested Henryk was old enough to feel left out of their future plans. Private time with the other man in Ania's life would be important.

Ania shared with Henryk why Samuel was coming. "Henryk, do you remember when you and Sam had some man-to-man talk between you? Samuel is coming this weekend so that the two of you can talk. The two of us have done everything together before, and this is no different."

Henryk knew it must have been important because Samuel was coming from Milwaukee to see him, but he had no idea how really important it was going to be. Three days later, Henryk was sitting at the top of the porch steps waiting for Sam.

Samuel wanted to walk from the train station and revisit the part Oconomowoc had played in his life. While the sidewalks and streets were not as busy as in Milwaukee, the people moved slower, especially when they came upon each other. Men and women took time for each other, smiling and laughing. Not barging by to get a space ahead. The difference between the two places was more than size and placement in the society pages. It was the celebration of self, as seen by others. People liked living here. Carrying a small valise for his overnight stay in one hand and a small gift-wrapped box in the other, Samuel walked up the steps of the Jameson's porch. Standing near the door, Henryk shook Sam's hand strongly.

"Strong grip, Henryk." Sam used the same words from their first meeting, now a signal of welcome between the two soon-to-be family members. "Are you ready to spend the afternoon together?"

"Yes, sir." Henryk led Sam into the house.

Sam saw Ania. "There she is. This is for you." He handed her the small box.

Opening it before her men, Ania's eyes sparkled as she pulled from the box a simple braided gold necklace with a centered gold heart. She looked at him in wonder. "It's so beautiful. Thank you, Sam."

Sam took her hands in his. "You will always have my heart."

"And my heart will always be yours." She pulled Sam into her arms to hold him tight. Breaking their hug, Ania turned to Henryk and then Sam. "Are my men ready? Then off with you. No lollygagging."

Ania smiled as the new man who had walked into her life turned the corner out of sight with her son, who had been the only man in her life. Her song was quickly becoming our song.

"Henryk, let's walk toward your school. Do you like school?"

"Most of the time. My teacher has to be mean sometimes because some of the boys in the classroom give him trouble. One of them finishing school this year is bigger than the teacher."

Standing in front of the school, Henryk reminded Sam of how he helped unveil its new name. "The teachers must think you're a good student if they picked you to do that. Do you want to finish school?"

"Yes. All the teachers say it's important to finish school and so does my mother."

"You know, after your mother's wedding, she's moving to Milwaukee to live with me. Perhaps we could ask Willy and Jane if you could live with them while school is in session and back home with us during school vacations. Can you go back and forth on the train by yourself?"

"I can do that."

"Let's shake on it. Then what, Henryk? What do you plan to do next spring when you finish school?"

"My mother and Willy think I should go on to Northwestern Prep School in Watertown."

"What do you want to do?"

"You and Willy went on to school, and I think I should, too."

"So do I. Let's shake on it."

"You have a strong grip, Sam."

"There must be an ice cream store somewhere in town."

"There is, but what about dinner at home?"

"There is always room for ice cream. Let's go."

Upon returning, Samuel and Henryk entered the parlor, where Jane sat. "So you two do know when to come home. Ania is in the kitchen finishing up our dinner."

Ania's men stepped into the kitchen filled with the smells of vegetable soup simmering on the stove. As she turned from the stove, Sam could see his gift was hanging around her neck.

"Do my men have it all figured out?"

"Yes, Mother. Sam is going to ask Willy and Jane if I can stay with them so I can finish school. I'll come home to Milwaukee during vacation times. We shook on it and then we went to the ice cream parlor. I had two bowls of ice cream."

"Two bowls? But your dinner, Henryk."

"They were small bowls," said Sam.

Smiling, she shook her head. "Sam, tell Willy and Jane that dinner is ready."

By the time the three of them were back in the kitchen, Ania had filled all five bowls with soup and had sliced a large loaf of bread that sat on a wooden board in the middle of the table.

After Willy offered the dinner prayer, Jane asked, "Have hotel arrangements been made for your family, Samuel?"

"They're all set. My brother and sister's young children are going to stay in Fond du Lac."

Ania chimed in. "I still have to make arrangements at the hotel for my sister and her daughter. Sam and I are going to do that after church tomorrow before he leaves on the afternoon train. I'm glad she is coming to the wedding. Aga probably has not had a whole week off from work for forever."

"Willy and I agreed that they can eat their meals with us. That will save her some money."

"I'm sure she will help wherever she can with the preparations for the meal after the wedding. We just need good weather, or we'll have to set up the tables for the meal on the front porch instead of under the trees in the backyard."

"The sun will shine. It will shine. Henryk and Sam can help me move the tables and chairs to the porch if we have to." Wrinkling his nose and lips, Willy repeated, "I put in an extra prayer for sunshine so the sun is going to shine."

"Oh, Willy! Did the pastor say we can borrow a few tables and chairs from church?"

"I plan to ask him tomorrow after the church service." Willy leaned toward Henryk. "Don't let me forget, Henryk."

Henryk nodded, digging into his second piece of sponge cake.

"Willy and Jane, we have a request of you. Ania and I are hoping that Henryk could live with you while he finishes eighth grade. Can he stay here with you?"

"Of course, Henryk can stay with us. We have always wanted him to finish school."

Jane added, "We would miss him dearly."

"Henryk says he can handle the train back and forth to Milwaukee, so we will send for him after Ania and I find a larger apartment. Thank you, Jane. Thank you, Willy."

The news of the upcoming wedding of Ania Sobieski and Samuel Thatcher was part of the after-service announcements given by the pastor. Kind wishes for the couple were shared at the church door. Watching, Willy thought back to the day when Ania first came to their home. He smiled broadly, saying to himself, *Jane was so right in encouraging me to invite her and Henryk to our home. They will always be a part of our family.*

Samuel and Ania hurried from church to his hotel to pick up his valise and to reserve a room for Ania's sister, Aga. Samuel planned to arrive on Thursday before the Saturday wedding and his family would arrive on Friday. Arm in arm, they walked to the train station.

Stepping onto the platform, Samuel took Ania into his arms and whispered into her ear. "Two more weeks."

Ania lifted her head off his chest and looked up into his eyes. "Two more weeks."

Ania was in no hurry to walk home and took the long way around, stopping at the water's edge near Milwaukee Street. The reeds of the cattails were already green, as the marsh was coming to full life. Ania paused, and while looking over the scene, a female red-winged blackbird flew to land on a tattered cattail. She sang immediately, and Ania thought no matter how pulled apart things might be, there was still a song that could be sung.

A week later, meeting her sister at the train station with the buggy on Monday afternoon, Ania wondered how her sister would react to her good fortune. They never had been close, even when they were young. Aga was the older of the two by four years, and she made sure Ania knew it. Recognizing her sister from the road with a little girl standing by her side, Ania waved and her sister waved back. Aga carried her valises in each hand while her daughter shuffled behind, off the platform, and across the tracks to the road. The smile on Aga's face was all Ania had to see to persuade herself to make this a new beginning with her sister. She was her only living family member, and since their future could break either way, Ania met her sister with love. It could be catching here.

The first stop was the hotel where Aga checked in and left their luggage in their room. In the buggy, the long day was wearing on the six-year-old, but Beata would not give in to sleep with all the new things she was seeing. Part of that excitement was meeting her cousin for the first time, whatever a cousin might be. Ania stopped the buggy in the backyard so her riders could step down, and then she told them to wait for her while she led the horse and buggy into the barn so they could enter the house together.

Walking toward the house, Aga said to Ania, "I can't believe it. You drive a horse and buggy. I wish our mother could see you."

Jane was busy in the kitchen and Henryk had just left the room after adding two more chairs around the kitchen table when Ania walked in the back door with her sister and niece.

"Jane, this is my sister, Aga, and her daughter, Beata.

Jane melted them with her smile. "Come in. Come in. Welcome to our home. I'm so pleased to finally meet you. This is my husband, Willy."

Coming back into the kitchen, Henryk stopped short at the entrance.

"Aga, this is my son, Henryk. Henryk, this is your Aunt Aga and your cousin, Beata."

Henryk took Aga's hand and shook it strongly, and then he bent down on one knee to do the same with Beata. Beata smiled at Henryk, still not understanding the word cousin.

"He's a tall one." Aga looked straight at Ania and smiled.

"You must be hungry and tired from your journey," Jane said. "We're going to eat early so that you can rest here for a while, and then it will still be light when you walk back to the hotel. Henryk can show you the way? The hotel serves breakfast in their dining room, but lunch and supper will be here, Aga. Is that all right with you?"

"You're most gracious."

"Can we eat now?" Willy said.

Tuesday would be the slowest day of the week for everyone. Willy was busy with a few patients, while Henryk tended to Beata. The three women finalized their plans for Saturday. Wednesday looked like rain again, but the day seemed to go by quicker as Willy and Henryk picked up the chairs and four tables from church while all the women went shopping for everything that would be needed for Saturday.

Back home, Ania was showing some nervousness when Jane took her aside. "What are you thinking about, Ania?"

Ania sighed. "I'm meeting Sam's parents for the first time on Friday and then marrying their son the next day. What will they think of me?"

Jane looked right into Ania's eyes. "The man you're marrying will take care of his parents. You can tell that he has put you and your son above all else, and that includes his parents. Be yourself and love the man that loves you. You're not marrying his parents."

Ania hugged Jane and laughed within. Then they laughed together and hugged again.

Sitting in the buggy at the train station Thursday afternoon, Willy and Henryk looked for Samuel among the disembarking passengers. Walking up to them, Samuel put his luggage for the hotel in the back of the buggy. Leaving the hotel on the way to the house, Samuel asked Willy if they could stop at the Townsend House Hotel. He wanted to reserve a special room for his first night with Ania and arrange for the hotel cab to pick them up at eight in the evening from the Jameson's house. Satisfied with the arrangements, Samuel reboarded the buggy and asked Willy and Henryk to keep this secret from everyone. Arriving at the Jameson's, Willy and Samuel got out of the buggy so they could go into the front door while Henryk drove the buggy into the barn.

Samuel walked through the entrance first and Willy followed. "The groom is here!"

Jane came out of the kitchen, wiping her hands on a towel, followed by Ania.

Stepping aside Jane, Ania went directly into Samuel's open arms and he whispered, "Two more days."

Ania leaned back and said softly, "Two more days."

Watching from the open kitchen doorway, Aga, with Beata at her side, approached slowly. "So, this is Samuel, Ania?"

"Samuel, this is Aga and her daughter, Beata."

"It's a pleasure to meet Ania's sister. Beata, hello. I'm Samuel Thatcher."

Ania then quickly said to Samuel, "We have to finish up in the kitchen. We're making the dessert for the wedding meal, and then we have to get supper on the table."

"I'll take care of the groom. Let's go to the front porch, Samuel. I have something that I would like to discuss with you."

Willy and Samuel sat down among the stacked chairs for Saturday. "What's on your mind, Willy?"

"I'm not getting any younger, Samuel. I love being a doctor. The day is coming when the workload will be more than I can handle. I'll soon be sixty-three years old. I'm asking you to consider joining my work here in the future and then when I can no longer carry out my responsibilities, you could take over my work completely. Ania and Henryk feel comfortable here. Maybe they'll like Milwaukee more than here, and maybe not. All of you could move back here if you wanted. Think about it."

"I don't know what to say."

"I didn't ask you to say anything. Just think about it. The door here will always be open to all three of you and I pray you will be blessed with more children. You and Henryk are like sons to me."

——

During dinner conversation, Ania placed her fork on the table. "Samuel, after dinner, I'd like to take a walk with you."

"Of course, my dear."

Jane caught the importance of some private time for them. "Go, you two. Aga and I can clean up in the kitchen."

Samuel and Ania walked hand in hand down the walk.

"It's a beautiful, clear evening. I hope we have the same weather on Saturday."

"What's bothering you, Ania?"

"I wonder what your parents will think of me, Sam."

"My parents have always trusted me to make the right choices, and I've not let them down. That trust I have earned ever since I left Fond du

Lac to become a doctor. My mother and my father know that I would never marry someone unless I knew she loved me. I believe you truly love me and they will see that also in you." Stopping in his tracks, Sam took Ania in his arms. "You are marrying me, Ania."

"I needed to hear that. I'd like to go with you to the train station to receive your parents. We can take the buggy from here and take your parents to the hotel and then onto the house. Jane has planned a dinner for all of us. She also said the kitchen will be crowded but full of love."

Friday morning at breakfast, Jane said to Willy, "This day will not have enough hours in it."

Willy sighed as only he could, and then turned toward his wife. "Jane, you have always made everything you set out to do special and I know this day will take care of itself with you in it. Don't you worry." Kissing her hand, he placed it over his heart. "Just ask me to do anything."

Ania was banished from the kitchen after lunch so she could prepare herself to meet Samuel's parents. She had decided to wear the wine-colored shirtwaist and skirt. It was her second best, but Sam liked it and maybe his parents would like her in it also. It was like skating with his parents on ice, but now was not the time to have a fall.

Coming down the stairs, Ania met Jane and Aga in the hallway.

Jane spoke first. "Remember, Ania, be yourself."

"You look very pretty, sister. May it stay with you."

"Thank you, Aga. Sam should be coming soon. I'm going to get the buggy from the barn and wait for him on the road."

Back in the kitchen, Jane asked Aga what she meant when she said, "May it stay with you?"

Aga leaned on a chair. "I have known two men. By them, I have three children. They have taken everything out of me so that I look like this and I am only four years older than Ania."

Jane put her hand on Aga's shoulder. "Perhaps you need a change."

Aga did not really hear Jane's words and asked, "What should I do next?" but Jane repeated the words to herself.

Ania could see Samuel walking up the street. She pulled the buggy up to him, and he jumped in.

"You sure are pretty this afternoon."

"Just this afternoon?"

"No, no, that's not what I mean."

"I know."

"Are you ready, Ania?"

"Yes, I am. Let's go meet your family."

After tying the gray to the horse head hitching post, Ania and Samuel walked across the tracks onto the train station platform. Waiting arm in arm as the two Pullman cars stopped alongside the platform, it did not take long to make out the Thatchers coming off the train. The six adults were all together, with the three men toting all the bags, and the three women looking down the platform between the other passengers for Samuel and his bride.

"There they are!" one said.

Soon, Samuel and Ania found themselves encircled by Thatchers.

Samuel greeted his tall, slender mother, kissing her on the cheek, and next he pumped his stocky father's hand.

Then Ania's new world parted before her when Samuel said, "Father, Mother, this is Ania."

By habit, Ania curtsied before them. "It is indeed an honor to meet you both. Welcome to Oconomowoc."

Mrs. Thatcher took Ania's hands in hers and turned to her son. "Ania is prettier than you wrote." Then she drew Ania into her arms and hugged her.

"My turn," said Samuel's father. First, he took Ania's small hand into his large weathered hand and gently shook it. "May I?" He held out his arms.

"Please do, Mr. Thatcher."

"Call me Pa. Sam does." He engulfed her in an embrace while being drowned out by greetings and hugs from the rest of the Thatcher family.

Leading the way toward the buggy, Ania turned to Sam. "There isn't room for everyone in the buggy. What are we going to do?"

"You take the women and luggage in the buggy, and the rest of us will walk to the hotel."

After the three women were on board, Ania said, "It's going to be a little tight."

"We'll manage," Mrs. Thatcher said. While the luggage was being loaded, Samuel's mother asked, "Who's going to handle the reins?"

"Ania is," said Samuel.

"Sam, untie the horse. Everyone ready? Let's go."

The four men stood there, watching as the buggy disappeared around the corner. Sideling up to his son, Mr. Thatcher asked, "She can do that, too?"

"Ania can do most anything she sets her heart to."

"I believe you're right about that, son."

By the time the men arrived at the hotel, the luggage was already in their three rooms. Samuel's sister turned to the men. "Now you fellows show up when the work is done."

Ania stood next to Sam in the lobby. "Since you haven't seen your family for a long time, you could show them the way to our house while I take the buggy back and get the horse into the barn. I'm sure they would like to talk with you."

Henryk was already posted at the door, watching for the Thatchers' arrival, while Jane looked over her table one last time. Finished in the barn, Ania joined her in the kitchen while Willy kept Beata and Aga occupied in the parlor.

Everyone was waiting.

It wasn't even fifteen minutes before they all heard Henryk yell, "They're coming!"

Willy went to the door and opened it when he heard footsteps on the porch.

Samuel stopped them at the entrance to introduce Willy to his family. "This is Doctor Jameson, my teacher and my friend." Jane was coming up to Willy from behind. "And this is his wife, Jane."

Almost in unison, they said, "Welcome to our home."

In the parlor, Henryk stood next to Ania, while Beata stood next to her mother.

"This is Henryk, Ania's son."

Henryk confidently stepped forward to shake the hands of all the Thatchers lined up in a half-moon under the arch.

Mrs. Thatcher broke the silence. "Samuel wrote to us about your son, Ania. You must be very proud of him."

It was all Ania needed to hear. *Leave it to Sam*, she thought.

"This is Aga, Ania's sister, and her daughter, Beata, from Milwaukee."

Then Samuel took it upon himself to introduce the members of his family and say a few words about each one.

After Samuel was finished, his mother turned to Jane. "Is there anything I can do to help?"

"Dinner for tonight is all set. Thank you for asking."

"Call me Emily. I didn't mean just tonight. We can help tomorrow."

"You're our guests."

"Guests can help, too."

"You're right. We're all becoming family tomorrow. Please call me Jane."

After dinner, Ania went to the parlor to spend time with her future relatives while Jane, Emily, and Aga stayed behind to clean up the kitchen.

Once they were finished, Emily wisely said to Jane, "I'll get everyone to leave as soon as possible. Everyone needs their rest for tomorrow."

Walking into the parlor, Emily started motioning with her hand that all the Thatchers should leave.

Mr. Thatcher finally got the message. "Before we go, I would like to thank the Jamesons for their very warm hospitality, and Mrs. Jameson your meal was delicious."

As the Thatchers slowly drifted out of the parlor, saying their goodbyes, Samuel took Ania into his arms and whispered, "Tomorrow. I love you, Ania."

"Tomorrow. I love you, Sam."

By eleven the next morning, with not a cloud in the sky, Emily and Mr. Thatcher showed up at the front door.

Jane opened the door to Emily. "We're here to help."

Willy came up to the door to see who was there and Mr. Thatcher said to him, "I've learned that our wives are on a first-name basis. My name is George. Call me George."

"My first name is William, but call me Willy."

"Good, Willy. I have something to ask you."

They stayed on the porch while the two women went into the kitchen to help Aga.

Willy came into the kitchen a few minutes later. "I'm going into town with George. We'll be back in a little while."

Time was passing quicker now. Willy and George were back, and with Henryk's help, they arranged tables and chairs under the arching boughs of the backyard box elder tree. Their next job was to cut white and purple lilac branches and place them into vases of all sizes in the parlor, on the porch, and at the tables in the backyard. Willy also tied a bouquet of lilacs with a white bow and placed it in a vase on the dresser in Ania's room. Arriving first, the pastor and his wife stayed out of everyone's way, sitting quietly in the parlor. Aga and Beata had already changed, and Jane finally left her preparations to do the same. Arriving next were four church friends of the Jamesons, and both couples joined the pastor in the parlor. Samuel and the rest of his family arrived last, but the smiles on all of their faces said it all.

After getting Aga and Emily from the parlor, Jane knocked on Ania's door. "May we come in?"

"Of course."

All three women streamed into the room, but skidded to a stop when Ania stood and faced them. A gasp of pure joy gushed from all of them.

"Beautiful, just beautiful," Aga said.

Emily kissed Ania on her cheek. "Welcome to our family, Ania."

After giving Ania her bouquet, Jane held Ania's face in her hands and, with tears falling from her eyes, kissed her on the forehead. "You are beautiful, my child."

Her eyes danced with joy. "Thank you, Jane, thank you for everything. I'm going to cry."

"I know." Jane turned away from Ania. "I'm afraid we're all going to cry so we better go downstairs."

A few minutes later, after the three ladies came down the steps, Samuel took his place under the parlor arch and waited for his bride.

Looking tall and lean, his wavy blond hair fell over the collar of his dark, vested suit.

Ania stepped into the hallway, carrying her lilacs, and stopped at the top of the stairs to reposition the heart of Sam's necklace to the center of her heaving chest.

Finally, seeing Sam among all the guests, the smile on her face broadened as she started her way down the stairs. Jane had added a white ribbon around the waist of Ania's light blue day dress, and her curled blond hair swept back fell gracefully across the nape of her neck.

Samuel stepped forward to take Ania's hand when she reached the bottom step. "Ania, you are beautiful," and together they made their way to the arch.

After the pair passed the doorway, guests from the porch poured into the hallway, and Aga and Beata made their way up a few stairsteps so that Beata could see.

The pastor stepped forward to join the couple under the arch, but before he could start the service, Samuel motioned to Henryk that he should stand alongside his mother. The setting was now complete.

After beginning the service with a short prayer, the pastor referred to the fine marriage example of Willy and Jane in his message to Samuel and Ania.

Looking into Ania's eyes, there was no doubt that Samuel meant it when he spoke his vows. Ania, in a softer voice but just as confident as Sam, then said her vows.

The pastor then asked Samuel to place the ring on Ania's left hand. Ania's head shook a bit in disbelief as she watched Samuel fish the gold ring out of his vest pocket. Holding the ring in his left hand, he took Ania's hand, and, while repeating the pastor's words, "With this ring, I thee wed," placed the ring on her finger.

Smiling at the pastor, Ania and Samuel joined their right hands so that he could lay his hand on top of theirs. While pronouncing them man and wife, he squeezed their hands tight, and then he made the sign of the cross above them. *So simple, so profound, and so forever*, Ania thought. Following the benediction, Samuel reached for his smiling Ania and kissed her warmly in front of everyone.

As Jane squeezed Willy's hand, he softly yelled, "Wahoo!"

When Ania and Sam turned to those standing in the parlor, everyone seemed frozen in place, reliving their own wedding minutes except Aga, who quickly sought Sam, and hugged him.

"I have had two husbands. They robbed me of my future. Don't do that to Ania." Aga then turned to her sister and kissed her on each cheek. "I wish you every happiness. Moja droga siostro."

"Everyone to the backyard so we can celebrate!" yelled Willy. "There's more room in the backyard. Follow me."

Like a colonel leading his troops in mass, the well-wishers followed him onto the porch and then around the house for the waiting reception under the extended limbs of the leafed-out box elder. White and blue ribbons tied to the limbs were hanging over the five tables set in a half-moon under the tree. Ania and Samuel were last and moved from one happy well-wisher to another.

Finally reaching Samuel's parents and holding hands in a small circle, Samuel's mother said, "Now, our family is complete." Then she took Ania to her daughter and daughter-in-law. "Your sister is here. Our family is complete."

Out the back door, Jane was leading Aga and Henryk, all carrying trays of small sandwiches for their guests. On cue, Willy and George appeared from the barn, each carrying two stacked cases of iced wine and placing bottles on each table.

Samuel stepped aside from his brother, who had just kidded him about a future child so that he could intercept Henryk before he went back into the kitchen. "You've done enough. It's time for you to stay at my side and then sit with your mother and me at our table."

Seeing the sandwiches almost gone, Jane asked Aga and Emily to join her in the kitchen. After a few minutes, they hurried back to the tables with trays filled with plates of shortcakes topped with strawberries and ice cream.

The low sun rays were still filtering through the branches, crisscrossing the faces of one happy family brought together by a young girl from nearly halfway around the world and a young man from a little-known town called Fond du Lac.

Willy waited until everyone was finished with their dessert and then he nodded toward George, and both stood together. Willy spoke first. "Everyone, raise your glasses. Jane and I have seen two wonderful people joined as one. As the pastor said, 'We wish them every blessing,' and I will add plus a little one or two."

Then George, his wine co-conspirator, added, "Ania and Henryk have joined our family, and now all of us have joined the Jameson family." He raised his glass. "Congratulations to all!"

Laughter filled the backyard in the evening air when a stranger appeared, walking toward them from the corner of the house.

Willy stepped forward to meet him when the stranger, in a formal black coat and top hat, said, "Did someone here order a cab from the Townsend House Hotel?"

"I did." Samuel turned toward Ania. "It's time for us to leave."

"Leave?"

"We are spending our first night together at the same hotel we had dinner together a year ago."

"You are full of surprises, Sam. Let me get a few things from my room."

"I'll be in front of the house waiting for you, my dear."

The combined families followed Samuel to the front yard to see them off.

Before boarding the decorated buggy, Ania stopped to hug Henryk. "I love you, son." She turned to thank Jane and Willy for everything. "We're family, son."

As instructed beforehand, the driver stopped near the bridge so that his riders could step out and look over Fowler Lake at the setting sun.

Ania and Samuel stood arm in arm, looking over the marsh. "Listen. Do you hear the red-winged blackbirds singing? The marsh is so full of life."

"So are we, Ania, so are we."

Chapter Twenty-Six

Settling into his former room in his parents' house was easy, even welcomed by Jakob. There were more rooms to get lost in, more servants, and certainly more sympathy from his mother than his wife. Avoiding his father was mutually agreeable with only either's death as a potential solution to a distasteful and embarrassing situation. Jakob was rarely seen on the street now, and never at the White Dove. Those in the business had learned of his condition, and so Jakob felt comfortable only in the presence of strangers.

Coming back into the house after one of his walks along Lake Michigan, the butler stopped him, handing him a letter. "This came for you this afternoon."

Jakob ordered the butler to stand by while he read the letter on the spot.

He crumbled the note from Danny in his hand. "I'll not be home this evening for dinner."

At the back door of the White Dove, Jakob said to the driver, "Give this to the guard inside the door and tell him it is for Danny's eyes only."

A few minutes later, the guard opened the door for Danny and he boarded the cab.

After greeting the Irishman, Jakob said to the driver, "Take us to Cullinn's Pub."

Greeting his friend, Jakob's loss of weight and drawn face was immediately apparent to Danny, even in the shadows of the cab.

Jakob recognized the look on his face. "I know, Danny. I know. I don't look myself, but I can still think, and I can still make decisions."

Danny helped Jakob step down from the cab, paid the driver, and then opened the door to the pub for Jakob. Sitting down at a nearby table, Jakob told the bartender to bring them the night's fair.

"What are you drinking?"

Jakob said, "Nothing for now."

"The potato soup will be on your table in a few minutes," said the bartender.

Jakob looked straight at Danny. "What is so important that you had to meet with me?"

"I've been trying to reach you for weeks. Since you don't show your face in the White Dove anymore, I sent a letter to your home address, but it was returned to me unopened, so I sent a note to your father's house, hoping that it would get to you. With things as they are in the city, Gretchen and I think it would be a good time to move on and put the White Dove on water."

"What are you talking about?"

"We move our business from a building to a boat."

"I still don't know what you are talking about, Danny."

"Our business is losing customers because of stories in the press about syphilis infecting good families and the murder of the two girls at the back of the Steamers House. The public wants the politicians to do something and those women do-gooders are tormenting our girls in public and encouraging them to quit. Bah! There is an old day boat tied up at the Goodrich dock. The two-deck steamer has a dining room and a number of cabins the girls could use for their work and leisure. We could clean her up and then move the furnishings of the White Dove onboard. More importantly, if one port gives our business trouble, we could move on to another. As the weather changes on Lake Michigan, we can move up and down the coasts of Wisconsin and Michigan.

"There is money to be made in more places than just Milwaukee. You could still make money and, over time, I could buy the boat from you."

Jakob looked straight into Danny's eyes. "Why didn't you come to me with this idea sooner? I sell the building at a profit. Buy a boat cheaply and we go on making a profit year after year. What is the price of the boat?"

With that question from Jakob, Danny knew the White Dove could soon be on the water. The news carried back by Danny to Gretchen this time would be better. Even while sharing Jakob's response at the pub, Danny could see past her eyes into the businesswoman's head. He knew she was already making plans for the transition and probably had already picked out the date when the White Dove would open dockside. Danny hoped Jakob could purchase the boat as quickly as possible so work could begin refitting it to the White Dove.

—⚬—⚬⟩

The first year for the newlyweds went by quickly, capped with Henryk's graduation from Garfield. The only blemish was not finding a suitable apartment for three, so Henryk could stay.

Finally, they secured the elusive two-bedroom apartment in a new building on Grand Avenue close to Samuel's office but safe enough away from the growing labor demonstrations in the center of the city. In two weeks, their new home was ready for Henryk's visit at the beginning of August. Staying for only three weeks before his first year at Northwestern Preparatory School, Ania wanted this time spent with her son to be special since they would not see each other again until Christmas.

Samuel eagerly helped his wife in their new home, wanting not only to be involved in something besides work, but because he wanted to please this woman who shared all of herself with him. They easily worked together, smiling, and just as easily laughed together when something went wrong. Satisfied with each day, they began each night with a kiss, and then Ania would wrap her body around her love, and Samuel, holding her close, would stroke Ania's hair until she would drift off into another well-earned sleep.

Henryk arrived on the last eastbound from Watertown, and while Samuel stayed with the cab, Ania made her way inside the station. She could see the platform, and when Henryk appeared, the first thought that entered her heart was that her son stood taller, looked stronger, almost flying on his own. The only thing missing was his very own red epaulets. *I hope he lets plenty of time pass for them to grow in*, she thought.

Seeing her, he hugged her tight. "You look wonderful, Mother."

"As do you, Henryk. You've grown again." They walked arm in arm. "Sam is waiting for us at the cab."

"Greetings, Henryk. You have a stronger handshake, son. We're headed straight home, but another day we'll show you more of Milwaukee."

As the cab headed north from the train station, the six o'clock work whistles blew around them, and immediately doorways and alleys heaved workers of all ages, clogging their path and bringing their cab to a standstill. Henryk watched as boys as young as himself, covered in soot, some swinging their lunch pails, oblivious to anyone close by, hurried in every direction. One lad, looking into the cab and seeing Henryk, spat on the sidewalk in front of him.

"This is only part of the city," said Samuel. "There's a lot more to see."

"People come from everywhere to work here. My parents did years ago, Henryk," said Ania.

"Even young men your age, Henryk, come here hoping to find work," added Samuel. "The city attracts them and soon they're attached to its sticky web. They first become laborers, mixing in with older men where they learn to take a joke, use their fists and hold a drink. They grow stronger and meaner. Some are smart enough to learn a trade to replace a man used up by the time he's forty. If he doesn't die in some accident, the foul air of the valley kills them. They die with oil and grease under their fingernails or embedded in the creases of their thick hands. The brick layers don't even have fingernails. They are just worn away over time from the bricks or cement and are covered up with calluses.

"Most of these workers hardly see the sunlight, working ten and twelve hours a day. The owners of the factories and breweries live up on the bluffs above the lake and above the valley where the air doesn't stink, and the soot doesn't foul their clean tablecloths whereas their workers live down in the valley, close to their jobs, because they have to walk to work. These men and their wives are just the slurry, the cement that holds the factories and businesses together, and then they disappear. It's all the same whether you work in a brewery, on the docks, or in a factory.

"I have to care for these people, Henryk. All of them. Some have diseases I can't even cure. The city is sick and soon it's going to erupt.

That's enough," Samuel pronounced. "There are some good things in the city, too. We have special plans for Saturday or Sunday, depending on the weather."

Finally, the cab broke free and continued north on Water Street and then turned west on Grand Avenue to the Thatcher apartment. Arriving in front of the four family two-story apartment, Henryk could see their building shared the block with three other buildings, with an alley separating the two buildings in the back and a small strip of grass crossing the alley.

"Where's the yard?"

"The whole city is your backyard," answered Ania. "In time, you'll be able to explore it."

Showing the way to their first-floor apartment and after unlocking their door, Samuel led Henryk to his room, holding only a bed and dresser.

Ania stepped from behind him. "It'll feel more like home by the time you return from school for Christmas vacation."

Raining Friday, the Thatchers agreed to move their outing to the beer garden on Brown Street to Sunday. They spent Saturday morning buying foodstuffs for the outing. Taking Henryk with her, Ania began the late morning trip with a visit to a Polish bakery located nearby to buy a round loaf of żytni bread and makowiec, a poppy seed cake. Turning the corner of the street, Henryk could not believe the long line at the door of the bakery. As the line moved, Ania admitted to Henryk that she wanted him to taste some original Polish food.

She beamed. "Just wait until you sink your teeth into some good Polish bread." She said it first in English for Henryk, and then repeated the words in Polish for him, and as the line shortened, Ania included herself in one Polish conversation after another while Henryk stood fast, listening to the rapid-fire foreign speech.

"It's been a while since I have been able to speak Polish. Speaking Polish reminds me of my parents and a long time ago. When you were a baby, I would sing Polish songs to you that my mother sang to me. They were called kołysanki. Would you like to learn a Polish lullaby I sang to you, Henryk?"

By the time Henryk had learned the first line, it was their turn to make their purchases.

Ania carefully placing the poppy seed cake and bread into the basket. "Now we have to get some zwyczajna sausage from the butcher shop."

Completing their purchase from Zeke's butcher shop, Ania and Henryk left the shop. "Mom, the sky is getting darker. I hope we get home before the rain comes."

Walking as fast as she could, Ania tried to keep pace with Henryk. Henryk urged her on, and, running the last block, they beat the rain home. Laughing as they entered their hallway, the downpour began.

Cutting the bread and sausage, Ania carefully readied the picnic basket, hoping the sun would shine the next day. Home from work, Samuel greeted Ania with a warm kiss and a swift hello to Henryk. Then Ania pulled a pamphlet from the cupboard for Henryk, and together they gave it to him.

"What's this, Mother?"

"It's a brief history of Milwaukee. We bought it for you so you could learn about this city that's now your home. In another week, you're going off to Preparatory School in Watertown and people will ask you where you live. You know a lot about Oconomowoc, but Sam and I want you to know something about your new home, Milwaukee. This will help."

As suddenly as the rain started, it stopped, so the three stepped outside to enjoy the cool air. Looking west from the front of the building, they could finally see the sun. A straight line of clouds crossing the horizon had freed the ball of orange so that it could dip below the horizon.

Samuel pronounced, "Tomorrow will be a good day to go to the park."

There was not a cloud in the sky on Sunday morning. As the cab headed north toward the park, Samuel asked the driver to stop before one of the large breweries on the way. Ania met the idea with a cringe, but recognized the reason.

Pausing in front of the building that held the large brass vats, Samuel went on and on about how beer was made, listing all the ingredients, when Ania curtly said, "Let's move on to the park, Samuel. We've spent enough time here."

Carrying the picnic basket, Samuel led Ania and Henryk under the ironwork archway entrance into the park. They couldn't help but notice the three-story observation tower on the hill looming ahead of them and walked in that direction to find a table.

"The trees and fields remind me of home," Henryk said.

"This is home," Samuel retorted. "This is our home for now."

Beckoning under a huge linden tree were four tables, and one of them was free of patrons.

"Let's take this one." Ania grabbed a low branch. "Can you believe the size of these heart-shaped leaves? In a few minutes, they'll shade us from the sun. Samuel, could you please hand me the basket?"

After laying out the tablecloth, they dove into the basket, and in a flurry, boiled eggs, a bowl of tomatoes, sliced bread, and sausage appeared, and the desired poppy seed cake. Looking up, Henryk saw that Samuel was already on his way to one of the stands to get two schooners of beer and one of lemonade.

Returning, Ania said, "I see you were thirsty, Sam," eyeing the half-spent schooner.

Sam placed the lemonade across from the two schooners of beer so that their places were drawn. Sausage and bread disappeared first, followed by the tomatoes and boiled eggs.

Ania knew how Henryk loved sweets. "The Poppyseed cake isn't going anywhere. Take your time, Henryk."

After the last small slice of cake was gone, Henryk heavily sighed. "I'm so full I can't move."

Sam offered, "Come to this side of the table and we'll watch people for a while before we go to the top of the observation tower." Then he quietly said to Ania, "I asked about the walkers at the stand. They will perform today at four near the concert pavilion if there is no wind."

Believing that their large lunch had settled enough, Sam asked, "Is everybody ready to climb the observation tower? Can you two clean up the table while I purchase the tickets?"

Holding the tickets in his hand, Henryk led the way. Climbing the stairs to the smaller top level, they looked east out over Lake Michigan and then south to the city spread out before them. Ania pointed out the docks where she had arrived with her parents, and then they looked for the train station. Following the Milwaukee River south, they tried to make out the corner of Water Street and Grand Avenue, tracing Grand Avenue to Samuel's office and then west to their apartment.

Feasting their eyes on the sights as long as they dared, Henryk was in awe. "Wow! There are so many tall buildings, factories, and chimneys."

Moving them on, Sam said, "We have just enough time to make it to the pavilion. Let's hurry." A crowd was gathering. "What's happening?" As he spoke, the crowd hushed as a man, and then a shorter woman appeared, walking above them between and over the tops of the trees.

Watching them make their way overhead, one woman buried her face into her hands, fearing a fall. No one spoke as the two daredevils made their way slowly over them, and then they were out of sight.

Ania looked up in astonishment. "Amazing."

Henryk's expression matched his mother's. "They must be very brave to do that."

"Brave enough to break their fool necks." Sam shook his head. "Let's get another drink before we head home."

After having their drinks, they walked north alongside the pavilion to the Brown Street entrance. Cabs were lining up to take the afternoon picnickers home.

Sam asked the driver to take a longer way home, heading first east to the lake and then south along the lake to Grand Avenue and home. Passing grand homes on the bluffs overlooking the lake, Samuel mentioned a person who lived in one of the extravagant houses was his patient, and did not have long to live.

Henryk was quiet as he pointed to one mansion and then to another.

Some of the stone homes were three and four stories tall, with stone border walls and ironwork gateways. A few people were strolling along their large kept lawns, oblivious to belching chimneys and horse manure in the streets of the valley not more than three miles away.

"We have some homes like these in Oconomowoc, but not this many."

Ania looked at her son. "Henryk, it makes no sense to compare."

After viewing the gold coast of Milwaukee, it was awfully easy that night for Henryk to compare what he saw to a week earlier when their cab stalled in the street and a soot-covered young worker spat in front of him.

Convinced her son had a good sense of direction, Ania said to him, "Take some walks while we're at work. I don't want the size of the city to frighten you. Just know your way back home and keep to yourself while you explore. Here are a few coins, so you can pay the bakery a visit on one of your journeys."

Each dinner was filled with new sights her son had seen, filling the night with conversation. Ania knew Henryk was growing into his own and that these shared conversations would disappear all too soon. For now, it was enough to hear her two men swap stories about their boyhoods becoming men. She pondered if only her time as a girl had not been all too short.

Thursday evening after dinner, Ania said to Henryk, "We have one more surprise for you. Saturday afternoon, we're going to meet Samuel at his work and we're going to the same restaurant Sam and I went to before I left Milwaukee after helping with all those fire victims. After dinner, we're going to take a walk about the center of the city. How does that sound, Henryk?"

"I can't wait. These weeks have been just grand, like Grand Avenue."

Saturday morning, after Henryk did some packing for his trip home, Ania sat across from him. "I wish you were not leaving for Oconomowoc and Watertown, but it's the right thing for you to enroll at Northwestern Prep School. I'm going to miss you. We are going to miss you. Jane and Willy are close, so if you need something, you can telephone them and they will telephone us.

"They are also paying half of your expenses, and I can't thank them enough, but that means we need to see a reward on our investment, and that reward is how well you do at school. You have been a good student, but you'll be away from home, so that means there will be all kinds of voices not to study. Don't listen to them. We and the Jamesons believe you can and will go far in life. We only ask that you try your best and remember that we all love you very much."

Standing up, Henryk walked around the table and took Ania's head to his chest. "Mother, I love you, and I'll be a good student for all of you."

Ania wrapped her arms around her son, and they held each other tight. There were no tears yet, just faces of pride and hope.

Ania loosened her grip. "After lunch, we can take our time walking to Samuel's office."

Approaching Samuel's office, a stranger turned his face from them as he shuffled quickly out the physician's door and hurried down the hallway. Henryk was delighted to see where Sam worked, and listened carefully as Sam described how medicine was changing.

"If a person does get seriously ill inside his body, there is not much I can do for him like the person who just left my office. He is slowly dying and I really can't do anything to help him but ease his pain. He comes at the end of the day because his face is covered with growing pustules, and he doesn't want anyone to see him. In fact, he wants me to see him at his home from now on. Enough doctor talk. Let's go eat at Bella's."

Since it was early, the restaurant had few patrons. Service was quick and Henryk's dinner did not disappoint his appetite.

Leaving the restaurant, Samuel pointed out to Henryk the small table in the window where Ania had joined him for dinner two winters ago. Turning the corner onto Water Street, they stared up at the Mitchell building before crossing the horse-drawn streetcar tracks to look into the windows of the shops shaded by large awnings on the east side of the street.

Past the banks, they came to the corner of the block where the Newhall House Hotel used to stand.

Samuel summarized for Henryk the awful details, and when he finished, Ania took Samuel's arm. "Lives can change quickly, even without your own initiative. Circumstance seems unforgiving at times."

They turned east on Huron Street, and, approaching Jackson Street, a growing crowd of men was making quite a ruckus, carrying signs with the same sentences in English, German, and Polish, which Henryk offered to read out loud, "Work eight hours per day not ten."

Seeing a policeman and a well-dressed man talking excitedly on the other side of the street, Samuel suggested, "I think we should turn back."

Turning back around on Huron Street, they turned north onto Jefferson Street, moving quicker than before.

"What does it mean?"

"Men working in awful conditions are beginning to harass their employers for a shorter workday, Henryk. I don't think they will get anywhere, but I respect them for trying. Eight hours in filthy air would be better than ten or twelve hours. It would be a start to improve working conditions for many people who give of their lives to make those who live on the lake bluffs we saw last Sunday rich. The problem is, if one worker complains too much, there are two or three other men who would be willing to take his job, so the owners of the businesses just replace the complainer so people who complain do so at great risk. Enough of this. Let's start back so that we're home before dark."

Sunday morning was quieter at the table. Henryk's train was leaving at one-thirty and he would not see his mother and Sam until Christmas. The goal for Henryk at school was great, but the distance for Ania was not.

She hid it well from Henryk. "We can't wait to hear about your progress at school. Write us when you can and tell us about your teachers, and schoolmates, and especially write about yourself."

Sam stood. "It's time to go. The cab has arrived."

As Samuel talked to the driver, Henryk helped his mother into the cab. The stillness continued in the cab to the train station, but as Ania walked with her son into the train station, her tears appeared. Samuel understood, and Henryk was beginning to understand, but of the three, Ania understood it the best. Even though people were parting all the time, no one's parting was more important than your own goodbyes and your own tears. No matter their value, Henryk was still going away.

Chapter Twenty-Seven

Gretchen's self-imposed date of October 1 was only a month away. Soon, she would have to tell her working girls of their plans to put their occupations on water. She reasoned that most of them would not mind leaving Milwaukee behind when the White Dove steamed away in the spring. If any of her girls did not like the change of venue, she would replace them.

Turnover had not been much of a problem before. A few of her charges found husbands, and a few had tired of the business and moved away, but most of her girls stayed put for six years as they could find nothing more suited for their talents. Bartenders, cooks, and servers will also have to be ready to work on the water for at least six months out of the year. Work is work, and they knew it.

Danny knew Gretchen was eager to leave Milwaukee behind. Too many people knew her role and the madam's anonymity on the city streets continued to shrink. This did not bother Danny much, but he further supposed his female partner was looking for something a little more secure. He did not see himself as a husband, much less a father, but the hints were becoming more obvious from thirty-year-old Gretchen. He did not blame her for wanting something more than a quality dress and managing whores. Her tipping point in life was drawing near and knowing Gretchen as he did, she would have little trouble making it known to him.

Coming from the docks, Danny said, "The carpenters are finishing work refitting our idea and making our steamer grander than what we already have at the White Dove. I found a large crystal chandelier to hang in the ballroom, and the bar will be longer than what we have now, plus a smaller second bar will be at the stern. Two stairways will lead to the rooms above. Our quarters will be above and larger than before, while rooms for the girls, crew, and rest of the staff will be below deck on each side of the kitchen. Jakob, so far, sees this venture worthy of his money. Let's hope he never changes his mind."

Jakob did not mind spending his money on this project at all. If Charlotte received less of his resources, then that was all right with him. If the beer heir spent more of his inheritance than he would ever fully enjoy, that was even better. All the possibilities Herr Schmidt hoped would bear fruit in his son, rotted on the vine, so that he was an embarrassment to him on his social level, and worse personally. Even though the heir did his father's bidding well in Chicago, Jakob felt his father let him down later by not giving him more business responsibilities earned by the future owner of the company, no matter that he was a drunk who needed to get sober. Hatred for his father was real. Whether it was his doomed marriage or the lack of having children that drove him to drink, it made no difference to Jakob. He found crutches and made no bones about using them. Taking the place of his father was Danny. Their venture may have been socially dubious, but the partnership Jakob forged with the Irishman and Gretchen was real. They trusted each other to follow through on mutual business decisions, and, more importantly, appreciated each other's stake in the business. Danny had no problem letting Jakob make the big decisions since Jakob had the money, and Jakob allowed Danny to make all the management decisions, since he lived with Gretchen on the premises. Jakob respected that and wished their roles were reversed.

Jakob and Danny stood at the Milwaukee River dock, two blocks northwest of the lighthouse, looking at the future repainted White Dove. "She looks great, Danny. When do you plan to open for business?"

"If we keep moving forward at our current pace, we can open October first."

"Spend what you have to, Danny, so we can move in on that date. You know what you're doing."

"We're going to have two gangways to enter our business. With your permission, I would like to stencil on each doorway our name White Dove and then put a small number two after the word Dove. We can honor our first business on land in this way."

"Do it, Danny. I love the idea."

"How should I get the new bills to you for payment?"

"I've opened an account for us in the Marine Bank, which is in the Mitchell Building. You can draw on the account to pay bills and future profits for me can be deposited into the same account while you're steaming about Lake Michigan. When do you think you'll leave on your first voyage?"

"The new compound engine will be installed early next spring, so I believe the White Dove can begin her first journey in May of next year. Once moved in, I can plan what ports we'll stop at in Wisconsin, Illinois, Indiana, and Michigan."

Jakob offered his hand, and they shook on it firmly. Then Danny gently laid his other hand on Jakob's shoulder and shook his hand again. It was the closest Jakob would ever come to the feeling of appreciation.

For months, Charlotte had been digging into the underbelly of prostitution with some success. Allies of prostitution are layers and layers of subterfuge, hiding at all costs, an appetite albeit natural, made more appealing behind closed doors with young women in addition to their wives. Not only did the girls work in the shadows, but so did those who issued the permits for buildings knowing their intended use, as well as the tax collectors who knew where the money was coming from. Charlotte tried to plow through those layers, making few friends among the politicians at city hall who had ties to the tax collectors or building inspectors. She was well known in the assessor's office, but for some reason, the assessor was always gone when she arrived to ask him some questions. It was gritty work, and she received no sympathy from the legions of men receiving a paycheck from the city, but at the same time protecting their employers from exposure.

Promises to receive copies of paperwork to build a case against those who profited from houses of prostitution never arrived. The only thing that was clear to Charlotte was that prostitution was big business in

Milwaukee and that it was of personal use to many who wanted it to remain hidden.

Clean water, safe milk, clean streets, the removal of brothels, and worker groups advocating for an eight-hour workday were all bubbling up from beneath. A tide of angry voters would someday break against city hall, but for now, no one could turn over the rock to expose the bugs below or in city hall above.

Changes for the working girls were apparent at the White Dove, as furnishings from their rooms were moved to their new home. The girls embraced the idea of steaming from one port to another, giving them longer periods of rest from their underlying duties.

Clients were also entrusted with the new address and the date of opening night on the water. The cab ride would be a little longer for most of their best clients, but the White Dove's new address could mean an additional layer of protection from the light of exposure.

The transition went smoothly, fueled by a curious interest in the new palace of comfort. Since the docks held their own mystique, security was provided along the streets leading to the entry gangways for those who made their way to their home away from home.

Gretchen kept track of those who came and went, but more importantly, those who had not yet come within the four weeks since they opened on the water.

Her words were comforting to Danny. "According to my tally, only seven former customers haven't appeared here."

"Can you guess why they've not shown up?"

"I think it's the distance they have to travel, but it needs to be monitored."

"Can you think of anything else we can do?"

"There's an idea I have and we could test it here. Since we have two gangways, we could have two kinds of clients."

"Are you suggesting we could open our place to kitchen door clients?"

"The satisfactions we provide dictate our prices and therefore the kind of client who comes to our door, but it seems to me as we steam to other ports, we'll not always be servicing men of means. Think about it. We could test it here. Especially if our girls have too much empty time on their hands."

"Your idea makes sense, Gretchen, but let's wait before we try this out. Since our clients don't want to be exposed, they treat our girls with respect, but the rougher the client, the more problems we'll have. Let's wait."

The afternoon mail was timely, and among the regular missives was an envelope from the assessor's office. Surprised that anything would come to her from there, as she perused the two pages dealing with two different transactions, the smile on her face turned to a scowl. Maybe the motivation of the person who sent this to her was to disturb her more than to enlighten her. Still, the facts contained therein made her boil. Her good husband had recently sold a building, housing the White Dove, and the other document confirmed he had recently purchased a ship to relocate the White Dove. As far as she knew, there was only one business called the White Dove in Milwaukee, and it was a house of prostitution. Charlotte was livid and decided on the spot that it was time to do some embarrassing of her own, but how and when?

No one among her crusaders needed to know, but Charlotte knew her instincts were twisted with a bit of revenge. She could cause quite a stir at the Schmidt house if she were to mail these two documents to Jakob's mother. Charlotte was sure she would pass them along to Jakob's father and that would be all the gratification she would need. A plain envelope would do.

The Schmidt house now labored as a doctor's office, too. Like clockwork, Doctor Thatcher came every month to check on Jakob.

Both knew there was not much that could be done, but pretended that something might change in the future or that a cure would be announced. The doctor remained loyal and comforting, but was now dreading the visits.

The setting was so out of place for the disease. Jakob Schmidt had everything at his disposal and there were no limits on the amount of money he could spend on a cure. However, hearing the same question from Jakob, "Have you heard of any news that might help?" brought about the same reply to everyone in the house, and especially to Jakob, "No."

All Samuel could do was check on the patient's condition, administer the salve at his own risk, and then leave. There was no need to say words of comfort or point Jakob to a myriad of possibilities, for there was only one end in sight. All the doctor was doing was closing one door after another as together they made the journey.

Coming back to his office, Ania could see the look of medicine's betrayal on his face. "Will he ever get better?"

Laughing, Samuel shook his head. "Death is eating away at him one bite at a time. The same must be going on internally. The day is coming when he will cry out for something to stop the pain. It'll be all that I will be able to do and even that will not be enough."

Charlotte waited until right after Christmas to send off her present to the Schmidt family. Even though she would never know how the recipients would receive it, it pleased her to know that this winter it would be warmer for her because she guessed it would be much colder at Jakob's parents' house. Looking out the window at the snow banks covered with new falling snow, Charlotte smiled and mentally put it to rest for now.

Quiet afternoons for Mrs. Schmidt were very long in the winter. Closed in because of the weather, she looked forward to the mail deliveries. Herr Schmidt received most of his mail at work, so there was always a chance there might be a letter for her when there was a mail delivery to their residence. The butler always furthered the delivery right to her hand, and an oversized envelope immediately caught her eye. There was no formal return address on the envelope, but because it was addressed specifically to Mrs. Elise Schmidt, she opened it first.

Quickly glancing at the enclosed pages, two things drew her attention. Both documents mentioned an establishment called the White Dove, and they came from the assessor's office. Her quick conclusion was the letter must have been for her husband and had been addressed incorrectly. Dismissing their importance, she placed both pages back into their wrapper and asked the butler to put the envelope on her husband's desk.

Heinriche's reaction when he read the two pages was quite different. Knowing of the White Dove and the document's purpose of registering the sale of one property and the purchase of another, it was quite clear to Heinriche that his son was the shadow owner of both properties and therefore, owner of a brothel. Brothels did not bother Heinriche, since he considered them businesses and had enjoyed their fruits within. What was more distressing to him was his son owned the White Dove, and worse, who mailed the letter to his wife and why.

Choosing not to draw attention to the issue, Heinriche obliquely asked his wife, while holding the envelope in his hand, "Elise, do you have any idea who mailed this letter to you?"

Handing the envelope to her, Elise shook her head. "I have no idea."

"Thank you, my dear." Heinriche took the matter out of her hands.

Controlling the impropriety and possible scandal was on the businessman's mind as he stormed into Jakob's room.

The sight laying in bed before him repulsed Heinriche. "Can you explain this?"

"Explain what?"

"This." He held the two documents in front of Jakob's face. "This."

Jakob took the two documents from his father's hand, and while examining them, a wicked smile crossed his face.

"What are you smiling about? What is so funny?"

Jakob rose out of bed and handed the documents back to his father. "Now you have proof that I'm a successful businessman. I've operated the White Dove at a substantial profit every year since it began, and I'm convinced that it will continue to be a profitable business. You're only worried about a possible scandal and how it may tarnish your good name. If you have not used the White Dove for your personal service, I'm sure you have used other establishments. You're the one who introduced me to take and use whatever I want, including women."

Heinriche stepped closer to his son. "Using women at a brothel is one thing, but owning a brothel is something that not all of my customers would accept."

"Don't worry, Father. The new White Dove is steaming out of Milwaukee in May and will take your scandal with her."

"Do you know who sent this letter to our house?"

"I have no idea, and I don't care. You don't care that I'm dying, so why should I concern myself about some little scandal that may enter your life?"

Fuming, Herr Schmidt turned to leave Jakob's room. "You could not give me an heir, but you have given birth to a scandal that could ruin me. Are you proud of your accomplishment?"

Without a moment for thought, Jakob smiled. "Prouder than you can imagine, Father."

⁓⊙⊙⊚

Reading Henryk's letter from school, Ania quickly noticed that the words he used were bigger. His sentences were longer, and the letter was laid out in proper form. One paragraph especially caught her attention: *Now that it is warmer, sometimes after class I walk along the Rock River with Hannah. She is the daughter of a professor and a year older than me. We talk about our classes and fellow students.* The letter closed with: *I will be home for summer vacation soon and I can't wait to work for the cream brick factory.* Smiling, as only a mother could, Ania laid the letter on the kitchen table for Sam to read.

Arriving unusually late from work, Samuel collapsed in a chair at the table. Knowing his schedule, Ania guessed his late afternoon visit to the home of his nameless patient must have been the cause of her husband's dread.

Sam did not offer a reason, and Ania chose not to ask. "There's a letter from Henryk on the table."

Sam read the letter with interest, ignoring the sentence that caught Ania's attention, referring only to the comment that Henryk was eager to begin his summer job.

"Henryk is old enough to work, Ania. He'll be fifteen, and the few dollars he makes can help pay for his second year at school."

"I know, Sam. Tell me again what he'll be doing?"

"He'll be digging clay from this side of the Menomonee Valley for the brick factory. The outdoor air will be good for him, and he could turn his extra weight into muscle."

"I'm glad he'll be working outdoors and not inside the brick factory. Other boys his age are stuck away in some dark hole doing awful things in cramped areas that bigger men can't get to. You're sure he'll stay outdoors?"

"That's what the owner of the factory said the last time I saw him in my office."

By now, Sam was ready to offer why he was so drained when he first came home. "I really wish I didn't have to see this patient anymore. I unwrap and rewrap his face and one of his hands each time I see him now. Most of his face is covered with gauze and the pain he's feeling from within seems to be getting worse. I've suggested he start taking a drug to ease that pain, but he refuses the injections. The man is being digested within. My visits are welcomed, especially by his mother, and the man knows I won't turn away from him so he can carry on a conversation with me, but it's hard to see him disintegrate right before me. I could use some time away from here."

Having nothing she could say to help, Ania walked behind Sam and squeezed his left shoulder. Sam placed his hand on hers and they left it there.

⚬⚭⚬

The same afternoon, the second test run of the White Dove's new compound engine finished, with the installer and captain pronouncing the steamer ready for open water service. Finishing work on the new engine delayed their departure by two weeks, but it also meant that the weather on Lake Michigan would be calmer when they headed south. Initial plans were to stop for a month of business near the money area of Chicago before Danny would point the White Dove northeast toward Michigan. Danny was not worried about how prospective clients would receive the floating palace. It was a nearby competition that might make it difficult for them to stay. He reasoned by the time they found a way to oust him from the waterfront, they would already be moving on to a new port. With all required shipping paperwork in order, it was time to get a message to Jakob that their business venture would be leaving home port on Monday morning, May 18, at eleven in the morning.

Making sure Jakob would receive the news, Danny dispatched a courier to deliver the sealed message personally to Jakob, giving him the date and time of their departure. On Monday morning, the butler recognized a different air about Jakob, even though it was quite early.

At the cab stand, Jakob hurried onboard, instructing the driver to get as close to the water as he could by the lighthouse at the mouth of the Milwaukee River.

Arriving, Jakob told the driver to wait for him, and then he hurried to the water's edge, waiting for the White Dove to appear.

Being early, he could reminisce on the White Dove's beginning with the huge Irishman, their good times together, and their mutual financial success. Most would call his situation bittersweet, but Jakob looked upon the boat appearing to his right as his baby.

Gretchen ordered all the girls to be dressed in their finest with the entire staff, to line the top deck before they left the dock and to stay in place as they paraded down the Milwaukee River. When passing the lighthouse, Gretchen wanted Jakob to see what he was sending on its way. Danny and Gretchen stood apart from the rest of their charges, waving so that Jakob could make them out from shore. Jakob waved his cane above his head in return. Danny then signaled to the captain to give four short blasts on the horn. Returning his needed prop to his side, Jakob watched the White Dove disappear, and with a big smile on his face, hobbled back to the waiting cab.

Ordering the driver to take him home, the driver asked, "Why are you smiling so much?"

"My baby should pleasure a lot of people after I'm gone."

Henryk's school year was ending on the last Friday in May, so the week before, Ania asked Sam if they could meet him at the Jameson's and then stay for a long weekend in Oconomowoc.

At first, Samuel hesitated. "We have patients to see."

Expecting the reaction, Ania used Sam's own words. "Not two weeks ago you sat in that same chair and said you 'Could use some time away from here.' I can rearrange the schedule and we'll only be gone for four days. It will do you good."

Realizing he couldn't disagree with his wife when he had set his own trap, Samuel agreed, and Ania planned the trip.

"Don't we have to ask the Jamesons first?"

"I have already called them. They're waiting for us to come."

Taking the first train to Oconomowoc the following Friday morning, Ania and Sam, each carrying their own luggage, walked first to the bridge near the hotel before they made their way to the Jameson's house. Ania wanted to hear her beloved red-winged blackbirds busy at work in the marsh.

"I miss these sounds. You just don't hear that in the city. They come back every year and find exactly what they're looking for."

Henryk had already arrived at the Jameson's, taking the train from Watertown. He was sitting on the porch with Willy and Jane and bolted down the steps when his mother came into view. Willy and Jane met the three of them five houses away with handshakes and hugs.

"Let's get out of the street," said Jane. "We're making quite a sight."

After lunch, they all returned to the front porch, where Willy watched Ania and Samuel drink in the clean air with deep breaths and closed eyes. "It's different here than in the city," said Willy.

Sam looked down the street at the lilacs and daffodils dotting the yards. "I love the work in Milwaukee, but it tears at your will when mostly all I do is hold death at bay."

"My offer still stands."

Ania looked at Willy with a tilted head. "What offer?"

"A year ago, I suggested Samuel join my work here, and when I can no longer continue to practice, take my place. We have no heirs, and we have to give the house to someone. Oconomowoc keeps growing, and a young doctor would bring new medical approaches to the area. All three of you would fit right in."

Ania was stunned and said nothing, waiting for Samuel's reply.

"Some days, your offer rings louder in my ears, Willy. I just might take you up on it."

Willy could see Jane smiling behind them. "Don't wait too long. I'm getting older."

"Let's leave these newlyweds alone for a while. Help me in the kitchen, Willy."

"Samuel, you never said anything."

"We needed to get settled first, Ania. Willy's offer is tempting, but we can't afford to make a change just yet."

Ania didn't even slump back in her chair because she knew Samuel was right. Still, she thought, *The red-winged blackbirds do come back.*

Early Monday afternoon, while Sam was enjoying his last moments on the front porch, Jane walked up the stairs and into the room where Ania was packing their valises. Looking at Ania from behind, Jane noted how Ania looked so comfortable being a mother first and now a wife.

"Do you need any help, Ania?"

"Almost done." Ania was cinching one of the bags.

"We'll miss you and Henryk. Willy needs my help more and more in the office, which means things around the house are not getting done. Could you persuade Aga to move to Oconomowoc and work for us? She and her daughter, Beata, could live with us. Beata could go to school here. It would really help us out. Do you think Aga might leave Milwaukee and come here?"

"As far as I know, nothing is holding Aga in Milwaukee except her work. I'll pass on your proposal to her as soon as we get back home."

Ania met her son and husband on the front porch. "It's time to go. We don't want to miss the last train to Milwaukee."

After Samuel and Ania said their goodbyes, Henryk was the last to hug Willy and Jane, and then the Thatchers were off down the steps.

As they headed down the street, Willy said, "Looks like a family to me."

"They sure do."

During the train ride back home, Ania relayed Jane's offer to Samuel. "While I was packing, Jane asked me if I would ask my sister if she would like to move to Oconomowoc and work in their home like I did. Sam, do you think it's a good idea?"

"Well, look at it this way. Their workload in the office has increased because of Oconomowoc's growth, and work around their home has not decreased and they're getting older. I think it would be a great idea. Your sister and her daughter would get out from under, move to a better situation, and help the Jamesons. Would your sister work as hard for Jane and Willy as you did?"

"She's used to hard work now, so I think she would do the same for Willy and Jane. Since Henryk does not start work for a week, he and I could visit my sister this coming Saturday afternoon."

"Would you like me to come along?"

"It's just a short cab ride to her house. We'll be fine."

Henryk took his time walking to Sam's office on Saturday afternoon. The noise of the city was exactly the opposite of what he heard around school. There was no silence here or bellowing cows. Instead, Henryk just heard sounds mashed together to make noise, and the closer he came to Samuel's office, the louder the noise became. His mother was waiting, and after saying goodbye to Sam, they hailed a cab on Water Street and headed for Aga's home on Pierce Street. Reaching home, Ania asked the cab driver to wait so they would have an immediate way home. This was no place for two strangers to be walking about, trying to hail a cab.

Aga greeted her sister and Henryk with kisses on each cheek as they did the same on Beata's cheeks.

"What brings you here?"

"Henryk finished his first year at school, and we met him at the Jamesons before coming home on Monday. While we were there, Jane wondered if you would consider moving to Oconomowoc and work in their home. They would pay you and you could live in their home like I did and Beata could go to school. I said I would telephone her after I talked to you."

"Me? Really! Live in Oconomowoc rather than here. Please call her and ask her when she would like us to arrive in Oconomowoc, and we'll be on our way. How wonderful."

"I'll call Jane from Samuel's office on Monday and then send you word, Aga."

"It's all because of you, Ania. I know it is. Thank you, dear sister, thank you." She took her younger sister into her arms.

"In two years since Sam and I married, we have only seen you two times until this afternoon, and now you're moving to Oconomowoc. I'm back here and you're going there. Things change too fast. Our cab is waiting for us, so we need to leave, Aga." Ania turned to Beata. "Looks like things are changing for you, too."

Boarding the cab, the driver headed back toward Water Street, and as he turned the corner, a large rally was gathering around a speaker standing above them on a wagon.

The driver approached the growing crowd carefully, hoping to break free without any trouble, when someone yelled, "There's the owner in the cab with his wife."

A portion of the crowd hearing his claim broke free from the speaker and surrounded Ania's cab with more than mischief on their minds. The driver, sensing trouble, told his horse to go, but someone tried to grab her halter and she reared up in defense, almost spilling the cab. Ania fell toward Henryk, jammed in the corner of the cab.

"Let's go!" The driver slapped the reins and grabbed for his whip. "Go!" His horse leaped forward, driving back the slew of people surrounding her, leaving danger behind. Running three blocks from the rally and convinced that they were safe, the driver stopped the cab to give himself and his horse pause. Stepping down, he went to his horse and stroked her nose to calm her, and then looked in on his riders. "Are both of you all right?"

Ania nodded. "We're fine. Can we move on?"

"Yes, let's move on." He uttered, "I'm never coming back here again."

Reaching home, Ania offered the driver more for his trouble, but the driver refused. "Thankfully, both of you are all right. I just want to get home. I have been a cab driver for seven years and now there are areas where I won't go any longer. There is a nervousness in the city and it's growing. Something is going to happen. Good day to you both."

Ania and Henryk sat at the table. "What happened could have been much worse. Please be careful at work. I think the cab driver is right that something is going to happen. I don't want you to get caught up in the debris that's left behind. Do your job and come straight home when your day is done. I don't want to say anything about this to Sam. He has enough on his mind right now."

"It's different here than in Oconomowoc or Watertown. I'll be careful."

Chapter Twenty-Eight

From the foot of their bed, Sam and Ania looked out the window at the yellow leaves of the big elm.

"I'm glad Henryk is settled back at school and I would suppose your sister is just as happy now that she is in Oconomowoc."

"Jane will, again, get the help she needs in the house and that will make Willy happy. . You were right, Sam. It was good that Henryk worked this summer. He seemed to be more of a man when he left for school."

"I know his handshake is stronger." Sam chuckled. "You know I love you, Ania, and because I love you, I want you to be careful on the streets, especially at night. Things aren't like they used to be. I know you'll go where you want and when you want, but please be careful, my dear."

"You be careful too, Sam. Now come to bed. We'll meet tomorrow's problems tomorrow. Tonight, we'll hold each other and sleep."

Looking out of a much different window, Charlotte was not at rest. There was more she felt she could do for the young girls and women of her city. Much like herself, they all initially felt the first flush on their cheek when a compliment was given by a man that life could be happy, full, and satisfying for oneself, not just satisfying a man's primal urge. They all had the same dream, but for too many, once love disappeared, used became their reality. Even shared wedding vows pontificated by many were just disillusioned voices that once knew the sweetness of love, but now had been soured and sullied by many. There must be a way to raise the voices of those who could not defend themselves or no longer wanted to defend themselves.

Still looking out of the window, Charlotte's hot, rambling thoughts coalesced and led in a straight line, up the street, to the house holding her deserting husband. Charlotte concluded at the window that a personal visit should be the next step after the Schmidts received her last Christmas present.

A storm was coming as Charlotte walked up the steps to the Schmidt's house. Standing before the door, she rapped once, and then again, and finally, a third time, laying aside feminine, well-mannered, courtesy. She was storming the castle, and it began here.

Recognizing Charlotte, the butler smiled and graciously welcomed her out of the weather. "How may I assist you?"

"I'm here to see Jakob Schmidt."

"His mother is with him at the moment, but wait here and I'll ask him if he'll see you now."

Coming back down the main stairs to the foyer, the butler said, "Jakob will see you now in his room. Follow me."

As they turned on the first landing, the butler looked back over his shoulder. "His mother plans to remain in the room, Miss Charlotte."

The butler led Charlotte into the room, and before he could announce her, Charlotte stepped around him and walked directly toward Jakob, who was laying in his bed, propped up by large pillows.

His mother was sitting on his left side. "Do you want to use this chair?"

"I have no use of the chair so it can keep you."

"Thank you for coming, Charlotte. My condition is worsening, so I'm very grateful that you've come to see me."

The sickening thrust and parry, as Jakob called it years before, had begun, and Charlotte had forewarned herself to hold her tongue and choose her words carefully but still slice away, slowly and deeply, covering Jakob's warped behavior with women, including the one standing before him.

"You don't have to thank me, Jakob. Is your condition worse?" *Put him and his mother at ease*, Charlotte thought. *It will be easier to cut his heart later.*

"I can't see well anymore. The pain in my stomach increases, and the doctor wants me to start using drugs, and you can see my face."

"I'm sorry for you. How did this all happen?"

"Charlotte, you know I have syphilis. I told you."

"But how did you get it, Jakob? You didn't get it from me."

"I got it from some girl."

"Some girl from where, Jakob? A whorehouse?"

"You might have known that, Charlotte, and I know it destroyed our marriage. I want you to have the home you're living in as a gift from me."

"Isn't that nice of your son, Mrs. Schmidt?"

"Oh, yes, Charlotte. It is very nice of him to do that."

"We could have had a son. Did you know that, Mrs. Schmidt? Our priest wanted us to raise, as our own, a beautiful child left at the church, but Jakob called him 'garbage with bastard's blood.'

"I once loved your son, Mrs. Schmidt. You know that. Did Jakob ever tell you how he treated me on our wedding night? He treated me worse than one of his whores. I became a thing to be used by him like the chair you're sitting on, Mrs. Schmidt. Nothing more than that. You are where you belong, Jakob, in the very bed you made for yourself. Good day to you both." Turning to leave, Charlotte stopped abruptly and pivoted. "The house is already mine, and it will be used as a home for girls and women you used and discarded, including me."

Leaving the room, Charlotte slowly walked down the stairs toward the front door and found her way out of the house. Charlotte's words hurt him far worse than the self-inflicted illness robbing his life.

His mother, now knowing more, said nothing as tears burst upon her face.

⁓⊙⁓

In late November, winds off Lake Michigan blew colder on all the grand houses on the Milwaukee bluffs, looking over the factories in the valley. Stacks at the tanneries, breweries, garment manufacturers, iron and steel factories, and lumber mills belched the soot of success for every owner and stockholder in Milwaukee. The worker laboring six days a week, twelve hours a day or more, for one dollar and fifteen cents pay per day or less, did not share in the success.

Colder weather ended worker rallies in the parks, but sentiments were not dying down this winter. Even if the newspapers would not print the national labor news of successful strikes in other parts of the country, union successes or losses made their way to the ears of men and women at labor meetings who, then embolden, butted up against the owners and especially their plant managers, battered in the middle.

Placards suddenly appeared on factory walls with words in bold type: **EIGHT-HOUR DAY IS OUR BATTLE CRY**. Although torn down as quickly as they were seen, the drumbeat was getting louder. The word on the street, repeated over and over again, moved westward from union meetings in Pittsburgh that something nationwide was planned for the spring of 1886.

More than one patient, using Doctor Thatcher's office, relayed their concerns to him, but it was the words from the owner of the brick factory where Henryk worked that stirred Samuel the most.

The conversation started innocently enough. "Henryk had worked well in the clay fields. If they cause trouble this year, business owners will be ready. We're hiring armed guards, so we can meet force with force if the police cannot protect our businesses."

Samuel's brows furrowed with concern. "You don't expect it will get that bad here, do you?"

"People died in the railroad strike out west last year and New York now hosts a Labor Day parade in September. Things are getting out of hand with the demands that workers are making, so I hope Henryk will have a safe place to work with us next summer."

Sitting at home and choosing to rephrase the words in a more gentle way for Henryk's mother, Samuel reiterated his concern for them both. "When Henryk comes home for Christmas next week, I think he should stay close to home. I hope he has enough schoolwork to keep him busy while he's at home and when we go anywhere, we'll go together."

Ania did not object, nor did she set it aside, thinking back to their encounter in the cab close to her sister's former home.

Henryk was fortunate that he could spend a few days in Milwaukee for Christmas. Most of his classmates traveled as much as two states away to attend Northwestern Prep. Those students stayed on campus for Christmas, sharing the spirit of the holiday with local families. This time, Henryk made the trip directly from Watertown to Milwaukee and would do the same when returning to school. Willy and Jane were not happy with the news, but they were busy enough with two new guests in their home. Easter vacation would be as brief, but Ania assured Willy and Jane that all three of them would be in Oconomowoc for a week when Henryk finished the school year.

This Christmas vacation, Henryk made no mention of Hannah. This actually pleased Ania, since Henryk's stature and strength as a man were becoming clearer each time she saw her son. Admiring Henryk standing next to the table, Ania wanted her son to be a student of life longer as he grew physically into a man. Thankfully, Hannah was not yet the tempter a young woman could be.

As usual, the winter temperatures turned brutal right after Christmas Day. Because of the cold, business was slow until mid-January when the telephone call came to Samuel's office, requesting that the next time the doctor came to Jakob's home, he bring with him the means to curtail the pain Jakob was feeling in his lower chest. Samuel always asked the caller if the request came directly from Jakob or from his mother, his caregiver, who often felt more pain than her son. This time the caller said the request for a painkiller came directly from Jakob and he was adamant.

The butler met him at the door. "It was good of you to come right away, Doctor." He glanced out the door. "It's awful gray outside. It looks like we're going to get more snow." Taking his coat and hat, the butler turned somber. "Mr. Schmidt is in terrible pain. He keeps rolling in his bed and grabbing his chest."

"I'm sorry to hear that about Jakob. Is he in the same room?"

"Yes, he is. His mother is with him."

"I can find the way."

Walking into Jakob's room, Samuel saw Mrs. Schmidt trying to calm her son.

Jakob was writhing in pain, throwing himself from one side of the bed to the other.

"Where does it hurt the most?" Jakob shouted.

Pointing below his heart, Samuel reached for his stethoscope and looked at his mother and a nearby servant. "Hold him still so I can listen to his heart and lungs. Try to hold still, Jakob."

Samuel worked the stethoscope down from his heart to his stomach and then back again, listening carefully. Then he pushed gently on the area below his heart and Jakob yelled out, loudly, cursing his doctor.

Fear masked Mrs. Schmidt's face. "What's happening?"

"The French disease is eating his insides as it is taking his nose and face." Samuel pointed below his heart. "There is an artery that carries blood from your son's heart to the rest of his body. It is bulging as the disease attacks his inner organs and it could burst."

"Is my son going to die?"

"We're all going to die, Mrs. Schmidt."

"Is my son going to die soon?"

"I cannot tell you when your son is going to die, but I will try to make his time left on God's Earth as comfortable as possible. Because your son is so stubborn, he refused to take morphine sooner because he knows how dependent he can become on it. I have to get ahead of his pain now with the right dose of morphine, and then your son will relax and his heart will not have to work as hard."

His words were comforting, and Doctor Thatcher knew it. Unfortunately, nothing would change. The destination was the same and inevitable, but the trip could have been calmer.

"I'll be back tomorrow morning to check on him unless the new snowfall prevents me. If that happens, I'll get here as soon as I can. Your son may sleep more now. Keep him warm."

Before they could answer or ask another question, Samuel made for the door and was gone.

This regimen of Samuel visiting the Schmidt home increased as Jakob's pain increased so that by Easter, Samuel was seeing his nameless patient regularly and slowly increasing the morphine dose along the way. Jakob didn't care anymore how often he was taking the drug or how dependent he was becoming. His spirits actually brightened. He was more relaxed and less demanding. Ania was hearing about the case almost daily, and it pained her to hear her husband say that his patient's mother actually thought he was getting well.

"My job," Samuel said to Ania, "is to make believe everything will be fine as I pat his mother's hand or squeeze his shoulder. Nothing is fine. Nothing at all. I have become a good liar, and soon everyone will know."

Home from school before Easter, Henryk took interest in the case and finally asked at the table, "How long will the man live?"

"No one knows, Henryk, but soon I may ask your mother to go along with me because it's so depressing going into that house. Would you go with me, Ania?"

"Of course, I will, Sam."

"There is something else that has made me very happy and your mother very happy, Henryk."

"What is that?"

"Your mother is going to have a baby in August or September."

Henryk rushed to his mother and hugged her, and then turned to Samuel and shook his hand.

Not letting go of Henryk's hand, Samuel looked at Ania, who nodded.

"We also have something to ask you, Henryk. I want to adopt you and make you legally a member of this family. You can keep your last name if you wish or take my last name. That's up to you. And, since you are older than fourteen, you can say no or yes. The decision is yours, Henryk."

"Sam, you have made me very happy and I know I belong. Give me a couple of days before I answer you."

"It's time for dinner," Ania said. "Sam, get the wine bottle from the top of the cupboard. We have a lot to celebrate."

After the Easter service at Grace Lutheran Church, the perfect weather made walking home an easy decision. Striding down Water Street toward Grand Avenue, Henryk, standing as tall as Samuel, took to Samuel's proposal with the surety that he belonged with the other three.

"Stopping at the corner, Henryk brought the subject up. "I'll always be a Sobieski in my heart out of love for my mother, but I want to become a Thatcher and I'm honored that you asked me to take your name."

Stepping off west on Grand Avenue, Ania looped her arms under the arms of the two men beside her and held them tight.

After Henryk boarded the Tuesday morning train for Watertown, Ania, riding the cab to her husband's office, noticed the streets were eerily quiet compared to a year ago when she and Henryk escaped from the crowd. Rage brewing for months within the factories and finally spilling into public view, was ready to boil over as the calendar marched toward May first.

The preview came on Wednesday. The first injury at a factory came to Doctor Thatcher's office almost as soon as he opened the door for business.

Two men brought the unconscious man into his office. "After blows to his bloodied head, he fell, and no one could bring him around. The mill manager decided it would be best if we brought him here. Is there something you can do?"

"Bring him down the hallway into my examining room."

While Ania cleansed his head wounds and Samuel checked the man's eyes, Samuel yelled to the two men. "Did you try smelling salts?"

"Yes."

Ania pointed out to Sam an obvious wound to the back of the man's head. "This man was hit hard on the back of his head with something."

Before Sam could look at the wound carefully, there was a loud commotion in the front office. As he walked out into the hallway, Sam saw another man bleeding from his head, stumbling toward him.

"Sit in this chair and I'll be right back."

The two men who brought the first case into the office were leaving. "Wait right there! What factory did the first man come from?"

"They both came from the Allis foundry. They were encouraging our workers to join the strikers of other factories and they were quieted. We don't know anything else." They left, slamming the door behind them.

Walking back to the examining room, Ania was washing the second man's wounds while the first man lay still on the table.

Samuel kneeled before him. "What happened to both of you?"

In his best English, the man said, "Both of us, before work, were speaking to small groups of our fellow workers when we were belted from behind. Since Janek didn't wake up, they brought him here in a cab but told me I could walk on my own."

Sam shrugged. "We'll take care of you. What is your name?"

"Call me Pawel. All we want is an eight-hour workday like the municipal employees and other factory workers, but Allis won't back down."

Thursday and Friday were not much different as more men came in off the street or were transported to Sam's office with the same kind of injuries, mostly from fights that were breaking out in factories all across the valley. Even their first case walked out of the office under his own power, looking for more. Each man they patched up made it clear they were not backing down this time. More ominous was the Friday morning call from the mayor's office, appealing to all doctors in the city to be ready for more bloodshed, beginning the next day, on Saturday, May 1. The call ended by informing doctors that the militia had been called upon by the governor to secure the citizens and their places of employment.

Putting the telephone down, Ania took the news privately to Sam in the hallway. Hearing the news, his face turned pallid as he looked at his wife's face and then lower.

Ania saw the concern on her husband's face. "We'll be all right. You worry too much."

Saturday was another long day for Samuel and Ania, tending men at their office with the same kinds of injuries from fights at their workplaces. Later in the afternoon, the one scheduled appointment for the day offered a different opinion.

Mrs. Walters was usually talkative, to begin with, but as the pregnant wife of a mill owner, she was beside herself with worry, spilling more details than her husband would have allowed. "My husband has put all of our savings into remodeling his factory, and he's worried that he could lose it all if this strike movement gets out of hand and there are damages to his mill or a fire that destroys his investment. People he does business with are worried about what could happen after the labor parade in the city tomorrow. He is only one man, and he employs over three hundred workers. What can he do against three hundred? The mayor should not have passed the law of an eight-hour workday for municipal workers or allowed the parade. These strikers don't know the risks owners take so that men can have a job. I hope the police and the militia are ready to put these strikers in their place."

Locking the door for the day after she left, Ania and Sam sat down across from each other. Dumbfounded, they recognized the real danger their city faced and how they could be caught up in the coming maelstrom.

Ania spoke first. "I know it's been a long week for us, but I think we should attend tomorrow's parade and see for ourselves where this is headed."

The weather was cloudy for the parade and many overlooking the city from the north were hoping for heavy rain. It didn't come, but the marchers and bands did by the thousands. The morning English paper the next day reported: *More than 25,000 Milwaukeeans watched 3,000 marchers, many in horse-driven wagons and just about every band in the city.* Workers of every occupation hoisted banners from their wagons, promoting the eight-hour day, or shouting it as their battle cry as they made their way to the Milwaukee Gardens on State Street for a picnic and rally. By the time the speakers at the rally finished, the entire crowd was ready to raise the stakes in the city the next day.

Workers arrived Monday morning to shuttered buildings, or they did not go to work at all, joining instead their compatriots on the streets, demanding those who were still working to walk off their jobs. The last operating brewery fell quiet when the strikers called upon them to quit. They joined those on the streets, now emboldened by their swelling numbers. Next, Allis Foundry, unprotected by the police, was forced to close its doors, and soon it, too, emptied its workers onto the streets. Surprisingly for Ania and Sam, there were no new patients for them to care for.

By Tuesday, the commotion had moved west of them into the valley and south of them toward the Bay View Rolling Mills, where the last large employer had not yet closed down. The lines were drawn between the strikers demanding a shorter workday and the management of the mill that had orders from their Chicago owners not to cave into the strikers' demands. Governor Rusk, now surreptitiously positioned in a downtown Milwaukee hotel, heeding the counsel of owners the night before, sent the Lincoln Guard by train to the mill to disperse the crowd.

By afternoon, the Kosciszko militia had arrived on foot to bolster the Lincoln Guard. The strikers met their fellow Poles in the militia with rocks and sticks, and their effort was met with shots into the air by a few rear guardsmen. Live rounds struck the walls and windows of the factory, alarming the strikers, who had nothing in their hands to meet the armed threat but their resolve.

Nightfall cooled tempers, but not the strikers' demands, nor orders held by these Polish guardsmen ordered to keep the peace and protect the buildings of Rolling Mills.

Early Wednesday would bring a radical change to their positions. Polish strikers at home for the night gathered early morning at Saint Stanislaus Catholic Church, two and a half miles from their objective. Leaving the church, streams of men, some women, and even a few children joined other strikers pouring down the street toward Bay View Mills. Thousands joined the men, left overnight in the field, and together they moved closer to the factory, renewing their demands for a shorter workday. Alarmed, the commander called the governor, who reaffirmed the order to fire on the strikers if they kept advancing. At two hundred yards, the strikers could not hear his command to stop. Drawing closer, the order was given for his Kosciszko guards to fire on fellow Poles and German workers.

All the strikers fell to the ground as if everyone had been shot. Then everyone rose as one to flee the field, leaving eight Poles and one German dead and more wounded. Their resolve was broken by a single volley from their countrymen that rang up the Menomonee Valley, covering again the stain of worker abuse for decades to come.

Two of those wounded made their way to Samuel's office and relayed their tales, confirming their regrets and bewilderment for their futures.

Samuel and Ania, concentrating on their duty to care for them, listened with compassion, perceiving nothing would change for many and hoping the worst was over for their city. A few days later, it was obvious that the workers' hopes for themselves were dashed. Family futures would remain stuck in neutral, business relationships were broken, and races would relocate, whereas the industry's muscle roared back to full strength. People living in fine houses on the bluffs overlooking the city had nothing more to worry about. The English newspapers confirmed it, praising the actions of the militia and the governor.

Chapter Twenty-Nine

The following week, the militia left and the workers, if not replaced, went back to their old jobs. Stability moved back into the city streets.

Feeling comfortable enough, Samuel asked Ania, "Can you join me at the end of the week and help me change the bandage of my patient at his home while I revise his morphine dose?"

"Of course. When do we go?"

"He is due another shot on Friday."

The cab was always waiting for Sam when he went to Jakob's home, but this time there would be two riders. For both, it was just another procedure they needed to do before they could go home.

Heading north toward the mansions close to the lake bluffs, Ania thought back to the previous weeks. "I wonder if the workers have ever seen these houses they've built with their labor?"

Sam shrugged. "I doubt it. They probably don't even know they're here. Why would they care?"

Ania was about to respond before Sam cut her off.

"We're here."

"Is this your patient's house?"

"It's his parents' home. Let's get this done. Thank you for coming."

Expecting him, the butler looked surprised to see a woman standing behind the doctor.

Samuel saw the concern on his face. "Your mistress knows my nurse would be coming with me."

Leading them into the room, the butler announced to Jakob, "Doctor Thatcher and his nurse are here for you, sir."

Jakob was writhing in his bed, demanding his shot, and then the next minute, begging for it like a baby. Yelling from his bed, he was like a petulant child. "I need more now, Doctor."

"After I give you your shot and you settle down, we'll change the dressing on your face and then your left hand. Do you understand?"

The shot did its work, and in a few moments, Jakob eased back against the pillows and his head softly fell to the side of the bed closest to where Ania and Samuel were sitting.

"First, Ania, soften the gauze with water and disinfectant. Do you have your gloves on?"

"Yes, Sam."

"Let's get started."

Jakob didn't cry out while they did their work, even as small pieces of flesh fell from his face as Doctor Thatcher unwound the gauze from his nose and face, placing the gauze in a wooden bowl held by Ania. Most of his nose was gone, and the open wound on the left side of his face grew larger each time Samuel changed the dressing. Ania then cut strips of new gauze in three-foot lengths for Samuel to wrap around his head and his face, repeating the process for his left hand. By now, Jakob was asleep as Samuel pulled off Ania's gloves and his own, throwing them into the bowl at the foot of the bed.

Leaving Jacob behind, Doctor Thatcher turned to the butler. "Make sure you burn the bowl and its contents. I'll be back on Tuesday to give him his shot."

Walking down the staircase, Mrs. Schmidt entered the front door and greeted the doctor with a smile.

"Mrs. Schmidt, good day to you. This is my wife and nurse, Ania."

"I didn't know you were married, Doctor. It's my pleasure to meet you, Ania."

Strangely, maybe, being in a great house, Ania curtsied, shaking Mrs. Schmidt's hand. "Good afternoon, madam."

Elise Schmidt recognized Ania's accent. "Are you Polish?"

"Yes, madam. I am Polish."

"Doctor Thatcher, when will you return to see Jakob?"

"We'll return on Wednesday to give him another shot and to change his dressing again. Be sure the butler burns the bowl and everything in it. We left it at the side of the bed. Good day, Mrs. Schmidt."

Ania turned quiet during the cab ride home, leaving Samuel to guess redressing Jakob's bandage was no easy task for anyone since his nose and a great part of his left cheek had been eaten away. Then again, Samuel thought Ania had handled tough cases before, but ever since he introduced her to Mrs. Schmidt, her mood had changed. By Sunday afternoon, Ania still was not saying much and she seemed to be miles away.

Choosing not to go through another evening like the previous two, Samuel stood in front of her. "Are you all right, Ania? Is something bothering you?"

Taking his hand, Ania pulled Sam toward the table. "Let's sit down."

Sitting at the table across from each other, Ania looked at her husband. "You need to hear this, Sam. Jakob Schmidt is the man that raped me more than sixteen years ago.

"He represented his brewery father staying at my employer's home in Sussex, and while there, he raped me. I was stunned at their door when you introduced me to Mrs. Schmidt and then she named her son, Jakob. That man raped me, Samuel."

"You're stunned, Ania?" Samuel jumped to his feet. "Thank God the bastard is dying. It can't come quick enough. You don't need to go along with me to his house, ever. I can handle him."

Ania rose to her feet. "We have a job to do, Sam, and we'll do it, but he needs to know that I weathered his attack and withstood the ensuing challenges to my life. I am whole. We are happy with a baby on the way and Henryk is ours."

Samuel took Ania into his arms. "The four of us will be fine, whether he's living or dead."

Wednesday cannot come fast enough, Ania thought. Jakob would not be able to run this time. Things needed to be said, and it did not matter who heard what she had to say to him. She planned the confrontation to be short, but wanted it to hurt as bad as the pain below his heart. Jakob needed to know he had a son he would never see or enjoy hearing about.

As before, the cab the Schmidts reserved for them was waiting at six o'clock outside the door of Samuel's office Wednesday evening.

Approaching the Schmidt's house, Samuel relayed to Ania that the greater morphine dose administered the Friday before allowed Jakob more time before slipping into agony and calling out for another shot.

The cab stopped before the house. "He should be calm and lucid."

The butler led Ania and Samuel into Jakob's room, and this time, his mother was sitting near his bed, talking to her son. Samuel greeted her while Ania pulled up another chair close to Jakob's bedside while Samuel stood behind her.

Elise Schmidt smiled. "Do you want me to move out of your way?"

Ania shook her head. "Oh no. You're fine right there."

Without hesitation, Ania looked at Jakob. "Jakob? Jakob Schmidt, can you hear me?"

Jakob nodded, fully aware of his surroundings, but not of what was coming next.

"Jakob Schmidt, my name is Ania Thatcher. Doctor Samuel Thatcher's nurse and his wife."

"Greetings to you, lady. Thank you for coming and helping me."

"I was hoping I would never see you again, but here I am and now I must tell you this."

Immediately, Jakob looked right at Ania, and Mrs. Schmidt dropped her indifference. "Have you met my son before?"

Ania looked from Mrs. Schmidt to Jakob. "Jakob, you know me. You knew me sixteen years ago. You knew me as a young girl who worked at a home in Sussex. More than sixteen years ago, you raped me in a field. You left me there and rode off." Ania looked at Jakob's mother. "My employer verified it that your son raped me."

Standing, Elise Schmidt looked rattled, but not totally surprised. Grabbing her only defense, she screamed, "Heinriche! Heinriche!" Turning to Ania, she yelled even louder, "Get out of my house."

Rising slowly, Ania looked down at her rapist and spoke softly. "I hate you for what you did to me. You will never see your fifteen-year-old son."

Hearing the screams, Heinriche Schmidt, joined by the butler, hurried into the room as Ania said a second time, "You have a son you will never see."

"Who has a son?"

Ania faced Heinriche. "I have the son. I delivered a boy after your son raped me."

Elise Schmidt was nearing eruption. "Get out of my house!"

Jakob stammered, "I…I…"

Motioning to his wife to be quiet, a wicked smile crossed Heinriche's face as he turned to Jakob. "You produced an heir after all."

"No, Father. Ania did."

Herr Schmidt stepped toward Ania. "My son is worse than a bastard, but he gave me my heir. When can I meet him?"

"That is for me to decide, not you." Ania marched out of the room.

"Your son, my heir! Let's talk."